Sign up for Michaelb
<u>And get FREE</u>

MW00636863

Sign up for the no-spam newsletter
(affectionately known as Michaelbrent's Minions)
and **you'll get several books FREE**.
Details are at the end of this book.

LIGHT-YEARS FROM HOME

By

Michaelbrent Collings

Written Insomnia Press
WrittenInsomnia.com
"Stories That Keep You Up All Night"

DEDICATION

To...

Gautham,
because it is irrefutable fact
that I couldn't have done it without him...

And to Laura, FTAAE.

PART ONE:

Intelligent(ish) life on Earth

1

My friend was dead, but that didn't keep him from shouting, "They're on our six, Max!"

"I know."

"On our six, man!"

"I know!"

"On our—"

"You say 'on our six' again and I'm going to stop dodging!"

"Why would you do that?"

"Because I'd rather be atomized by a Gro'nid plasma net than hear 'on my six' again!"

"But *you* just said 'on my six'! Does that count?"

I flinched as the fighter behind us fired again.

I was lying: given the choice between hearing a ghost shout, "On our six!" again and death at the hands of a bloodthirsty alien, I'd choose the first one.

But it was a close call.

"Max, he's still there. Still on—"

"Don't say it!"

"—our tail!"

"I know. I *know!* Couldn't you have just found a penny? A paper clip? A bobby pin?"

"Dudes don't carry bobby pins, dude."

"Well you should have done...have done...anything but what you did."

Do I sound confused at this point? I hope so, because I was. It's not every day that a guy misses school due to alien kidnapping, then ends up in the middle of an interstellar war.

If this were a movie, I'd follow this tense moment with a

blazing victory, then a bit about getting the girl in the end.

But this wasn't a movie. It was just me, light-years from home, trying to survive.

Though, technically, this did start with a girl. Unfortunately, not the "hottie who falls for the nerdy kid" type of girl. Just my eight-year-old sister, Chloe.

And sure, my current predicament wasn't *technically* all her fault. But if she hadn't let the other girls bug her, hadn't run into the forest, and (above all) hadn't let that stupid Walkman-wearing tree grab her, none of us would be in this mess.

Unfortunately, she did all those things.

And, for funsies, brought me and Noah and the girl of my dreams along for the ride.

2

I wasn't there when it all went to pieces. But I heard about it later. And, like so many other problems in the universe, it started with nothing more than a family squabble.

Family squabbles aren't rare, and neither was this one: arguing about who was supposed to pack what on the trip, and whether there would be fuel enough to get to the destination. Arguing about the particulars of the adventure, and about the expected results. All normal. Boring, even.

The only thing of interest about this particular gripe-fest was its location: ten miles above the surface of the Earth.

And falling fast.

***

The argument—and the arguers themselves—did not fall straight down. The descent had been carefully planned, painstakingly plotted. Threading between satellites, skimming through the atmosphere in a broad arc that would bring their craft down *just so*. The entire thing was timed out to the nanosecond.

So when one of the aliens (not sure which—accounts differ as to whose fault this part was) looked away from the control panel in order to snap at the other, neither of them noticed the blinking light that should have told both to veer left instead of continuing forward.

They spotted it quickly enough. A seemingly minor problem, easily overcome by a race as advanced and intelligent as theirs. The pilot had to veer a bit so as not to blow a hole in San Francisco's beautiful Golden Gate Bridge, then another minor trajectory shift to avoid vaporizing a humpback whale that had chosen a poor moment to breach in the harbor.

Then they were back on course, with a whole new set of things to argue and assign blame over.

But the argument hadn't been part of the plan, and nothing that followed was, either.

Which, if you think about it, is probably the most accurate thing that can be said about any history, or any major historical event: it's usually the result of a screw-up.

And where was my little sister, Chloe, during all this?

Lost in the woods, dancing away her fear: in short, being Chloe.

***

In the interest of understanding (an important thing to have, as events will show), lemme back up a bit.

To start: everyone in this story is neurotic or crazy or, you know, *an alien.* So Chloe being Chloe wasn't the only crazy thing that happened. But it made her a target to the Trio of Terror, which made her upset, which made her have to go with me to the forest, which made her run off, which ended up with Noah repeatedly screaming "on your six!"

And who are the Trio of Terror, you ask? Simply, they are a trio of eight-year-olds who had been making my sister's life miserable since day one. Three little girls who wear clothing so expensive it borders on obscene, whose hair is creepily perfect at all times, and whose parents own much of the city.

And, worst of all, who continually badgered, dismissed, and belittled my little sister.

***

Case in point: the day it all began.

The day when, somewhere in space, preparations were being made to visit Earth, for reasons bordering on the nefarious.

Chloe was headed home from school, riding her skateboard. I gave it to her for her birthday (over Mom's objections), and she's been glued to it since then. Only thing that even comes close to being that cool to her is her iPod with the retro Walkman headphones I gave her for the next birthday.

So Chloe was riding home, listening to her tunes, and she came upon the Trio of Terror:

First, we have Jessica. Picture an attorney—the kind that charges a thousand bucks an hour, who makes CEOs tremble, politicians weep, and mobsters turn to putty with a well-placed glare. Now, shrink her down to eighty pounds and put her in a Forest Camp Girl outfit. That's Jessica.

Next up: Sierra. You know the ditzy sorority girl in every horror movie? The one who snipes passive-aggressive comments at the other girls and whom you hope-hope-*hope* will be murdered gruesomely by the end of the second act? That's Sierra.

Which leaves only the alpha: Becca.

Becca is, at eight years old, one of the most frightening creatures I've ever encountered—and yes, I include the Gro'nid kill-mongers in the comparison sample. Becca's father was some kind of software genius who sold his first company to Google for "an undisclosed sum" when he was twenty-five…then went on to make *real* money.

Becca's mom, from what I understand, is some kind of pageant queen—Miss Delaware or Miss Connecticut or some other Miss Place-Full-of-Rich-White-People. And from what I can tell, she's been grooming Becca to become the *next* Miss Golden-Stick-Up-Her-Butt since five minutes after her egg was fertilized.

Quite the little death squad. So when Chloe rolled into school (yay, skateboard!) the first day of school, it took Becca and her minions all of five seconds to realize that Chloe wasn't going to be one of "them." Why would she be? Chloe: hair perpetually mussed, jeans with scuff marks on the knee. The one not-rich kid at a school littered with the spawn of the wealthy.

Right from the start, Becca sensed blood in the water. The first day, she was tripping Chloe, shoving her in the lunch line. Or rather, getting someone else to do it—Becca's too smart to put herself in the sights of the authorities.

At first I didn't believe it was as bad as Chloe made out. But a month after school started I went to a bake sale for Muir Elementary and ended up at a table where Becca & Co were selling "*Exquise Brownies de Chocolat Tres Magnifique*" (yes, that's what the sign actually said).

Two minutes later I stumbled away in a daze, holding a Brownie de Chocolat that cost two weeks' allowance and feeling like I'd survived an MMA match against the love child of Genghis Khan and the entire cast of one of those Real Housewives shows.

After that, I believed everything Chloe said about Becca, including that she once cut off a teacher's braid because it was "too 2018 to be permitted" and got off with not even a slap on the wrist because the entire school administration was scared of her.

Not of her parents.

Of *her*.

***

So there was Chloe, skating home, not a care in the world aside from whether her big bro (me) had scarfed all the Oreos Mom bought the night before (spoiler alert: I had).

They were just waiting for her to ride by.

"Chloe! Chloe!"

Chloe looked over and saw Becca running toward her, trailed by twin demon-shadows/cronies, Jessica and Sierra.

Chloe told me later that she suspected they were up to no good; thought about ignoring them. But they were wearing their Forest Camp Girl outfits, which to Chloe epitomized coolness: sashes laden with badges for everything from Woven Pleather Skills to Social Media Mastery, forest green skirt-and-shirt combos tailored just for them, bright red berets worn at just the right angle.

And, being Chloe—which is to say, being a creature of infinite hopefulness—she thought, *Maybe this time they're going to be nice.*

So she didn't ignore them. She waited.

Becca got there first. Breathless. "Oh, my *gaaaawwwwsh,* Chloe! You look so cute today! Doesn't she look cute today, J?"

"Obvies, totes," said Jessica. "Right, S?"

"Obvies, totes," Sierra mirrored. "To the cutest of the max."

"So's your mother," said Jessica.

"No, so's *your* mother," said Sierra. They both laughed.

After they finished with this witty repartee, Chloe—terrified, hopeful—whispered, "What's up, B?"

Hearing about the whole thing after, I knew that Chloe was just trying to be nice. The Trio of Terror always referred to each other by their first initials, so Chloe was trying to respect their preferences.

But calling the girls by their pet names without permission? In their eyes, it was just one more sin (like being poor, or having a soul).

But Becca managed to pull a smile out of her bag of Insincere Expressions, plaster it on, and say warmly, "Oh, I have great news for you, Chloe!"

"What is it?"

"Well, I know you're interested in being a Forest Camp Girl."

"I—" Chloe wasn't expecting that. "Why do you think—"

"Hayley T. told Hayley L. that she overheard Principal E. tell Mrs. R. that you'd told her you wished you could be a Forest Camp Girl, so Hayley L. told Maddison and then Maddison told Bella and Bella told Hayley J. and Hayley J. texted me," said Sierra, holding out a phone in a case covered in enough bling to star in its own rap video.

"Oh, but I—" Chloe began.

"I know, I know," said Becca. "You can't be an FCG without

being sponsored by one of the charter sisters, but we think we found a way around that." Her grin widened. "Not that you could be, like, *in*-in the Forest Camp Girls. But you could be, like, a mascot."

"Wha—" Chloe's head was spinning hard. She *had* told the principal once that she would love to be a Forest Camp Girl, but knew it would be way too expensive. Dad's a teacher and Mom's a firefighter—so we have enough to get by, never been hungry, but we also don't have much extra. So when Chloe found out that being a Forest Camp Girl cost five hundred bucks a month just for dues, she did her best to put the idea out of her head.

But now, Becca seemed to be telling her that there *was* a way. And Chloe couldn't help but think:

What if I could be in the Forest Camp Girls? What if I was friends with Becca—or B—and J and S as well? What if I actually felt like I belonged?

"I know," Becca said. "Totes cool. You'd make a great mascot. Super-important."

"Totes," agreed Jessica.

"Obvies," said Sierra.

"O-okay," stammered Chloe. "How—"

"Simple," said Becca. "Me and J and S are selling FCG Cookies. If—I mean, *when*—we sell five hundred boxes, we get a new tablet computer with an official Forest Camp Girls case. But we're off the day's quota. So you make up the shortfall, and we get you in as an FCG Supporter. It's like getting in for doing a good deed, instead of being, you know, actually *wanted*."

Chloe still didn't understand what was happening. But her head was filled with that siren song of belonging. "Supporter?"

"An *official* Supporter," purred Becca. She snapped her fingers, and Jessica and Sierra each whipped out a box of cookies and thrust them toward Chloe.

"FCG: Lighting a fire in the camp of your girls' hearts since 1972,"

intoned Sierra and Jessica together in tones typically reserved for cult and multi-level marketing meetings.

"Exactly," Becca said. "So we need you to light your own little fire, and buy these boxes off of us. Puts us back on track for our quota, and we put in a good word for you at the next meeting."

Chloe's a really good kid, and thinks the best of people. So all she thought at this point was that Becca, Jessica, and Sierra were finally reaching out. It fried her circuits a bit, and she didn't even think about what she did next. She just scrounged around in her pockets for some money—because in the whirl of the moment, the one thing that she did understand was that she was expected to pay for something.

"Sixteen dollars each," said Becca.

"Thirty-four dollars total," said Sierra.

"Thirty-*three*, dummy," said Jessica.

"Right. Thirty-three. I forgot," said Sierra.

Chloe had already pulled out the contents of her pocket: some lint, a ball bearing, and a buck-fifty in change.

Becca examined Chloe's outstretched palm. Her lips curved downward in a mockery of sadness. "Oh, *poe iddle baby*," she said. "That's not nearly enough, P."

"It's C," said Chloe. "For Chloe."

"No, I'm pretty sure it's P," said Becca.

Sierra and Jessica had been waiting for their cue. At Becca's final word, they shouted together: "For *Poor*!"

Chloe finally realized she was being invited to nothing but mockery, and decided it was time to go. She tried not to cry as she jumped on her skateboard, and rode away to the sound of three girls laughing at her.

3

And where was I during all this? Same as Chloe: coming home from school—a moment I dreaded.

I need to be clear: I am not one of those teens who wish their parents were dead. I love them. I want the best for them.

But I was (still am) a teenager. Which meant the thing I wanted most was for my parents to be the social equivalent of air: good to have around, but never really noticed. Not cool. Not *un-cool*. Just there...and invisible.

What kind of parents do I have? The worst of both worlds.

Mom's definitely cool. She's smart enough to keep up with my dad in a conversation (more on that in a moment), she's pretty enough that I've seen classmates openly checking her out when we bump into them at the mall. Even worse, she's a firefighter, which means she's strong and tough and has tons of amazing stories involving battling burny stuff and saving lives.

And on the other end of the spectrum? Dad. The uncool one. A straight-up oddball. And if you don't believe me, just check out my front lawn.

The house itself is pretty blah—one story, three bedrooms, two baths, and a two-car garage. But no one notices that. They notice the yard filled with things like the following:

A Huffy bike with a full-size catamaran sail welded to its frame, a robot that looks like a cross between R2D2 and the Terminator with its arms chained to a lawnmower, a swing set covered in gearboxes and wired to a pile of solar panels. I could go on.

I used to think it was fun and cool. My dad was a real-life mad scientist! But by the time I was ten I started to notice that everything he made—*everything*—had some crucial flaw that would render it useless. Sometimes it was a little thing: a missing wire or a blown fuse. Other times the entire concept was flawed from the get-go—like, what's the point of a solar-powered umbrella?

By the time I was twelve it was embarrassing.

By the time I was fifteen, I felt like a leper.

Even moving a few years back hadn't helped; somehow my dad's rep as a mad scientist/inventor had gotten around the school by the end of the week. The best I could do was pretend to be dumb as an attempt to distance myself from him. I didn't even wear my glasses, because I thought they made me look too much like Dad. Like a nerd.

***

So just as Chloe was getting mocked all to pieces, I was coming home to see Frankenstein's Yard. The garage door hung open, which meant Dad would be fiddling with his newest "breakthrough."

"Crap," I muttered.

"What was that?" asked Noah, a refrigerator masquerading as a high-school student. Six-foot-four, solid muscle, able to shatter walnuts with his biceps. Captain of the football team, the baseball team, and the wrestling team. Wikipedia's entry for "babe magnet" just has a picture of Noah and a caption that reads, "'Nuff said."

Despite all that, he's always been pretty cool to me. He's never threatened me with death or maiming (which makes him the only holdout on any of the aforementioned teams), and he even lets me mooch rides home—though being crammed in the back of a 1985 Volkswagen Beetle that's ninety percent rust is not the most pleasant of experiences.

We also play video games online a few times a week, usually an online shooter of some kind. So far, I have yet to beat him. Sooner or later in every game I hear him say, "I'm on your six!" in my headphones and I know I have about two milliseconds before he kills me.

Are we close? Not really. But he drives me home and we love the same video games, and those two facts easily qualify him as my "best" friend. Which, yes, is very, very sad.

"Did you hear me?" he said. "Did you say something?"

"No," I said as the VW coughed its way to a halt in front of my house.

In the garage, something sparked loudly, a small mushroom cloud puffed out sideways through the open garage door, and I heard my dad say, "Blast it!" in angry tones, then repeat the words as more of a command: "Blast. It."

Noah squinted. "Is he trying to Death Star a watermelon?"

"How should I know?" I muttered.

Noah opened the door, then grunted as he released the catch on the side of his seat and leaned forward. I waited for a sec, but when Noah showed no signs of getting out of the car to make my exit easier, I did my best to squeeze through the four inches between the back of his seat and the doorframe.

Of course my bag got caught. Of course when I tried to get it loose my feet twisted up. Of course I ended up falling out onto the pavement.

And of course, all this happened in front of the girl of my dreams.

4

Leya Taylor is a mystery.

She just showed up in the middle of the term and took my breath away. Literally. She was exiting the class I wanted to enter, and when she opened the door it slammed into and knocked the wind out of me.

Flat on my back, I immediately realized this was the most beautiful girl I'd ever seen in my life. Her helping me to my feet was like being rescued by an angel. Who looked incredibly sad.

"It...uhh...it's okay," I stammered. "It didn't hurt." Obviously a lie, since I had to gasp the words, so I pulled myself together and tried to add a joke: "No more serious than a minor car crash. I give myself at *least* a sixty percent chance of full recovery."

She started crying, and rushed away. A personal best for me: plenty of girls rushed away when I tried to talk to them, but no one ever actually *cried* before.

After school, I saw her with Noah, getting into my best/only friend's car and tooling off.

My jealousy surprised me—I'd never wanted to murder Noah before.

Next day I asked him about her during homeroom, trying to act casual. Noah wasn't really listening to my question—he was too busy accepting thanks for throwing yet *another* game-winning touchdown the night before, so the conversation was fragmented, but I got that she lost her parents in a car accident.

This made sense of the crying after I joked about dying in an accident—and also made me want to crawl under a rock and stay there until my shame died or the universe ended, whichever came first.

Noah also let me know that she'd been staying with friends

and relatives while people tried to figure out where she should stay on a more permanent basis.

At this point, Noah told me to shut up because Amari Robinson, the Homecoming Queen three years running, had just come in. He wanted to focus his attention on her very short skirt, which I thought was tacky given that he obviously was with Leya.

I called him out on it, and he glared at me, then said, "She's staying with me, idiot."

"So...you're not interested in her?" I asked. "You're her family?"

He gave me a funny look, then said, "You like her?"

"I didn't say that." Noah kept staring at Amari, so I had to prompt: "Well? You're not interested in her?"

He flicked a glance my way, and got an amused look on his face. "I didn't say that."

***

I couldn't get much more out of him after that, but that was fine because I didn't really feel like talking. What I did feel like was walking in front of oncoming traffic. Because Noah had just intimated she was not related, so she was fair game, which meant I had the same chances with her as the Titanic about ten minutes after the captain announced, "I think we might have hit something."

I mean, not only was he interested, but she lived with him. Literally a captive audience to his undeniable charms.

I tried to lock my heart away to avoid further soul-crushing pain. It didn't work, mostly due to the conclusions I reached in the following weeks:

1) She was smart (which, call me crazy, I think is *way* attractive), and artistic. She and I had the same English class, and she wrote a poem about sadness that was so depressing

it made me want to kill myself.

2) No one knew much about her, though rumor held she was staying with Noah's parents after she got expelled from her last school for burning off the eyebrows of a girl who teased her about her folks dying.

3) When she wasn't writing sad poetry or refusing to make eye contact with the world, she was really funny and sarcastic.

4) As previously noted, she was the most beautiful girl I'd ever seen.

Call me shallow, but it was mostly #4 on my mind when I rolled out of Noah's car and pancaked on the pavement. Because Leya was in the car, sitting in the passenger seat, watching as I doofused my way out of the vehicle.

It made sense that she'd ride with Noah, of course, which made mooching rides complicated for me. I liked the chance to see her, of course, and she even started talking to me. But every time I saw her in Noah's car I could tell she was that much more firmly under his spell.

So I mooched rides a lot less, though there were still days when he just offered without me even asking, and I didn't want to act awkward about it so I took the rides. And inevitably ended up looking stupid, just like I did in that moment, tripping out of his car and ending up flat on my back.

***

Noah laughed as he leaned the seat back to its regular position. "Sorry you had to ride in the back, but…you know." He rolled his eyes in Leya's direction. I think. I wasn't wearing my glasses, so he was mostly a blur. "She called shotgun."

"*I* called shotgun," I muttered as I got to my feet.

Noah shrugged. "I didn't hear you."

"Talk louder next time, rockstar," Leya said. I'm pretty sure she grinned, which was nice. She didn't smile much.

Noah pulled the door shut, then gunned the VW's engine. The car lurched forward three feet, then gasped like a dying asthmatic before coming to a stop. Noah gunned it again, and the car managed another six-foot lurch, coughed, then died. Noah punched the steering wheel, then looked at Leya, who sighed and got out.

"Come on, rockstar," she said to me.

As she took up position at the bumper, I gaped at Noah. "You're going to make *her* push?"

Noah looked irritated. "She doesn't know how to drive stick. Just get back there."

I joined Leya at the back of the VW. "You guys on my six?" shouted Noah.

Leya rolled her eyes and mouthed, *"On my six?"* I rolled my eyes back, and we both started pushing.

"What say...you and I start...a crowd-funding site...devoted to...Noah's crappy car?" she panted.

"Sure," I said. "Or he could just, you know...get a job or something." I tried to sound cool and nonchalant, like talking to the most beautiful woman ever invented was a normal thing for me.

"I heard that!" shouted Noah.

"So you don't hear me when I say shotgun, but you hear me when I point out you—*auuugh!*"

The car coughed, barfed out a cloud of smoke, then lurched forward, causing me to fall flat on my face in front of Leya for the second time in as many minutes.

I felt a breath on my neck. "See ya, rockstar," Leya whispered in my ear. Before I could scramble to my feet, I heard her crunch across the pavement, then the passenger door thudded shut and

Noah and Leya were gone.

***

Behind me, there was another micro-nuke explosion, another curse. "Blast it, blast it, *blast it!*" A pause, then, sadly: "Why won't you please just blast it?"

I sighed and turned around to face Dad. Or rather, to face the general direction of the blur that I suspected to be my father. I pulled out my glasses. No need to be blind here—the one benefit of a family that thinks dorkiness is cool.

As the world came into focus, I saw my dad throw down a comically tiny screwdriver, then stomp into the house, slamming the door behind him.

"And another one bites the dust," I said to myself.

I went into the garage. Picked up the screwdriver and turned to face Dad's latest: a high intensity laser he called the StormLight. He had talked about it a lot the last few weeks— going through the science of it, the construction, the engineering. Scientists had known for years that lasers could both trigger and direct lightning strikes—basically using them to create photonic lightning rods—but Dad was convinced that they could do even more. Could move from controlling the electrical discharge of a cloud, to controlling the cloud's movement, even whether it rained in a specific location or not.

It was all very thrilling to hear him talk about it: droughts averted, storms stopped before they could turn to floods. Mom and Chloe always geeked out about it when he talked about the laser work he was doing, conveniently forgetting the most important fact: he had yet to make anything actually *work*.

I looked at the scribbled notes Dad had left on his whiteboard, immediately spotting three math errors. They weren't as basic as some of his mistakes—at least that was an improvement. Still, a scientist should be able to handle conversions using nonlinear eigenvalue problems without blinking. *I* could.

I began erasing the incorrect values on the white board, replacing them with the correct equations that hopefully would allow Dad to move forward a bit farther with his dumb weather machine.

Next up was the laser itself. Several of the wires were loose, and there was a circuit board I suspected would prove to be flawed in design. I'd have to redesign it on Dad's computer when he—

A clatter of plastic on cement shocked me out of my science-coma, making me jump. I looked over to see Chloe shucking off her elbow and knee pads, then stripping her helmet. Her hair was all over the place—no surprise, the girl was immune to all styling products known to humanity—but even for her she seemed a bit on the ragged edge.

"What's with you?" I asked.

Chloe frowned and said, "You're not supposed to mess with Dad's stuff."

I snorted as I popped out the questionable circuit board and examined it. "If I didn't, he wouldn't accomplish anything."

"Still broken?" asked Chloe.

"Still broken," I said. "But I think that I can—hey." I finally realized that Chloe's hair wasn't the only thing that was a mess. Her eyes were shining, she looked on the verge of tears. "What's up?"

"Nothing," she said. She sniffled.

"Obvious lie, kid. *Nothing* looks like Dad, trying to invent something that works. What's happening here definitely looks more like *something*. So I say again: what's up?"

Chloe hitched in a breath, struggling against tears. "It's—" Another hitching, gasping breath. "It's *them*."

I knew immediately who she was talking about. If Hitler, Mussolini, and Stalin got their children together for a playdate, I'd expect them to look just like Becca, Sierra, and Jessica.

"What'd they do this time?"

"They're just so *mean!*"

As she recounted the Trio of Terror's taunting invitation to "help out" and the extortion attempt that followed, I felt my jaw clench. I shoved the circuit board back into place and started working on the laser again—tinkering calmed me.

Chloe got to the end of her story—the part where the girls mocked her for her poverty—then gave a little scream of frustration and threw her helmet down to the garage floor. It hit the concrete floor of the garage, bounced off at an angle, banked into the wall, then ricocheted straight at me.

I yelped and ducked, barely avoiding a knock on the noggin.

The laser wasn't so lucky. It didn't dodge, but sat, silent and sullen, right in the path of the errant helmet bounce. A spark, a smell of ozone, and suddenly it felt like all the hair on my head stood on end. Light flashed, so bright it left everything a blur even with my glasses.

When the blur faded, I saw Chloe looking at a small hole in the wall. I stuck a nail in it; now it looked like just one more tool-hanger.

"We should tell Dad that we got his laser to work," said Chloe, sniggering.

"*I* got his laser to work," I said. Trying not to laugh, I said, "And I think we should just let him discover it himself." I hung a crescent wrench on the new hanger. "I wish..."

"Wish what?"

"I wish Dad could get his act together and make something that actually works for once."

Chloe shook her head and put her little fists on her hips. It made her look surprisingly grown-up. "You know, you should give people more credit."

I cocked an eye. "How so, oh wise one?"

"Just, you go through the world thinking everyone stinks. But everyone *doesn't* stink. Not even…"

"Not even…?"

"Not even you," she said.

Then she was off and running, the way little kids always do—to get to the next excitement, the next moment in a never-ending adventure. The connecting door to the house swung open, slammed shut. I was alone.

I shook my head, smiling in spite of myself. Chloe was a candle in a dark universe, insisting that there be light. It made it all the more mind-boggling to me that people like Becca and her sycophantic followers could treat her so poorly. What did she ever do to them?

The answer came swiftly to my mind:

Nothing, man. But the universe doesn't need a reason to mess with us. It does it because it can.

5

Even without hearing about Chloe's misadventures, it had been a pretty crappy day. Dinner just continued the trend.

"So, Max, who was that girl?"

I stared at Mom, uncomprehending, unblinking, unbreathing. My brain ran through a dozen questions before finally settling on the ever-eloquent, "Huh?"

"The girl," Mom said. She leaned in close and bobbed her eyebrows up and down. "The one you were getting googly-eyed with outside."

"I wasn't—"

"You were," said Chloe. She attempted a version of googly eyes, which for her meant looking around in circles as fast as she could, then weaving in her chair like a drunk sailor caught in a storm.

"Traitor," I whispered as I kicked her under the table.

She yelped, but covered the sound with a wheeze and a yell: "So *googly*! So *crazy*. So…*in love*."

I had to laugh at that. Chloe was a pain, but pain or not, she had a flair for the dramatic, and a good sense of humor. Plus, I worried if I didn't laugh, she'd keep spinning her eyes around like that until they fell out of their sockets.

Still, laughing didn't mean I was going to just tell everyone my deepest and darkest, you know? So I went for the time-honored, classic avoidance technique of switching topics.

"Why do you smell like smoke?" I asked Mom.

"I think that's just her lasagna," said Dad.

Mom mimicked punching him. Dad flinched, but he was grinning—they both were. Good thing too—at least for him. If Mom ever did take a shot at him, I'm pretty sure she'd shatter him like an overcooked piece of toast.

"I cook very good lasagna," Mom insisted.

"It's great, Mom!" Chloe shouted.

"Very good," agreed Dad. "It's not every woman who can both cook a meal *and* give her fellow firefighters a workout by burning the house down—*oof.*"

Mom punched Dad in the shoulder hard enough to swing him half around in his chair. He winced and rubbed his shoulder, but the grin never left his face. It got wider, if anything. So did Mom's.

My parents are weirdos.

"I smell like smoke because we're doing acquired structure live fire training for the rest of the month," Mom said, passing the lasagna to me.

"What's that?" asked Chloe.

"We've got a bunch of old buildings out in the foothills that have been condemned. The county bought them, and we get to burn them so we can practice putting out fires in real-life conditions."

"So you can save people better?" asked Chloe.

"So we can save people better," Mom agreed.

"Cool," said Chloe.

"Very cool indeed," agreed Dad. "And highly sexy." He winked at Mom, who winked back and managed to do a booty-shake while still sitting down.

Chloe mimed barfing. Then everyone was silent for a moment, the eating begun in earnest. All joking aside, Mom is a pretty good cook. Most firefighters are—they have to spend long shifts together, and they share meal prep responsibilities, which means that you better learn to make decent food or you're going to tick people off when it's your turn to cook. And you don't want to rely on someone who's ticked off at you during a fire.

***

When I finally judged it safe, I looked at Mom. "Could you

please pass the—"

"So who's the girl?" Mom interrupted.

"Could you just pass the sal—"

"Sure," said Mom. She held up the salt shaker. "But it's gonna cost you."

"*Mom*, for the love of—" I looked at Dad, wearing my best "Help a bro out" expression.

Dad just raised his hands: a silent "You're on your own, kid."

"Fine." I held my hand out.

"You're going to tell?"

"I'm going to tell. Jeez, Mom."

She handed me the salt. I shook it out, very…very…*slowly.*

"Max, you're stalling. And oversalting."

"Fine. Fine. Her name's Leya."

"Is she Noah's girlfriend?" asked Dad.

I shrugged. "I'm sure she will be sooner or later."

"Is she new? I don't remember seeing her at any of the football games."

I nodded. "Pretty new. She's from Portland."

"Where's that?" piped up Chloe.

"Oregon," said Mom.

"Where the White House is?" asked Chloe.

"No, that's Washington, DC," said Dad. He steepled his fingers in his best professor pose. "Interestingly, the reason that the state was named—"

"No," said Mom. "Don't let Max change the subject, hon." She held a finger up. Me and Chloe called it her Doom Finger—it meant things were about to get serious unless we listened and obeyed. Slowly, the Doom Finger pointed at me. "Spill. The. Beans."

I sighed. The Doom Finger had been leveled; obedience was the only option.

Not like Mom was big on punishing people, but the next step after the Doom Finger usually involved her tearing up and saying things like, "I'm a terrible mother." That kind of thing should be outlawed by the Geneva Conventions.

I held up my hands in surrender. "Her parents were in a car wreck last year and they got...uhhh..." I glanced at Chloe. She was listening with wide eyes. "They were...snuggled."

Mom's hand went to her mouth. She glanced at Chloe as well. "How...*snuggled* were they?"

"They died," Chloe said brightly. Everyone looked at her in shock. She shrugged, shoveled enough lasagna in her face-hole to choke a lumberjack, then said (mouth full), "What? Everyone at school knows about it." She leaned in close to me and, speaking out of the side of her mouth like some 1940s film noir sleuth, said, "People talk, ya know?"

Dad laughed. "They do indeed."

I picked at my food as I said, "I guess Leya's been living with different relatives. Now she's moved on to friends of the family, so it's Noah's family's turn. And just so it's clear, I wasn't getting googly-eyed."

For a second, I thought Mom was going to ask for the grim details—or Chloe was. But Mom could tell I was uncomfortable, which I knew because she motioned everyone to shut up.

Thank you, Marla Rose Abernathy, I thought. *Though able to guilt-crumble tall buildings with a single tear, you are, at times, also a classy person.*

Mom put a hand on mine. Then, wide-eyed and innocent, she said, "No one would blame you if you *were* getting googly-eyed."

I guess I spoke too soon, I thought. *You're a demon trying to torture me, Mom.*

Everyone at the table cracked up (except me). Mom took her

hand from mine, shrugging. "She's cute. And probably in need of some human connection. Maybe you should—"

"Don't say it, Mom!"

"– ask her on—"

"Please, Mom, don't go there—"

"– a date."

Chloe, predictably, jumped on that: "*Oooo-ooooh*," she cooed. "A *day*-ate!"

Chloe has the power to turn single-syllable words into polysyllabic events when at her most annoying. Like now.

"I'm just saying, Max," Mom was continuing. "You're at 'that age' now."

"Mom, I'm begging you."

"You may be starting to experience—"

"Please, Mom, for the love of all that's holy—"

"– *changes*."

As Dad laughed hard enough to cause an aneurysm, Chloe's eyes went saucer-sized again. "What kind of changes, Mom?"

Dad finally let me off the hook. He waved, dried his eyes of laughter-juice, then said, "How about we *change* the subject?"

***

Over dessert, Dad said, "Max, I have that new inventor's presentation later this month and I'm still working out the kinks on the mini-laser. Thought maybe you and I could work on it together this weekend."

"Sorry, Dad," I said. "I already made plans with Noah to go up to Muir Woods."

"With Noah, huh? And that cute girl?" Mom asked, wearing that dumb wide-eyed-innocent expression again.

"No!" I shouted. Then sighed. "Yeah. Noah got assigned to do a science lab, gathering different flora specimens."

"And she's in his class?" asked Dad.

"No," I said, "but I heard she got assigned as Noah's tutor to help him keep his GPA up so he can stay on the team."

"What team?" asked Chloe.

"All of them." I pushed around my food with my fork. "Leya said she was looking forward to helping him because plants and green places reminded her of Portland, so I told her it sounded like Muir, and that it might be a good place to gather stuff for Noah's assignment."

"Oh, I bet you jumped on that, didn't you, Casanova?" shouted Mom, using the same tone as a cop might use when triumphantly stating, "Admit it, *you* killed Colonel Mustard in the conservatory with the candlestick!"

Chloe, meanwhile, apparently thought she'd gone too long without contributing to the conversation, because she shouted, "*CASANOVA!*" in a tone that said clearly she had no idea what the word meant.

"Chloe, shut—"

Mom's voice rode right over mine. "You jumped on it because..." She rapped her palms against the table in a makeshift drumroll. "...you *like* her."

"Mom, I—"

"You want to *date* her," Mom sang.

"I don't, I—"

"You want to *kiss* her," Mom continued.

"Please, just—"

"You want to *marry* her." That last came from Chloe. Everyone stared at her for a second. She blushed, then screamed, "*CASANOVA!*" again before shoveling pudding into her mouth.

"Marla, please," Dad said. "Let's not bother him about it."

"Thanks, Da—"

"I mean," said Dad, "if Max wants to do anything he can think of to avoid helping his old man out—"

"I'm not trying to avoid anything! I'm just saying I already have plans. And no!" I added, shaking my own (albeit less effective) Doom Finger in Chloe's direction. "No, my plans are *not* to marry Leya, or anyone."

Chloe made a face and whispered something. I'm pretty sure it was "Casanova," but it just came out as a murmur of syllables and a bubble of chocolate pudding.

"Okay, okay," Dad raised his palms.

"And *I'm* just saying," said Mom, putting her hand on mine again, "it sounds like a date."

"It's not a date. Two reasons why: first, Noah likes her, which means I'm never going to have a chance. Second: it's not a date, it's a *science project*."

"Really?" Mom leaned in close. "I think it'd be good if it were a date. You push people away, Max."

"No I don't. I just—"

"You do," Mom insisted. "Going on a date will be good for you and—"

"*IT'S NOT A DATE!*"

I could immediately tell I'd gone too far. Much as it pains me to admit, Mom and Dad are pretty good sports—we hassle each other, and they take my shots as well as they give out their own. That said, there are pretty strict rules about actually *yelling* at a parent.

Mom's eyes narrowed. "Fine. If it's not a date, I guess you won't have a problem taking Chloe with you. You can teach her science."

She grinned, smug. She thought she had me cornered, calling my bluff. But I wasn't going to give in now.

"Fine," I said evenly.

Everyone was quiet.

Finally, Chloe asked a question that had obviously been bothering her for a while:

"What's a Casanova?"

6

Sometimes I feel like a ghost. I bet every teenager does.

The high school years are just a slow-motion viewing of *The Exorcist*, only from the point of view of the unwanted, acne-ridden spirit: unseen by the people we wish would notice us, unable to influence the things that matter most. And, it has to be said, half the time when people *do* notice us, it's just to scream at us to get away; that we don't belong.

That's how I felt after dinner. Mom finally got a clue and realized that no, I really *didn't* want to talk about my non-date with Leya. But by then Chloe was fully invested in "her" upcoming adventure in Muir Woods and kept pestering me about it until I finally hollered at her, which triggered Mom hollering at *me*, which triggered Chloe crying, which prompted Dad to start "calming us all down" by talking about all the problems with the mini-laser and asking for my thoughts on possible solutions, which prompted me to tell him to try figuring out his own inventions for a change, which got me invited to excuse myself from the table.

Which I did.

I didn't even care that I hadn't finished dessert—I just wanted to get away. From my beloved-but-irritating little sister. From my meddling (and far-too-cool) mother. From my professor dad, who—in a surreal turn of events—kept asking *me* to finish *his* homework.

Of course, once I left the table I was immediately bored. Another reality for we who haunt the teenage years: there's never anything fun to do.

I'd beaten all of my meager supply of video games, and Noah texted to let me know he'd be late for our weekly online battle. No books I wanted to read, and since Mom and Dad forbade me from watching TV in my room—not sure why, but since when do parents make sense?—I basically sat on my thumbs for the next few hours.

Eventually, because I am a ghost cruelly cursed with an overdeveloped conscience, I started to feel pretty bad about how dinner had turned out.

I shouldn't have yelled at Mom. She was just being involved, showing she cared.

I shouldn't have hollered at Chloe—she just looked up to me, and wanted to do everything I did.

I shouldn't even have sniped at Dad, though the guilt I felt there was a bit less defined.

Still, whether I totally understood why I felt guilty or not, I wanted to do something to fix it. So I hauled my ghost-self out of the bed from which I'd been staring at the ceiling for what felt like the past several thousand hours, and drifted down the hall to Mom and Dad's bedroom.

***

The door was open a crack, and I could see Mom sitting on the edge of the bed, rubbing lotion on her arms. I couldn't see Dad, but I heard the slip-slide-clack of plastic hangars being moved around and figured he was probably doing his nightly ritual of deciding which of his ten *identical* tweed blazers and burgundy Stanford sweaters he was going to wear tomorrow.

I could hear their TV on too, because obviously whatever dire danger came with watching TV in your room didn't apply to parents. Some news reporter was talking about conspiracy theories. Then the sound changed and I heard a bunch of different voices:

What sounded like an old man: "Rumor 'round the coffee shop is that it's a laser show for one of those rock-and-roll concerts." I could actually *hear* the air-quotes in his voice as he continued, "Buncha kids staying up too late and smoking 'the pot,' as they call it. The 'Mary Jane.' The 'chronic.' The—"

The newscast wisely cut away from the geezer at this point, switching to the voice of someone younger: "Weather balloon maybe? Or like, a new pizza delivery system?"

And then the words of someone of undetermined age, but very determined levels of crazy: "Some kind of advanced military tech. Super-secret, deep state black ops, military tech. Probably the Russians. First the lights, then they take you away and next thing you know you're being brainwashed in Leningrad! Commies every all—"

Then back to Newsy McNews-reporter: "Numerous theories, but the official position of the police department is that these unidentified objects are nothing more than drones being flown by local teens in violation of city ordin—"

I turned away. Any conversation, I realized, would undoubtedly turn into another discussion about me, about my lack of a social life, about Leya. Pass. *Hard* pass.

So I went to Chloe's room. Her door was open, the lights were already out. I peeked in, surprised to see that she was already in bed. I must have been in my room longer than I thought—maybe even drifted off without realizing it.

"Chloe?" I whispered. The Chloe-shaped lump in her bed didn't move. I tried again, a bit louder—trying for that sweet spot where she'd definitely hear me if she was awake, but I wouldn't wake her if she was asleep. "Chlo?"

No movement. I stayed in the doorway for a sec, looking around her room. The lights were out, but her window allowed enough illumination for me to make out the devastation and clutter my sister left in her wake wherever she went. That and the skateboarding posters plastered to every available surface were the key features of her room, twenty-four hours a day, three-hundred-sixty-five days a year.

I suddenly felt really bad. She was eight, she wanted attention. And instead of giving it to her I yelled.

And, standing there, I saw something I'd never seen before—or rather, never *noticed* before: in addition to skating posters, Chloe had maybe a dozen framed photos of various events. A class party at the park, a field trip to a waste disposal plant—even a picture of the infamous bake sale where I learned to fear Becca.

None of that was really new—I'd been in this room hundreds of times, if not thousands. I'd seen the pictures before. But I'd never realized that, in all of them, Chloe was alone.

Other kids in the photos held hands, had arms around each other's shoulders, or just clustered so close you couldn't tell where one kid ended and the next began.

Except Chloe. Always off to the side. Always alone, no matter how crowded the room was.

A sound came from the shadows of Chloe's bed. A long, drawn-out sigh. And suddenly, I knew with absolute certainty that Chloe was awake. That she was lonely. And that she'd pretend to be asleep no matter how loudly I called her name.

She was a ghost too.

I turned away, deciding to make some changes. There was nothing I could do about my own problems, but I could sure try to help Chloe out. I could be a bit nicer, more encouraging. I could help her find some way to be...

Not alone.

I made a silent promise to myself that tomorrow would be different. I'd yell less, and hug more. Maybe I'd even do something about Becca and the Trio of Terror. Dress up as a bear and prowl around their windows at night or something.

Well, no. That was dumb and creepy. But I was going to try and make some changes. Chloe deserved better than she'd gotten in life.

***

I checked my watch and saw that it was late enough Noah should be online. Five minutes later, back in my room and running around a deserted warehouse in a first-person shooter 1v1 match, Noah killed me for the third time.

Usually he had an infinite capacity for shooting me online, but this time he sighed and said he was bored and asked if I wanted to play a different game. I was kinda surprised to find out he wanted to play a *Star Wars* game. Seemed a little nerdy for him. But, five minutes later, he was shouting at me again—this time calling for help as an alien fighter ship got ready to vaporize him.

"He's on my six, Max! On my *six!*"

Side note: you folks who are paying attention may be thinking, *Ah*-ha! *We've finally gotten to the part at the beginning!*

Sorry, but no. But now you're privy to one of the secrets of the universe: Noah screams about being on other people's sixes, or them being on his. A *lot*.

"On my six, Max!"

"I know, I know."

"Do something! I can't shake him. Who *is* this guy? Where did he even come from? *What kind of gamer tag is UsernameUncertain74?!*"

I didn't answer, too busy lining up a shot. "Boom," I whispered as I clicked my mouse. UsernameUncertain74 disappeared as the phase torpedoes I'd sent his/her way atomized the ship that had been hunting Noah.

"Boo-yah!" shouted Noah, sounding as though *he'd* been the one to shoot down the attacker.

"You're welcome," I said. I checked my ship's heads-up display. No blips nearby—we had a second before some other fighter on the alien team found me or Noah. Now was as good a time as any. "Oh, hey," I said. "About our field trip to Muir—we gotta bring my little sister."

"*What?!*" Noah's shout came through loud enough to make me wince. "What kind of dumb—"

"I know, I know, but it is what it is. My parents are turning it into a package deal: either we both go, or neither of us do."

Noah sighed. "All right, dude. We'll make the best of it. Right after I whale on you a few more times."

"I gotta go, actually."

"Studying?"

I didn't want to lie to him, but I tried to keep my studying on the down-low. So I answered his question with one of my own: "Don't *you* have to study? You mentioned a science quiz tomorrow."

"Dumb bio class," said Noah. "We have to watch some dumb *Blue Planet* show about dumb birds doing dumb stuff to each other. Like dumb-dumbs."

"*Blue Planet's* fun," I said without thinking. "My dad always watched that with me when I was five…teen. Fiveteen. Fifteen."

Noah didn't seem to notice I'd just highlighted that he was studying, now, today, in his current high school classes, stuff I'd covered before I finished kindergarten. Thank goodness. He just snorted and said, "*Blue Planet* is a snooze-fest. The only good show I ever saw in a science class was one about Albert Edison."

"I think you mean Albert Einstein. Or Thomas Edison."

"Whatever. Did you know the guy electrocuted an elephant to show off how dangerous electricity was? An *elephant*, man. They put him on a wire and *zzzzap!* That was a cool video. *Blue Planet* is dumb. It always cuts away right before the good stuff so you never get to see any—CRAP ON A CRACKER!"

That last was less about his low opinion of BBC nature documentaries than it was about the alien ship that appeared out of nowhere and blasted Noah's fighter out of existence.

I checked the stats screen. "Guess who just murdered you?"

A short pause—Noah no doubt looking at the same information I'd seen. This suspicion was confirmed as he shouted, "Curse you, UsernameUncertain74!" I laughed, then laughed harder as Noah shrieked, "Noooooooooooo!" in his best Emo Darth Vader impression.

I realized that we weren't just playing. We were actually kind of connecting. It felt strange, but good. Yes, he was a bit of a lug in a lot of his classes, but he was a good gamer, and actually kinda funny. Who knew?

I expected UsernameUncertain74 to go after me next—I *had* just killed him/her just a moment ago—but apparently whoever it was only had a vendetta against PullMyFinger4Evah (yes, Noah is a class act as an online gamer), because the fighter didn't even wait for Noah to be done evaporating before warping to a different sector on the map.

I waited a second. Then, softly, with a voice full of caring and sympathy, I said the words I'd been waiting to say: "You didn't check your six, did you?"

This time Noah didn't yell, "Noooooooooooo!"—though he *did* holler several other words which would have changed the rating of any *Star Wars* movie.

7

Lots of stuff happened the next day, but nothing of much import, so I'll skip it. Noah's always complaining about stuff in books being unrealistic, which makes me laugh. No one wants *realism*—if stories were *real*, they'd be thirty percent sleeping, thirty percent drudgery, and the rest would be either going to the bathroom, or worrying about what you'd look like next time you saw yourself in the bathroom mirror.

No one wants that.

And no one wants to hear about the stuff that happened between my gaming time with Noah and the Big Important Stuff. So I'll skip it. But I *will* give you a quick synopsis:

I woke up. Went to school. Argued with my dad over whether I was going to help him with the StormLight. Argued with my mom about arguing with my dad. Packed a bag. Slept. Woke up. Went to the woods.

And at this point, the *interesting* stuff (which is what people really want, not "real life" stuff, which is boring as all get-out) started to happen.

***

A bit of background for those who have never been to Muir Woods. First thing you have to know is that it is *legit* woods. Old when the Crusades were just a twinkle in some king's eye.

The coast redwoods of Muir stretch hundreds of feet high, with trunks so thick around it boggles the brain. Standing at the feet of living things the height of a twenty-five-story building really gives you a sense of—I dunno—how unimportant you are, *and* how important you are.

Standing there, among the tallest things ever born, you feel like you're more than a speck in the universe.

Standing there, among the tallest things ever born, you feel like less than the dust of dead stars.

And in the mornings and evenings, when the ocean breezes stir up mists that float through the forest, you feel like anything could happen, and like most things—eventually—*will*.

It's a magic place. And that magic was more than just the wildness of it all. It was also the one place I could be me, and no one would mind. The trees didn't care if I was smarter than them, or if I might blow the curve. They didn't care how popular I was—or wasn't—or if the right people invited me to their parties.

In Muir, I just *was*.

So I was almost bummed when I mentioned the place in an atypically outgoing moment and next thing I knew, Noah had volunteered me to be his wilderness guide.

But there was a pretty amazing consolation prize: that Leya was coming.

***

Noah showed up ready to hike: comfortable jeans, Keen hiking boots. He would've looked pretty experienced were it not for the most noticeable item in his ensemble: enough Hydro Flasks to make it through a week in the Sahara. Carabiners fastened a good two dozen of the metal thermoses to every available surface, so every step he took sounded like epileptic church bells.

Leya, on the other hand, was wearing exactly the same clothes she wore every day: black jeans, black boots, a shirt with some punk rock band from at least thirty years ago (this time it was The Ramones).

Maybe not the kind of thing you'd see gracing the cover of a teen magazine letting all the girls know "How to Dress to Catch THAT Guy's Eye." But to me, she looked gorgeous, even through my no-glasses perma-haze.

So much so that I found myself staring at her until she asked if I was trying to hypnotize her. Then I looked away until she asked if I was avoiding her or something.

Following that, I tried not to look *at* her too much, or *away* from her too much, and as a result probably looked like I was having a series of tiny seizures as my gaze bounced from her to the forest to her to the bugs to her to the mist, etc. etc. etc.

"So what exactly are we supposed to do here, anyway?" asked Noah. "And how do we avoid predators?"

"Wait, *predators*?" Chloe said. "We're supposed to avoid *predators*?" She looked scared, then confused. "What's a predator?"

"Something that comes to eat you when you ask too many dumb questions," I said, already forgetting my commitment to be nicer.

"Aw, go easy on the kid," said Leya, and honest-to-goodness tousled Chloe's hair.

I thought it was kind of adorable.

Okay, I thought it was a *lot* adorable.

Leya punched Noah on the shoulder. "Just relax and enjoy the sights and sounds of nature. It'll be enlightening."

Noah looked dubious. "I think I'd be more enlightened by the Internet."

"We can just head back," I said, kind of torn between hoping he'd agree so that I could keep Muir to myself, and hoping he'd turn me down so I could hang with him. And Leya.

Leya was already shaking her head. "You do *not* want to head back, Noah," she said.

I looked at her, surprised. "You've been here?" Leya nodded. "I thought you lived—"

I slammed my mouth shut so hard it made a click that startled a pair of birds out of the nearest tree.

Stupid, stupid, stupid! I thought. *How could I bring up where she lived before she lost her parents?*

Leya got a bit pale, but she took a breath and said, "Yeah, I lived in Portland. But we visited this idiot plenty," she said, pointing at Noah. "And every time we did, I'd ditch him as fast as I could and come here."

She looked around, lifting her head slightly as though to take in more of the sunlight that filtered through the trees.

"Pretty," said Chloe, and looking at her I wasn't sure if she was talking about the forest or Leya.

"Yeah," I agreed. I was definitely talking about Leya.

Noah looked from me to Leya and back again. Scowling, he said, "Fine. But if I see a bear I'm taking it down."

Rolling her eyes at Leya, Chloe said, "I'm not sure these testosterone monsters have it in them to be enlightened by the spectral beauty of this forest."

My jaw dropped. "You don't know what 'predators' means, but you know 'testosterone' and 'spectral beauty'?"

Chloe shrugged. "I watch lots of *Blue Planet* on Netflix."

Leya laughed and high-fived Chloe. "Preach, girl—I love that show!" she shouted. Then she put her arm around Chloe's shoulder and the two walked ahead of me and Noah, chatting like besties.

I hurried after them.

"Dude, Max, wait!" Noah shouted. Running to catch up, the Hydro Flasks bouncing along, he sounded like an insane windchime.

Leya looked back at him, laughed. She caught sight of me too, and, though it's hard to tell since my glasses were still tucked in my pocket, I think she winked.

Probably not. Probably it was just my over-hopeful imagination. But my blush was as real as they come.

***

We strolled along for about an hour. We had decided to take the Canopy Trail—it's an easy enough hike for Chloe, but still gorgeous, with trees reaching across the path to create a near-constant awning that captures the fog and mist and turns the world into something out of a fairy tale.

Leya did most of the talking, pointing out the various flora and fauna that inhabited the place. I was shocked—and thrilled—by how much she knew about the wildlife.

She was cute, she was funny, she was smart.

"She's out of your league, bro," Chloe whispered once when she caught me staring. I couldn't even get mad, because she was right.

After an hour, Noah found something interesting on one of the trees—some fungus he insisted was something he'd heard you could make LSD out of, no matter how much Leya and I tried to convince him otherwise. She and I kept walking then, but Chloe hung back to ask him what LSD was, and suddenly I was alone with the girl of my dreams.

"So, Max, Noah tells me you're hella smart."

I glared at (blurry) Noah, who was still staring at a shelf fungus and talking to Chloe about what LSD did. Chloe was animated, happy talking to him.

She really needed a friend.

"Well?" Leya prompted, drawing me back to what I was doing.

"I'm not," I finally managed. "Hella-smart, I mean." I did my best to smile, failing pretty miserably. "Just a normal guy."

"Don't wanna be labeled a bookworm, that it?" She nodded toward my chest. I'd worn a t-shirt which featured a pair of big lips on it and the words ROLLING STONES across the top.

Did I buy it to bond with Leya? I plead the Fifth.

But yes. Yes, I did.

"So you just a rock-and-rollah?" Leya asked. "The fast lane for you? Nothing but the hottest parties and the hottest girls?"

41

She bounced her shoulder around as she said that last. I laughed, even though I was mortified. How do women manage to be so consistently interesting *and* so constantly embarrassing?

Desperate to change the subject, I looked around. "So the trees..." I began. I tried to think of something to follow that up with, but my mental hard drive had glitched. "They're...uhh...green, right?"

Leya wasn't buying it, and wasn't about to be put off. Shaking her head, she said, "I work in the school office fifth period."

"I know that!" I blurted. Then clapped my mouth shut again because it sounded like I wanted a prize or something.

Leya didn't seem to notice. "The point is that I do data entry for some of the teachers—some of *your* teachers. So I know that you get low grades, then high grades."

"Lots of people do better when they re-take—"

"Uh, uh," she interrupted. "Lots of people do better, but *no* one gets *exactly* sixty percent on the first test—every single time, mind you—and then a hundred percent on the re-take. That's purposeful, Max."

I didn't know what to say. I looked around, staring at Noah, at the interesting mushrooms, at the trees. Anywhere but at Leya. "I don't know what you're talking about."

She shrugged. "Whatever you say, rockstar. I'm just saying: the *Rebel Without a Clue* bit doesn't suit you."

I got a bit irritated here. What did she know? She was smart, sure, but she was allowed to be, because she was also gorgeous and dripping with cool. I bet she'd never been shoved in a locker or dropped in a trash can or made fun of in every single PE class she'd ever participated in.

Of course I didn't *say* any of that—I'm not a total idiot. But Leya must have realized I was annoyed, because she waved her hands around in the air and said, "Don't get mad, dude. There's always some reason people have a hangup about something like this. Some issue they can't get past."

"I guess you'd know," I said.

All right, maybe I *am* an idiot.

Leya went bright red—which my dumb, hormone-addled body couldn't help but notice made her somehow even cuter.

"Yeah," she said. "I guess I do."

"I'm sorr—"

"Hey, what are you guys doing?" Noah asked, walking over to us, stealthy as a doorbell convention.

Leya covered her embarrassment—anger?—with a forced smile. "Just psychoanalyzing your best friend is all."

Before Noah put his two cents in—to let her know I wasn't his best friend, or ask what the word *psychoanalyze* meant—I blurted, "I don't have a hangup. And I'm not trying to act dumb."

An awkward silence ensued. Noah looked from me to Leya and back again, then said, "Hey, I thought we were here to, you know, commune with nature and stuff."

"Not with you sounding like an accident at a gong factory, we're not," said Leya. Then, rounding back on me she said, "What's your mom like, Max?"

"Uh—" I said, while Noah said, "Leya, this is a sore—"

"I mean, it's got to be someone close to you, right? So what's your mom like?"

"She's *fine*, you know. She's—"

"And it's not Chloe, I can tell you adore her."

"I wouldn't exactly say—"

"So it must be your dad."

"It's not my—"

"Sure it is."

"No, he—"

"I mean, it has to be. That's all that's left."

"No, I—"

"What's your dad like, Max?"

"Well, he—"

"What's he like?"

"I don't—"

"What's your dad like?"

Leya almost shouted the last, and that's probably why I *did* shout back at her:

"He's *ridiculous.* That's what my dad's like. He blows every penny we have on one stupid invention after another and he's never able to make them work completely. Even when the answer's staring him right in the face. There, that the breakthrough you were looking for?"

I was panting, and I could practically *hear* the veins throbbing on my forehead, even as I heard myself shouting internally.

Good job, rockstar! *Way to scream at the coolest girl you've ever met! Way to make her feel like junk! Way to ruin any chance of—*

Only Leya didn't seem mad. She was grinning. "That's a good start."

"Uh, guys?" Noah said quietly.

Leya wasn't finished, though. "Though not a breakthrough— technically it was more of an acknowledgment."

"Leya?" said Noah.

"I'm really not sure you're qualified to go all Dr. *Fraud* on me," I said, getting angry again. Geez. Hormones suck. I've heard Noah make fun of a girlfriend or two for acting like lunatics during their periods, but I always point out that guys get every bit as hormone-induced bonkers—just women have the basic decency to schedule their crazy in advance, and with guys it's random as a lightning strike. Like now, with me. "It's not like—"

"Max?" said Noah.

Leya put her fists on her hips—cutely, it must be admitted—sniffed, and said, "Maybe I've been through a thing or two that you don't understand."

"Guys," Noah said.

Continuing right over him, Leya now snarled, "And maybe I have a little perspective on relationships with parents that you don't know. Maybe—"

"Guys?"

Like Leya, I ignored Noah. I put *my* hands on *my* hips and snarled right back, "Oh, really? Well then tell me, how is it that you—"

"GUYS?!"

Both Leya and I rounded on Noah, screaming as one: *"What?"*

Noah looked embarrassed. He fidgeted with a Hydro Flask. Then looked at me for a second and asked in a small voice, "Uh, where'd your little sister go?"

"What?"

Leya and I both said it together, then both of us spun around, looking up and down the trail. This part of the path was fairly straight, going on for maybe a quarter-mile in each direction before curving out of sight.

No Chloe. In either direction. So far as any of us could tell, the forest had swallowed my little sister.

Of course, the forest hadn't done any such thing—and while sitting around doing nothing on the mothership (which is coming soon, trust me), she told me about what *did* happen. So for the sake of story clarity I'm going to tell you now—instead of making you wait until the part where *I* actually found out. 'Cause I'm nice like that.

Where were we? Oh, yeah: the forest hadn't eaten her. Though it *was* about to knock her down, console her, then kidnap her.

***

The problem, as it turned out, started with the fact that Noah wasn't the only one who brought stuff that he didn't really need (one Hydro Flask would have been fine; eighty-two of them jangling around like demented cowbells was a bit much): Chloe had brought along that iPod I gave her.

She loved that thing. And yes, her music was awful. And yes, she drove me nuts 'cause she constantly sang along to music no one else could hear. But I always liked seeing her wearing the retro-80s-style headphones I'd bought her along with the iPod. She'd bounce around, singing whatever earwormy stuff was popular that day, and I knew when I saw her doing it that she was happy.

Unfortunately, she also had a habit of putting on the headphones, blasting the music, and tuning out everything around her. So about thirty seconds into Noah's examination of the mushroom—with him using a lot of words she didn't understand, and continually referring to a TV show called *Breaking Bad* that she knew she wasn't allowed to see—she got bored, put on the headphones, and began to wander.

That's a bad idea in Muir Woods.

Not like you'll get eaten by a bear, but there are plenty of sightings of coyotes, bobcats, and mountain lions: exactly the kind of things that would describe Chloe less as "cute" or "precocious" and more "potential appetizer." Plus, like I said before, Muir is a place where the trees loom so huge, the fog gets so thick, that it's easy to lose sight of the trail.

Chloe knows better than to wander off, but it was either that, keep listening to Noah rave about becoming the world's lamest drug dealer, or watching me (as she later put it) "look like a crazy-head instead of just telling Leya you're totally in love with her!"

So she moved away from Noah. Figuring she'd just go a little way. Maybe hide, to see how much we freaked out when we didn't see her. But what really happened was (typical Chloe), three steps into her plan—three steps off the trail—she started dancing, and then she just flossed her way into the forest to the sound of the traditional hiking anthem "Moves Like Jagger."

Props to her: she didn't panic when she realized she was lost. She just turned around and started walking back where she'd come from. Only "back where you came from" is a tricky thing when you're an eight-year-old who's been dancing for ten minutes, spinning in circles the whole time, and bopping along without the benefit of either a compass or decent dance moves.

She started to panic when she saw a bunch of fungus that she figured was Noah's new business startup, but no Noah, no Leya, no annoying older brother. And no trail.

She started spinning. "Max!" she shouted. No answer. The trees and the forest floor just soaked in the sound like water—there wasn't even an echo.

At this point, she did panic. I don't blame her. I would have too. And as easy as it is to talk about just stopping and staying where you are, waiting for Someone In Charge to find you (that's what you're supposed to do when lost in the forest), it's hard to actually do it when you're alone and terrified and worried about getting turned into a coyote's version of carry-out.

Chloe ran. And in under ten feet managed to do something amazing by running smack dab into a tree.

Normally, running into a tree in the forest isn't particularly spectacular (other than being spectacularly dumb).

But when the tree you've just run into: a) wasn't there a second ago, b) falls down like you've just chainsawed it to pieces, then c) *scrambles back to its feet* (or roots, I guess)...that definitely qualifies as amazing.

8

As all this was happening, I was busy being terrified; barreling through trees and brush, trying to find my lost little sister. Noah and Leya followed close behind, shouting as well, both sounding nearly as worried as I was.

Chloe has that effect on people: people worry, never quite sure if they're worried what will happen to her, or what she'll do if no one's watching.

So Noah was shrieking, "Kid! Kid, come out! These woods are infested!"

Leya, who'd been shouting Chloe's name with the precision and regularity of a metronome, broke off her shouts with a groan. "*Infested?* With what?"

Noah shrugged. "I dunno. Deer."

"Deer aren't worth getting worried abou—"

"*Rabid* deer," Noah insisted.

I did my best to ignore them. Alternating between shouting for Chloe, muttering dire threats, and griping her out for always wearing those dumb headphones so she never knew when anything important was happening.

I heard something shuffling around behind me, like someone was wrestling in the dirt or something. Figuring it was Noah and Leya, I turned around, ready to shout at them to knock off their screaming at each other and switch back to screaming for Chloe.

The sound I'd wanted to make died in my throat as I saw something move. I still wasn't wearing my glasses, so things were on the blurry side. I patted my pockets down until I found the bulge where I'd hidden them, slipped them on as quickly as I could, and saw…

…nothing.

Just trees. The two trees closest to me weaved a bit in the

wind, swaying back and forth in a way that made it easy for me to imagine they were communicating, whispering to each other about the little girl lost in the woods.

Leya and Noah hadn't stopped moving while I did my spot-check. They were about twenty feet away from me now, but close enough that I heard Leya hiss, then say, "Over here! I think I heard something."

I turned away from the talking trees, barreling after my friends as they disappeared into the woods. Moving fast, still scared. But a thought kept worming its way out of my subconscious, demanding attention. An image:

The two trees, weaving back and forth in the wind.

Something was wrong with that picture. I tried to push the thought away, to ignore it and focus on, you know, the eight-year-old lost in the woods. But the mental snapshot of the trees kept coming back, coming back.

And finally I realized what the problem was: there was no wind. Not even a breeze. Certainly not enough to make a pair of trees move.

I turned back to look, my instincts shouting at me that something was wrong. Me arguing back, *Nothing's wrong. It's just—*

My internal voice cut off as I saw, again, nothing.

Only this was a different kind of nothing. Last time, I'd seen nothing of the friends I expected to see. Just two trees, weaving back and forth in a nonexistent wind.

This time, it was the two trees that were missing. Gone, like they'd never existed at all. Just empty space where I'd have sworn two short trees stood, waving in non-existent wind.

"Guys?" I shouted. "Someone come and check this—"

My mouth shut. What was I thinking? *Chloe* was missing, and I was worried about foliage?

Besides, even if we had the time for extra-curricular arboreal investigation, what was I going to say to Noah and Leya? "Uh, guys, do you see any trees that aren't there now?"

Yeah. Right. Noah'd never let me hear the end of that. Leya would hardly be impressed, either.

So I shut up and pressed on and did my best to pretend I wasn't hearing noises all around me. Movement on a previously still day. Enough to convince me that something was definitely going on, and I was about to call out to the others when a pair of people rounded a tree.

I relaxed.

We're fine, I thought. *It wasn't ghosts or talking trees or whatever. Just hikers.*

And sure, part of me knew that was a lie. That hikers didn't explain breezeless tree movements followed by complete lack of tree-ness.

But that's what humans do when we face uncomfortable truths: we lie to ourselves, doing our best to convince our brains that all is well despite all evidence to the contrary.

***

The newcomers on the trail, a man and a woman, were tall and thin, in the middle of passing a bag of Trader Joe's organic granola back and forth. That bag, plus the sandals, plus the fact that both had what looked like natural-fiber hemp scarves cinched around their waists instead of belts, told me pretty much everything I needed to know about them. So it wasn't a surprise when I got instant judgment-face from both.

"That's what we've been hearing, Graham," said the woman with a sigh that immediately communicated her long-suffering nature in the face of all adversity.

"I figured as much, Greta," said the guy, heaving his own sigh. Staring at me, he added, "Some people have no respect."

"Either of you guys see a little girl around here?" I asked.

Greta and Graham the Granola Twins stared. Finally, Graham said, "A girl?" in kind of the same tones you or I would say, "A piece of dog poo?"

"Yeah. Girl," I said. "Eight. Wearing Walkman-style headphones. Probably doing Fortnite dance moves and/or looking like she's about to get into trouble?"

Graham and Greta stared at each other. "A girl?" said Graham.

"A girl?" said Greta.

"Yes. We've established it's a girl," I said. "That's not the issue. The issue is: have you seen her?"

They slowly turned to look back at me. "We have not," said Graham. "We just came out for a nice hike—"

"A nice *commune*," Greta interrupted.

"—a nice commune," Graham said quickly, sounding somehow both agreeable and penitent. "And we have seen no girl, no Walkman, no…" and here his nose wrinkled with disgust, "…Fortnite dances. Just people who don't respect the woods," he added, staring at me hard so that I would know I was "people."

"Who don't respect our right to quiet," Greta added.

As if on cue, behind me I heard Leya shout, "Chloe? Chloe?!" off in the woods.

Greta sighed again. She was a professional-level sigher. "All we wanted was—"

I didn't care to hear the rest of their sad story, so I turned and walked away, hearing Greta huff as Graham said, "Well, I never!"

She responded, "I know, Graham. We should find the park ranger and let him know someone's disrespecting our right to quiet."

"Isn't *that* true, Greta?"

"Good," I shouted, already heading back to my hunt for

Chloe. "Find a park ranger! And tell him a girl's missing!"

Greta huffed. "I don't take orders from you, you teenage defiler of sacred forest—"

The rest was lost to the woods as I ran into the trees, searching for my sister and my friends.

***

I found Noah and Leya a moment later, standing rigid in the middle of a small clearing. Both startled visibly when I came into view.

"What's going on?"

"We thought we—" Noah grimaced, obviously embarrassed.

"We what?" I prompted.

Noah just grimaced again. Leya rolled her eyes. "We thought we heard something."

"Like what?" I asked. And I have to admit that, even at this crossroads of Scary and Terrifying, my heart still pounded just watching her talk. Yeah. I had it bad.

"Like, *noises*," said Noah. I frowned, thinking of my own experience a few moments before. Noah must have mistaken the expression for disbelief. His fists balled up and he half-shouted, "Seriously, dude. Noises!"

"Whoa!" I said, raising my hands. "I believe you. I just—"

A loud *crack* cut me off. All three of us spun toward the sound. I was still wearing my glasses—my little sister was missing, so no way was I going to risk not finding her so I could look cool—but now I regretted that fact. "Glasses on" made it harder to explain why I thought I'd just seen a tree *walk off* into the forest.

"Did you see that?" I asked.

"See what?" Noah said. He sounded guarded, and I knew right then that he'd seen *something*. But whatever it was, it had to have been something different than my thing, because he was looking in a totally different direction.

"Leya—" I began, my question cutting off unspoken when I saw that she was staring—pale, silent, frightened—in a third direction.

Something made a sound, deep in the woods. A series of echoing clicks. A moment later, more clicks answered.

"What makes that sound?" Noah whispered.

"I've never heard something like that," I whispered back.

"I think we need to find Chloe and get out of here," Leya said.

"Yeah," said Noah. "Fast."

9

Back to Chloe.

After she bounced off the tree—and after it fell down, then hopped back up again and then drove its naked roots back into the ground before going still as...um...a tree—Chloe stared at it for a long minute.

The tree did what trees usually do: nothing.

Chloe kept staring at it, and (according to her), "I wasn't scared or anything at all and didn't run into the woods screaming but maybe a little pee came out." All of which, for the record, I believe.

So instead of doing what any sane person would do—run away, or at least walk quickly in any direction but treeward—she headed right for the offending plant.

From where she'd been standing it had looked like a tree. But up close?

Up close, it looked even *more* like a tree.

Again, at this point any normal human shrugs or screams or something, then walks/runs/crawls away.

Not Chloe. She reached toward the tree. An inch at a time. Closer, closer. She said later that it sounded like the tree's leaves were rustling, like "They were nervous or maybe scared like maybe the tree had tree-peed a little too."

And, as often happens when you reach toward something, soon she touched it.

The bark flickered, like the rough tree skin was just a video on a faulty phone screen. The bark appeared again, then disappeared. Flickering. Only each time it flickered, it looked less like deep brown wood and more like grayish scales.

Chloe watched it all, more fascinated than scared, rooted (no pun intended) to the spot. This lack of movement gave the tree a chance to wrap two branches around her upper arms, and this finally clued my little sister's brain to the fact that what was happening was both abnormal behavior for a tree, and also potentially dangerous.

She opened her mouth to scream. As she did, the tree's leaves shifted, revealing (back to Chloe's description): "A gray thing that was like a face but it wasn't a face because trees don't have faces also this one had way too many eyes and was creepy but also funny so I wasn't sure whether to laugh or scream."

Chloe: Undisputed Queen of the Run-on Sentence.

That laugh/scream dichotomy did her in, because she opened her mouth wide, then just froze, not sure what to do next. Which gave the tree a chance to open *its* mouth wide, and Chloe realized it was mimicking her.

Again: not normal tree behavior. Again: any normal person would have screamed, peed themselves (a lot this time), struggled, or all of the above. If that had happened, Noah, Leya, and I would have come running, and maybe this would have all turned out differently.

But Chloe isn't normal. So she did not struggle, scream, or pee. Instead she tested the mimicry capabilities of the tree by sticking out her tongue.

The tree did the same. Chloe giggled. The tree didn't giggle, but it did open its mouth and mimic her giggle-face.

As she had been opening and shutting her mouth, the tree's "face" had held a dark tone, a "black glow," as she later described it. But as soon as Chloe laughed the glow turned pink. It soothed Chloe, so she laughed again, harder.

This time, the tree *did* make noise as its mouth mirrored Chloe's. Clicks and whistles came from it.

Chloe's upper arms were still being held by the tree's branches, but she was able to raise her hand and point at the tree. As she did, another branch extended to mimic her gesture. And I do mean "extended": it grew out of the tree's trunk, going from nothing to a fully-grown-looking branch with five offshoots that curled and pointed just like Chloe's fingers were doing.

Chloe giggled again. "Who—what—are you?"

The finger-branches curled up, making a fist. Then one of the branches swiveled so the tree was pointing at itself.

The tree clicked. Chloe stared, confused. The tree repeated the gesture, then the sound.

"That's your name?" Chloe guessed.

The tree gestured. Clicked.

"Click?" said Chloe.

The tree clicked.

"Click," Chloe said. Then, satisfied with herself for being the first gradeschooler ever to name a talking tree, she said, "That's what I'll call you. It's a good name. I'm Chloe. But you can call me C. Or Chloe. Whatever."

The finger-branches curled again, and Chloe got the impression the thing was trying to say her name. More clicks came out of the "face" in the middle of the trunk. As they did, more and more of the trunk's bark shifted to scales, and more and more of the leaves melted into the branches—which in turn melted into globs of gray matter that were absorbed into the thing holding Chloe.

Which, in case you hadn't figured it out by now, was definitely not a tree.

***

But it wasn't very scary looking, either. About Chloe's size, it was kind of an amorphous mass that Chloe said reminded her of one of the Pac-Man ghosts, "Only more gray and scaly than a ghost and without Pac-Man. Also it smiled and it had four eyes and feet with three toes."

That's right, Chloe saw a tree/blob/glow/video-game-ghost-

56

with-three-toed-feet making a weird expression and called it smiling, which is part of why I do love her so much. Because it's a kind of magic to see the world in a good light, and Chloe had that magic.

One of the blobs reformed, turning into something like an arm with a long-fingered gray hand at the end of it. One of the fingers angled at the headphones that were now dangling around Chloe's neck.

Chloe touched the headphones. "Music. You like music?"

"Click's" mouth closed. Then it opened and Chloe saw something that looked a lot like her own face, open in laughter.

My little sister didn't know what that meant, so she did what she usually does when she's confused: ignore the confusing thing and keep talking. "Do you even know what music *is*?"

Click's head cocked a bit, like it was unsure.

Chloe lifted her hands. Click flinched.

"Don't be scared," Chloe soothed, slowing her movements. "I'm just gonna show you some Maroon 5."

She pulled the headphones from her neck, then lifted them until they had settled over Click's bulbous excuse for a head. Again, the creature flinched, but it didn't move away.

Chloe smiled—and so did Click's mimic-face. Then she hit the Play button on her iPod.

The response was immediate. Click stumbled back, letting go of Chloe's arms. A dozen pseudopods erupted from Click's body, flailing around in terror. Then they straightened and hardened, going from gray to brown and then to green, which meant…

10

...that Leya, Noah, and I stumbled out of the woods just in time to see Chloe staring at a large bush wearing Walkman headphones.

It should tell you how scared I was that I didn't even think to question that. I just knew I'd found my sister, and now I wanted us both to leave the forest as fast as possible.

Of course, the relief I felt mixed with my terror and came falling out as a jumble of annoyance. "There you are!" I shouted, stomping her way. "Don't you know better than to run off and get—"

"I'm sorry," said Chloe. "I was listening to music and I just didn't—"

"You scared me, Chloe. You know that?"

Chloe smiled a little, and I could tell she was pleased to hear I cared. I should have stopped talking, but sometimes your brain has something planned, and it's going to happen no matter what. So I kept hollering as I approached. "Mom and Dad would ground me until a month after infinity if they found out I let you out of my sight!"

Chloe's expression fell and I knew I'd just hurt her. At the time, I wasn't sure why, but that didn't matter. Guilt wracked me, immediate, and harsh. I felt terrible. So bad, in fact, that I didn't even think to question why Chloe had given her headphones to a shrub. I simply went to grab them, intending to put them back on her head, then give her a squeeze and say I was sorry.

My clever and loving plan was immediately derailed when, as I reached for the headphones, the bush *leaned away.*

I think I blew a fuse for a sec, because instead of doing the sane, wise, safe thing (running, followed by maybe burning down the forest), I snarled and darted my hand out again, like I was mad the bush refused my will.

A very loud crack sounded. My hand stopped six inches from the bush. The bush had made the noise, but it wasn't like a twig cracking or wood shifting. More like a New Year's Eve popper. The sound repeated, shocking me into movement. I snatched the headphones away from the Bush Of Noisy Sounds, jumped backward—

"*Ughoof!*"

That's the sound you make when you launch away from an aggressively noisy shrub and slam into the trunk of a tree that wasn't there a second ago.

In that moment, the whole world seemed silent. Nothing but me, Chloe, the Walkman headphones, and the thing I'd jumped into.

I felt behind me.

It felt like a tree. Rough, barky.

Then, it didn't. The bark started to slide around under my fingers, like it had dissolved into putty.

I pulled my hand away. Very…very…slowly.

I reached out and took Chloe's arm. Also slowly.

Then I ran. Not slowly.

***

"Hey, where are you—" Noah began.

"RUN!" I shouted.

I heard Noah and Leya start running after me and Chloe. Chloe tripped and I hauled her to her feet. Loud pops and whistles and cracks and clicks sounded all around us. The noises reminded me of the old-fashioned video arcade that Dad drags us to once in a while. Lots of blips and bleeps and for a short moment my brain expected a short Italian plumber to jump out of one of the trees and scream, "It's a-me, a-Mario!"

Then it was just running. Running and not looking back, because looking back is, statistically, the number one killer of kids my age in every movie where something goes wrong in the woods.

We ran faster, faster. I heard Noah and Leya shouting behind us, but it felt like we were outrunning the sound of their voices because I didn't understand a word. Or maybe it was just that Noah's Hydro Flasks were still jangling like bells in a tornado.

I didn't care. I just needed to get Chloe away, out of Muir, back home where all she had to worry about was Becca and her cronies and hopefully we'd never see another tree again.

"Max! Slow *down!*"

I finally turned. Leya had been the one to shout, but it looked like that was everything she had. She collapsed to the ground. Noah patted her back, water bottles clattering.

"We have to keep going!" I shouted. I was out of breath too, but terror-induced adrenaline was doing its thing, keeping me upright while shrieking to every part of my body that it had to keep running; that we still weren't safe.

"WHY?" Noah bellowed (he was, of course, hardly out of breath at all).

I gaped. Hadn't they realized what just happened?

I looked at Chloe. Her hand was still in mine, and the pained expression on her face told me I'd been holding on way too hard. I loosened my grip, but didn't let go as I turned to Noah. "Didn't you see?" I asked.

"See what?" he managed.

"See *what?*" I mimicked, my eyes bulging. My arms windmilled. "The trees!"

"It's a forest, moron!" Noah shouted.

Leya rolled over and picked herself up as she said, "Trees are kind of the point."

My eyes bulged a bit more as I realized: they didn't know. They'd heard me shout to run, and ran...but hadn't seen any of it.

For a moment, I doubted my own sanity. Was I going nuts?

"What about the noise?" I asked. My voice cracked, but I was so freaked I barely felt embarrassed at all: turns out total terror is a great cure for self-consciousness.

"What noise?" asked Noah. He turned as though looking for sound, the dozen Hydro Flasks clipped to his waist clanking as he swiveled.

Leya's eyes did their own bulgy-surprisy-thing. "You didn't hear? All the pops and whistles and—"

"Clicks," Chloe said.

"Clicks," Leya agreed.

Noah shrugged. The four Hydro Flasks clipped to his shoulders clanked. "I thought those were, like, forest noises."

"*Forest* noises?" Leya shouted in surprise. "Noah, when you were born did your parents drop you, or did you play with lots of lead-painted toys, or—"

There was more, but I didn't register it. Too busy turning on Chloe. Just like before, I meant to say something different. Better, more loving. And just like before, fear infected my intent, turning what should have been reassurance to anger.

"Don't you ever run off like that again!" I shouted.

Chloe had been on the verge of tears. Now she got angry. "What's the big deal?" she shouted. "Not like you would have noticed if I died! Not like *anyone* would have noticed, or cared, or like it would have mattered to—"

"It would have mattered."

The words were soft, but piercing. Both Chloe and I turned to Leya, who was looking back at us with an unreadable expression as she continued, "Losing someone always matters."

Chloe must have been dealing with the same anger-inducing fear I was, because instead of doing something Chloe-esque, like hug Leya or offer to give her a quarter or something, she shrugged and pointed at me. "What's the big deal? *He* wouldn't have cared."

Leya shook her head. "Yes, he would." Her eyes got shiny and she blinked, obviously trying not to let the tears well over her cheeks. "There's nothing worse than losing someone you love. Trust me. It's a very big deal."

The moment lengthened out. Chloe stared at her feet. I looked at Noah, who shrugged as if to say, "Girls with dead families. Can't live with them, can't keep 'em from sleeping in your family's guest room, am I right?"

"Chloe?" I said quietly.

She shook her head and turned, crossing her little arms in a gesture of defiance that would have been cute if it didn't make me feel so rotten.

"Chloe, I just—" I touched her shoulder.

She shuddered, shaking my hand away. "Leave me alone," she said.

My gaze hardened. "That's enough, Chloe." I tried to take her hand—

And that was when all the trees around us exploded.

11

Maybe *exploded* isn't the right word. They just came alive. And it wasn't really all of them, either.

But when you're standing there after running away from killer trees/not-trees, thinking you're maybe safe, and three trees tear themselves away from the ground and lurch toward you, it sure *feels* like they're exploding.

One of them rushed Noah, who immediately grabbed two of his water bottles and swung them back and forth, trying to keep the attacking greenery at bay.

The other moved toward Leya, who shouted, "What the—" before screaming and diving away from a pair of branches that quested for her, bending bonelessly (or woodlessly, I guess), like the arms of an octopus.

The third one went for me and Chloe. I shoved her back. "Get behind me!" I shouted. I didn't have a weapon, but I curled my fists and got ready to go down fighting.

Chloe wasn't interested in protection. She tried to move in front of me. I pushed her back. She moved ahead of me. I pushed her back.

CLONG!

One of Noah's water bottles made contact, bonking the tree on its—uh, trunk? middle? woody bits?—which looked less and less tree-like with every passing second. The branches started melting like candles. The bark started sliding, turning gray and scaly.

Noah panicked. "AUGH!" he shouted, and tried an advanced double-bonk flask attack.

Two branches intercepted the water bottles, morphing into grey pseudopods that wrapped around the Hydro Flasks and jerked them out of his hands.

Noah went white—whiter, I guess, he was already pale as a ghost—but wasn't about to give up. He unclipped another bottle from his belt; tossed it to Leya, who held it like the world's stubbiest baseball bat; then grabbed two more and returned to his attack stance.

"Don't!" shouted Chloe. She finally managed to shove away from me. "They're not going to hurt us!"

***

Everyone froze. I think it was just the ludicrousness of it all finally sinking in. Even the trees stopped moving—thankfully.

Chloe stepped forward. I reached out to grab her, but she shook me off. "Chloe!" I shouted, lurching for her. The tree that had headed for us—the littlest one, the one that had been wearing her Walkman headphones a few minutes ago—didn't seem to like that. It clicked, and a vaguely branch-like pseudopod shot out of its center, wrapped around my chest, and body-slammed me to the ground.

As I tried to coax the air back to my lungs, Chloe leaned in and said, "He's just trying to protect me."

That was a surprise. "Who is?" I said. Actually, I was still gasping for air, so technically all I said was *"Ooooz?"* before my voice trailed off to a whistle.

Chloe must have understood it because she pointed at the maniac shrub and said, "Click."

"Click?!" I gasp-shout-asked. "What the—"

The bush melted into a gray, blobby puddle. Then it shot up again. Patterns appeared on its flesh. Scales. A bit like a lizard's, but somehow less icky. Gray, but iridescent, casting rainbow tones over the blob.

Two eyes appeared. Then a mouth. Only the mouth didn't seem to actually go anywhere—it was like someone used a big melon-baller to scoop out a cave in the thing's face.

It smiled.

I realized then that Chloe was smiling too, and the thing's smile was a pretty good mimic of hers.

"What...what's..."

I tried to get up. Froze when the thing's smile disappeared.

Bong.

"Ow!"

I glanced Noah's way. He was holding his head with his hand, and the tree nearest him—which had also turned into a gray Pac-Man ghost-blob like the one standing near Chloe, only taller—tossed away the Hydro Flask it had just bopped Noah with.

The thing had feet—or at least, slightly thicker tentacle-things at its base, each of which had three toe-like appendages. And as I watched, one of the feet lifted and used its three toes to itch the back of another tentacle-leg—a shockingly human gesture that made everything even more surreal.

Noah rubbed his head a few more times, then actually *growled* as he unclipped yet another water bottle from his diminishing supply.

"Stop!" I shouted. The tree by Chloe—Click?—flinched a bit, so I lowered my voice and repeated the word in a whisper. "Stop."

Noah lowered the bottle. The tree facing him, which had raised its own remaining Hydro Flask when Noah did, also lowered its "weapon."

Taking that as a good sign, I stood. Slowly. In as soothing a voice as I could manage, I said, "Let's just think this through, whatever you are—"

"Freaky space-monsters?" Noah bit out.

I glared at him, trying with everything I had to wordlessly express, *Don't piss off the aliens.*

Noah looked abashed. I turned back to Click and the two other "trees"—both of which were now in what I took to be their natural gray Pac-Man ghost forms.

I noticed, too, that each of them had a small green band around their midsections. Didn't look like it was part of them, but more like a weird belt. Wasn't sure what it was, so filed that away in the "To Think About After Not Dying" part of my brain.

"You guys probably don't want anyone knowing you're here," I said, speaking calmly. "And we don't want to make you mad, so we're just going to walk away…" (I gestured at Noah and Leya, who slooooooowly started moving in my direction) "…and pretend we never saw you."

"Yeah," said Leya, carefully putting down the water bottle she'd been holding. "All good." She looked at Noah.

He nodded. "No probe, no foul, right?" He tittered, his voice cracking a bit mid-giggle.

The Pac-Man-ghost-tree-aliens now all had what I assumed to be eyes: four perfectly round orbs about four inches across, with no color whatsoever save a purple dot in the center.

The eyes tracked Noah and Leya as they shimmied toward me. I flicked a glance at Chloe, hoping she'd follow. She didn't.

"Chloe," I said, trying to manage my terror. "Please come over here."

Chloe took a step my way. I gathered the aliens didn't like this, because the monsters immediately started clicking and chirping and beeping. The littlest one—which, in its "natural" form was only a little taller than Chloe—wrapped a pseudopod around her hand.

I tried to strangle my terror, imagining what I'd say to my parents if something went wrong: "Honest, Mom and Dad, it wasn't my fault her brain got melted!"

"Chloe," I said. "Please come here."

Chloe turned to Click. She smiled. Click mimicked her with its toothless, tongueless, throatless smile. "It's okay," said Chloe. She squeezed the tentacle that was holding her hand. "I'm glad I met you." She looked sad. Trust my sister to feel sad when getting away from a monster.

She turned to me and held out a hand. I realized I still had her iPod and headphones in my hand, and handed them over without thinking. I mean, what would *you* do?

Chloe turned back to Click and held out her prize. "Here," she said. "My present to you."

The tentacle that had held her hand withdrew, and Chloe put the iPod in it, then put her headphones on Click's "head."

She smiled, then stepped back to me. Noah and Leya had drawn even with me too, and we all started shuffling backward. The monsters didn't move, and for a second I thought we were going to get away.

Then Greta and Graham the Granola Twins burst in on us and ruined everything.

The Granola Twins weren't alone: a thin, harried-looking guy in a too-big park ranger uniform followed, and the second they saw us Greta stabbed her finger our way and screamed, "There they are! There are the ruffians who aren't respecting our rights to silent communion!"

"You tell 'em, Greta!" shouted Graham.

The ranger sighed. "Sorry, folks, but these high-maintenance loons are right. You are obligated to keep the noise down in Muir Woods."

"You tell 'em, Greta," whispered Graham.

Remember earlier, when my eyes bulged? This time I felt like they were going to pop out of my sockets then fly around like deflating balloons.

Why aren't Ranger Rick and the Granola Twins freaking out about the monsters? I thought. *Didn't they see?*

No. They didn't. Because Click and his friends were "gone." Once again, we were surrounded by nothing but trees—though, granted, one sapling was wearing Walkman headphones.

Ranger Rick noticed that little tidbit, and his mouth firmed into a line. "All right, kids," he said, a lot more seriously than he had before. "Who did this?" He glared at Noah. "You?" At Leya. "You?" At me. "You?"

"I, uh—"

I didn't know how to finish my sentence, and that was fine because the ranger wasn't listening anyway. Stomping toward the tree, glaring around as he said, "If I find out that you guys are the ones that have been painting on trees and putting up signs that say 'Rabbit Season Open,' and—" He reached for the headphones. Frowned. "What the—"

I couldn't help it. None of us could. In spite of everything that had just happened, we all craned our necks to see what he saw. Even the Granola Twins did.

The headphones had been "worn" by the bush, which was odd enough. But far odder was that the bush appeared to have grown a branch *around* the accompanying iPod. The ranger tugged on it. It didn't budge.

"Uh, sir," began Noah, while at the same time Leya said, "I don't think that's a good—"

The ranger silenced them with a look. Turned back to the iPod. Tugged on it. Tugged again. Tugged a third time—hard.

There was another one of those cracks, followed by a bunch of clicks, all of which was swallowed up in the madness of what happened next.

***

The trees surged around us. "Branches" shot out, knocking down Ranger Rick. Graham and Greta shouted something that sounded like, "The noble but bloodthirsty spirit of the forest!" as they dove out of the way.

As for the rest of us, we found ourselves tangled up in things that were half tree branch, half scaly pseudopod. The ground shook, and a moment later I heard the sound of wood breaking. I had about a half-second to wonder what *else* was out in Muir today, when a trio of round silver discs about ten feet in diameter and maybe six inches tall sped through the air, heading in our direction.

"What are those thing—*auuggggh!*" Noah shouted.

I was shouting too. So was Leya. Only Chloe seemed unconcerned as the trees "jumped," dragging us into the air along with them just as the silver discs got to us.

The discs flew into the narrow gap between us and the forest floor. A metallic scrape sounded. The three discs shivered, and windows seemed to sprout from the top edges of the discs, rising up and meeting at the top so that Chloe and I found ourselves inside what looked like a crystalline egg, along with Click, who held us tightly and made (of course) a bunch of clicking sounds.

The other discs had also egged out, and I had enough time to see Leya sealed in another egg with Tree Number Two. Noah stood in the third, trying to Hydro Flask Attack his way out of Tree Number Three's branches.

The discs shuddered. The hairs stood up on my neck.

And three seconds later we were no longer on Earth.

12

This one time in history class the teacher showed us interviews with various astronauts. They used words like "serene" and "awe-inspiring."

Me, Noah, Leya, and Chloe would have agreed on a better word: "screaming."

I know, because I heard my and Chloe's shrieks in Eggship One; and I could see Noah and Leya doing the same in the other two eggships as we blasted into space.

As we flew, Leya struggled against her ghost-alien-monster, which held her calmly. For some reason I got the impression that it was a bit amused at her antics.

Noah, on the other hand, must have been a bit too irritating for his alien host, because he'd been shoved up against the outer wall of his eggship, his face all smooshed and his nose bent sideways.

But he was still screaming, no doubt about that.

The screaming redoubled as we left Earth's gravity and started to float. My feet left the floor of my eggship and I looked out to see Noah in his, still held by his Pac-Man tree, but now frantically trying to "swim" in the air. Looking toward Leya, I saw she was holding herself utterly still, frozen in terror.

A new sound drew my attention. I glanced toward Chloe's gasp and saw my sister looking straight up, her eyes so big I could see the whites all the way around her irises.

I'd been mostly looking either at my friends or straight down to this point, seeing Earth go from literally my entire world to a grapefruit-sized thing below my feet. Now I looked up.

I couldn't see it at first. Just a shimmer against the infinite night of space.

Then the shimmer solidified. And suddenly, above us hung a

ship. It loomed larger and larger, stunning me to silence by its sheer enormity. Parts were silver, parts were the same gray as our new alien "friends." Red and green lights glimmered in various spots, and I suddenly flashed to the half-listened-to news report my parents had been watching the other night.

As we approached, the ship changed, going from kind of a pyramid shape, with most of the red and green lights along the bottom edges, to something that vaguely resembled the shapes of the aliens when in their natural Pac-Man ghost configurations.

At that point I started screaming again, because it sank in that we were going *very* fast, the alien mothership was getting *very* big, and we were on what looked an awful lot like a collision course with the thing.

***

Chloe squeaked in fear, then switched to a full-throated roar of terror. I tried to shout some encouragement, but Chloe didn't seem to hear. I looked up again, realized we were about to do a bug vs. windshield thing, and switched to terrified screaming as well.

I glanced over at my friends' eggships. Leya and Noah were both screaming, heads tilted upward, mouths formed into wide round "O"s of horror as they foresaw their doom. I couldn't hear them, of course—we were beyond Earth's atmosphere, which meant no air between us, so no way for sound to get to us from them—but their screams rang in my mind.

So did my regret. There was so much I hadn't said. So much I hadn't done.

I hadn't thanked Noah for being my only friend.

I hadn't told Chloe how much I loved and appreciated her.

I hadn't told Leya—

My brain was saved from having to finish that thought as the eggships all zigged to the side, moving toward a large, blank field of gray metal (or whatever the mothership was made of). Death loomed, but at the last second a pair of bay doors flipped open, allowing our eggships to slip into a trio of claws that lay behind the doors.

There was a *thunk,* and that was the first time it really hit me how quiet it had been. Sure, Chloe and I were screaming, but other than that, there'd been no noise. None of the background sounds of machinery or nature or other people that enfold us constantly day to day. Just a blank, muffled nothing.

It hadn't really sunk in to this point that I was weightless. Now it did, in the instant the eggships clipped into their waiting bays. I wasn't floating, though, because Click still held me fast, and though Chloe and I were hanging there in mid-air, he/she/it seemed to have no trouble staying affixed to the floor of the eggship.

The bay doors slid shut. I caught one last glimpse of Earth, and then it was dark.

Sound returned outside—louder and harsher than I could have believed—which meant there was atmosphere of some kind. Hopefully nothing that would boil, melt, or scorch our tender Earth flesh and lungs.

Metallic squeals sounded, and I felt something moving the eggship in the darkness. A second later, the free-floating nausea I'd been experiencing from the moment we left Earth's atmosphere settled into a hard lump of lead in my stomach, and I realized in the same instant that gravity had both gone and then returned. And just about threw up at the implications.

***

For those who don't know, "artificial" gravity isn't really that tough to create. All you need is a gigantic wheel in space. Spin it up, then put living rooms on the outside rim, the "top" of each room facing the center of the wheel. Anyone in those quarters will feel the wheel's centrifugal force pushing them away against the centripetal force of the floor holding them in, and *voila*! Gravity.

The bigger the wheel, the faster the spin, the higher the "gravity."

But all that requires a big wheel in space. Which, the mothership thing definitely had *not* been. No spin-up, either, with mounting "gravity" force against our feet as the spin began.

I just went from floating weightless one moment to standing on my feet at pretty darn close to Earth levels of gravity.

It was already obvious that we were dealing with an advanced race of creatures. But the fact that they were so advanced they could actually *create* a gravitational field out of nothing horrified me. We were still decades away from anything like this on Earth, and I had visions of Click and the other tree things attacking us, focusing artificial gravitational fields on Earth, ripping big chunks of the planet away and sending them spinning into space. Or just altering gravity so *we* all floated away, leaving the world nice and empty for its new owners.

I tried to find Chloe. Found her hand in the complete darkness. I squeezed it and whispered, "It'll be okay."

"Baloney," she whispered, but she squeezed my hand back. I couldn't tell who was comforting whom at that moment.

I realized I could hear screams.

Noah? Leya? I thought. *What are they doing to my friends?*

The possibilities were endless, and endlessly horrifying. Were the aliens vivisecting my friends? Planting alien babies in their stomachs? Forcing them to watch Justin Bieber videos?

Another *thunk*, followed by that metallic sound. A draft of air hit me and I knew the eggships' walls or shields or whatever they were had withdrawn back into their metallic bases.

Something shoved me. The eggship wall gone, I tripped forward a full ten feet before finally managing an ungraceful fall that bruised my shoulder and ribs.

Screaming accompanied my tumbling routine. It got suddenly louder and I realized that Noah's and Leya's eggships must have opened as well.

Okay, I thought, *we're together. But where?*

***

I got my answer a second later as a soft glow nearby turned into a ball of green light hanging in mid-air about ten feet above us, allowing me to see.

Click and his buddies had disappeared, leaving Noah, Leya, Chloe, and I alone in a cavernous room that stretched as far as I could see. Nothing else in the room, just us and the light-ball hanging about twenty feet away.

For once, I didn't try to hide my glasses. If ever there was a time to see clearly, that time was now.

Near me, Leya was spinning around, looking everywhere and nowhere, eyes wide with terror as Noah did a bizarre panic-dance and kept on screaming.

And Chloe? She was just standing there with a big dopey grin on her face like this was the coolest thing that had ever happened to her.

I tried to think of what to do, but Noah's shrieks kept getting in the way of my thoughts. "Noah, shut up!" I shouted. His response: continued screaming.

I marched over to him, shouting even louder, "Dude, quiet!"

Screams.

"Noah!"

For a second I thought I'd gotten through to him, because he stopped screaming. Then he started again, and I realized he'd just needed to take a breath.

I slapped my palm over his mouth. "Dude, chill! I need to think!" Then I yanked my hand away, disgusted. "Did you just lick me?"

Noah barely heard. He was mimicking Leya's spin-in-place move.

"What's there to think about?" Leya said, her voice jittery.

"We've been abducted. What happens next?"

"The probing," Noah whispered, his voice almost reverent.

"The probing?" said Chloe. "What's that?"

The sound of my little sister's voice changed something in Noah. He seemed to realize for the first time that he wasn't alone in this. He straightened, squared his shoulders. Looked at my sister and, with only minor quavering in his voice, said, "Don't you worry, kid. That ain't happening. Not on *my* watch."

At which point Noah whipped back his head, gave out a war-whoop of some kind, and charged toward the far end of the big room. I have no idea what he intended, but I couldn't really blame him for reacting like this. Whether he screamed or sucked his thumb, whether he charged at no one at all, or started dancing in place and shouting, "Happy birthday, I'm a chicken!" — anything would be equally reasonable under the circumstances.

In this particular situation, he got less than ten feet before there was a bright flash, and Noah reeled back, stumbling in reverse for a few steps before going down hard on his caboose.

Leya rushed forward, shouting, "Noah!"

I was close behind her, opting for a strangled, "Bro! You okay?"

Noah was looking around with a dazed expression, a nice big goose egg forming on his head.

Leya knelt beside him. "You back with us?" She held up two fingers. "How many fingers am I holding up?"

"Two."

"Who was the first President?"

"John Hancock Adams?"

Leya looked up at me with concern. "I think he might have a conc—"

I shook my head. "Not necessarily." I looked at Noah. "Who won the 1959 World Series?"

"Dodgers, four games to two against the Chicago White Sox."

Leya looked at me. "Is that right?"

I shrugged. "How would I know?"

Noah kept talking. "It was a cool game. Chuck Essegian set a World Series record with his second pitch-hit homer of the series off Ray Moore, and I think we can all agree," he continued, his voice now rising, "that the best part of the game was that no one got abducted or probed at all!"

Leya and I both looked at each other and said, "He's fine."

A bit of an awkward moment. Leya lowered her gaze and murmured, "Jinx."

I grinned, then turned and walked—slowly—to the approximate place that Noah had bounced off nothing. I held out my hand, palm forward. I took a step. Another. Anoth—

All the hairs on my arm rose up at once, like I'd just shuffled across the world's deepest shag carpet. Only there was no sense of electrical build-up, like there would be on such a rug. Just the hairs standing up, which was my cue to stop moving.

"What is it?" asked Chloe. She ran to me, already reaching out her own hand.

"Don't!" I hollered. Her hand jerked back. Good.

I rather doubted Noah's probing theory, but that didn't help us know what we were dealing with.

***

Glancing at the light orb above, I turned my head slightly and leaned down, angling my body to the side.

"What are you doing?" asked Leya.

"Looking for—there!" I shouted the last as I saw a flash of light, a quick rainbow flare in the air about six inches ahead of my still-outstretched hand.

"What?" shouted Noah.

"What?" hollered Leya.

"What is it?" said Chloe, sounding totally calm.

"Some kind of energy field," I said.

"How can you tell?" asked Leya.

Without thinking, I did what I rarely do in class at school: answered accurately. "Some kind of polarization effect. Can't tell if it's refraction or scattering, maybe both, but the EM intensity reduction is almost nil and that's—"

I broke off, realizing that everyone had gone silent.

"Duuuude," said Noah, sounding awed, which surprised me.

Chloe winked at me. As for Leya, she wore an expression I'd seen before: I had just been filed in the "Super Geek/Social Leper" file in her internal hard drive.

Flustered, I tried to think of some way to backtrack the jargon that had just fallen out of my mouth. "It's...uh...there's like, a forcefield," I said, trying to sound like I was taking the recommended-for-teens daily dosage of Vitamin Duh.

"No way!" shouted Noah. Apparently recovered enough to stand, but not recovered enough to think clearly, he shouted, "Not on my watch!" and started to charge the forcefield again.

Leya stopped him by standing in his path with her fists on her hips. "Ease off the thrusters, Noah!"

Noah did. It kinda surprised me how fast he acquiesced.

Then I saw Leya's face, and witnessed a strength in her features I hadn't seen there before. Everyone knew she had tragedy in her past. That fact made her seem sad, maybe even broken. But that tragedy had forged steel into her soul as well.

I liked it. More than liked it. I was blushing just *looking* at it.

Leya turned her head, caught my eye, and winked. "Don't hold it against the big idiot. He thinks he has to be everyone's protector. The burden of the jock mentality."

"Protect us from what?" asked Chloe.

Everyone swung in her direction. She was standing there, looking as sincere as I'd ever seen her.

"Uhh, C? We've just been kidnapped," said Leya.

Chloe took a moment to revel in being called "C" by a cool—

(*And smart and gorgeous and—augh, get a grip of yourself, Max!*)

—older girl, then shrugged and said, "They're not going to hurt us."

"How do you know that?" asked Leya.

Noah threw his hands in the air and growled in frustration. "Look, kid, these *things* are not our friends! They're our captors!"

Chloe frowned. "They're the little words on YouTube videos?"

That took Noah aback. Surprised me too. Leya took it in stride. She knelt before Chloe and held both my sister's hands in hers.

"That's cap*tions*," said Leya. "Noah said cap*tors*. Which means kidnappers. People holding us against our will."

"Only not people," said Noah. And he said the word everyone had been thinking, but no one had said:

"*Aliens.*"

***

I shivered. So did Leya. Noah's fists bunched, which was how I knew he showed fear.

"*Doy,*" Chloe said, monumentally unimpressed. "Of course they're aliens." She shrugged. "But they're friendly."

"Are you totally out of your—"

I cut off Noah's bellow with a gesture. Kneeling in front of Chloe (and trying to ignore how close Leya was) I said, "How do you know that, Chloe?"

She opened her mouth, trying to find the words. "I just feel it."

Noah and Leya shared a worried glance. I felt the same, but when I looked in Chloe's eyes and saw no fear, only certainty.

Crazy, I know. Tree-shrub-bush-Pac-Man-ghost-monster-aliens had kidnapped us and now we were in a spaceship that could be anywhere in the galaxy by now. If there was ever a time to panic—or even to just calmly assume the end was near—it was now.

But Chloe believed we were safe. That the aliens meant us no harm. And, seeing her calm expression, the absolute lack of fear in her eyes, I couldn't help but believe it as well. At least a little.

And all that calm went away when Chloe said, "So what do we do now?"

I looked at Noah, who stared back at me with the same question in his eyes. Then at Leya, who wore a similar expression.

"Why are you all looking at me?" I squeaked.

Noah shrugged. "What *do* we do now?"

"How should I know?"

Noah's remaining water bottles (four after the legendary Hydro Flask Battle for Muir Forest) clanked lightly as he shrugged again. "You're the smart one."

I know it was stupid. I *know* it, so you don't have to say it (even to yourself). But I'd been pretending to be anything *but* the smart one for so long that my response was sincere and automatic: "I'm not the smart one." I looked at Leya. "You're the smart one. What do you—"

She was still on her knees right beside me, but Leya's fists immediately went back on her hips. "Why do you do that?"

"I don't know what you—"

"That," she insisted. "Why do you pret—"

A rumble went through the floor. Something had just shaken a ship the size of an apartment complex, I could tell from the worried glances of everyone but Chloe that it had shaken us as well. It stood to reason that either something was wrong, in which case we were in big trouble, or something was right—which would be even worse.

Because I could only think of one thing that would shiver the ship, or make my stomach feel heavier.

We were moving.

13

It was shockingly mundane.

We didn't shatter into a trillion particles while some sentient computer dreamed us from one point in space-time to another. We didn't get cartoonishly distorted as we popped through a wormhole that turned us into living stress balls as it transported us from one galaxy to another. No bright lights, no sparkles.

Just that first, thrumming shiver. It went on for a few seconds, then lessened, becoming a hum, then nothing at all.

No one spoke. The questions were still there—What next? Where are we going? How do we escape? How do we get *back*?— but suddenly they seemed too hard to think about when put against the enormity of our situation.

We weren't merely the first pre-adults in space. Not even simply part of the first contact with an alien race. The ante had been upped since, so far as we could tell, we were being taken somewhere. And I would have been willing to bet anything that if we looked out a window we would no longer see Earth outside—or even the planets of our own solar system, the stars of our own galaxy.

Noah was the one who said it: "We're going. Leaving Earth. Leaving home."

After that there was just silence. How long, I don't know. The bulb that glowed near us didn't change. It hung in the exact same spot beyond the force field, growing neither brighter nor dimmer.

Funny thing about space adventures: you never hear about the little things, the normal things. Like the fact that I'd knelt down to talk to my sister, but the floor was hard and now my knees ached.

I stood up. As I did, Leya held out her hand. I stared at it. "It means help me up, dopey," she said.

"Oh, uh...yeah." I helped her up, praying that my hand

wasn't a sweaty mess.

Once she was on her feet, Leya started walking slowly away, hands out, in the opposite direction of the force field that had knocked Noah on his keister.

"What are you doing?" Noah asked.

"Checking to see if we're stuck here or—" She yelped as light flashed. Not as bright as it had when Noah ran into the force field, but there was no mistaking what had just happened. She shook her hand, then stuck her fingers in her mouth.

"Did it burn you?" I asked, worried.

She shook her head. Took her fingers out of her mouth and inspected them. "Feels like my hand fell asleep."

Noah's Hydro Flasks clanked as he went in a third direction, checking the boundaries of our cell on that side.

In the end, we discovered that the force field confined us to a square of floor about fifteen feet by fifteen feet. Noah jumped up to see if he could touch a "top."

Noah has a pretty impressive vertical jump—almost three feet from a standing start—but he couldn't find a ceiling of any kind. Just as well; I had visions of him jumping straight up and breaking his neck when it turned out the ceiling was only six inches above him.

We did discover something hopeful, however. I thought at first that Noah had caused the force field to react forcefully because he ran into it, while Leya only had her fingers get numbed. But when Noah found the third "wall," he reported no pain or numbness. He said the hair on his neck and arms got goosebumpy, but even that went away.

"Why is that wall different?" Leya asked.

"Maybe—"

She looked sidelong at me. "Maybe what, rockstar?"

Instead of answering (or making eye contact), I walked back

to the first place that Noah had bounced off of. Reaching out, I felt for the invisible wall, my body hunching a bit in expectation of a flash and then some not-good feeling.

It didn't happen. No pain, no numbness, not even goosebumps this time. It just felt flat, a little cool, like a concrete wall. I considered a second, then backed up a few paces, gave a little psych-me-up yell, and ran at the wall.

Everyone shouted—variations on "Don't" or "Are you crazy?" but when I hit the wall, it didn't hurt at all. Well, it *hurt*, but in the same way as running into a normal wall hurts. It hurt because the wall yielded less than my muscle and bone.

I still ended up the same way Noah had: going down hard on my butt, then continuing down until I was flat on the floor, rubbing my newly bruised arm.

Chloe was the first to get to me. "You okay?" she said, looking sincerely worried for the first time—a bit insane, under the circumstances, but touching.

Leya got there a second later. Kneeling down, she said, "You hurt? Anything broken? Are you insane?"

"Yes, not much, no, and no," I said, nodding to Chloe and Leya as I answered their questions in the order I'd received them.

"Bro, you shouldn't have tried to break out," said Noah. "I mean, no offense, but if *I* couldn't do it, then..." He looked pointedly from his own well-muscled arm to my own significantly noodlier appendage.

"Offense definitely taken," I said. I felt a hand wiggling under my back, and another gripped my wrist as Leya helped me sit up. "I wasn't trying to break through."

"Then why—"

"It got less painful every time," I answered.

Noah blinked. "I don't get it."

Leya did. "The first time, it knocked you on your butt with

this explosion of light."

Noah felt his head. "Thanks, I'd forgotten," he said sarcastically.

Leya cocked her head. "Pain, then numbness, then nothing. Which means—"

I nodded. "They're changing the wall—or maybe it's programmed to change itself. To acclimate to us."

Leya stood again, went to a wall, and laid her hand against it. Looking at me, she said, "If I closed my eyes, I'd just think it was concrete or brick or something."

As she lay her hand there, the wall darkened. Nothing above, but the places we had found the wall on all sides grew opaque. You still got the sense you could see through it, but it was like looking through smoke. Looking around, I realized our cell wasn't a square, but a circle.

"Okay, what does any of that mean?" asked Noah.

"Obvies," said Chloe. "They don't want us to get hurt. They changed the wall so it wouldn't hurt us, then changed it again so we could see it and wouldn't bump our noses."

"Or heads," said Noah. Feeling his goose egg, he asked, "Then why keep us here at all?"

Chloe had no answer to that.

Leya, her hand still against the wall, said, "Either they want us safe so they can be the good, 'We come in peace' aliens, or..." She gulped.

"Or what?" asked Chloe.

"Veal."

"What's veal?" asked Chloe.

"It's a kind of steak," answered Noah. "Tender, juicy, delicious steak."

"Tender, juicy, evil, *mean* steak," said Leya. "Which they make tender and juicy by keeping baby cows in cages small enough that they can't hurt themselves. They can barely even move."

No one said anything for a while. Finally, Noah said, "Mooooooo!"

I'm sure he meant it as a joke. No one laughed.

***

I'd like to say that after that we acted like the plucky band of misfits, thrown together by chance, but destined to get their act together and save the world by the time the end credits rolled.

What we actually did was just stand—or sit—quietly for a while. What else was there?

Noah asked Chloe what had happened before we found her, and she told us the whole story, starting from her flight from Noah's drug kingpin aspirations, bringing us up to the moment we crashed her moment of music-sharing with Click.

The whole thing surprised the rest of us. Noah asked my sister repeatedly why she thought it was safe to walk away, while Leya kept asking why Chloe would enter into discussions with a sentient tree. To both, Chloe just shrugged and answered: "I just knew," until everyone got tired of asking her the same questions and fell silent.

After a while, the light dimmed. Almost as though the area sensed our exhaustion and was, again, accommodating itself to us. Encouraging us to sit down, take a load off, and relax.

Noah moved to one of the now-darkened walls, laid his hand against it. He turned and leaned back, sliding down until he was lying on the floor, his shoulders and neck propped against the wall like a pillow.

Watching him, I suddenly felt very, very tired. I started to sit down next to Noah, then realized that would put us at a disadvantage should anyone creep up behind us. So I went to the opposite wall and followed Noah's suit.

The human body is kind of miraculous, if you think about it.

Incredibly frail compared to so many other animals, but at the same time it can endure a lot, and get used to things you wouldn't believe it could. Pain can become commonplace; the impossible can cease to matter.

My body didn't care that I'd just gone through the weirdest day of my life (or, I figured, just about anyone else's). It was just tired, and a second after I sat down I felt my eyelids start to droop.

Some time later—a minute, an hour, a year, I don't know—I felt something leaning against me. I cracked my eyes open just far enough to see a head resting on my shoulder.

It was Leya.

I knew then that I'd fallen asleep. No *way* would she sit beside me—not when there were other perfectly good spots to rest against, like near Noah: someone much stronger, more athletic, and generally much better boyfriend/shoulder-leaning material than me.

Another indicator that this was a dream: Chloe, standing by the wall. It had darkened further, as though—again—sensing our needs. Shifting to allow less light to bounce around, fostering a restful environment.

My little sister was staring at a part of the wall that looked like a shadow had fallen against it.

Not Chloe's, though. The outline she stared at was gray, vaguely cylindrical. Something was on the other side of the smoky wall, looking in at us.

"Chloe?" I—or my dream-self—said.

She jumped. Turned to me and said, "Click's here."

"Where?" I said, feeling blurry and stupid and also wanting her to stop talking so I didn't wake up and leave this beautiful dream where the girl I adored was resting on me like I had a chance.

Dream-Chloe jerked her thumb at the shadow. "Other side of

the wall."

Dream-me confirmed her observation by hearing a clicking noise. I looked at Leya. She had her hands threaded around the crook of my arm, cuddling up to me like a blanket.

Yup. Definitely dreaming.

"Go to sleep, Chloe," I said.

"I can't."

"Try."

My eyes closed again, and the dream melted away. Everything was dark and I could no longer see the floor of the spaceship, the force field wall, or Noah or Chloe or Leya.

Just a black abyss that I somehow knew led either to a world of dreams and light, or to a place of fear like nothing I'd ever known.

14

Screaming woke me.

A second to register what was happening, then my brain finally realized what I was seeing and I started screaming as well.

The floor had disappeared.

I could *feel* it below me, vibrating and humming the way it had when we started moving. But I couldn't see it. I flashed to how the entire ship hadn't been there when we shot up in our eggships, then just suddenly appeared out of nowhere. Now it was happening again, in reverse. The ship had disappeared around us, including our circular force field wall.

Meaning as far as our eyes could tell, Chloe, Leya, Noah, and I were all standing in the middle of deep space.

My throat tightened, my brain suddenly convinced there was no air. How could there be, in the middle of a cosmic void?

Slowly, my screams petered out as my brain pieced together the facts that there *was* a floor and there *was* air. So we were still in the ship, and the smart part of my brain forced the dumb, screaming part to calm down and figure something out.

I went to Chloe first—she's my sister, after all—and held her tight. "It's okay," I shouted. "We're safe! It's just like when the ship appeared out of nowhere before."

Chloe's screams lessened and then ceased, but she held me in a death grip. She let out a little yelp as the (invisible) floor vibrations changed. Everything shifted positions around us as the ship moved, going from a dead stop to speeds so great the stars blurred around us.

Noah was still screaming, actually clawing at the invisible walls of the force field, shouting, *"No-no-no-no-no!"* over and over. Leya was closer to me, standing totally still, her entire body a clenched fist of panic.

Keeping one arm tightly around Chloe, I reached out for Leya. She jumped when I touched her, but one eye opened a crack and she threaded her hands around my outstretched arm the way she had done in the dream.

I drew her a bit closer, into an awkward three-way hug between me, her, and Chloe. I felt strong arms encircle all of us, and Noah, through jags of tears, managed, "Will someone please explain—" before starting to scream again.

The stars blurred, shifting from pinpricks of light to long streaks of every color imaginable. Then, abruptly, it all stopped.

There was no inertia shift that I could feel, but all of us swayed as the blur around us abruptly became a view of static starfield, our eyes tricking us into feeling like we were moving even though I absolutely knew in my bones that if I'd placed a marble on the floor it wouldn't have rolled a millimeter.

The starfield shifted, back and forth like whoever was driving this thing was getting his/her/its bearings. Then the stars blurred again for a second or two, and then we were in a different location. Still moving, incredibly fast, judging by how quickly things shifted around us—but slow enough that it was all in focus, rather than blurs of light and motion.

Despite the terror that still wriggled its way up and down my spine, I gasped in wonder at the sight of the four of us floating through a field of planets and stars that I had never seen before.

A bright dot appeared below us, growing quickly to a marble. It grew and grew, until it had grown so large it was all we could see below us. The entirety was green, so deep and rich it made me feel like I was looking at something verdant and lush and full of life.

It was a *lot*, so none of us noticed Click was there until Chloe gave a delighted little shriek and shouted her new "friend's" name.

I had a moment to notice that the green belt-thing the aliens had been wearing back on Earth was gone, then the creature held out a slender tentacle-arm. Long gray fingers at the end unfurled to reveal what looked like torn-apart pieces of a yellow dish sponge. Click held them out, obviously intending for Chloe to interact with them somehow.

And, Chloe being Chloe, she immediately went over to Click and took one.

I tried to stop her, a highlight reel of every "It Came From Outer Space" horror movie I'd ever seen playing at high speed in my head, but I reacted far too slowly to stop my nutso sister. She took one of the sponge-things, which immediately slid up her arm and disappeared under her shirt sleeve.

Noah hadn't tried to stop her from grabbing the sponge, but his reaction to the thing going up her sleeve was near-instantaneous.

"*Alien!*" he shrieked.

I'm pretty sure he was referencing the movie, worried like me that Chloe had been chosen to be an incubator for some vicious thing that would consume her from the inside out.

Chloe just giggled and tried to reach whatever it was as it roved around under her shirt. I grabbed at her, intending to yank her shirt off, find whatever the thing was, and stomp it to goo. I even got as far as grabbing the bottom hem of her t-shirt, lifting it an inch before Chloe shrieked and pushed my arm down.

"Max, what are you doing? There are *people!*" she shouted, gesturing at Noah and Leya with one hand while using the other to keep me from removing her shirt.

"I don't care if all of YouTube is watching, Chlo," I said, still struggling with her. "We have to—"

Long gray fingers wrapped around my arms, yanking me backward. I tried to resist the grip, but Click was stronger than he looked. *Much* stronger.

"Noah, help—"

My shouted request died in my throat as Chloe suddenly stiffened. I glimpsed a tiny yellow dot slithering into her ear, then I was screaming again.

***

Lots of screaming today, and my throat was getting raw, but this was my *sister*. Who knew what kind of grotesque alien parasite baby was now growing inside her? Who knew what horror would burst out of—

"No, he's not usually like this," said Chloe matter-of-factly.

I blinked. "What?"

Chloe waved me to shut up. "He's just worried, I guess," she said.

That was when I realized she was talking to Click.

The alien whistled.

Chloe laughed. "He's my *brother*, silly." More retro arcade sounds, and Chloe laughed again. "I know, but it's how he is. He doesn't mean anything by it."

Noah and Leya had grown silent, staring at Chloe and Click as they communed. I barely noticed the green planet still coming up below us, enveloping more and more of our field of vision, resolving a bit into rolling mountains and valleys and plains, all of them greener than anything I'd ever seen or heard of on Earth. My attention centered on Chloe, who laughed again, then took one of the sponge-bits and held it out to me. "Stick it in your ear, Max!"

Normally that kind of talk would earn her a rebuke from Mom. But Mom was a bijillion-and-one light-years away, so it was up to me.

I didn't rebuke her, instead opting for, "What? How? What? Wait! What? No!"

Not my most eloquent moment, but I was under a lot of pressure. So much so that when Chloe took a few quick steps toward me and held her arm out, my muscles didn't engage. I didn't knock her arm away or run or anything. Just stood there like an idiot as the little spongy dot suddenly quivered, then leaped through the air and—

Someone shoved me, pushing me out of the range of the parasite or egg or whatever it was. Leya! And it worked—the little yellow mystery missed me completely...but got my dream-girl instead. She screamed as it hit the side of her head, disappearing into her hair.

"Leya!" Noah shouted.

Too late. Another glimpse of yellow sliding into an ear, and this time Leya was the one who went motionless. A burst of expressions crossed her face: confusion, fear, and delight.

Click beeped like an Atari, and her face broke into a smile. "Was that you?" she asked. Click booped this time, and Leya actually blushed. "Why thank you," she said.

Noah, eyes wide, whispered, "Are you being..." His lips moved as he searched his vocab for the right word. "...*probed* right now?"

Leya winced and shook her head. "Of course not, you idiot."

I felt something tickle my cheek, and it registered at last that, while I'd been watching Leya, Chloe had taken another sponge-bit and tossed it at me. I screamed and raked my fingers over my cheek. I thought I caught it, started to peel it off my face. Then it oozed through my fingers, leaving a greasy feel behind, and I felt it slither into my ear.

My body clenched in anticipation of the inevitable chest-bursting as Click flailed its tentacles and started making noise.

"*Beep-boop-beep-rrrrrk*—elax it'll be much easier on you and then we can move on to your large friend, though I suspect we might need to tranquilize him first. Is he stupid? He seems stupid."

"Woah!" I shouted. "I heard you!"

Click turned to me. Actually, no; one of the alien's *eyes* moved over his head, sliding across like a boat on an oil slick, to stare at me while the other colorless orbs remained in place, the purple dots at their centers focused fixedly on Chloe.

It fascinated me; apparently Click's species had a near-infinite control over their bodies' structure and appearance.

"Of course you heard me," Click said. "You've heard me many times; just now you *understand* me."

I could still hear his little clicks and beeps, but they'd seemed to fade into the background. What I mostly heard was a voice in my head. It was confident, but high and warbling, almost the voice of a young boy. And familiar—

"Hey," said Leya, interrupting my thought. "I understand you!"

The floating eye moved to take in Leya. "Yes. We've established that. Now please be quiet, both of you; your leader and I need to chat."

Noah had backed away during all this. Now he leaned down and picked up his belt with the remaining water bottles clipped to it, brandishing it like it had magic attack powers. "Guys?" he said, keeping his gaze glued on Click's hand and the last little sponge bit. "You still there? Or am I talking to the hive mind now?"

I sighed. "It's us."

He frowned. "Prove it."

"You're an idiot," Leya sniped.

He relaxed. A little. But not fully. "Anyone could say that."

"Yeah, but I'm the one who *means* it," she responded, obviously irritated.

I held out a hand to stop the impending argument. "Geez, you guys argue more than most brothers and sisters," I said. Then, looking at Noah, I added. "It's cool. I got your six."

Noah still wasn't convinced. "You hate when I say that."

"Yup. But it's always true. You've got my back, I've got yours."

Noah nodded. He lowered the water bottles. "So what just happened with the yellow booger things?"

"They're translators," I said. "They—"

"This is foolish," Click interrupted. And, faster than any of us could react, the limb that he was using to hold the last yellow translator thing shot out, elongating and thinning as it whizzed toward Noah.

Noah screamed and tried to dodge, but he wasn't fast enough, and a second later he underwent the same emotions that Leya, Chloe, and I had already experienced.

"Now, as I was saying," said Click. "I need to talk to your leader." All the purple dots of his eyes roved over to stare at Chloe. "There are some things you should know before—"

"She's not our leader," I said.

An eyeball floated my way. Shocking as it is to say, I was actually getting used to it by then; even found it kind of cool.

"Oh?" said Click. "Then who is?" He made a sound like a modem farting, which translated in my head as a sardonic chuckle. "You?"

"No!" I almost shouted, my need to avoid attention taking over automatically. "I mean, I'm just—"

"As I suspected." Click's eyeball showed his dismissal by winking and then sliding over to join its fellows, focused again on Chloe. "Now, we should—"

"Is that your home?" asked Chloe.

It's a pretty good indicator how wild the last few seconds were that we had all pretty much forgotten that we were rapidly flying toward the planet that had now overtaken our field of vision. Close enough that I was starting to be able to make out individual trees, and even see some things I thought might be lakes, though the water was just as green as the rest of the land.

"This is—" Click modem-belched, clicked a few times, then made a sound like two pieces of steel wool mating. There was a pause, and I felt like the translator sponge was really gearing up for something. I heard the word "Heaven," then had the strange sense the brain-sponge was going for something more grand.

A second later, in a tone of awe and wonder, a single word rang in my mind:

"Celestia."

PART TWO:

So...this is Heaven?

15

I filed the brain-sponge's pause away for later thought, realizing as I did that all the others were looking at me.

What the heck do they want me to do?

I had no idea, but they were waiting, so I said the only thing that popped in my head:

"Your planet, huh? Um…cool."

Something flashed in the distance, and the ship's vector changed, bringing us in line to intersect the flash.

"Is that a city?" Noah asked, squinting. He had much better eyesight than I did, even when I *was* wearing my glasses.

"Yes," said Click. "My home." Another series of beeps and whistles and grunts. The brain-sponge finally barfed out, "San Francisco."

I guessed then that when the brain-sponge paused, it was trying to figure out how to translate a word from Click's language into ours when there was no precise analogue: in this case, it looked for the closest thing in our memory banks.

Leya verified that by saying, "It's called *Portland*?" while Chloe said, "Washington DC?" and Noah surprised me by whispering, "The Cloud City of Bespin?" in a kind of awed voice.

Click nodded to all of us. "Correct," he said. "But I have been away a long time. Traveling with my *beep-boop-deep-dop-Morb-Drxx*." The brain-sponge paused, then completed with: "…parent-halves, Morb and Drxx."

"What kind of names—" Noah began.

I interrupted, "So Morb and Drxx are your parents?" an upsetting suspicion forming in my mind.

"Correct. I already said that. Is your brain-sponge not—"

"So you're a kid? A child?"

Click bobbed his upper half. "Correct again. It is good that not all of you are stupid like the maniac with the water vessels." Two of Click's tentacles came together and slapped, and a moment later I got the impression that he was clapping in delight. I think that was the brain-sponge doing its thing, translating not just the words, but the expressions the alien was making. "Very good that you are making not-stupid statements. Good boy!"

I resented that the brain-sponge translated his words into something that sounded like how you'd talk to a dog that finally managed to piddle on the newspaper, but tried to focus on the bigger issues.

Make nice with this thing, get home, I thought. *That's all that matters.*

"It must be tough, having to go on work trips with your, uh, parent-halves," I said.

Click's tentacles waved—a shrug, the brain-sponge told my brain. "I do not mind. I do not have many friends on my planet anyway. The other young Celestians are more studious than I. I prefer adventure. But still, it is good to be home."

When he said that he preferred adventure, I suddenly realized why his voice sounded familiar: he sounded like a male version of Chloe. Again, that must be the brain-sponge, somehow using my own thoughts and experiences to craft appropriate "sounds." Click was a young, adventurous kid who probably had impulse control issues, so he sounded like Chloe to me.

Why like a boy version? No idea. Maybe it said something sexist about me—but of more pressing interest was the fact that Noah was shaking his head so fast I worried it might pop off his neck. "That may be your home, alien-kid, but it's not ours. So why don't you tell your mom and dad, or whatever your double-sized doppleburgers up there are, to flip a U-turn and Uber us back to Earth ASAP."

Click beeped: "I do not know this doppleburgers word."

Leya sighed. "He means dopplegangers."

"Ahhh," said Click. His eyes went back to Chloe. "Your large pet is very stupid."

Noah roared. Leya clapped her hand over his mouth. "He's not a pet," she said. "He's protective. And he's right. You can't separate people from their homes and families. It—"

She swallowed hard, unable to finish the thought that obviously hit painfully close to home (in the farthest-from-home way possible).

Noah shrugged away from her and stomped toward Click, obviously intending mayhem, but Chloe jumped in front of the alien, her arms flung wide. "Lay off! It wasn't his fault!" She cocked her head. "Or her fault. I'm not sure which."

"Actually, my people are all hermaphroditic. We reproduce by—"

"I don't care!" shouted Noah.

He might have said more, but all of us went still as we heard faraway sounds that the brain-sponge started to translate for us:

"...cannot *believe* you took souvenirs."

"What was I supposed to do?"

"Literally anything other than that!"

"I panicked!"

"That's an understatement. And what are we going to tell the Elders?"

"The truth; that we went on an expedition to study humans and accidentally brought back samples."

Just like with Click, the voices sounded strangely familiar. Only this time I knew what was happening, and was able to pin them down: they sounded like my parents.

An ugly thought hit me. I looked quickly to Leya.

She was standing there, frozen by a combination of grief and horror. "Mom?" she whispered.

I ached to go to her. Noah beat me to it. Faster at running, faster at first-person shooters, and faster at comforting too. "Don't worry," he said, putting his arm over her shoulders. "It's just the alien mind-babies talking."

Morb and Drxx were still at it, arguing away when they suddenly appeared. I didn't fully understand the optics of the alien ship, but I guessed they'd been walking toward us from another room, and whatever light-bending technique enabled us to see through the walls also made people in other rooms invisible to us. My guess was that Morb and Drxx had just turned a corner into our area.

"And what was that on the way in, Drxx?" asked Morb, the mom-sounding one. "Were you *trying* to bump into every planet on the way here? Or was that just a lucky accident?"

"Side-seat driver," said Drxx, sounding just like my dad when he was trying to be patient right before starting an argument.

They finally noticed the four Earthlings. Several tentacles burst from Morb's body and tapped its forehead, and I got an image of Mom with her hands on hips, getting ready to level the Doom Finger at someone. "We told you not to come in here, Click!" she said.

Click shrunk into himself a bit. "They deserved to know what was happening to them."

Morb's tentacle stabbed toward Click. I met Chloe's eye and she nodded and mouthed, *"Doom Finger."*

"I told you to go to your room!" Morb shouted.

"You're deflecting," said Click calmly.

Morb bristled visibly; more so when Drxx whispered (or at least, a whisper is what the brain-sponge turned his exceedingly loud eight-bit coughing sound into in my head), "Click's right; you *are* deflecting."

Morb glared at Drxx with one eye, but her other eye was fixed firmly on Click as she said, "You do know this is your fault, don't you?"

"Beloved parent-half, I—" Click began.

Morb wasn't having it. She slashed a tentacle through the air: apparently parents told their kids to shut up exactly the same way across the universe. "If you didn't wander off and engage with the humans in the first place, we would not be in this mess."

Click's head bowed until he was almost folded in half, though his four eyeballs migrated as they did, so that he was still looking at his mom/dad/parent-halves. "I know, and I'm sorry, but before you say anything more, I—"

"Hush!" Morb's tentacles started telescoping in and out. Now, when I heard her voice, it sounded a lot like my Mom when she guilted us with one of her rare weepy jags. They were highly effective; I'd rather get punched than make Mom cry. "I suppose it's because I raised you wrong."

"You didn't, Morb," Click insisted. "But you should know, they—"

"It's all my fault that you interacted with one human, so we had to snatch up all four. I hope you're happy."

"That's enough," said Drxx, quietly but firmly, in the tones of my dad on the (very rare) occasions where he disagreed with Mom enough to bring it up in front of us. One eye roved to Click. "It's not your fault," he said.

"Not entirely," sniffed Morb.

"No, not entirely," Drxx agreed. One of his eyes turned to Morb. "It was *your* fault as well."

Morb's tone changed immediately. "*WHAT?!*" she shouted. "Exactly how do you—"

"Your hotshot flying on the way in—how in the *world* did you think we wouldn't be seen?"

The two started arguing so quickly and loudly that the brain-sponge couldn't keep up. I just got snatches:

"...don't hotshot *bee-beep-boop* fly..."

"...-ecause you wish I flew *beep-boop-boop-BEEP* like your parent-half..."

"...stop bringing *boop-beep-boooooop* in-laws into this..."

"...*beep-bee-bee-eep* cooks better than I do too..."

"MORB! AND! DRXX!"

Click's shout was like a klaxon going off in my temporal lobe.

"You shouldn't yell at your parent-halves, Click," said Drxx quietly.

Click's three-toed foot tentacles stomped down in frustration. "I wouldn't if you'd *listen*."

Morb looked like she was going to take Click to task for that, but Drxx held up a tentacle. "All right, child-meld. We're listening now."

With all attention on him, Click grew reticent; yet again, I was reminded of Chloe: always wanting attention, but so often unsure what to do when she got it.

"I just wanted to let you both know that—" Click gestured at all of us, four tentacles erupting from his side, each pointing at one of the Earthlings. "The humans have been brain-sponged."

Morb was aghast: "You *brain-sponged* them without permission?"

Drxx crossed his tentacles. "You know better than that, young child-meld."

Click bowed low again. "They deserved to hear what was happening."

"They already heard every—" began Morb.

"And *understand* what they were hearing," Click clarified.

Surprisingly, Chloe reached out and held one of his tentacles as though to support him. Morb and Drxx took note of this. Both seemed to soften a bit.

"That was for the Elders to decide, not for you," Drxx said quietly.

"They're too slow. And my friends would have been confused and scared the whole time."

Morb laughed. "Your *friends*?" More laughter, much louder. "Click, that's the most ridic—"

"Hey!" Chloe had finally had it. Stepping forward, she shook a little fist at Morb. "Stop being so mean to your kid! Click's just watching out for us, which is more than anyone else on this dumb invisible jet."

Morb drew herself up to her full height, stretching and thinning out until she was well over fifteen feet tall. I'm sure it would be daunting to others of her kind, but it actually relaxed us—me, at least. Hard to feel threatened when you're facing off against a piece of scaly gray linguini.

"How dare you, you...you...*Earthling*. Didn't your parent-halves ever teach you any manners? Didn't—"

Drxx laid a calming tentacle across his spouse's back. "The irritating baby is correct, Morb. We have not been fair to them."

Morb snapped back to her normal size. "Don't tell me you're on their side!"

"I am on your side, my dear. But that means letting you know when you—when *we*—have made a bad choice."

"Well, I don't—"

"Besides," Drxx said soothingly. "We're here."

With that, I felt the floor fall away beneath us. A short drop, then the metallic click I remembered from the eggships, and we were all whisked away to an alien planet.

16

In stories, first contact between aliens and humans is always either glorious or terrifying. The reality was that we spent the first bit arguing, the next falling on our butts.

The whole time we'd been arguing, the spaceship had been closing in on the planet, bringing us right smack into the middle of the Celestians' city. None of us humans had noticed, which may sound odd, but try getting into an argument with aliens after a thing has just jumped into your ear and see how observant *you* are.

So after the eggships flew us down, their shield windows deactivated, the cylinders tipped to the side, and all of us fell the last few feet to the ground.

We said "oof!" and picked ourselves up, and then we humans got our first up-close-and-personal look at a Celestian city.

It was massive, with building after building stretching as far as the eye could see. The edifices themselves were amazing, and completely backward from how we did it: the lowest levels—the ones actually touching the ground—were tiny. Each level higher, however, was a bit thicker, reaching outward and upward for fifty or sixty feet, then splitting into multiple towers that further arced up and away from the buildings' foundations.

It was a bit like looking at a city made of upside-down chandeliers, an effect heightened by the silvery, semi-transparent material the buildings were made of. The material also reflected and refracted light in a way I'd never seen, making each building seem less like a visible structure than kind of a vague glow in the air: another reason we hadn't noticed the city, even with a full view through an invisible spacecraft.

The buildings were there, and standing right among them on ground level, they were easy to spot. But I could tell that, from above or from any distance, they'd be tough to see. Like the

Celestians themselves, the aliens' buildings bent shape and light to hide in plain sight.

The ground around us was moist, lush. Everything that wasn't a building seemed to be either a tree or bush or some kind of moss that felt like damp memory foam. Which was a good thing, given that we'd been tossed out onto our butts from ten feet up.

***

Unlike the humans, the Celestians had landed easily. Not sure if that meant their physiology had cat-like landing skills, or if they had just been more ready for the ejection than we were. Regardless, by the time Noah, Leya, Chloe, and I picked ourselves up, Morb and Drxx were walk/slide/slithering toward the closest building, Click close behind them.

Chloe ran after. "Where are we going?"

None of the Celestians stopped moving, but one of Click's eyes shifted to the back of his head. "To meet the Elders. My parent-halves must explain to them what happened."

I headed after them as well, channeling some of my ongoing terror and confusion into a stern, "I'd like to give them a piece of my mind about that myself."

Click turned toward us. The brain-sponge turned his sounds into an urgent whisper: "The Elders are very important, and they believe in rational decision making. Heightened emotion rarely resolves—"

"What the heck are you blabbering about?" Noah asked.

Chloe shook a tiny version of a Doom Finger at the big teen. "He's saying don't make a scene, dude."

"Don't make a *scene?*" Noah was incredulous. "First of all, I never make a scene. I've got class coming out of my butt. Second—hey, wait!"

Click had resumed following his parents, which triggered Chloe's "follow like a puppy" instinct, which in turn made me and Leya run after her. Noah charged in last, grunting in irritation as he huffed across the alien sod.

Morb, Drxx, and Click were almost at the building now, which I belatedly noticed was the biggest one in view. I looked up for a second to see if I could gauge exactly how high it was, but found it difficult to do—hard to eyeball a building that moves out and up and splits into a hundred different branches. But I did spot the mothership, hanging off one of the building's upper towers like it was some kind of docking space.

In front of us, a portal opened on the wall. Not a doorway, exactly—there was no door swinging in or out, or even sliding into the wall *Star Trek* style. The wall itself just irised open, leaving a breach big enough for a Celestian to walk out.

The Celestian looked pretty much like all the others, only with an orange scarf of some kind. It rushed straight at us, and I had visions of the traditional "Eat The Humans" homecoming moment. But he angled slightly away from us, rushing to Drxx. Tentacles erupted from both of them, and the tentacles intertwined.

"Yuck," murmured Noah.

Chloe tugged on Click. "What's going on?"

Click hesitated, then whispered, "That is Drxx's—" He shook his head, then pointed at me. "What is he to you?"

"My brother," said Chloe. "But what does that have—oh."

He needn't have explained, because the new Celestian said something to Drxx that only one brother would say to another: "You are *totally* busted."

"How am I busted?" asked Drxx. A tentacle touched the other Celestian's scarf. "And what's this?"

The new Celestian glowed amber, and the brain-sponge pulsed the image of someone puffing out their chest directly into my brain.

"Like it?" asked the Celestian.

Drxx shook his head. "The Elders must be getting desperate if they've promoted you to the Corps, Brxx."

The brother(-half?), Brxx, punched a tentacle at where Drxx's shoulder would be if he had shoulders. "Exhale my spittle," he said, which confused me immensely. I felt another one of those pulses I was coming to understand as the brain-sponge rejiggering its vocab, and heard this time, "Suck it, bro."

The building we were standing in front of pulsed a weird black.

"Uh-oh, the Temple of the Elders calls," said Brxx. He disentangled his tentacles and said, "See? Busted." Then he leaned in close and whispered, "I am glad to have you back," before hurrying off to wherever Celestians hurry off to. Hunting Pac-Mans, I guess.

Drxx watched his brother-half go, then Morb tugged him toward the still-open portal Brxx had just exited. "The Elders await," she said. Drxx nodded and followed Morb and Click into the building.

I hesitated when they disappeared inside. Maybe it was a bad idea to follow aliens into their house—or their local shopping mall, or perhaps human-meat-processing plant.

Then again, what else were we going to do? Besides, Chloe had already followed Click inside. So I squared my shoulders and pushed on as well, trusting the others to do the same.

As soon as we were through, the wall-hole disappeared behind us. Watching it happen, I realized these might not even be buildings. At least, not the way we thought of them. From inside, watching the way the hole disappeared, and the peculiar way light continued to dance and deflect across the surface of the "wall," I realized that what I thought of as walls and buildings were more likely made out of the same force fields that had acted as both chassis and windshield for the eggships.

That would also explain how the upside-down chandelier structure worked, given that the design would have fallen to pieces under its own weight if constructed of things like concrete, glass, or steel.

I heard a sound and turned to see Morb, Drxx, and Click hurrying down a long, shimmering hall. The walls played tricks on the light, so while everything was vaguely translucent, I couldn't quite see through the walls. Sort of like our little cell back on the mothership.

The Earthlings followed the Celestians, and at the end of the long hall, the corridor opened up to a huge room. At the center of the forty-foot-high space, a swirling vortex of smoke and light curled and writhed in a chaotic mass that reached almost to the ceiling. It was awe-inspiring, beautiful, and more than a little frightening.

Drxx, Morb, and Click did their versions of bowing, their Pac-Man ghost bodies bending at the waist—which was when I noticed that, like Click, they no longer wore the green belt-things I'd seen back on Earth. I wondered if they were like the scarf on Brxx, or—

Movement drew my attention to Click and his family. The Celestians' eyes extended, stalks growing from their heads and then wilting forward so their eyeballs dangled inches from the ground in obvious obeisance.

I could tell we were somewhere capital-I-Important, even before one of Drxx's eyes rotated to look at us and made a sound like a modem being drowned in maple syrup, which the brain-sponge translated to, "Bow your heads to the Elders!"

"I don't bow to no—"

Noah was cut off by the sound of a million circuits fizzling, which the brain-sponge converted to a deep, thrumming voice that sounded—I kid you not—exactly like Darth Vader, saying only a single word: "KNEEL!"

We did. Immediately. Hard not to, given the situation.

Chloe whimpered a bit, obviously terrified. I put an arm over her shoulder, and was surprised to feel something already there: one of Click's tentacles, patting her back.

"KNEEL!" screamed the Darth Vader voice again. This time *all* of us whimpered.

Noah seemed especially affected. He clapped his hands over his ears and I saw a tear squeeze out of his closed eyes as he shouted, "I will, I will, I'm so sorry, I—WHAT?"

***

Noah's *"WHAT?"* echoed the shock I too felt as the owner of the enormous, booming earthquake of a voice exited the maelstrom of smoke and light in the center of the room, coming into plain view.

All twelve inches of him.

A second later, several more foot-tall versions of Pac-Man's nemeses hove into view. The giant smoke and light show pulsed as each of the "Elders" presented themselves for our awe-filled gazes.

Only it's hard to be awed at a dozen creatures that look like a prize you'd get for winning a round of Whack-A-Mole at a cheap midway.

Other than their diminutive size, the Elders looked almost exactly like the other Celestians we'd met. The only difference was that they had green, hairlike filaments coming out of their heads. The filaments writhed like Medusa's snakes, creating a strange mirror to the whirling smoke and light behind the Elders. Also, where I'd noted Click's color changing several times as he spoke to us, the Elders glowed pure white.

"You gotta be kidding me," murmured Leya.

"SILENCE!" shouted one of the Elders. A different one this time. The first one had sounded a lot like Darth Vader. This one sounded, for some reason, like the Queen of England talking through a megaphone. "WHAT ARE THESE SPECIMENS?" she shout-thought.

Interestingly, though the Elders' speech came only from the cloud, the brain-sponge made it very clear to me which Elder was talking each time. I would have thought it super cool if I weren't so worried about my survival.

"They are humans," said a very meek-sounding Morb. "From the planet Earth."

Elder Number Three (who sounded like Thor from the Marvel movies) said, "WHY ARE THEY HERE ON CELESTIA?"

"Why do they keep talking about Bespin?" asked Noah.

"Dude, you and I have to talk," whispered Leya, at the same time as I hissed, "*Shhh!*"

"What happened was—" began Drxx.

"We were surprised," Morb interjected. "Caught off-guard and, attempting to protect the secrecy of the mission, we determined it would be best to bring back the specimens."

As Morb said it, I saw Drxx reach a small tentacle out to her. I was reminded of moments where my mom and dad were fighting, and one of them would do something nice—clean the dishes or put away the other's laundry. Hugs and thanks would be shared, and the fight would officially be over. It was both touching and oddly comforting to see that kind of family moment play out here, on an alien planet so far from my own home.

Elder Vader said, "WERE YOU ABLE TO ASCERTAIN WHETHER EARTH WOULD SUIT THE MISSION PARAMETERS BEFORE YOUR PREMATURE EXIT?"

"The research was not yet complete," Drxx said quickly, and I got the feeling that, just as Morb had tried to cover for him a moment before, now he was trying to shield her from blame by being the one to deliver the bad news. Again, surprising—and surprisingly reassuring.

Elder Thor didn't share my sentiment. "THIS IS UNSATISFACTORY. IN ADDITION TO—"

"Can you not be so yelly?" Chloe shouted.

"Chloe!" I hollered.

"Quiet!" hissed Leya.

"Don't piss off Emperor Palpatine!" shouted Noah (I *really* needed to talk to him about his surprising *Star Wars* fanboying).

Elder Thor's eyes swung to look at Chloe, its green head-filaments started twitching like an electrified toupee. Then it turned its eyes back to Morb and Drxx. "IN ADDITION—"

"Are you just always angry?" asked Chloe, all wide-eyed and innocent. "Or do you just have to go to the bathroom or something, because when I have to go to the bathroom sometimes I get yelly, especially when Max is in there and he's spending too much time because he's popping a zit or shaving even though he doesn't really have to because he barely has much whiskers and—"

"Chloe! Hush!" I shouted, not sure whether I did so to avoid the Elders' ire or just further embarrassment in front of Leya.

Elder Thor's eyes swiveled in Chloe's direction for a moment, Then, doing his best to ignore her, they swiveled back to Morb and Drxx. "IN ADDITION TO—"

"I guess it's okay though. My mom gets yelly sometimes, but then she makes cookies or puts out a fire and feels better."

Silence. Even the swirling vortex behind the Elders seemed to pause.

"In addition to failing—" Elder Thor began, his voice significantly quieter in our minds.

"See, doesn't that feel better?" Chloe asked.

"**SILENCE!**" shouted all of the Elders at once (I couldn't make out all the voices, but in addition to Darth Vader, sinus infection Queen of England, and Elder Thor, I was pretty sure I heard the

President of the United States, Principal Carter from my high school, and Nicki Minaj).

"You don't have to shout is all," muttered Chloe.

The Elders waited a moment. When Chloe said nothing else, Elder Thor finally managed to finish speaking to Morb and Drxx: "In addition to failing to collect the necessary data to formulate an assessment, you may have imperiled us further if the Earthlings come in search of their offspring. These specimens' presence here heightens the danger to our world."

"With respect, Elder Thor," said Drxx, "that is unlikely. The Earthlings are not yet capable of travel beyond the immediate reach of their planet."

"Be that as it may," said Elder Nicki Minaj, "your mission must be completed, and urgently. You shall return to Earth immediately, returning the humans to their proper environment and completing your assignment."

Chloe turned to Click and whispered, "What exactly *is* your mission?"

Click hesitated. He glanced at the Elders. I don't know if it was because they were testing him, or if my little sister had simply annoyed them to the point where they figured it was just easier to let her questions be answered. Either way, they were silent, waiting until Click said, "We are tasked with finding a new home for our people."

"New home? Why?" asked Chloe.

Click sounded absolutely beside himself with terror. "Because the…" (and here the brain-sponge did that little hiccup I was starting to realize was the equivalent of it saying, "You guys don't have a word for this part in your memory banks so I'm just gonna do the best I can and leave it at that") "…*Gro'nid* are determined to take our current home. The Gro'nid are going to take Celestia."

I looked at Leya and Noah. They both shrugged. So I leaned

in close to Click and asked the question on all our minds: "What's a Gro'nid?"

All of the Celestians—and I do mean all of them—gasped, the brain-sponge making it clear in my head that I had just asked the equivalent of, "Who *is* Hitler, and was he really that bad?"

But before they could answer my question, the universe did the job itself, introducing me, my sister, and my friends to the Gro'nid in the scariest possible way.

17

Slight pause from the story here—at least, the story of what was happening in the Temple of the Elders—as we whiz a few thousand miles due up.

I had already had a chance to see, if only briefly, how beautiful Celestia was from space. I had also seen some of the other planets and moons and stars. Amazing, beautiful. More than any Earth human had ever realistically hoped to see, and we were there for it.

But we hadn't seen *everything*. We certainly didn't see the flotilla of massive, angular ships that had clustered above Celestia in the moments when we four little humans were scurrying after Click and his family as they entered the waiting door.

We didn't see the smaller ships, either: hundreds of them, shaped a bit like boomerangs, the leading angle of each bristling with sensors and weaponry.

But they were there. And as we were listening to the Elders chew out Morb and Drxx, the boomerang fighters dropped toward Celestia. The lead one was painted with splashes of red, and on the underside, close to the front windows, there was a painting of what I suppose was the equivalent of a pinup on a World War II fighter jet: an alien wearing the equivalent of a bikini for a creature mostly made of mucus and elbows, with a single eyeball on an eyestalk winking sensually at the universe.

The rest of the boomerang fighters followed the one with the alien pinup, searing through Celestia's outer atmosphere in a tight formation of flaming red streaks, then heading for the Celestians' capital city and four humans about to find themselves right in the middle of an intergalactic war of extermination.

***

At exactly the moment when I asked, "What's a Gro'nid?" the first missiles hit the city.

They smashed into a tall building on the outer edge of the city. The field structure of the building shimmered, then shattered into thousands of glassy shards. Celestians who'd been outside scattered, trying to find safety as the missiles rained down.

Inside the Temple of the Elders, we heard a BOOM, followed by a sound that was half explosion, half shattering mirror, half short-circuit (yeah, I know that's too many halves—there was a lot going on).

The Elders all started glowing black, which I guessed was a Celestian fear response. They all started chattering, and I got a few minor snippets of panic before the brain-sponge threw its nonexistent hands into the air and just gave up trying.

I was able to hear Morb and Drxx, though, as they intertwined their tentacles with Click and started rushing him out of the Temple. Chloe followed, of course, which meant that Leya, Noah, and I were hot on her heels.

The first round of explosions was still happening, and as we exited a missile slammed through a tall building nearby. I heard that explosion/shatter/short-circuit sound again. This time I realized it was the sound that the fields holding up the Celestians' buildings made when they lost their fight against gravity.

A building tumbled. Another.

I barely heard or saw them. I just saw the Celestians. Dozens, maybe hundreds. Big ones like Morb and Drxx, smaller Celestian children like Click, even a few tiny Elders. All of them scurried around and a part of my mind that was desperately trying to run from reality thought they looked even *more* like Pac-Man ghosts right now.

Maybe it would have been funny any other time. Not now though, with explosions going off and sparkling tracer fire sparking out of the boomerang ships, tracking their way across the buildings, stitching needle-bright flashes into and through Celestians.

I saw two Celestians darting down a mossy side street, their gray skin turning green as they did. It camouflaged them from sight, so a boomerang fighter that had seemed to be cruising after them flew right past as they flattened themselves against the ground, becoming almost invisible.

Another group wasn't so lucky. Two big ones—parent-halves, I guessed—were clasping tentacles with two Celestians about Click's size. They started to shift coloration as well, but weren't fast enough: the boomerang fighter I'd been tracking opened fire and the Celestians were slammed into the wall. They stayed there for a long, horrible moment before they slid slowly to the mossy ground. Their bodies dulled as it happened, going from the iridescent gray I'd come to associate as "normal" coloring, to a dull, empty shade. Dead.

I heard screaming.

Chloe!

Turning around, I saw she'd run back into the Temple. She was in the hall we had first entered, staring back at the destruction.

I began running. Before I'd made half the distance, Leya was at Chloe's side. She practically fell on Chloe, turning my sister away from the devastation outside, holding her tight.

I was there a second later. I put my arms around my sister too. An instant after that, I felt Noah's arms wrap around all of us. It's something we do, as humans—as all thinking creatures: we hold to what we love. We do it mentally, all the time, and holding those things defines the shape of our lives.

Then something else joined us. Click sprouted a dozen tentacles and wrapped them tightly around Chloe and the rest of us.

A second later, I saw Morb as well, tapping her tentacle against Click's fear-blackened head.

"Stay here," she said softly. A tentacle tapped the wall, and

116

the field aperture shut. The sound outside dampened immediately, though we could still see a lot of what was happening. Too much.

"What's going on?" I whispered.

Click spoke, sounding strangled even before the brain-sponge translated. "The Gro'nid are attacking. For many centuries, they did not even know we were here, and we hid in plain sight. We saw them, but thought it would be best to present this area as uninhabited." Click's mouth did a little wiggle. The brain-sponge nudged the image of someone grimacing into the front of my brain. "Little did we know that an uninhabited planet would look quite appealing to them."

"Duh," whispered Noah. "Haven't you ever seen *any* alien movies?"

"Probably not," whispered Leya right back. I didn't need a brain-sponge to translate the scorn in her voice.

I suddenly realized that I wasn't just holding my sister. I was also holding Leya—right in front of Noah. I immediately tried to pull away, but Leya grabbed my arm and wouldn't let me go. Neither would Click: the tentacles around us all tightened, binding all of us into a close knot.

Click continued talking to keep the fear at bay. "There is little we can do now except wait—"

Leya shook her head. "You can't hide from—or just wait out—a bully."

"Yeah," said Noah. "Don't you know that?" He winced as another explosion sounded, and his big arms tightened around us.

"Fighting back...it is not in our nature. We are not warriors, so our response efficacy has been limited. And the Gro'nid are so powerful."

Another explosion. Click cried out, and Chloe screamed as well. The intensity of the noise shocked me: it sounded more like she was actually in pain than like she was watching what happened outside the Temple's shielding.

I started to ask if she was hurt. But before the words formed, I found myself screaming in exactly the same way. Because I was suddenly somewhere else. Someplace far more dangerous than a hallway in the middle of a war zone. Chloe was there too, and my terror ratcheted up a notch, because I knew one or both of us would be dead in moments.

18

It was all a jumble at first. A confused mix of sensory inputs that made little sense. Sudden heat. Pain in my limbs, like they'd all fallen asleep at the same time and were now waking up in the most excruciating fashion. Bright red lights whipping across my field of vision.

The sensations increased in speed, as did my terror and confusion. Then everything collapsed to a single point: a singularity. I fell into the singularity too. Collapsed around myself, then into myself, then falling into the brightness that was everything and nothing at once.

I felt something beside me. Chloe. I looked at her, and as I did the singularity exploded outward, instantly expanding to fill the entire universe. Chloe's mouth was open, she was shrieking in terror, but I heard nothing.

In the instant I realized that sound had not returned to the universe, it did just that, and did it *big*. I could hear the explosions of a moment before, only this time they were louder. I could see them too. They weren't hitting the shield-walls around me, they were hitting…what?

The ship. I was back in the mothership that had brought us all to Celestia. I didn't know how, but that's where I was. Chloe too. She didn't seem to notice me. She was just screaming that silent, terrifying un-scream. I was still holding her, just as I had been in the Temple. And I realized that Click was there too, holding us both. He looked different, though. The graceful movements of his people were gone, replaced by complete rigidity. Eyes kept popping open everywhere on his body. They'd swivel around wildly, like they were trying to take in the whole universe in an instant, then disappear into his flesh.

That was when I decided I must have gone crazy. As I thought that, eyes erupted all over Click's body, and all of them looked at me. "Not crazy," said Click. "*Joined.*"

"What does that mean?" I started to say. But the words never came. Another explosion did. The mothership rocked, and I heard twin shouts.

Looking to the side, I saw Morb and Drxx, sitting in front of some kind of control console that kept fading in and out of focus. It was hard to see the details, but I somehow knew they were staring out the mothership's main viewscreen, tracking the mass of Gro'nid boomerang fighters that wove in and out of the Celestians' city, bringing destruction at every turn.

A few big, flaming orbs that reminded me of cannonballs arced upward. I knew, the same way I knew we were in the mothership, that these were Celestian armaments: the best the peace-loving creatures had figured out how to make, and woefully inadequate against the Gro'nid.

The Gro'nid fighters dodged and tightened into a knot. Drxx screamed. "No!" An eyestalk whipped toward Morb. "They're creating a destruction formation around the Temple."

Noah! Leya! I thought.

Again, all the eyeballs on Click's body flicked toward me. "We're in danger too," he said.

Or did he? I heard his voice, but it wasn't the same as when the brain-sponge translated. More like it was my own mind translating the words.

No, that wasn't right either. It was like, for that moment, in that place, I just spoke the lingo myself.

That feeling was confirmed as I heard Drxx shout, "Do you hear me, Morb?" They were speaking Celestian, but I understood the language like I'd been born to it. Drxx shouted again, sounding utterly panicked. "They're going to destroy Click and the humans!"

Morb finally spoke. "Quiet! Let me concentrate."

I understood her, just like I understood Drxx. But interestingly, both still "felt" like they were speaking a lot like my parents would: Drxx the permanently off-kilter dad, Morb the analog to my calm, capable mom.

A series of lights swept across the inner wall of the mothership. They were Celestian communications, but just as with the words spoken by Click, Morb, and Drxx, I understood them:

Estimated time to Temple destruction:

25...

24...

23...

A few more fireballs arced up. The boomerang fighters slid away, easily avoiding the Celestians' meager attack, then returning to the formation that was tightening around the Temple of the Elders.

20...

19...

"Dear..." said Drxx.

"I know," said Morb. She flipped several switches, and the view of the city and its attackers changed, zooming in close on one of the boomerang fighters.

The fighter didn't look like it had taken any direct hits, but scorch marks around its mid-section—including one on the weird, winking creature that was all elbows and snot covered up by an alien bikini—showed that the Celestians weaponry had rattled its chain a time or two.

Morb touched another button. "Attention all Celestian defense personnel. Stand down on current targets and focus all firepower on the ship with the Gro'nid prostitute on the fuselage."

A series of voices came in over whatever Celestian radio

system Morb had spoken into:

"Can't find—"

"Negative, target is not—"

"Lost my gun capabilities—"

"Targeting needed—"

"Drxx!" shouted Morb.

"On it!" Drxx flipped several switches and suddenly the Winking Gro'nid was highlighted in orange. Another tentacle came out of his back, questing through the air until it joined with a matching one that had erupted from Morb.

The two appendages twined around each other. Like humans holding hands in terror, a moment where physical contact made shared emotion bearable.

As they touched I felt a sudden jolt, deep inside the part of me that was still just Max Abernathy.

The universe shifted again. Faster this time, and instead of collapsing to a singularity and back again, it collapsed into something I barely had the mental makeup to understand. It was like looking at that singularity through a diamond: the facets split my vision into multiple pieces. Each facet showed a different event, as though I was looking through many different eyes at once:

Through one set of "eyes," I saw the sky, filled with Gro'nid ships. I felt terror, and knew that it wasn't my own fear, but that of the Celestian whose eyes I was looking through.

(10...

9...)

On another facet, I saw the image of a Celestian I'd never seen before, trying to move a dead friend away from a scorched, heat-twisted hulk of something I somehow knew had once been a cannon.

(8...

7...)

On yet one more facet of this sight-diamond, I saw a new Celestian, who I recognized as Drxx's brother, Brxx, due to the bright orange scarf he wore. Brxx plopped in the seat of what I could tell—in the same way I could understand Celestian speech, and read the countdown still going on the wall—was a cannon. He gripped the cannon's controls (which looked a lot like a joystick on a 1980s arcade game), and the weapon rotated. Brxx shifted a pair of eyestalks toward a readout on the side of the cannon, and my view shifted to another facet...

...where I saw, through another Celestian weapon operator's many eyes, the image of the Winking Gro'nid on its targeting system. From this angle there was no way the Celestian could see the creepy pinup model on its fuselage, but the Celestian said, "Got it."

(5...

4...)

How can he know he's got the right one? I thought.

And as I did, I saw yet another facet of that diamond. It was Click, whispering a word he'd used before: *"Joined."*

(3...)

The Celestian gunner rotated the joystick just a hair—

(2...)

"Now!" shrieked Drxx back in the mothership, and in his voice I heard every fear I could ever imagine, all distilled into the terror I knew he and Morb were both feeling: that of losing a child.

The boomerang ships all started to glow, and lights streaked out from each, connecting the ships to each other at the corners of a giant, deadly web of light.

(1...)

The Celestian gunner hit the fire button.

A flurry of cannonballs launched upward from the side of a small building to the right of the Temple of the Elders. Most missed, harmlessly zipping past the Gro'nid ships. Several passed between the attackers, crossing through the lines of light that had connected the boomerang fighters. As each cannonball hit the strands of the web, there was a flash and when the flash cleared, the cannonballs were just gone. Disintegrated. That was what would happen to the Temple of the Elders—and Noah and Leya, and even Chloe and Click and I, who were in the Temple, even though we were also somehow *here*.

(0...)

The Gro'nid ships dropped toward the Temple. But an inch before the web touched the structure, a lone cannonball arced up. It slammed into the side of the Winking Gro'nid.

The result was instant. The web flickered away, leaving the Gro'nid ships descending quickly toward the city, without the benefit of the disintegration weapon they had been about to unleash. A few of the ships slammed into Celestian buildings, and though the Gro'nid's missiles could penetrate the shield-walls, the ships themselves were another matter. They ricocheted off the buildings, struggling for control.

The Winking Gro'nid fared even worse. Smoke erupted from its engines, and a gout of fire coughed out. More cannonballs hit—from a different angle this time—and as they did, my diamond view of the universe shifted again.

Back in the mothership. The whole thing rattled, the invisible walls of the ship going bright, then dark, then bright again. Through the flashes I could make out several boomerang ships. Either they'd broken away when the net failed, or they'd always been on the outer edges of the fighting. Either way, they had spotted the mothership, and were now firing on it. Some kind of plasma beam, it looked like. Whatever it was, I could tell that the mothership was in trouble.

"They're not going to be able to take that for long," I heard someone say. Noah?

Maybe. But he sounded wrong. Split in pieces, like my view of the universe: he sounded like he was right next to me, speaking into my ear as we all cowered together in the Temple of the Elders, and at the same time far, far away from me as I stood with Chloe and Click, watching Morb and Drxx in the mothership.

Morb was still piloting the ship, but Drxx had brought out a new set of controls that my strange inner connection told me was a gunner's setup. He pressed a button and more of the cannonball things spat out of the mothership. They exploded against the Winking Gro'nid, rocking it. Another wave of shots from the Celestian gunners in the city smashed into it a moment later.

The Winking Gro'nid swerved around the next barrage, then returned to its place in the original formation. It looked scorched but otherwise okay.

The mothership wasn't faring so well. Bright lights started appearing everywhere, and something like whale song on speed—the mothership's alarms—started to sound.

"Morb—" Drxx began.

"I know," she said. "Keep firing."

"Click is Joined with us." In Drxx's voice, I heard a concern that surprised me. And I knew with absolute certainty that the concern wasn't for himself, or even for his spouse. He wasn't worried about dying, but about dying in front of his child.

"I know," whispered Morb. "Keep firing. I'll try to keep us alive and—"

Another round of shots from the boomerang fighters sliced into the mothership. The impacts felt like they were going to tear the ship apart around us. And even though I knew somewhere deep inside that I wasn't really here, that I was just experiencing this through some kind of Celestian mind-meld, I wanted to scream in terror.

The mothership's shudders increased. One more hit and it—they, we—were all done for.

One of the Winking Gro'nid's wings, I was guessing weakened by the Celestian bombardment, sheared off. The wing shot sideways, bouncing harmlessly off a nearby building and out of sight. The remaining part of the ship started spinning. It was maintaining its height, more or less, but obviously had no control beyond that.

"Yeah!" I screamed, and beside me I heard Chloe yell, "Booyah, jerks!" even as, in the mothership, the alarms flared on again, even brighter this time. The whale song went completely manic.

"We've sustained significant structural damage," said Drxx, deathly calm.

The mothership canted hard to the side. As it did, the Winking Gron'nid stopped spinning and dropped like a rock, straight toward the Temple of the Elders. It hit one of the upper tower arms of the building.

The impact shuddered the Temple, and as it did I felt my balance shift. I stepped back. My mind was in the ship, with Morb and Drxx—and in a dozen other places too—but my physical self was still in the Temple, and the Gro'nid ship's impact made me stumble.

I felt Chloe trip in a different direction, and at the same time Click staggered, his tentacles no longer touching me as he struggled to remain upright in a collapsing world. As he broke contact, the diamond view of eternity sheared away, fragmenting and then disappearing from my mind. The many facets of reality collapsed, leaving me no longer *"Joined."*

I was alone, and the feeling was so terrible and wonderful that tears erupted from my eyes.

As he tumbled to the side, Click screamed, *"Parent-halves!"*

I understood the word, but only because the brain-sponge gave me the translation. The psychic connection between me and the others had been severed.

If it happened at all, I thought. *That might have been nothing but intergalactic shell shock.*

Something to figure out later. When we're not in danger of dying.

My brain had a point.

I looked up and could see the wounded boomerang fighter ricocheting off the Temple's towers above. Once, twice, three times. Then it hit the ground, landing at the bottom of the Temple almost directly in front of us.

Click was scurrying away, and for a second I thought he was going to rush the downed Gro'nid ship. Once again, Chloe was on his heels as he ran, shouting, "Click! Wait! It's okay!"

But Click wasn't listening. We all followed him and Chloe— it was getting to be something of a habit—as they ran outside the Temple. Click's eyeballs grew stalks, and the stalks shot straight up, straining to their limit as though extending an extra inch would guarantee he saw good news.

We looked the direction he was looking. I finally saw the mothership, which was flickering into and out of sight. No longer a pyramid, now it looked like something between a Mobius strip and a pretzel: all intersecting tracks that ran together in ways my eyes insisted were impossible, studded with crystalline structures that I guessed were the camouflage projectors.

As it flickered in and out of sight, Click kept screaming, alternating between his parent-halves' names and wordless sounds of terror.

The mothership finally winked away completely. I worried it had been disintegrated. But one look at Click told me the disappearance was a good thing. They weren't disintegrated, just getting the ship back up to function after the Gro'nid—

I gasped, realizing that we were still in the middle of an attack! In all the rush of the "Joining," then the pain and confusion right after, I'd somehow forgotten that we were in a war zone.

Only the war zone was gone. The boomerang fighters—all but the downed one—streaked higher in the sky, obviously on the run. A moment later, the Winking Gro'nid coughed and then slowly, wobbly, rose into the sky and shrieked away.

"I don't get it," said Noah. "They were kicking your butt."

"Well, they're retreating now," said Chloe. Noah actually gave out a cheer, and Chloe clapped.

"Why do you applaud?"

I turned to see Elder Thor coming out of the Temple, followed by Elder Queen of England, Elder Nicki Minaj, and all the rest.

"We won, right?" said Chloe. She was patting Click absently, obviously still worried about her friend. I loved her in that moment probably more than I ever had. We were on an alien planet, light-years from our own, and had somehow gotten stuck in some kind of interstellar conflict, and she still managed to find that caring for the people—er, aliens—she loved.

"A short-lived victory at most," said Elder Vader. The brain-sponge was really pulling out all the stops too, because at the end of the sentence I could have sworn I heard the robotic asthma sound he always makes in the movies. "The Gro'nid will return. And we must now begin the task of surveying the damage. I assure you, there will be no cause for applause."

"Buzzkill," whispered Noah.

A shadow flickered in and out of existence, something blocking the sky for an instant, disappearing, and then appearing again.

"What the heck is that?!" Leya shouted. She'd barely made a sound this whole time, and a part of me had admired her strength and courage. Now I suddenly wondered if she'd simply been terrified to silence. Certainly her voice held the jagged edge of panic right now.

I reached out, thinking I'd pat her shoulder or maybe even put my arm around her. Noah beat me to it, of course. "We've got this," he whispered, hugging her.

"Yeah," Leya answered, sounding thoroughly unconvinced.

Looking up, we saw the source of the weird lighting: the mothership flickered in and out of sight directly above us. It docked at the temple, and a couple of seconds later, smoke billowed out of it.

An eggship shot out the side, and I saw Morb and Drxx inside, moving into a portal atop the Temple, while other Celestians raced out of the same opening, presumably to put out the fire and start fixing the ship.

Not long after that, Morb and Drxx came into the hall where we were still standing. Click shouted with joy, and rushed to his parent-halves. The little family embraced, and it was beautiful (in a weird way).

I heard Leya choke back a sob, which tempered the beauty of it. Her expression was clear as glass: the Celestians were in a fight for their lives. But at least Click still *had* his family.

Again, I wanted to reach out to her. Again, Noah beat me to it, holding her tight and whispering what were no doubt very manly sports metaphors into her ear.

Nearby, Click was click/screech-crying. The brain-sponge transformed the sounds into hysterical weeping.

"It's okay," whispered Drxx. His tentacles fluttered over Click's back. "We're okay."

"Are we?" whispered Morb. She was staring over my shoulder. I turned my head, glancing in the direction she was looking.

The Celestian city, so bright and beautiful only moments ago, now looked singed and scorched. Fires leaped out of breaches in the shield-walls. Pieces of alien machinery sat in burned-out heaps on the streets.

And they weren't all that had been burned.

I put my arms around Chloe, trying to keep my body between her and the devastation. Not easy to do when the entire building you're in is mostly transparent. But I had to try.

It didn't work. I could feel Chloe shaking in my arms, and she suddenly sobbed and buried her head in my stomach and I knew she'd seen it all.

Morb was right. Things definitely weren't okay. Not okay at all.

And about to get worse.

19

After the battle the Elders put their heads together—literally. They bowed close, and the neon toupees atop their little ghost heads seemed to weave into each other. The Elders started pulsing, their bodies turning different colors in rapid succession (mostly black and red) as they "talked."

Click told me this was how they had private conversations, via direct contact. He said that Celestians were able to converse mind-to-mind, sometimes whether they wanted to or not, so tentacle-talk was the only way to ensure privacy.

I almost asked him why he was explaining this, given that I'd just had my own out-of-brain experience, but one look at his face (area) convinced me not to. He was still just trying to hold it together after nearly losing his parent-halves. Morb and Drxx seemed just as on-the-edge as Click, but Drxx suddenly detached from the rest of his family and ran outside. Click and Morb followed.

For once Chloe didn't just run after. She looked up at me with a mixture of trust and hope in her eyes that made me want to cry: her world was falling apart, but she was sure I could keep her safe. That I would know what to do.

And she wasn't the only one. Noah tapped my shoulder. "Uhhh, what now?"

"How the heck should I know, Noah? Why do you think I'd have any better idea than you on what to do or where to go or how to act to get out of this stupid, impossible mess?" is what I wanted to shout, but didn't. Instead I looked at the Elders having a wig-chat, then at the rapidly retreating forms of Click and his parent-halves.

I shrugged. "Come on," I said, and followed after the three Celestians who were our best chance of getting back home.

***

We had to run to keep up. Chloe tripped and almost fell over some debris strewn across the street, but Noah scooped her out of the air and tossed her onto his shoulders like she weighed nothing. She screamed—first in terror, then in delight—then held tight to Noah as he ran.

We passed numerous other Celestians, but none of them seemed to mind or even notice us.

"You think they get a lot of Earthlings?" Leya asked, breathing hard. I was panting a bit—cardio, like anything else vaguely physical, is not my thing.

Noah, of course, seemed to breathe easier with every step.

"I think...they don't care...so long as we...aren't Gro'nid," I said.

Leya nodded. She threw me an odd look too, one I couldn't really parse out. Almost looked like she thought I'd said something smart or something. Like she liked me.

Yeah, I thought. *That'll be the day.*

I also covertly took off my glasses. Dumb? Undoubtedly. Irrational? Likely. But habits are habits, and I didn't want to look even nerdier in front of her—not with Captain America running along with sixty pounds of kid on his shoulders without seeming to notice.

Ahead of us, Drxx abruptly halted. Tentacle-arms erupted all over Drxx's body and he leaned back and shrieked pure eight-bit sadness into the smoky sky, then rushed toward a gray shape on the mossy ground.

Drxx arrived at the shape, and fell to his...whatever Celestians have instead of knees. He kept screaming, though, even as he wrapped his tentacle-arms around the shape and began rocking back and forth.

Morb was there a second later. She tried to put her arms around her spouse, but Drxx shook her off and kept screaming.

"What's going on?" Noah whispered.

"It's Drxx's brother," Leya said. For a moment I wondered how she knew that, but the answer came almost simultaneously.

She recognizes the grief Drxx is feeling, I thought. *She knows what someone looks like when they've just lost family.*

Brxx must have remained at his post, firing on the Winking Gro'nid even as it fell, making sure the threat was ended. A hero. A dead one.

Click was closer to us than to his parent-halves, and now he turned and came over to join the Earthlings. I couldn't blame him; I tried to imagine how I'd feel if my dad started going on like that, and I think I'd go anywhere but there too.

"I'm so sorry about your dad's brother," said Chloe.

"Brother-half to my parent-half," Click corrected absently, sounding detached and in shock even without the brain-sponge's help. A tentacle writhed absently out of him, reaching up to Chloe as she sat atop Noah's shoulders. She took it like she was holding the hand of a friend. Which, to her, was exactly what she was doing.

Drxx was still keening, his head glowing the deepest blue I'd ever seen.

"I'm so sorry," Chloe said.

Click started toward his parents, but didn't let go of Chloe's hand. Like he wanted to go to them, but needed strength that only his new friend could offer.

Noah resisted, obviously not wanting to get any closer to the grief zone, but Chloe pounded her little heels into his chest and said, "Giddyap!"

Noah grunted in pain and moved forward. Click reached his parents. He touched them. Their many arm-tentacles wrapped around his, and he started making grief-sounds like his father.

More Celestians started weeping, their sobs becoming a shared song that rose up to the sky.

Chloe started wailing. I ran to her, worried that something had hurt her, but then realized she was singing along, her child's heart touched in a way I could never hope to understand.

I joined in, singing the grief as best I could, mimicking the sounds, feeling the pain of a planet facing the end of all. Leya followed suit, and a moment later Noah shouted the grief-song as well.

I had known that terror and pain and grief could divide people. Heaven knew I'd seen enough of that on Earth, where not sharing your neighbor's opinion meant you might be fighting with each other until one of you died. But here, on Celestia, terror and pain and grief brought the people closer. It didn't make it *good*. It didn't even make it all right.

But at least this way there was a measure of comfort. The pain could be borne more easily, because it was shared. And sharing the pain brought understanding. It brought love.

Not good.

Not even all right.

But…enough.

20

The next few hours were tough. I felt like the air had turned to Jell-O—every movement took more effort than it should have, every word I spoke was hard to formulate. Chloe had a dazed look on her face, and I could tell she was feeling the same way. I knew we'd been through a lot (and if that isn't the understatement of the century, I don't know what is), but even so, I sensed something was wrong. I was about to ask Click what was going on when I saw Chloe weave on her feet, then fall.

I tried to catch her, but the Jell-O universe got in my way. Not only was it hard to move, but just like Jell-O, reality seemed to wiggle and stretch: with every centimeter I reached, Chloe pulled away too.

I'll never catch her, I thought. *Never save her—*

Leya leaped forward and caught Chloe. She stared at my little sister, fear written clearly on her face. "What's going on?" she said.

I tried to answer, but my knees buckled and I fell. The green ground rushed up at me and I had a second to wonder if the mossy stuff would keep me from breaking my face.

A strong arm shoved between me and the ground. Noah, catching me just like Leya had caught Chloe.

And then I was out.

***

Every color in the rainbow waited for me in whatever place my mind had fled to. It was beautiful—so beautiful that, even though I knew I should be worried about what was happening to me, and downright *terrified* about what was happening to Chloe, all I felt was calm and peace.

The colors shifted. Some brightened, some faded away. Soon I mostly saw green, with various browns and reds and pinks slivered through the shifting emerald tones. The colors slid over each other like oil over water. Then the chaotic dance of hue and tone slowed. The shadows grew sharper, the lines between colors more pronounced. Trees formed, then the ground, then the sky over all—and a moment later I was back at Muir.

For a moment, the invisible line between what had happened, and what was about to happen, I thought, *I must have tripped or something. Conked my head on a tree and been knocked out.*

The trip to Celestia, the Gro'nid attack—nothing but a dream, and now I was waking up.

But if that was the case, why was I already standing? Why was I watching the park ranger we'd run into in the woods as he talked to a concerned-looking cop?

Please, please, please let the kids be okay. Wherever they are.

My brain gave a little jump inside itself. The thought that had come wasn't mine. It was...

It's Dad's.

(it's mine)

Then why am I the one thinking it?

(because i'm dad)

The ranger finished talking, and came toward me. I looked down, and saw someone holding my hand.

Marla.

(mom?)

I saw the hand. The hand of my mother. The hand of my—

(wife)

Okay, I knew Mom wasn't really my wife (our family has problems, but not *that* kind of problems). But when I looked at her hand, what I thought wasn't, *"Mom's hand."* Instead, my thought was, *"I'm glad Marla's here. She'll keep it together. My wife always does."*

And with that, I knew that one of two things was happening.

136

Either I was asleep/unconscious, and my brain was having a long-overdue panic attack, or this was like the feeling earlier, when Chloe and I were *"Joined"* to the Celestians.

Only now, I was Joined to my dad.

The police officer was talking. He jerked a thumb over his shoulder, pointing at a pair of hikers —

(greta and graham the granola twins!)

— standing off to one side. Greta looked irritated. Graham looked terrified.

"They saw them," said the cop. "I guess those tree huggers over there were complaining that your son and daughter's group were getting' all rowdy —"

I felt Marla's hand —

(no, not Marla's. *mom's hand.)*

— close tightly on mine. "My son and daughter are not *rowdy* people, officer."

"Not the point right now, hon," said Dad's *(my)* voice, and his *(my)* hand tightened around Mom's.

The cop waited, wearing an expression of borderline-fear that made me think he probably knew Marla Rose Abernathy, at least by reputation, and wasn't suicidal enough to interrupt her when she was obviously worried and ready to fight.

When Mom said nothing else, the officer added, "So the Forest Avengers over there went to the kids to…" He checked his notepad, reading, "'Warn them about the sanctity of the forest and unsullied nature.'"

Again my father spoke. It was disconcerting to say the least, hearing his voice coming from the place my mind insisted was my mouth. "And what happened then?" he asked.

I felt his panic. He wasn't just worried, he was on the verge of losing it. The intensity of it surprised me.

The cop shrugged. "Said the kids ran off."

Greta had been leaning on the tree, looking dazed. Now she spoke up: "I didn't say they *ran off*. I said they *disappeared*."

The panic feeling came again, stronger this time. My dad spoke, terror lending jags and cracks to his voice that I'd never heard before. "What does that mean, 'disappeared'?"

"Means the trees took 'em, man!" Graham shouted.

"Preserve the holy silence of the forest!" Greta shouted back.

Graham ignored her. He waved at the woods and screamed, *"THE TREES TOOK THEM, MAN! THE TREES!"*

Mom stood up. Dad tried to hold her, but she shook his hand loose and walked toward the Granola Twins with obvious mayhem in her eyes.

"Honey, let's—Dude, wake up!"

No, that wasn't right. Dad was saying something else, trying to keep Mom from murdering a pair of innocent forest enthusiasts, but I just heard Noah's voice screaming, "Dude, wake up!"

I blinked—or did Dad blink? Probably that was more accurate. Only instead of the fraction of a second of nothing that most folks see when they close their eyes, when Dad blinked I saw Noah leaning over me.

Noah disappeared as Dad opened his eyes again. I was back in Muir, watching the cop try to keep Marla Abernathy from momma-bear-mauling the Granola Twins.

Dad's vision got hazy as tears pushed free. The curtain made him blink—and again, I was staring at Noah.

This time, though, the vision remained. Glee replaced the concern on Noah's face. "You're awake!" he shouted.

***

I felt a weight, and realized that Chloe was curled up beside me, both of us lying on something vaguely bed-like. That was when I realized we weren't in Muir, and we weren't standing in the smoking ruins of the Celestian city. We were inside a small, round room. No windows, no doors. Another Celestian cell?

Maybe. All it held were the four of us, four of the bed-looking things, and something that looked like it might be a chair, if chairs were capable of undergoing severe mental disturbances.

It also held a table, on top of which —

"How did *that* get here?" I asked, sitting the rest of the way up, pointing at the table with its shocking cornucopia.

Noah cracked a smile. "Pretty cool, huh? They asked what we eat and when we told them we got *this*."

"Not true," said Leya. "When you told them, we got a lot of confused stares and questions about our reproductive systems. When *I* told them, we got this."

She handed me one of the McDonald's Happy Meal boxes that sat on the floor, then gave one to Chloe, who was looking around with the confused expression of someone coming out of the deepest sleep. "Or rather, when I told them, they looked really confused, but then Click talked to Morb and Drxx and —" She shrugged. "I got the words 'scanning' and 'human nutritional databases,' but most of the rest I didn't have the right vocab for, so it just came out as clicks and whistles. But whatever it was, they brought us these for dinner while you guys were conked out."

I examined the box in my hands. It looked like a Happy Meal box. It felt like a Happy Meal box. When I opened it, the smell of hamburger and fries wafted out.

I hadn't realized how hungry I was, but my stomach loudly told me to dig in. I heard smacking lips and knew that Chloe had gone from "Just Waking Up" mode to "Best Meal Ever" setting. Half her burger was already gone, and fries stuck out of her mouth, gradually disappearing as she chewed her way to the finish line.

I took a bite too. Partly it was the hunger, partly the fact that several empty boxes clearly showed that Noah and Leya had already eaten and hadn't expired of alien food poisoning (though I did find out then that Leya was a vegetarian and so had subsisted on fries and apple slices).

Plus, Chloe had already eaten, and if something happened to her because of it, I didn't want to be the only one to survive and have to tell my parents about it.

I flashed to Mom, stomping toward the Granola Twins, ready to murder them for impugning her children by calling them "rowdy." As I did, Chloe said (through a mouthful of food), "Glmpgh glurg glumb."

"What?" I said.

"Don't speak with your mouth full, kiddo," said Leya, then blushed brightly and looked sad.

Probably something her mom told her, I thought. The pain of being so far from my own mom was almost crippling, but at least she was there—battling tree huggers for profaning the integrity of her children, if dreams were to be believed.

What would it be like if she were gone? If Dad was dead instead of just annoying?

The pain of that thought motivated a strange bravery. I looked at Leya, waiting until she looked back, and then—gearing up internally—instead of looking away I smiled and gave her my best "I'm here if you need to talk" smile. She smiled back (I think; my glasses were in my pocket), then looked away.

Chloe finally swallowed, said, "I was Mom. Isn't that wonky-wacky-weird?"

I cocked my head. "What do you mean?"

"I dreamed I was Mom," she said. Another bite, and she said, "Mom is terrifying."

"Where were you?" I asked.

Chloe finished her burger, then pulled a little bag out of her

Happy Meal box, and I realized the Celestians had even reproduced the cruddy little toy that comes in every Happy Meal. Frowning, she said, "Aww, I already have this one."

"Chlo? Focus?"

"What's the big deal?" asked Noah. "Don't you—"

I put a finger in front of his face to silence him as I said, "Chloe? Where were you in the dream?"

Chloe pulled a chocolate milk out of her box and shouted, "My favorite!" before unscrewing the cap and taking a long drink.

"Chloe, answer me," I said sternly.

She finished her drink with a satisfied little burp. Leya laughed at it, then cut off and looked (beautifully) embarrassed.

Chloe chucked the now-empty drink bottle into the Happy Meal box and went searching for errant fries as she said, "I was in the forest. Those dorky people who yelled at us were there too. Dad was trying to keep her from murdering them, I think." She shook her head and repeated, "Mom is terrifying."

Leya was looking from Chloe to me and back again. "What's going on?"

"I had a dream too," I said, more to myself than answering Leya. Turning to Chloe, I asked, "What exactly did you see?"

Before she could answer, a hole opened in one of the walls and Click entered. "Good, you are awake," he said.

"Hi, Click!" said Chloe. "Thanks for the Happy Meal!"

"You are welcome. I am glad you—"

"*HEY!*" Noah roared. "Will someone *PLEASE ANSWER MY QUESTIONS.*"

Everyone went silent. Finally, Click said, "What questions do you have?"

The direct response seemed to take Noah by surprise. He opened his mouth, then shut it. He reddened, then looked at me and muttered, "Help me out here. Ask something smart."

I glanced at Leya and, though I know it's ridiculous, I flashed to all the times I'd been mocked in school for being the "smart one" or the "nerd." All the guys who'd made it clear that I was worth only as much as how far I could(n't) throw a football. All the girls who'd made it clear that their dating interests were more "guy with sixteen-inch biceps and no neck" than "weakling who can tell me the value of pi to thirty places."

"Why am I the one who—" I began.

Leya broke in, addressing what to her must have been the most obvious, important thing to say. "I'm so sorry about your, um, uncle, Click. So, so sorry. But is everyone else…"

Click gave a courteous little bow. "Thank you for your concern, Leya." He made a sound halfway between a record skipping and a busted hard drive, which my brain-sponge interpreted as a sigh. "We will survive. Hopefully."

Leya had obviously taken some Hostage Negotiation course, because she looked around and, spotting the Happy Meals, said, "Thank you for the food. Where did you get it?"

Smart, I thought. *Ask how they got our food, then lead into how we can get to that place, aka, Earth.*

"Do you like it?" Click asked.

"The fries and apple slices were…very good," said Leya.

Noah started to say something, but I pinched his shoulder and mimed zipping my lips. He glowered but shut up to let Leya work her magic.

Click's tentacles waved in agitation. "Did you not like the rest?"

"No, I'm…" I could see Leya struggling, trying to guide the conversation that would get us out of here and back home. But she's a vegetarian, and one thing I've noticed about vegetarians is they never pass up a chance to talk about being vegetarians. "I don't eat meat."

Click's tentacles flailed again. "Meat? There was no meat."

Leya's brow furrowed. "What about…" She held up a cheeseburger in its greasy paper wrapping.

"Oh! I see." Click's tentacles quieted. "That is not meat. That is a simulation, based on your description of alimentary necessity, our research into human physiology, and the big guy's description of teenage preferences."

He pointed at Noah for the last sentence. Noah puffed out his chest and said, "Big guy," in a pleased tone.

Great. Even the Celestians crush on him, I thought.

Leya was looking at the cheeseburger. "Then what is it?"

Click answered in the best show-don't-tell manner possible. His mouth opened wide, but he didn't speak a word. Instead, he made a *hrrk, hrrrk, hrrrrrrk* sound (which the brain-sponge kept pretty much intact in my head).

And he barfed up a Happy Meal.

"Cool!" Chloe went to it and opened the cardboard package, dumping out a burger, fries, apple slices, another junky toy, even a plastic bottle of chocolate milk with the Golden Arches on the side.

"That's…that's what…we were…eat—" Leya made little *hrrk hrrk* sounds of her own. I stepped toward her, but she waved me away, her other hand plastered against her mouth.

Noah, of course, was allowed to comfort the damsel in distress. He held her while she got her gorge under control, then kept his arm over her shoulders while he glared at Click.

"Are you unwell?" asked Click. "Did the regurgi-food not suit you?"

Leya went *hrrrrrrk* and shrugged away from Noah before going to a corner. Noah watched her go, then turned to Click and said, "Hey, here's a question: when do we get to go home?"

"Noah—" began Chloe, sounding embarrassed at the question.

"It is all right, Chloe," said Click. To Noah, he said, "I am not sure. The ship you came here in—"

"The mothership!" shouted Noah, sounding oddly triumphant.

"The mothership? The mothership. Mothership." Click sounded like he was trying the name out. He must have liked it because he said, "The mothership is the only vessel currently capable of high-speed intergalactic travel."

"Look, dude, I don't need a history lesson. When are we going home?" Noah crossed his big arms over his chest.

"Noah, don't be rude," said Chloe in a surprisingly tough voice. She sounded like Mom about to flatten a granola-chomper.

Noah looked down and actually rubbed his toe on the floor. "Sorry, Chlo."

"Don't apologize to *me*, Noah," she said, again sounding just like Mom.

He heaved a big sigh, then looked at Click. "Sorry, Click."

"It is all right, Noah. I would not have handled any of this nearly as well as you have."

Noah beamed, which surprised me. I wouldn't have thought someone as popular and cool as him would get a rise out of an alien's praise. I added that item to my Things To Ask Noah About Later file, then returned my attention to Click.

"We are trying to repair the ship as quickly as possible," Click was saying, "but it will be a few days."

"A few *days?*" shouted Noah.

"Mom is going to be *mad*," whispered Chloe.

"So we're *stuck* here?" shouted Leya, then went *hrrrk* again and sat down on one of the chairs.

Click was bobbing that little courtesy-bow at all of them. "I know. I am so sorry. We will do our best to make you comfortable until then." He turned to the still-open hole in the wall and stepped through.

"Wait!" Chloe grabbed one of Click's tentacle arms in her tiny hands. "I'm really sorry about—about everything. I wish we could do something to help you, Click."

Something seemed to pass between the alien and my little sister—something that disquieted me. I stood up, intending to pull her away from Click, maybe give her a reminder course on stranger danger; remind her that just because Click seemed nice didn't mean he was really our friend.

As I stepped toward them, Click cocked his head. Chloe nodded and smiled and said, "Sure I'll come."

"No!" I lurched at them, but as always: too slow. Chloe stepped out of the room with Click, the "door" shut behind them both, and they were gone.

"Hey!" I shouted, pounding on the wall with the flat of my fist. "Hey, bring her back!" I hit the wall again, hard enough I knew I'd have a nice purple bruise later. I didn't care. I hit the wall again.

Leya joined me, pounding on the wall and shouting for Chloe and Click. Noah came over a second later and "helped," though even his massive fists made barely a whisper as they hit the walls.

I slumped and slid to the floor, my back against the wall, my legs splayed out in front of me. Leya sat beside me and squeezed my forearm. "I'm sure she's fine."

It was a measure of how worried I was about Chloe that the touch barely registered.

***

Noah pounded on the wall intermittently for maybe ten minutes. "No one hears. No one cares," Leya said dully. Then turned to Noah as he sat down and picked up a "burger." "You're seriously going to eat that?" she asked.

Noah shrugged. "It still tastes like a Happy Meal. And I gotta keep my strength up in case we get a chance to run."

"Run where?" I asked dully.

Noah stared at me. "You know how many video games I play?"

I didn't get that immediately, but Leya did. Her mouth dropped open and she said, "You think that's going to qualify you to steal the mothership, then fly us across the universe using tech so far ahead of ours that it might as well be magic?"

Noah stared right back at her. "Unless you have a better idea, then...yeah."

Leya looked like she wanted to argue, but didn't. She didn't say a thing. Neither did I. Because Noah was right—not that his idea was a good one; it was ludicrous.

But it was still the best idea we had.

21

Not sure how long we stayed there like that. We all had our cell phones, of course (we *were* teenagers), but it wasn't like there was a recharging station around. The cells were just dark pieces of metal and plastic. The only way to measure the minutes passing was to count the number of times Noah whispered, "This is lame," in between times he pounded on the wall.

After ten *this is lame*s, Leya stood and started sweeping her palms up and down on the room's circular wall, like she was trying to find a hidden switch. She gave up after a while.

I was sitting on a bed, thinking. I hadn't come up with anything, and all possibility of that changing disappeared as Leya sat beside me.

It was an alien world, not my room, but—and I cannot emphasize this enough—the *most beautiful amazing wonderful interesting girl in the world*s *was sitting on a bed with me*. So all my critical thinking skills went bye-bye.

Silence for a long, long while. She glanced at me. I glanced away. Thinking what to say, the only thing coming to mind was, "You're perfect," which even no-lady-skills me knew enough to know was a bad idea.

She inhaled.

She's going to talk to me. She's going to talk *to me.*

"I—"

Noah hit the wall too hard and yelped. The sound broke the silence, and shattered whatever had been about to happen. Leya glanced at me one more time, then went over to make sure he hadn't hurt himself. Moment over.

Just as well, I thought. *She was probably going to ask me to stop staring and creeping her out.*

I patted my pocket, feeling the glasses that hid there. Other than that, I didn't move. I just sat. Thinking. Thinking of ways to get out (none). Thinking of ways to get home (few). Thinking of all the times I'd made a bad impression on Leya (many).

To my surprise, the thought that came back the most in this spiral of doubt was how I'd failed Chloe. The hopes of her heart, the friends she so desperately wanted. Was that because of me? Because *I* didn't act like her friend, so she was lonely?

And what about now? Sure, Click sounded friendly, but what if this was all some devious plot? The definition of *alien* was something that differed to the point of incompatibility—meaning there was no way to be certain that what the (also alien) brain-sponge whispered was "kindness" wasn't actually their equivalent of marinating a steak. Getting us nice and tender before eating.

The thought took life. I had an image of Celestians encircling a big table, each of them barfing up silverware, then Click reaching out a tentacle to lift the lid of a big silver serving tray, revealing Chloe, tied up and with an apple in her mouth.

How am I going to get us out of this? I thought. And the answer was the most deafening silence I'd ever heard.

***

As I sat there, stewing in despair, thinking of Chloe, I could almost hear her say, "You look so serious," and giggle.

At which point, Leya screamed, "Chloe, you're alive!" and I realized that I actually *did* hear her say that, because Chloe was back.

My sister waved over her shoulder, and Click waved his squiggly spaghetti arms from the other side of an opening in the round cell, then the hole disappeared and the humans were trapped again.

I barely noticed, and cared not at all. I just hugged Chloe and tried not to cry too much.

"Can't…breathe…"

I let go. Let her catch her breath. Then hugged her again. "Where'd you go, what'd you do, what happened, why'd you leave, don't you ever leave like that!" I whisper-shouted into her ear.

"Still...can't...breathe..."

When I finally let her up for air, she told me where she'd gone: "We just walked around," she said. "They're already rebuilding the city. Or growing it, maybe? I dunno." Her face wrinkled a bit. "I think they barf most things."

"Most things?" Noah asked.

Chloe nodded. "Yeah. Like one guy says, 'I need a piece of wall!' and the other guy goes, 'Coming right up!' and then goes *hugghhh, hughhh, huuuuuuuggghhhhh* and pukes up a section of wall and can I have the rest of those fries?" she said, all in one breath. That, and the way she started gobbling barf-fries told me that she was okay, and I finally let loose the breath I'd been holding since I saw her.

Between fries, Chloe continued, "Click took me to a building that looked like an egg with a tree on top, and then another one that looked like a cloud, and another one where his class was—did you know he's a student?—only he doesn't go to school like we do, he's kind of an outcast; that's not the word he said, but I think it's the right one because they don't really let him play with them and they don't invite him over to parties—did you know they have parties?—even though they used to but now they—"

"Whoa, whoa, *whoa*!" I finally managed to break in. "Chloe, first answer me: were you hurt? Did they...*do* anything to you?"

She looked at me like I'd fallen off the highest part of the Stupid Tree and hit every Idiot Branch on the way down. "*Duh.* Didn't you hear anything that I just—"

I hugged her again. Thinking only, *She's okay, she's okay*, with an intensity that surprised me. I knew I loved her. More than loved, I couldn't think how anyone *wouldn't* love her—part of why I detested Becca and her Forest Girl friends was that I just didn't understand why they didn't like Chloe.

But now, seeing her—alive, whole, with me again—I realized that what I'd thought of as love was the tiniest part of my feelings for my sister. I'd seen the tip of the iceberg, but having her gone showed me a bit of what hid under the surface of my thoughts.

Nothing can happen to her, I thought as I hugged her. *I'll die before I let anything happen.*

I saw Leya looking at us. She had a strange smile, but I was so deep in the moment of revelation that for once Teenage Guy Thoughts had no power over me. I was just there, and Chloe was with me, and as long as my sister was safe I could figure out a way to fix all this. To get us home.

***

When I finally let Chloe come up for air, I peppered her with questions, mostly about if she'd seen anything that would help us get back to—or even just communicate with—Earth.

To my complete lack of surprise, she hadn't noticed much in that area. Even less surprising: she was more worried about the Celestians' situation with the Gro'nid and with Click's situation with school than anything else.

"...so I was super happy that their school didn't get bombed or whatever, even though it kinda woulda served them right because they're so mean to Click, even though he's a lot smarter than any of them, I just know it; and besides, he said a really, really, *really* cool thing, he said—"

"Wait, Chloe!" I almost had to shout through her words, waving my arms in front of her to break through the stream-of-consciousness recounting. "I'm glad they're okay, Chloe, I really am, but—"

"What was the cool thing he said?"

Chloe swiveled to Leya and asked, "Who said?" her brain already fluttering like a moth over to the next thought, leaving the rest behind.

"Click," Leya said. She smiled a sad little half-smile that betrayed deep emotion barely controlled. "What was the cool thing he said?"

Chloe lit up like she'd just won the lottery. She did that a lot—got excited when Leya talked to her. Again I felt a pang that my sister was so in need of friendship, so desperate for connection.

"I said that maybe they'd be more interested in him, maybe let him crash their squad, if he was more interested in *them*. Like, if he hung out and talked to them and asked them how their day was and what grades they were getting and what their favorite thing to barf up was and then they'd all barf the same stuff and play with it and they'd like him because that's what people like about people: when they talk and find out they like the same stuff."

"That's pretty good advice," said Noah. Everyone looked at him. He blushed and mumbled, "What? It is good advice."

I knew I should keep asking Chloe for details that might help us, but I wasn't about to interrupt her now. Earlier, sure. But that was before I saw Chloe's expression. Telling about her advice to Click, I again saw her longing to belong. I remembered the empty pictures in her room and winced.

Focus, Max, I reprimanded myself. *Get her home and safe first, figure out how to make her one of the Cool Kids later.*

"What did he say back to you?" asked Leya. And, watching her, I felt like there was more to the question than the obvious. Something important, something I wasn't seeing.

Chloe seemed to, though. She hugged Leya, hard. I saw every muscle in Leya's body go rigid. Then she relaxed. She held tight to my sister.

"When I told him how I thought he could fit in by being like them, he said, 'Why would I do that? I am me, and they are them. There is no need for me to be one of them.'" Then Chloe released

Leya. Leya knelt before her, and Chloe took her face in her hands and added the final words Click had said to her, and which she now spoke to Leya: "'Plus, *you* are my friend. What more do I need?'"

For some reason, Leya was crying. I didn't fully understand why, and wanted to—needed to—ask what was happening. To ask how I could help. But doing that with your sister is one thing. Doing it to the most beautiful woman in the world? Impossible.

I was saved by a subtle change in the air. I turned and saw that the wall had opened, admitting Click with Morb and Drxx. Click's head was glowing blue and yellow like an alien siren, (my brain-sponge nudged the word "embarrassed" into my mind). Morb nudged her "child-meld" and said, "Well?"

Click's glow turned a honey color.

Determination, I thought. *Thanks, brain-sponge.*

Click finally geared up enough to speak. "Come. We can tell from all of your vitals that it is time to eliminate your wastes."

"Wait, wha—" I began.

Talking right over me, Morb looked at Chloe and said, "Click told us you walked with him today, and that you were kind." Her voice deepened and lowered, like she was about to whisper something incredibly important in the middle of a church meeting. "So we would like to invite you to join our family-branch as we relieve ourselves together."

Noah's hands swatted the air like he was fending off invisible bees. "No way. Kidnapping is one thing, but telling us we have to group-poop is a bridge too far."

Morb's tentacles gave a little flutter that the brain-sponge told me was how Celestians say, "What the heck?" as she said, "We are not on a bridge."

"And you're not watching me drop the kids off at the pool!" Noah shouted.

"Look, Drxx," said Chloe, again sounding surprisingly like Mom. "I gotta go with Big N on this. And why would you want us to be with you when we..." She looked right, looked left. Like she was a spy in a bad movie, she then whispered out of the corner of her mouth, "...*twosie.*"

"Suit yourself," said Drxx. He and Click and Morb all grabbed tentacles.

"Wait, what's happening?" Noah's hands went from bee-swatting to frantic pushing. "Are you going to do that *right here*?"

Click and his fam were making some very new sounds. The brain-sponge translated them. But because I am a very classy guy, I will not repeat them for you. Trust me, though: they were loud.

Noah started gagging halfway through. A second later, Leya started making strained sounds as well. I thought she was trying not to barf again, then realized she was trying to hold back laughter.

The cutest giggles ever escaped, which triggered full-body laughs. Chloe joined her, and a moment later the two girls were rolling on the floor as Click's family finished doing their thing. It was a lot like the process for making our food, which made me wonder if we were eating Barfy Meals or Poopy Meals. I decided not to ask.

At the end of this "special moment," the three Celestians let go of each other. Drxx picked up the results of their—ahem—hard work, which looked like three little pebbles.

Through all this, I became aware of something. Something uncomfortable. Something ugly. But it was also undeniable, and had to be dealt with.

I really *did* have to go to the bathroom.

"Morb?" I said. "You've been watching us? Observing humans?"

"For some time," she agreed.

"Okay. Well, for humans, *elimination*—"

"Ew," said Chloe.

"—is something very private."

"Ahhh," said Drxx, sounding like my dad making a discovery (usually one I'd pointed out). "That explains much. We simply thought that humans lacked the emotional capacity to come fully together."

Leya frowned. "So you never saw…" she glanced at Chloe. "Humans…making other humans."

The Celestians' tentacles all went crazy, and they glowed every possible color. Finally, Morb managed, "Of course we saw such things. But as any thinking creature will tell you, the second-greatest of the two great indicators of sentience are the need to eliminate with loved ones."

"What's the first-great—" Noah began.

But matters that had been mentioned were now, well…pressing. Talking quickly, I said, "What's important right now is that humans go to the bathroom differently, but we need to be private. Totally alone."

"Thank goodness," Leya breathed. "I've been trying to figure out how to bring this up for *hours.*"

She grinned at me, and I couldn't help it: I flashed forward twenty years. Me and her, married. Talking to our kids. "Well, kids, the truth was, I didn't love your father for his brains *or* his body. It was all about how he was the first one to ask about a bathroom break."

***

The quick version of what came next is that, after considerable embarrassment—some ours, some theirs—the Celestians touched a spot on the wall that opened four little rooms they called their "privacy thought nooks." A bit more talking and they provided appropriate "cleaning materials": little blue napkins they barf-pooped just for us.

154

At that point, I didn't care. You could have handed me a porcupine and told me to work with what I had and I wouldn't have cared. I. Had. To. *GO.*

Everyone went into their rooms. And we all tried very hard not to look at each other or say anything as Click, Morb, and Drxx swept in the moment each of us finished to "take samples." Though Noah couldn't resist leaning in and whispering to me, "Think they'd ever show *that* on *Blue Planet*?"

22

I didn't know if it was Chloe's kindness to Click, or what happened after, in our "privacy thought nooks," but a lot of the chill that had existed between the humans and Celestians had thawed. Morb and Drxx were a lot less stiff-seeming with us, and we with them.

They took us out of the room we'd been in, which turned out to be one of the only undamaged rooms in the Temple of the Elders, where they put us simply because it was close and convenient.

"But after much discussion," Morb explained as we exited, "the Elders determined that lower life-forms are unlikely to pose a danger to us at this time, and we might learn much about your habits and limitations if we leave you to wander a bit."

"Gee, thanks," said Noah as sarcastically as possible.

"You are very welcome!" Drxx replied, pleased as can be.

***

On the way out of the Temple, Click, Morb, and Drxx each grabbed several small, silver discs that leaned against the wall. When we were outside, they threw them on the mossy ground. Each stood on one of the discs, and they instructed us to do the same. Drxx touched something on his disc, there was that metal *snick*ing sound, and the discs turned to miniature versions of the eggships.

Eggpods, I thought. It was hardly a cool name, but it fit.

Morb shifted in her eggpod, and we must have been linked together, because all our pods lifted about ten inches, turned as one, and started gliding through the still-rebuilding city.

Celestians turned to watch as we passed by. No one said anything, but this time there were plenty of stares. Disconcertingly so, given that Celestians could create as many eyes as they wanted at any time. And no matter how many eyes the Celestians focused on their tasks, there were always six or seven new ones just for us.

Responses to this varied. Chloe waved in her eggpod. Noah clasped his hands over his head and shook them every once in a while, like he was the Grand Marshall of the world's tiniest parade.

Morb would wave occasionally, calling out words of encouragement to the workers. I'd seen my mom on the news once, being interviewed after a giant house fire that had claimed the lives of two people. She'd sounded just like Morb now did: sad, but trying to remain hopeful in the shadow of misery.

Drxx said nothing. He didn't wave. His head glowed a steady, dull blue that increased in intensity with every broken building— or body—we passed. A lot of the other Celestians had that same glow. Grief.

I watched in silence. So did Leya. I glanced at her whenever I could, thinking of her face when Chloe talked to her: *"Plus, you are my friend. What more do I need?"*

I suspected that Leya would be glowing blue as well, if she could.

Something shifted in me. She was still interesting, smart, beautiful, amazing…but she was also hurting. I wanted to stop that hurt. Not for any of the obvious reasons. Just because…

Because she's your friend.

I almost laughed aloud. Maybe the Celestian air was making me hallucinate. I mean, sure, I'd be *her* friend. But for her to slum it by hanging with *me*? No way.

That was true, I knew. But I also knew it didn't matter. Whether she ever liked me or not, I wanted to help her. To heal her.

Actually, that was wrong. I didn't care if *I* was the one to help her or heal her. I just wanted her helped and healed, by whoever could do the job. If it was me, that would be a dream come true. But if it was Chloe who helped Leya find hope and happiness? If it was Noah who helped her smile, and to do so without the edge of sadness that haunted her?

Well, that would be just fine.

***

Sooner than I expected, we left the main part of the city. Beyond the big buildings, green fields stretched in straight lines, separated by shimmering orbs of various sizes.

Click pointed at three of the orbs that were connected by thin tubes of the same shining material and said, "Home."

The eggpods set down and the shields disappeared. The Celestians made no move to pick up the discs, but as we stepped off they zipped back toward the city. I watched them go for a second, then followed the rest of the party as it moved toward Click's home.

I decided to call the individual orbs "lifepods," both because calling it a "house" seemed weird and to keep the branding consistent. As we approached the lifepods—perfectly round on the sides, reflecting the green of the fields just as the city's buildings had done—Morb and Drxx reached out tentacles and briefly wrapped them together. Drxx's head was still glowing blue, and when he and Morb touched, her head took on the same tone. Like she'd pulled his sadness into her. They separated, and each headed to different lifepods. Click seemed to expect this, and headed to the third in the grouping.

The wall opened as we approached. Several eyes appeared on the back of Click's head. Apparently satisfied we were still following him, he walked into the orb. We entered as well.

The room was similar to the one we'd waited in at the Temple of the Elders. A table, some Celestian chairs, and four beds. I figured at first that it was prepped for us—hence the four beds—but then, where would Click sleep? Was this just how all

Celestian rooms were set up?

So many questions. So few answers.

But we're here for a few days. Definitely time to gather data.

For once, I didn't quash the nerd-thought. It was an optimistic one, for one thing. Gathering data assumed I'd be around long enough to either make sense of it or share it with someone who could. My dad or some other scientist—probably the latter, given Dad's track record with turning data into usable form.

I'll get home. I'll get us all home.

***

As soon as we were all inside, the wall opening disappeared. Noah muttered, "*Aaaaaand* we're prisoners again."

Click's head glowed violet: confusion. "You are not prisoners, Noah. You are in my home."

"I don't care what you call it, if there isn't a way out, it's a prison."

Click stared at him for a long time, the colors in his ghost-head pulsing continually. Finally they leveled out, then dissipated, leaving behind only the palest hint of purple. "You don't know how to open the wall-shields?"

"How would I know how to do that?" Noah asked.

"Amazing," Click mused. A pair of his tentacles writhed toward Noah. When the big guy shied away, Click wrapped one of the tentacles around Chloe's wrist instead. He leaned in and whispered to her. "Do you understand?" he asked a moment later.

She nodded, then turned to the wall. Little brow furrowed in concentration, she clicked her tongue against her mouth. The wall opened. The opening wasn't the perfect, clean oval that Click and the others got; looked more like an egg that had had a severe stroke and now kind of leaned to the side. But it would let us in or out.

159

Chloe grinned and clapped. "Cool!"

"How did you do that?" asked Leya.

"The shield-walls open with the right keywords," said Click.

"Why'd you need to touch her?"

"The wall only accepts instructions from its owner, or people who have been keyed to it in the presence of the owner."

"So we *were* prisoners," I muttered.

Click either didn't hear me or ignored the observation, facing Noah as the big guy said, "Like a security system, huh?" Noah looked around. "Got a big B&E problem here, Click?"

"I do not understand this B&E, Noah," said Click. "The security is a new feature, because we are at war. Some of my people have seen our enemies at the edges of our city, making strange sounds that we believe are intended to terrify and demoralize. Under such circumstances, it seemed unwise to allow the walls to open for whatever monster should wish to wander in."

"Show me!" said Leya, holding out her hand.

"Of course." Click held her, then repeated what he'd done with Chloe. This time I heard the whispering, which was just Click saying, *"Repeat after me,"* followed by a clicking sound the brain-sponge didn't translate.

Leya tried. The wall opened to a perfect circle. "Nice," I said.

Leya looked embarrassed. "When I was a kid I took piano. The teacher always said I had a good ear." She glanced at the wall. "Guess she was right."

"I'd say both your ears are pretty perfect," I said. Then looked away fast, because I hadn't meant to say it and didn't want her or Noah to get mad at me flirting. "Show me?" I asked Click, going for the world record for Subject Change (subcategory: Dork Moves).

Click touched my hand, repeated the sound. My hole wasn't

as lopsided as Chloe's, but it was far from the perfect opening Leya managed.

Noah's attempts brought only vague burping sounds from the wall, which made me secretly happy. Petty, I know, but it was nice to actually be better than him at something.

"Ahhh!" He waved dismissively at the wall. "Who needs you anyway?"

Click spoke, sounding amused. "We are glad you are here, you know."

"Yeah, about that. Why are you—" I was going to ask Click why we had been grabbed. What the deal was with the Gro'nid. A thousand different things, and that was just to start. But in that moment, I noticed our group had lost someone. "Where's Leya?"

***

I looked around and saw a new hole in the wall. Looking through, I saw the tube connecting Click's orb to one of his parents'. I entered it, worried almost as much as if Chloe had disappeared.

The hall was surprisingly tough to walk through. Low enough I had to crawl, the corridor was a perfect circle made of the same shimmering, reflective material the Celestians favored for their other buildings. Moving through it was a bit like crawling into a funhouse mirror: dizzying, disorienting.

When I finally got to the end of the tunnel, I found another shield-wall, with another one of Leya's perfectly circular entries. I looked through and saw a lifepod much like Click's: four beds, some chairs. A table. Only this table looked more complicated, with buttons and levers on it. I flashed to all the times my parents told me "no computer in the bedroom!" and wondered if Click had a similar rule, so his table was just a table, not the complex machine that Drxx was currently operating.

The alien moved a lever, and the table hummed. A cloud of shimmering dust puffed into the air, like spores escaping a mushroom. The dust settled, coalesced. Became a shape I recognized: a Celestian in miniature. The Celestian waved its tentacles at Drxx, and as it did I heard a clicking through the room:

"Drxx, turn the recorder off," said a familiar voice.

Then I heard Drxx's "voice," from the same hidden speakers. "Make me."

The dust-holo recording waved its arms again, and I heard laughter. "I'm going to tell our parent-halves. You'll be *totally* busted," he said, and I finally placed the voice.

It was Brxx, Drxx's brother.

The real Drxx flipped a switch and the sound cut off, though the dust-holo kept on playing. He sat there, watching in silent sadness, the blue glow of his head steady and sorrowful.

"Just so you know, you're not alone. I've been there."

Drxx swiveled to look at Leya, who'd been watching him as he watched the dust-holo. A few of his eyes opened and shut.

"She means she knows what you're going through," I said.

Leya must not have noticed me coming in. She gave a little jump, but flashed me a quick smile. Turned back to Drxx and said, "I know it sucks to lose a family member. Puts a hole in you that you can never fill."

Drxx's eyes swiveled back to the recording, the image of his dead brother-half pulsing orange, its tentacles slapping together as it clapped at something out of the recording's view.

"I find it difficult to think of anything else," Drxx said, the blue of his head so deep it was almost midnight.

My turn to jump as Noah clambered past me into the room and said, "You just need a distraction, dude. You guys have YouTube? I know a good try-not-to-laugh video."

Drxx shifted to look at Noah. "We have an entertainment device, not unlike the televisions and computer we have seen you use on your planet. But based on my review of your physiology and your basic mental capabilities, I think that turning it on now would be a bad idea."

"Why?" I asked, genuinely curious.

"Because you might very much enjoy the visual stimulus—"

Noah rubbed his hands together. "Cool, sounds like just what the doctor ord—"

"—or it might make you physically ill, have a seizure, and die."

Noah stopped rubbing his hands together. "Not exactly a great ratings gimmick." Leya snickered, and the sound was lovely. That and Noah's bright "let's help a bro out!" attitude broke a bit of the sadness in the room.

Another hole in the wall opened, and this time Morb entered from what I assumed was her lifepod. Looking at Drxx, she said, "I see you are feeling better."

It was true. Drxx's literal blues had lessened in intensity.

"A bit," he said.

"Good. There is much to do."

That brought me back to reality. *Time to gather data,* I thought, as aloud I asked, "What was that attack about?"

"The Gro'nid," said Drxx. He made a grating noise that my brain-sponge turned into the sound of someone spitting.

"They inhabit a planet one galaxy away from ours," said Morb. "But from what we have been able to determine, they have destroyed it—exploited and abused its resources. Now they must find a new place to live and to destroy."

"Why would they destroy the planet?" asked Chloe, she and Click clambering into Drxx's lifepod. The whole party was here now.

Morb's head weaved back and forth. "The planet will survive. Whether our people will or not is less certain."

"What about your army, dude?" Noah asked. "Can't you like, *pow, ka-pow, k-k-k-k...*" He mimed shooting a machine gun.

"I do not understand your animal grunts, but we have never needed an army," said Morb. "We never knew such things existed until the Gro'nid came. Even then we didn't understand fully until we analyzed your own planet's military and realized what the Gro'nid intended."

"Well you definitely need an army now," said Noah. "Take the fight to them. Bam! Pow!" He punched the air a few times.

"Animal grunting aside," said Leya, rolling her eyes, "he's not wrong."

"At least take the fight to them," I said. "I mean, we know your ships can travel across the galaxy. Go to their world and —"

The blue glow on Drxx's head deepened. Staring at the still-cavorting image of his brother-half, he said, "We have weapons only for defense. Unlike the Gro'nid, or your people, we have never felt the urge to murder one another." He heaved a big, snap-crackle-pop of a sigh. "The Gro'nid are much better at fighting than we are."

"Not true," said Noah. "You fought them off today, right? And if they're so scared of you that they run away as soon as they see your weaponry hit one of their ships —" He shrugged. "I bet you'll be fine."

"That is not what happened," whispered Click, now standing right behind me. "They have seen our weapons before. Many times. Today was the first time we have managed to bring down a single ship of theirs."

"Then why'd they run?" I asked.

"They're bullies," said Leya under her breath.

I thought she was just calling them a name, but Morb nodded. "They like to hit, but are afraid to get hit back. If we damage one of their ships, they retreat. That is why we focus as much firepower as we can on a single ship when they attack."

Staring at the holo again, Drxx said, "Though this time they stayed longer. We had damaged the Winking Gro'nid early in the attack. It stayed far longer, until we destroyed its wing." His head section twisted back and forth. "It does not bode well for our future chances."

"And even if it *does* stay status quo," I said, "you endure so much destruction just to destroy a single ship."

"That is indeed our dilemma," said Morb. She moved to Drxx's side. One of her arms waved over him, as though trying to wipe away the blue grief-glow. It didn't work.

"What about other cities?" Noah said. "You're all high and mighty about not murdering each other. So why don't you cooperate with other Celestians and just wipe them out with overwhelming force?"

Morb twisted to look at Noah. "What other cities?" When no one spoke, she added, "Celestian reproduction is complicated, much less disgusting than how you do it, and takes a great deal of time. And we have no need to continually multiply in the fashion that humans and Gro'nid favor. Creating so much life the planet dies is not our way." She waved her tentacles. "This is the only city. This is all of us."

"Can you disperse? Just hide?" I asked, then answered my own question. "No, then the Gro'nid would just move in unimpeded and hunt you down one at a time."

"You need bigger weapons," said Chloe.

"She's right about that," Noah said. "Or at least more of 'em. You can't have all your forces focused on one ship, while everyone else is getting blasted to pieces."

"That's what I said: you need bigger weapons," Chloe repeated.

"We have none," Drxx said. He sounded like my dad after a long day of working on his inventions, finding nothing but failure after failure. "And we do not understand the mechanics of war well enough to make anything useful in the time we have left. It is all too new to us."

Chloe shrugged. "It's not new to *us*. Humans are awesome at war. And Max could make you some weapons."

Suddenly, every eye in the room (two from each human, several dozen from each Celestian) was on me.

"Uhhhh, Chloe? I don't think—"

"Sure you could," she said brightly. "You could make Dad's StormLight into a gun. Remember what it did to the garage wall?"

"What is this StormLight?" asked Morb.

"Can it help us defeat the Gro'nid?" asked Click.

"Do you guys have a bathroom?" asked Noah.

Looking from Chloe to Morb to Click and back again (I ignored Noah), I said, "Chloe, I can't—"

"You *can*," she insisted. Then, moving into the run-on mode she entered whenever excited, Chloe said to the Celestians, "StormLight's what our dad does—well, he tries to but he doesn't but he means well and he's my dad so I love him plus his birthday cake is *uh-MAY-zing* so he's got lots of good points but he tries to make stuff but doesn't so Max does 'cause he's better at it even if he tries not to let anyone know."

Everyone was looking at me again. I looked down and saw my glasses, poking out of my pocket. Sighing, I was about to do my usual thing: deny I knew anything at all. It wouldn't even be a lie this time. I mean, I was on an alien world, talking to a race so technologically advanced it made humans look like we were still trying to figure out how to evolve thumbs. What could I do? Nothing.

But I looked up, and caught Leya looking at me. And something in her expression changed my mind. Made me want to be...different. More.

Better.

Which is why, as though from a stranger's mouth I heard myself say, "I'll need to see your weapons."

23

The next few days were a blur. Click convinced his parent-halves that they had nothing to lose, then his parent-halves convinced the Elders. I saw that argument, and it wasn't flattering to humans in general or me specifically. Imagine trying to convince the President of the United States to appoint a dung beetle as Secretary of Defense, and you'll have a rough idea of the conversation. Elder Thor in particular seemed to have a low opinion of anyone who couldn't glow.

It was a mark of how desperate they were that the Elders eventually gave in.

After that, the only person left to convince was me, but it seemed *that* was an optional feature to our little science project. Whether I wanted it or not, I was going to help them.

After the excitement of me saying, "Show me your weapons," wore off, I decided to bow out. Maybe telling them to shove it, then crying for my mommy and daddy. I cooked up a lot of options—all of them negative.

Again, Leya changed my mind. Not with reasoned arguments, but just by laying her hand on my arm and saying, "I'm glad you're helping them."

Which is how I ended up half-buried in the guts of one of their cannons, Morb explaining how everything worked, while Leya ran errands, taking an eggpod back and forth from building to building to pick up various things the Celestians designed and barfed-to-order for me, and Noah sang a consistent refrain of, "I don't know what that word meant!"

The Celestians' tech was *way* more advanced than ours, so though they listened intently to everything I told them, I often felt like the world's dumbest baby in a room full of Nobel Prize winners. There were some fun bits, though. Seeing how they made small tools and machinery was a fascinating process. Even more interesting—and gross, if I'm being honest—was watching giant blob-creatures they called "factories" barf up bigger items, like giant pieces of machines or entire lifepods, furniture included.

Watching Celestians catch onto the idea of lasers and finally understand why I needed two reflectors (one total, one partial), was almost as fun. For the first time in my life, I wasn't being avoided for my brain—I was being sought after.

Oddly enough, one of the hardest parts was explaining conduction to them. I was telling them what level of power I thought I'd need, then realized none of them understood anything I was saying. I backed up and tried again. Still no dice.

After maybe a half an hour, I realized what the problem was: they didn't use electricity the way we did. It should have been obvious: they were alien. They would have developed different kinds of technology, because they lived on a different planet, and had different physiological necessities and limitations. They had taken a different evolutionary path, and that path hadn't included Ben Franklin flying his kite in a lightning storm.

After that, I discovered that not only were they unclear on the concept, but electricity was incredibly dangerous to them. The green "belts" I'd seen on Click and his family back on Earth created an electrical dampening field, and they had to wear them from the moment they entered Earth's atmosphere, because the smallest spark of static electricity could cause "catastrophic effects" on a Celestian.

The implications of that boggled my mind—from the fact that all their tech functioned without AC, DC, or any other kind of current, to the fact that walking across a shag carpet could kill a Celestian. I also figured we were totally screwed: how could you make lasers without electricity?

But I'd forgotten who I was working with. One of the Elders showed up and started asking questions. It was super terrifying, because it was the Elder who sounded (to my brain-sponge's discerning eye) like my high school principal. And Principal Carter was, to put it lightly, terrifying. All she had to do was glower and say, "And just what do you think you're doing, Mr. [fill in last name of terrified student here]?" and the most hardened juvenile delinquent of a high schooler would slink away, promising to turn over a new leaf and never cross her path again.

It took a while to get over feeling like I was about to be expelled from school, but once I did, the process kickstarted back into action. I answered questions for an hour, then Elder Principal Carter nodded and her toupee started glowing bright green. The heads of the other Celestians started glowing green as well, the lights all pulsing in time as some kind of knowledge-surge passed between them.

Elder Principal Carter spoke with her machine-gun precision. "We have conferred. We understand the concept now."

I frowned. "What do you mean you *understand*—"

"We understand," Elder Principal Carter repeated, the threat of detention in every word. "It is an interesting concept, given the impact that it has on the much weaker gravitational force, and the precision available via the electrostatic manipulation of subatomic particles certainly lends itself to interesting possibilities within the realm of—" and the rest turned into a bunch of whistles and clicks that I didn't understand. The brain-sponge gave off a vibe like it was shrugging its shoulders and saying, "You wouldn't understand even if I told you."

"Whoa, whoa!" I half-shouted. "Where did you learn—*how* did you learn all of that so fast?"

Another burst of clicks and whistles and electroburps from Elder Principal Carter, which after a long pause the brain-sponge managed to turn into "Celestian Wikipedia."

***

After that, no more lessons were necessary on my part, at least as to the basics (or most of the advanced aspects) of electrostatic theory. Either they grasped everything I said instantly, or there'd be a short pause followed by an Elder doing the toupee-glow Celestiapedia infodump, and we'd be good again.

After the basic barrier of understanding electricity was hurdled, the next big issue turned out to be finding conductors. Again, the Celestians' tech was different than ours, and I was shocked to learn that their planet was home to a lot of things, but almost none of them suitable for creating the machines I described.

Again, I thought we were D.O.A. Again, I was wrong. Whenever we needed a metal of some kind that they didn't have and couldn't fabricate with barf-tech, an Elder (usually Elder Principal Carter or, ironically, Elder Thor) would appear, glow-burst some instructions, and then someone would be dispatched to some unknown place. They'd return in a few hours, and a Celestian wearing a green dampener band would hand me just the thing I'd asked for. The pieces were always the same color too: electric blue.

When I asked them why they liked the color so much, the Celestians all said variations of: "It's how it grew." When I asked where they were getting the alloys, I just got a cryptic, "Another place," and a look that my brain-sponge told me meant, "Drop it, buster."

A few of the Celestians acted twitchy after that, throwing me Celestian side-eye(s) and muttering among themselves. I didn't understand why me teaching them (or at least, getting them started on teaching themselves) about electricity would do that, until I finally cornered Morb and asked about it. She looked abashed, but finally admitted that the Gro'nid were carbon-based as well, which made humans suspect to some of the Celestians.

I shivered a bit, and worked all the harder the next day. I didn't care if the Gro'nid were carbon-based or silicon-based or had evolved out of hyperintelligent peanut butter. But I knew enough to worry about being "like the enemy." History was littered with stories of people "like the enemy," and how whether they were guilty or not, they eventually got rounded up and tossed into a deep, dark hole.

***

Around the time we had our short dissertation on electricity, Noah gave up on understanding what I was doing, and started teaching some of the Celestian kids how to wrestle. I'd find him rolling all over the mossy ground with them, roaring as they inevitably pinned him. He outweighed them, but they were extraordinarily strong.

And in a wrestling match it's hard to put someone's back on the ground when that person can literally alter their body's composition. Every time Noah had one of them on the ground, the Celestian just turned themselves inside out so what had been their back was now their front, and vice-versa.

Leya wasn't idle, either. She hunkered down and started learning the Celestians' language—not via brain-sponge, but directly. I was glad she was doing it, mostly because I found it impossible to concentrate or talk without stuttering when she was watching, so it was nice to have the Celestian engineering team to myself. Still, I was curious why she'd go to the trouble, given the brain-sponges.

Her response to the question was cryptic. "Just want them to know what we can do," she said.

Chloe and Click were mostly absent. Every time I asked what they were up to, I got a Celestian telling me, "They're fine. Having fun. Explain what kind of gain medium we need to sustain emission," or "Don't worry about them. They're alive. What kind of specifications on the energy source?" You know, the usual.

***

Because of its position relative to its two moons and three suns, Celestia stayed bright for about thirty hours (though it was

172

noticeably dimmer when one of the suns disappeared over the horizon), then got totally dark for four, so it was hard to say how many "days" we were there like that. More than a week, less than a month. I worked from when I woke to when I slept.

I dreaded sleep. I'd lie there, Chloe curled up against me (she didn't like being alone in the lifepods for some reason), and steel myself for the pain that I knew would follow closing my eyes.

Sometimes I dreamed I was Mom, hassling the cops for updates, or Dad going back to Muir to look for any traces of us. One time I dreamed I was Mom, hanging on the back of her station's biggest fire engine as it went up and down the streets in the neighborhoods near Muir. It would drive half a block, stop. She'd jump off long enough to staple a "MISSING CHILDREN" poster to a telephone pole, then jump on again and off they'd go.

They both looked so tired.

I wondered if they *were* dreams. I'd tried asking about the whole *Joining* thing several times. But whether they were avoiding the answer or just genuinely didn't understand the question, all I got was silence when I asked Click or his parent-halves. The closest I got to an answer was when Elder Thor told me to stop asking about things I'd never understand.

I asked Chloe once if she was having the dreams. Her face twisted with worry. "Do you think Mom and Dad are worried about us?"

"Of course. But they're okay too."

"I don't know about that," she said, then ran off with Click to figure out how to build a mattress out of Celestia moss or plot how to take over the universe or whatever it was they did all day.

Little kids are funny. They're small, so there's limited room in their brains for ideas, their hearts for feelings. Whatever they are—happy, sad, angry—that's *all* they are. When a new feeling comes along, it bumps the old one out and off they go on their new course.

I envied that kind of clarity. It frustrated me to no end sometimes, but how I wished I could just have that single-minded focus. It would at least keep me from noticing Leya while I worked. Keep my mind from wandering constantly to her smile. To her wry comments. To her…other good features.

***

On the fourth or fifth "day" of work I stopped to eat. Cranky, tired, worried. My state of mind wasn't helped by the fact that, though the Celestians had managed to perfectly reproduce the Happy Meal, that was *all* they had managed to properly reproduce to this point. And as much as I like a burger and fries, or six almost-but-not-quite chicken nuggets, having them every day for all three squares was getting a bit tiresome. They'd tried "making" other things, but they always came out wrong enough that the Happy Meal was our only option.

Leya suffered the most, of course. She finally broke down and ate the burger and chicken nuggets, which Noah hassled her about until she pointed out that neither was really meat, but had been "excreted" by one of our Celestian friends. She won the argument, but neither one ate anything that day.

So yeah…tired, worried, cranky. Lonely too.

Leya had been gone all day, visiting various Celestian lifepods to observe their ways and learn more of the lingo. Noah was there, but paying no attention to me. He'd somehow convinced a Celestian to dye a square of moss gray for him, then barf-install four poles and some ropes to create a legit WWE-style wrestling ring.

As I sat there, gagging down my billionth chicken nugget and trillionth fry, Noah jumped into the air, screaming, "The People's Elbow for the win!" before slamming down onto a Celestian kid who was lying on the mossy floor. The kid immediately turned half to goo, to the click-whistle-scream-laughs of delight of the three dozen Celestian kids who now showed up for Noah's interstellar version of Monday Night Raw. Noah continued screaming, now yelling, "He slimed me! Foul, foul, foul!"

Yup. Everything totally normal here. Everyone having a grand time but one Max Nathan Abernathy. It put me in a foul mood which was probably why, when I asked Drxx where Chloe was and got the inevitable stonewalling response, I put my foot down. Refused to help any further until I saw what was happening to her. Just feeling petulant and lonely, and wanted to get my way.

So Drxx and I walked away from the weapons rig I'd been working on. We took two eggpods through the Celestian city, heading in the general direction of the lifepods outside of town. Before we got to them, Drxx veered the eggpods away from the living area, taking us somewhere I'd never been.

***

Like most places on Celestia, it was green and moist, everything perpetually in a state of verdant chaos. The farther we got from the city, the more flora surrounded us. Tall trees started to loom, some of them dwarfing the more earthly variety I remembered walking through at Muir.

Drxx slowed the eggpods, and a tentacle tapped my wrist twice: Celestian for "we're here." I looked around. We were more or less out of the trees now, standing on a small hill that looked down over a field of what looked exactly like a beautifully-maintained lawn of softest Kentucky bluegrass, only every single blade of "grass" was about ten feet tall.

The grass started waving back and forth in one spot thirty feet away. A moment later, I spotted Click, the height of my vantage point allowing me to see as he burst into a patch of moss-floor where no grass grew. The way he was moving, I could tell he was running from something, which worried me. My mind coughed up a dozen possibilities, all of which involved Chloe being eaten, inhaled, melted, burnt, or some combination thereof.

I opened my mouth to yell something heroic—either, "We've got to help them!" or "Eeek!"—but then Chloe exploded into the same grassless spot. She spun, spotted Click, and smacked his back.

"You're it!" she screamed.

Click stopped. "I am what?"

"It," Chloe said. "You're *it*."

"I thought you said I was *Click*."

"No, you're *it*. I tagged you. Now you have to tag me, and then *I'll* be it."

Chloe had had her hand on Click's back (which turned to his front as she spoke to him; Celestians didn't really turn around, just moved their front-parts to the back, and their back-parts to the front). Now she took it off. "Trust me," Chloe said, "it's fun. Here, try to tag me."

She stood back a few feet. Click held out his own tentacle, slow and unsure. Chloe waited…and when Click was maybe a centimeter away from touching her, she danced backward in a sudden, surprisingly graceful move that took her half into the grass.

Click's eyes bulged. I think he was worried, maybe offended.

Chloe took another step back, disappearing into the grass. But she had her hand extended, still visible and waving around. "Come on. Come and get me…"

Click's tentacle shot out again, faster this time. Chloe gave an excited little giggle-shriek and ran into the grass. And I saw Click get it: the sudden, surprising, delicious realization that this was a new game, brought to him by the Human.

Click whistled—a giggle of his own—then ran after her. Chloe appeared and disappeared as she barreled through the bare spots in the "lawn," Click right behind her each time. I saw her whirl, try to juke to her right. Click sidestepped, reading her motion, cutting her off and slapping a tag on her shoulder. Then four other tentacles burst out of his chest, all of them smacking down on her shoulders and arms as he proudly shouted, "You're *it*!"

Chloe beamed, and I almost *felt* her happiness. Felt that one-emotion-at-a-time purity welling up in my own heart. She pulled away, Click's tentacle-arms sliding off. Then I felt the wicked edge to her happiness; saw her smile become a devilish grin as, viper-quick, she smacked Click right between two of his eyes, and said, "Tag back!"

She spun and was back in the grass in an instant. Click stood alone, flabbergasted. Then he hollered, "Tag back! Tag! It!" as he chased her. Chloe giggled, a musical bell-tinkle of a laugh.

Hearing that, for the first time I thought we might just make it through all this. You can't laugh like that in a universe where all roads are dark.

"Peace," said Chloe's laugh. "All is well—or well enough to play."

I wished my phone had juice. If it had, I'd have taken a picture of her, playing tag with an alien friend a million light-years away from San Francisco. I'd have taken a *hundred* pictures, and printed them out and put them in all the picture frames she had in her room. I'd have replaced all those pictures of her loneliness with visual proofs of this moment when, for her, she was one of only two people—the only two people who mattered in the world, the solar system, the galaxy, the universe.

"Someday, Chloe," I whispered. "Someday you'll know."

I left her that way: playing, laughing.

Happy.

24

From laughter to war. A few hours later I was sitting beside the newly-modified Celestian cannon. It had been moved from its upward-facing position to something that paralleled the ground for purposes of this little test, pointing at a mountain several miles away with nothing between us and it but a few moss fields.

Noah sat in the gunner's position (with strict orders not to blow anything up without permission), and a dozen or so Celestians stood in a half-circle around us. Morb and Drxx were there, as were all the Elders we'd seen, along with a few new ones.

Leya was there as well, a fact I tried to put out of my mind as I spoke to the assembly. I had my glasses on, but the second she appeared, I turned around and shoved them into a pocket.

I pointed out the basic features of the laser cannon, explaining the modifications I'd made as I did so. I'd checked and double-checked, then double-checked my double-checks, so I was pretty sure everything was where it should be.

I still felt nervous. I had taken my Dad's basic design, stripped all the errors, and then worked with a *highly* advanced alien race to strengthen it. Everything checked out. No reason to fear.

Except the chance I blow everything up. And the weird way Leya keeps looking at me.

After I rambled for another minute or so—my voice only cracked seventeen or eighteen times, very manly—Noah finally sighed theatrically. "Come on, let's see what this baby can do!"

"I still have to—"

Noah flicked a switch, then pressed the big red button on the joystick control. "Boo-yah!" he shouted.

I flinched. Again, very manly. But what if I'd been wrong? What if instead of a new weapon, I invented the first murder-suicide machine capable of interstellar use?

There was a bright flash and then a deep rumble. I looked at the mountain the laser had just shot.

At first, nothing happened. Not surprising: it was a laser, not a mortar shell. We'd have to send someone to the hill to see if there was a burn mark, and note the size and intensity of the destruct—

Another big rumble, then the ground bucked so wildly I stumbled to the side. When I righted myself and looked at the mountain, half of it was gone.

Not burnt. Not shattered. *Gone.*

I spun to look at the Celestians, who were click-murmuring to each other. "What was—how did—" I couldn't figure out how to finish either sentence. "I didn't design that! I didn't make that happen!"

The nearest Elder (the one who sounded like Nikki Minaj) looked at me for a long three-count, then said, "Once we understood the basics of what you were doing, we were able to make some slight modifications."

"Slight modifications?" I spun and looked at the big empty space that used to be a mountain. "That wasn't a slight modification, that was thermonuclear war! That was—"

"Yeeeee*hawwwwww*!" shouted Noah, spilling out of the cannon gunner's seat. He held his hands out, obviously a bit dizzy from what had just happened, then he was going up and down the line of Celestians, high-fiving everyone (whether they wanted it or not).

I looked around, not sure what I was looking for, and saw Leya sitting on the ground. She must have fallen when the cannon went off. I ran to her, my emotions funneling to panic as I shouted, "Are you hurt?" and held out my hand.

She took it, hoisting herself up and then slapping dust off her pants as she said, "Well done, rockstar."

I smiled, and leaned (what I hoped was) nonchalantly on part of the laser cannon housing. Which promptly shuddered and fell apart, dropping me to the ground. Leya laughed, and then it was her helping me up. Embarrassing? Yeah.

But not as embarrassing as the fact that, once I was on my feet, I *kept* holding onto her hand.

And holding it.

And holding it.

"Dude, what are you doing?"

I turned to see Noah bearing down on me, his eyes practically spitting fire. I looked from him to Leya to him to our hands to him.

I had time to wonder if Celestia had an urgent care where I could get a cast for whatever bone Noah was about to break. He was five feet away. Four. Two. One…

He shouldered past, shoving between me and Leya and breaking our grip on each other as he rushed to the piece of shielding that I'd knocked loose.

He picked it up and started trying to jam it back into place. "Dude, you can't break stuff like this! Not 'til I've blown up more stuff! Smooth move, Max!"

I looked at him. Hard. Then at the cannon. Then…well, everywhere but Leya. Waiting for her to leave.

Only she didn't leave.

Finally, I looked back to her. The second we locked eyes, she grinned, looked at the hand I'd been holding. Then she looked at me again and said, "It *was* pretty smooth, Max."

"Uh—I didn't—I mean…uhhhh—"

Noah's inner rage-demon came to my rescue. "Abernathy, get over here and *fix this!*"

I rushed over to help him reattach the shielding. A few seconds into it, I looked over my shoulder. Leya was gone.

***

Once I'd finished helping Noah fix the laser, I tried to talk to him, hoping I could find some roundabout way to reassure him I wasn't making moves on Leya. He wasn't interested in chatting, though. Just making sure everything was secure on the cannon.

"We gotta do another test. For science!"

That terrified me, so I badgered him until he promised not to "do science" unless I was there to help. I was pretty sure he was lying, planning to start shooting the second I was out of sight, so I added, "Besides, without re-priming the cosmic nucleotide, all you'll have is antineutronic values that could result in irradiated states of Higgs bosons."

When Noah looked askance, I pointed at his groin, then mimed an explosion.

Noah backed up slowly, hands over his pants, his eyes wide. "Woah. What—" He gulped. "What do we do to stop that?"

"Have to add dihydrogen monoxide," I said. "You want me to get some?"

"Yeah," he said, his saucer eyes never leaving the cannon, like it had turned into a snake that would bite him if he blinked.

"Fine. I'll go get some. But promise you won't—"

"I don't want to get irradiated!" he said.

"Okay."

I turned away—fast, before I started laughing at the fact that I'd spouted a bunch of scientific gibberish and then, when asked, "What do we do to stop that?" had answered using science-words that essentially meant, "Just add water."

***

"Where'd you learn all that stuff?"

I jumped, surprised out of my reverie. Turning toward the voice, I saw Leya pushing off from where she'd been leaning against one of the Celestian buildings. She put her hands in her pockets, then sauntered over.

I watched her approach, my body and brain as usual locked into Terminal Stupid by Leya's presence. She stood in front of me, then cocked her head and gave a little smile that made me feel like singing, or maybe howling at the moon.

"You wanna ask me something?" she finally said. "Or are we just having a weird staring contest?"

"Uh, no. I just—um, I just…About lasers?"

Her turn to look confused. "What?"

"You asked me where I learned all that stuff," I said, the words tumbling out as I tried to deflect her attention from my massive embarrassment. "So lasers? You must be talking about lasers. Lasers, right? Probably. Lasers."

She gave a little laugh. "Sure. Lasers." Growing slightly more serious, she added, "I mean, I'm in AP Physics—"

"Of course you are," I whispered.

"What?" she asked.

I held my breath. "Of course you're in AP Physics. Because you're smart and amazing at English and nice and also let's not forget drop-dead-beautiful so of *course* you're in the hardest science class at the school, probably acing it like you do at everything," is what I absolutely did *not* say, even though I wanted to.

What I did say was, "Huh?" even though I didn't want to.

Leya squinted at me. Shrugged, but kept staring at me, beautiful eyes boring into my soul. "Like I said, I'm in AP Physics, and I don't remember them talking about anything like what you've been doing."

I shrugged. "I picked up a thing or two from my dad."

Leya smiled.

Oh my gosh I made her smile I made her smile PLEASE KILL ME NOW I MADE HER SMILE.

I also didn't say *that*. Leya seemed to be waiting for me to say *something,* so I added, "Well, I learned from his mistakes."

Leya laughed the best laugh ever. "That's how you learn, right?" She moved closer to me and added in a low voice, "From your mistakes?"

She took another small step. So close now I could smell her hair. It smelled like strawberries.

How can she smell that good after days without a shower? I thought. *And how do I probably smell after days without a shower?*

I edged back a few paces.

She closed the distance. "But I have to admit, mistakes are a less fun way to learn," she said.

"Less fun than what?" I asked, hoping she didn't notice my voice cracking right in the middle of the sentence.

"Learning by..." She stepped forward again. "...experience."

And the way she said that last word, her head tilted up toward me and standing so close and it didn't matter in that moment that she was probably Noah's girlfriend. It just mattered that she was right here in front of me, and he was far away.

I leaned in, waiting for her to smack me, not knowing what came next—

Am I about to KISS LEYA TAYLOR?

—and at that moment Click walked past, wearing Chloe's shirt and headphones, proclaiming triumphantly, "Look at me, I'm Chloe! I am a human girl and I wear clothes for some reason I do not understand!"

He continued past, disappearing around the side of a building. Followed a moment later by Chloe, rushing after him, wrapped in some kind of towel and shouting, "Click! Click, gimme back my clothes!"

Even the most hormone-ridden teenage guy knows that once he's seen an alien run past wearing his little sister's clothing, said little sister following after wearing next to nothing a moment later, any romance that might have been in the air is over.

I looked at Leya, gave her the best grin I could muster under the circumstances, then ran after Click and Chloe.

***

I caught up with them near Click's lifepod. Chloe was yanking her clothes off the alien, then running inside the pod.

I started after her, got a shouted, "Don't you dare!" and thought better of it.

I turned to Click, a million questions at the ready.

"Why do you put those things on you?" Click asked. He pointed at my shirt. "Chloe says they are 'mostly for protection or something but mostly just, like, to rock my style but underneath I'm normal and you ask a lot of questions but that's okay because I like you and you're nice to me, nicer than anyone else at school, that's for sure.'" He blinked. "I am not sure I understand everything she says."

"I'm not sure I understand *anything* she says."

"Chloe told me she has no friends. Is that true?"

I started to deny it. I knew what my parents would say: "Of course she has friends. Everyone loves Chloe." But I wasn't a parent. I was Chloe's older brother. And she deserved the respect of my honesty.

"I don't know for sure. I think it's true, at least at her school."

Click was silent, digesting this. "She said she does not miss any of them because they are not her friends. But she does miss her family." He brightened and stared at me with the same intensity Chloe has when pronouncing some eight-year-old wisdom. "I do not want her to be sad and miss things. So you will be my family now, so she has family here and does not have to miss things."

Chloe came out of the lifepod as he said it, still pulling down the shirt that she'd just put back on. "It doesn't work like that. I

184

have a mom and a dad—two parent-halves of my own—and I'd like to see them again."

Click was silent a long time. He touched Chloe on the forehead. Longing, and togetherness, and empathy showed in that gesture. "I understand," he said.

I realized then that through all this, Click had stayed with Chloe. Morb and Drxx were more likely to be talking to me than to him. I'd assumed that was because they were basically at war, but now I realized that it had started before we saw the Gro'nid attack. Even on Earth, Click had found Chloe while the two of them walked alone in the woods.

I grabbed them both in a hug. Again, I felt that many-faceted image of the moment. I was Max, holding tight to the kid sister I loved and never quite knew how to help, and to the alien kid who had somehow come to mean so much to her. I was Click, experiencing a wealth of new moments, right in the center of things. I was Chloe, being held by her brother and by her new—her only—friend.

So many of the moments were infused with the feeling of "for the first time." Which you'd expect, given that this was still First Contact stuff. But most of the "first time" feelings weren't about that. They were...

...first time someone's held me like this.

...first time I've felt safe.

...first time I felt seen.

In that moment there was no war, no homesickness; even teenage hormones disappeared. It was just us, holding each other. Someone thought, "This is how the end happens. This is how we fix the universe." And I don't know if it was Click or Chloe. I just know it wasn't me.

I'm too close to being an adult, and am no longer wise.

25

Morb found us a bit later. She gave us a look just like the one Mom hit us with whenever she came in a room just after we'd cleaned up all evidence of some kid-crime.

"Everything good here?" she asked.

"Sure," said Chloe. Then, impishly, added, "Mom."

"Chloeeee," I said.

"What?" She gave me a dose of the wide-eyed innocence for which humanity has yet to develop an effective defense. "Click said we were family."

Click made a noise like a burp farting (my brain-sponge insisted it was a giggle). Morb glanced at him, then said, straight-faced, "It doesn't work like that."

"That's what *I* said," Chloe shouted, almost gleeful.

By now I sensed there was something in the air. Motioning Chloe to silence, I said, "What's up?"

Morb permitted herself a Celestian grin: her flesh rippled like a pond with a rock tossed in it, and briefly went every color of the rainbow. "You are going home."

Have you ever seen an eight-year-old told they were going to Disneyland after hitting up a candy factory? Well that was *my* reaction.

Chloe took it somberly. When I asked why so serious, she wouldn't answer. I couldn't press her on it either, because Noah appeared out of nowhere, screaming, "We're going *HOME, BRUH!*" He then did a dance which was mostly fist pumps and pelvic thrusts, followed by gleeful screaming of words I had to keep telling Chloe I'd explain when she was older.

We found Leya, and told her. She was happy, but neither candy-factory-Disneyland-happy like me, nor pelvis-based-chicken-dance happy like Noah. She kept looking at me funny, and I was worried she was going to either tell me never to talk to her again, or beg me not to tell her boyfriend about the moment we'd had right before Chloe did her streaking act.

I wanted to hear exactly zero of those things, so I "respected her space" (aka I avoided her).

The Celestians asked if I could tune up a few things on the laser cannon prototype before bed, and I said sure. It was mostly a pro forma request: the laser was done, and they were just tinkering with esthetics. Designing a control system for a many-tentacled Pac-Man ghost is different than what you'd do for a human, and there were a few kinks to work out.

The Earthlings settled in for our (hopefully) final Happy Meal secretions—Noah putting down his chicken nuggets every once in a while to do a triumphant "We're going home!" twerk, the rest of us mostly silent—and then slept.

And dreamed.

***

I was Dad.

I moved through the garage with a fury. There was a circuit board on the floor and I stepped on it, barely noticing the crunch as I ground a piece of my life's work underfoot.

It was disorienting. So much anger in my head. So many thoughts flying through my mind:

Enough fliers?

Never enough. Need more.

Gotta get them back.

It's enough for now. Can print more later.

What was that?

The armature of the laser was extended into his path, and he batted it aside.

Stupid—get that thing out of the way. Not worth anything without Max to fix it.

That last bit bounced around in whatever part of the dream was me, and I felt sadness. Not Dad's—he was just drumming his fingers as more "Missing Children" posters slid from the printer we had in the corner of the garage.

The sadness was all mine. Max Abernathy's. In my dad's head, realizing in this moment that he knew exactly how bad he was at his job; that he needed me to do the hard parts. What would happen to him if we didn't get home? How would he take care of himself?

There was also a deeper, darker thought: was that what I was to him? Even now, was his main thought in getting me back so that he could fix his stupid inventions?

The printer finished. I (or rather, Dad) snatched the thick pile of pages, glancing at them quickly to make sure the contact info was there, the pictures of a teenage boy and a little girl were clear and unsmudged.

"The guys are here."

I turned to see Marla—

(mom)

—dressed in her San Francisco Fire Department uniform, standing in the door to the house. She slapped the button on the wall nearby, and the garage door started reeling up.

She walked to me, grabbing the papers out of my hands. She gave me a peck on the cheek, then turned to the still-opening door, where a fire truck waited. She would plaster the posters all over the neighborhood, as she had every day since the kids—

(since chloe and i)

—disappeared.

The dream-me grabbed Marla/Mom. I kissed her, hard, and I felt Dad's thoughts even as he said them:

"We'll find them."

She held on so tight I felt my ribs creak on Celestia.

Then she was gone. Off to cover the city in images of two children who were so far beyond "Missing" there wasn't even a word for it.

***

I woke up to sobbing.

I dreamed the terror and confusion of a parent, and woke up crying for my mommy and daddy. Confusing, to say the least. Even more so when I realized I wasn't actually the one crying.

It was Noah.

I rolled to face him, trying not to wake Chloe. "You okay?" I asked.

He sat up in his own bed, wiping his eyes. "Yeah. Dream. Sorry."

"What was it about?"

Leya sat bolt upright from her own bed. "Mom and Dad," she said, in a voice so hushed and haunted I thought I would remember it forever.

At the same time, Noah said, "Nothing. Just dream stuff."

The answers deflated me. I'd wondered if anyone else felt the "Joining" feelings. But how did you ask that? Just walk up to your best/only friend, throw your arm over his shoulder, and ask, "Have you been mind melding with people recently?" Not easy.

And really, what was the likelihood I had been gifted with psychic powers? Especially when compared to the far-more-realistic option: I was just dreaming. My mind creating a made-up world where I was wanted, loved. A way to cope with a reality that had far outstripped any dream.

A polite knocking sound interrupted my musing, and the wall of the lifepod opened to admit Click.

"Ready to go?" he said.

The mood changed. "Am I ever!" shouted Noah. He was out of bed and through the door in an instant, shouting, "Will there be an in-flight movie or something this time? That last trip was *way* too long. I could have…"

His voice trailed off as he walked away. Click sprouted two limbs and did a passable imitation of a human shrug, then followed. Leya went as well, wiping tears from her eyes.

Just Chloe and I remained. She was still in bed, looking around with the dazed look of someone jerked out of a dream. "Mom got *mad*. Or was it me?"

I went to her. Helped her out of bed, giving her a little shake. "Chlo? You good?"

She nodded, but her eyes didn't focus. "This *is* an emergency."

I frowned. "What?"

Chloe finally looked at me. "It's what I said. The lady at the bakery got mad when I put the paper up and said, 'Aren't you supposed to be dealing with emergencies?' so I said, 'This *is* an emergency,' then the lady said, 'How long they been gone?' and I said, 'To a mother? A lifetime.'"

I frowned. "Chloe, what exactly did you dream about?" I asked.

"Home," she said. Then she shrugged out of my grasp and ran after Click, leaving me alone and wondering. *Were* the dreams real? Were we reaching across time and space to our parents? No way to tell. Not here, not now.

And Chloe had been right. The only answer, the only thing that mattered right now, was that one word: "Home."

***

I hustled out of the lifepod. When I caught up with everyone, Noah and Leya were standing so close their hands kept brushing. It actually seemed to bug Leya (joy!), so she solved the problem by threading her arm through the crook of Noah's (despair!).

"What do we tell our parents when we get back?" Noah was

190

asking. He turned red, and started to stammer out an apology to Leya. "I meant in general. What do we tell people? Like my parents, or Max and Chloe's. What do we tell the world?"

Leya shrugged. "The truth. I mean, why wouldn't we?"

Noah grimaced and shook his head. "Aside from the fact that the truth will buy us one-way tickets to the cuckoo farm?"

"Everyone will believe us," Chloe said, with the perfect confidence of inexperience. "Right, Click?"

"I do not know what any of you are talking about," he answered.

"Join the club," I said.

"Not true," Leya said. "You know more than anyone." She flashed a smile over her shoulder. Predictably, I blushed and looked away as my dumb body tried to turn inside out.

Soon we arrived at the Temple. Numerous eggship discs were on the ground below the hovering hulk of the mothership docked above us. Morb and Drxx were already there—each standing on a separate disc.

It didn't take the Celestian version of a marriage therapist to see that something was going on between them. Morb had about a hundred tentacle arms all folded across her chest or thorax or whatever. Drxx had only two eyes, instead of the usual four-plus, which I figured was Celestian Eye Contact Avoidance 101, a theory backed up by the fact that both of his eyes were looking pointedly away from Morb, and his head was glowing red.

"What's up?" Click asked tentatively, sounding just like Chloe when she knows Dad and Mom are having an "adult disagreement."

"Ask Drxx," said Morb, the words sharp enough to slice steel.

Drxx turned to us and said a very uncomfortable nothing at all.

"Uh-oh," said Chloe and Click almost simultaneously.

Noah shrugged. "Don't know, don't care. So long as we're going home."

Lonnnnng silence.

"We are going home, right?" said Leya.

Drxx finally looked at Morb. Now it was Morb's turn to avoid eye contact, which she did in dramatic fashion by sprouting a dozen more eyes and very slowly and dramatically pointing them all away from her spouse.

Drxx sighed, then looked at us and said, "There's been a delay."

"*What?*" Noah whispered, stricken.

"No. Huh-uh," said Leya. "We *have to…*" Her words thinned out and disappeared into the heavy silence.

"Click?" said Chloe.

"I do not understand," said Click. To his parents, he said, "What possible rea—"

"It's easy!" Morb finally shouted, turning to look at us. "The Elders have *deliberated*." She grew about a hundred arms and threw them all in the air as she said the last word, which is when I learned (via brain-sponge) that air quotes are a universal constant.

"Deliberated? What's that mean?" asked Noah. "They're the boss-guys, right? So they're—"

"Not going to let us go," I realized. "Because they're worried that if the new weaponry fails, they won't be able to fix it. Without me."

It wasn't the brain-sponge. It wasn't "Joining" (real or imagined). It was just my subconscious gathering data behind the scenes to arrive at the only possible conclusion.

"But they would not do that. They—" Click flailed helplessly.

"They would and they did," Drxx said. "Whether we like it or not." And his tone told me the reason he and Morb were fighting:

Morb wanted us to go home, and Drxx had argued to keep us here.

"Whether we *like* it or not? Whether we *like*—" More tentacular air quotes from Morb, followed by a disgusted sound. She turned to us. "I am so sorry. My understanding was that we were to complete our mission immediately. I was prepared to return you to your homes while I continued my work."

"*Your* work? *YOUR* work?" Drxx shrieked.

"Fine, *our* work!" Morb shouted right back. "Not that you care about that anymore. And just because your brother-half is dead doesn't—"

She cut herself off, but it was too late. You could have heard a feather falling in the silence that followed.

After a few seconds, Morb visibly pulled herself together—literally, her arms all telescoped in, then disappeared into her body and she was just smooth Pac-Man ghost flesh again. Coldly, she said to Drxx, "You do not understand. The humans should be with their families."

I looked at Leya. Noticing her stiffen at the last word. Noticing even more how Noah reached out to comfort her and she grabbed his big hand in both of hers.

Drxx turned to us and spoke to me with the voice of a doctor telling you, "Now, this won't hurt a bit" right before sticking a twelve-foot-long needle into your butt. "I know you anticipated reunion. I know you wanted to go back. But the wisdom of the Elders cannot be questioned. We have not yet fired the laser cannon against the Gro'nid, and might require a man of your skill to assist us." Chloe started to cry. "It's just until after the next battle, and then--"

"It is not fair to these humans," said Morb.

"We will do our best to return them—"

"They should not have been taken in the first place!" Morb hollered. "We *must*—"

"But we *did* take them!" Drxx shrieked. Visibly calming himself, he added, "No one is happy about this. But our work must continue, and our people must live. Asking them to wait until the laser is tested in battle is a small price to pay."

"And what if the laser fails?" I asked.

Drxx stared at me. "Then the question of going home becomes moot."

He tapped his foot and the eggpod enclosed him. The craft zipped up and disappeared into a hole that opened on the mothership.

I put an arm around Chloe and hugged her. Click did the same. Once again, an embrace between me, my little sister, and an alien kid who didn't understand the concept of a t-shirt were the closest things to an island of safety in the universe's ocean of insanity.

26

I expected Noah or Chloe to explode—their emotional ages being the closest—but Leya surprised everyone by giving out a little scream and stomping away.

"You going after her?" I asked.

Noah shrugged, hopeless. "Would it do any good? We're still stuck on this moss planet full of nothing but shattered dreams and McBarfy Meals."

"Someone should check on her. To make sure she's fine," Chloe said, and gave me a nudge. That surprised me. It surprised me even more when she nudged me again, this time adding a sly wink. "You think she's fine, right?"

I fully expected her to burst into flame due to the look I shot at her. Instead she winked again. And again. I decided I had to get away before her single entendres prompted Noah to punch a hole in me.

I rushed in the same direction Leya had gone, and found her staring at the Temple of the Elders with a look that could have paralyzed small woodland creatures.

"Trying to make it explode with your mind?" I asked.

She barely looked at me. "Going all *Firestarter* wouldn't do any good, would it?"

"Stephen King reference. Nice," I said, going for jollity. Her expression didn't change. I looked at her, thinking how tough she was. Chloe, Noah, and I were all worried because we'd been taken from our homes, but that happened to her long ago.

"What?" she asked.

She'd caught me staring. I tried to think of something not-creepy to say, so of course my brain coughed up the worst thing possible: "You kinda remind me of my mom."

Leya looked utterly surprised at that. A laugh forced itself out of her. "Really?" She blinked as though trying to figure out how to respond, then bobbed her shoulder around in an over the top come-hither motion. "I didn't know you cared."

My blush could probably be seen on Earth.

Leya laughed. "You're too easy to mess with, rockstar."

I laughed too, and then she turned toward me, so close that for a second I thought/feared/hoped she was going to kiss me. Instead, she gave the shoulder bob again and said, "So are you like your dad?" She heaved a melodramatic sigh. "What does that make...*us*?"

"Uhh—"

She laughed again. Shook her head ruefully. "Boys are so dumb."

That irritated me. Everyone always seemed to know more about what was going on than I did, and having that pointed out to me poked a sore spot in my heart. "I guess if I'm dumb then I'm definitely like my dad. Not that that's a compliment."

"Why do you say that?"

I couldn't answer. How to tell a girl who'd lost her family how much your own family bugged you?

She seemed to guess what I was thinking, and surprised me by saying, "Just say it, Abernathy. Whatever's bugging you—"

"I just...don't know if you'd be the right person to complain to about family problems."

She shrugged and looked away. "Why not? I know a lot about family problems. Shuttled from one distant relative to another, none of whom really want me there. Now it's Noah's poor parents who got stuck with me, so—"

"*Stuck* with you?" My lower jaw nearly unhinged. "Have Noah's parents ever acted like you were a burden? I've seen you with them around town, you know. At the mall, at a restaurant, even at the movies once. They didn't seem like they were having a bad time, or like they didn't want you there. *Noah* sure likes having you around. Heck, everyone likes having you around. Hadn't you noticed that?" I shook my head. "And it's not like you're all alone. You have people. You have Noah, and his parents, and—" I shrugged.

"You?"

Every time I thought my blush had maxed out, Leya managed to kick it up a notch.

"Me?" I squeaked. "No. I mean...uh...yeah. Sure. No. What?"

Leya didn't laugh. She didn't make fun or anything else, either. She stepped in close, so close she was the only thing I could see. "How about this: I'll start accepting that maybe there are a few people out there who like having me around and don't think of me as a burden, and you start accepting that you're a pretty smart, capable, likeable guy."

I laughed. Couldn't help it. "Sure. Yeah, obviously that's true. What with all my friends, and the constant parties, not to mention all the girls clinging to me all the time. I'm Mr. Popular." I snapped. "Oh, wait, I'm thinking of Noah."

Leya shook her head. "Abernathy, you are the *stupidest* smart person I know." Sighing, she added, "I remind you of your mom. But you don't want to be your dad, so what does that mean about—" She shook her head. "Forget it. Let's just enjoy what we have for the moment."

I did not have a clue what that meant. For a moment, my brain swung back and forth like a pendulum on meth. I thought she was going to hit me. I thought she was going to hold my hand. I thought I was going to faint, or maybe kiss her. Everything was possible, nothing was possible.

Now, I thought. *If you're ever going to try anything, now's the—*

The moment passed. Sanity returned and I was left trying not to look at her, but also trying not to *look* like I wasn't looking at her. And if that sounds confusing, good. Because it definitely confused me.

***

Morb came barreling around the side of the Temple. "There you are!"

"What is it?" I shouted, suddenly fearful the Gro'nid had returned; that Chloe was in danger.

"We're going on a trip!"

"Home?"

She didn't answer, just waved for us to follow and set off at a fast pace. We caught up to her back at the mothership, where Noah was asking Click, "So, if we're not going home..." He caught my eye and shrugged to ask, "Do you know what's going on?"

I gave him my best "No idea" shrug in return.

"We are all here, as you said we must be," Click said to Morb. "So tell us what is your 'big idea that you are going to do no matter what and if Drxx does not like it he can go soak his tentacles'?"

Morb reeled off a long series of clicks and whistles. My brain-sponge was silent. But Click understood what she was saying and freaked the heck out. Arms and hands and eyes and a couple things I have no name for kept shooting out of him, sucking back in, shooting out again. He made a constant stream of noise that my brain-sponge translated as various shades of "Woohoo!"

Chloe, Leya, and Noah were all sharing confused looks. "Anyone get that?" asked Leya.

"Nope," said Noah.

"Must be something good, though," said Chloe, clapping excitedly as Click continued cavorting.

"For them, maybe. But what if it's finally...the probing?"

I was about to answer Noah when the brain-sponge finally coughed up a translation in a completely new way: for a moment,

198

all I could see or hear was a YouTube commercial, complete with the grayed-out "Video will play after ad" banner that meant I had to watch the whole thing.

First: music. A soulless fusion of techno and something vaguely reggae-esque playing over quick cuts of blue water, beaches, people laughing, playing in the sun, volleyball. Two people kissing as the Caribbean sun set and a welcoming voice encouraged me to call 1-800-Sandals.

"Did any of you get that?" I asked.

Noah and Leya looked baffled. But maybe Chloe's brain-sponge was better, because she got a big grin, ran over to Click, and started jumping up and down with him, while he screamed "Woohoo!" and she shouted "Legoland!"

***

The discs I hadn't noticed we were all standing on activated. Click and Chloe barely noticed, dancing around their eggship together. Leya and Noah, sharing their eggship with Morb, looked confused and irritated as they zipped away.

I got my own egg all to myself. Lucky me.

The trip from ground to mothership lasted only seconds, but when my eggship dropped me off, Noah all but jumped on me to scream, "We're going on a picnic!"

As he explained, I got why my brain-sponge had given my brain a YouTube commercial for a getaway: because that's what was in store.

We were going to some kind of vacation spot for Celestians. It was too warm for them to live there all the time, and there was far too much static in the air—they had to wear their green electrical dampeners at all times while in the planet's atmosphere. But they loved visiting the place, and from what Click explained, going to it was a rare and expensive treat.

I'd been right that Drxx was one of the main reasons the Elders decreed we must stay. He wanted vengeance for his brother-half, and figured having me around would increase the chances of the laser blowing the Gro'nid to itty-bitty pieces. He convinced the Elders of this (over Morb's objections), but while I was talking to Leya, Morb had a quick mental powwow with the Elders and convinced them that, if we weren't allowed to go home, at least we could have a good time on their dime.

I had to admit to curiosity by now. What kind of place would Celestians view as a retreat?

We took off in moments. The mothership looked the way it had when we first saw it: a silvery pyramid with flashing lights. I asked Click why it was like that sometimes, and transparent others. He babbled an answer that my brain-sponge turned into static and white noise. Looked like the reasons lay beyond my simple Earthman understanding.

We lounged in the same room we'd originally been "imprisoned" in on the way here. Someone had very considerately barfed up a table and chairs for us, so we lounged around and gagged down some of the ever-present Happy Meals for an hour or so, chatting amiably. Everyone was trying hard not to be bummed that we weren't going home, and mostly succeeded.

Click showed up and asked if Chloe would come with him to "see something fun!" I'm a good big brother, so I didn't object. But being a good big brother, I followed after to make sure I'd also see whatever the fun thing was. For science.

I followed Chloe and Click at a distance. They chattered about everything from the reasons for clothing to how the Celestians secrete to whether Ariana Grande was a "good" singer or "the best singer who ever lived ohmigosh!" Though I have to admit the last one was mostly Chloe talking and Click looking confused.

When they turned the corner, I heard Chloe scream. I ran, my mind exploding with images of murder and mayhem. When I turned the corner, I didn't scream.

But it was an effort.

The outer wall of the ship had gone transparent, so Chloe and Click (and I) were now standing on a shimmering floor looking out into space as we passed through some kind of asteroid field. I worried that several of the big rocks were going to crash into us, but the mothership just zigzagged through, so fast the asteroids seemed to jump away the instant before they hit us.

Soon the asteroids thinned to reveal a planet beyond. Predominantly green and blue, but with random-seeming stripes of orange scattered over its surface that looked a bit like Band-Aids some celestial being had slapped on the planet. Maybe that's why my brain-sponge translated Click's next words as they did:

"Band-Aid," he breathed. "The funnest place ever discovered. The closest planet to ours, and for eons, we did not even know of its existence."

"How could you miss an entire *planet*?" Chloe asked.

"It is the asteroids. There is something about them that we do not fully understand—even now. Something of the material that forms them confuses our scans—there!"

Click pointed, and I saw a shimmer in the distance, a rainbow that arced between two of the asteroids. When it ended, they had changed places. Or had they? I squinted and, after checking to make sure no one was around, slipped on my glasses.

It didn't help. The asteroids kept eluding my attempts to pin them down visually. They were there one moment, somewhere else the next, transported across vast spaces in the blink of an eye.

"Are they going through wormholes or something?" asked Chloe, and I felt pride at my smart sis.

"That is the part we do not understand fully," said Click. "Something about the asteroids resists not only our best scans, but the way we see them. As the popular saying goes, 'you should not trust what you see while passing through the anomalous asteroid field between Celestia and Band-Aid, because if you do you might find an asteroid embedded in your tentacles.'"

"Catchy," Chloe said dryly.

"Indeed," Click said. "It took us hundreds of years to work out the calculations necessary to make it through the asteroid field, and we were shocked when we discovered that the asteroids' qualities masked not only their own movements, but the planet that hangs in the center of the field, moving with the asteroids as it orbits our suns."

Chloe gave a little squeal as one of the largest asteroids swerved straight at us.

"Do not worry," Click said. "We have worked out the likelihoods of each shift to within a billionth of a percent."

Sure enough, the huge rock blipped out of existence with a rainbow flash, and blipped back into being hundreds of feet away from the ship, swerving wide of us in its new trajectory.

It was amazing, beautiful. And obviously a bit scary to Chloe, who gulped audibly before saying, "It seems dangerous anyway. Why are we going to a planet in the middle of blipping asteroids?"

"It is a treat!" Click said. "Band-Aid is a resort planet, where we occasionally vacation." When Chloe jumped again, he turned a pair of eyes her direction and said, "You are always safe with me, Chloe. Always." And a tentacle extended to hold her hand.

Chloe cocked her head. Then said, simply, "It's beautiful," in a way that told me she trusted Click utterly, and knew that they would get to Band-Aid just fine.

It was magical, in a way. Chloe was so completely present, enjoying the moment. We weren't going home, but there were delights to see, and she would enjoy them with her friend.

She was safe.

She was happy.

And that was more beautiful to me than all the quantum

asteroids that may (or may not) have been in the universe.

***

When I returned to Noah and Leya in the opaque room, Noah was playing Rock, Scissors, Paper with himself. Shockingly, not every round was a tie, which I filed away as just another of the Many Mysteries of Noah.

"Where are these Martians taking us, anyway?" asked Noah.

"They're not Martians," said Leya.

"Poe-*tay*-toe, toe-*may*-toe," said Noah.

Rather than unpack all the things wrong with that sentence, I piped up from the doorway as I entered, "You were the one who told me we were going on a picnic. You forget?"

"No, but I been thinking," said Noah. His right hand lost against his left (third time in a row), and he gave up the game. Staring at me and Leya in turn, he said, "These things kidnapped us. And now they're taking us to *another* planet? For a picnic? I don't buy it. I bet we're going where they take all the humans they abduct, forced to be in slave labor camps or permanent probing volunteers." He shook his head, then slowly flexed his arms. "Not this guy. I got a plan."

"Which is what, exactly?" said Leya.

"Overpower them. Catch them off-guard while they aren't expecting it and—"

"And what? Pin them? Brag about your bench press stats?" Leya rolled her eyes, which made my heart do a little flip-flop.

"Naw. I'll take over the ship and—"

"And then we all hold on tight while the spaceship crashes into a quasar?" Leya snapped. "How does that get us home?"

I tried to concentrate on the words they were saying, though most of my brain was alternately pointing out that the shine was off whatever relationship they had and screaming "Yippee!" Such are the ways of the heart.

"Better than waiting here," said Noah.

Leya shook her head. "I appreciate that you want to protect everyone around you, Noah, but you need to use your head. Be smart about this."

Noah glared at Leya for a second, then at me. I raised my hands. "I just work here," I said.

Noah turned on his heel and started walking away. "Where are you going?" I called out.

Without looking back, he snapped, "Don't worry. I'm not going to crash anyone into a quasar. Whatever that is."

I looked at Leya. She looked at me. "We should—" I began.

"Yeah," she agreed.

We ran after Noah, catching up to him as he spun around and, pointing a finger at both of us, shouted, "And for your information, it's three-hundred-seventy-five pounds, and it's the school record!"

Then he was stomping off again. Leya looked at me, seeming to expect a response. "Your boyfriend's really strong," was all I could think to say.

She looked super upset for some reason, and stomped off after Noah. I hurried after them both, asking myself what I'd said wrong.

27

When I caught up to Leya I resisted the urge to ask what I'd done to make her mad. Partly because she was glaring at me and I didn't want to risk it, partly because at that moment we followed Noah around a corner and found ourselves in a room we'd never seen.

Not that we'd seen a lot of rooms in the mothership—we'd sat in the cargo bay, we'd seen through the whole thing when it went transparent, and we'd walked through a few corridors. Still, by any objective standard, this room was new. And stunning.

It looked like some kind of garden, only instead of trees and bushes and flowers, giant purple mushrooms grew everywhere. I marveled at the Celestian shielding. What else was hidden behind transparent walls? Indeed, when I turned around, I could still see all the way to the cargo bay, with only the slightest distortions marking where the walls were.

Noah seemed incredibly unimpressed. He tore through the place, not even noticing the enormous violet fungi or the ten-inch pink worms with neon green mohawks that appeared to be tending to them. He just turned a corner, and was gone again. Leya followed and I ran after, with one last glance at the amazing garden. We ran into an adjoining room full of little creatures flying through the air, each of which looked like a cross between a bat and a hummingbird.

Again, Noah didn't care. Again, Leya ran after him, and I ran after Leya. Room after room, with marvels I couldn't begin to describe, let alone comprehend.

After a half-dozen rooms, we found what Noah'd been after. "Intergalactic GPS," he said quietly as he slipped inside.

Alien in design and makeup, but there was no denying that we were in the navigation and command room. The transparency settings of the room were set so the far side was completely invisible, allowing us a clear view of the blue and orange stripes of Band-Aid—

No, that's too lame, I thought. *How about Bandia?*

Better.

Morb and Drxx, sitting beside each other, moved knobs and levers on a table similar to the one in our lifepods. I wondered fleetingly what size factory had vomited this ship up, and shuddered just thinking of it.

I looked over at Noah, and caught a look that surprised me: elation. He drank in every movement, his eyes alight with excitement. Made sense: he loved gaming, and here was something that put the best VR gaming rig to shame.

Appendages sprouted from Morb's base, her feet pushing down a pair of levers, while a third appendage gripped a stick. The view shifted, and Noah pumped his fist.

"What?" I mouthed.

"It's a frickin' stick shift!" he laughed.

Eyes appeared on Drxx's back, glaring at us. "You should not be here," he snapped.

"They can be here if they like," Morb snapped back, her tones cold enough to give my brain-sponge an ice-cream headache.

Drxx glared. "They are going to get in the way."

In the most overly pleasant voice I've heard on any planet, Morb said, "Come in, Earthlings. Sit down and enjoy watching everything we do. It is our pleasure to have you with us, for an extended period of time that *some* of us thought would be a good idea but now perhaps are regretting."

I knew from my parents' upsets how this was going to end: lots of sulking and silence, and the kids unsure whether to stand there and be uncomfortable, or just go be uncomfortable somewhere else.

Noah did neither: one more reason he's him and I'm me. "Can

I drive?" He literally rubbed his hands together.

"I think that's going a bit—" began Morb.

"No, we should definitely let him drive. After all, as you have made it clear, we should encourage them to participate as much as possible," Drxx insisted, obviously enjoying turning the tables.

"I think letting him crash the ship is going a bit far to make a point," said Morb.

"And I suppose that will be my fault too, won't it?"

When I was in fifth grade I went to a friend's house and witnessed what later turned out to be the final fight in his parents' very troubled marriage.

I was more comfortable that day than I was now. Looking at Leya, I saw she felt the same. Noah was the only one who seemed unaffected:

"Soooo...can I drive?"

I laughed; I couldn't help it. Leya joined in. A second later, my brain-sponge informed me that the sound like two yaks clogdancing on a cheese grater was Celestian laughter.

And Noah got to drive.

Morb firmly drew the line at him piloting through the asteroid belt, but as soon as we were past it, she and Drxx showed Noah the controls and let him have a go.

Click and Chloe showed up midway through the practice session, Chloe looking green around the gills and wondering "what's going on and who's flying because they're terrible and are we going to die because this is supposed to be the fun part of the trip?" which just caused more laughter.

Morb seemed to warm up as Noah piloted the ship. She even offered to let me and Leya try. Leya's face went white as a sheet. I remembered her previous comments about not driving stick and wondered if that was much more about what had happened to her parents than just an avoidance of non-automatic transmissions.

I passed, because I had no wish to look bad in front of Leya by being worse at driving a space ship than her boyfriend was.

Soon enough we closed in on the planet, and Morb insisted Noah relinquish the controls. He wheedled a bit first, trying to convince Drxx ("come *on*, mah dude!") to let him land. But Drxx said, "Landing is different. If your calculations and movements are off by more than a meter, we are atomic dust," and that was that. Noah settled for watching like a hawk as Drxx took over and landed, and the look in Noah's eyes told me I might be witnessing the planning of the first-ever interstellar joyride.

Noah kept edging in close, and Drxx finally snapped at him. "Back off!"

"Don't yell at the human!" Morb shouted back.

"We're entering the atmosphere, and if it's all right with you, I'd rather not become a *beep-click-tick-boop*!" The brain-sponge didn't give any translation, but Drxx slid on the green electrical dampener he'd been wearing back on Earth, so I figured it had to do with the danger of static charges in Bandia's atmosphere.

Morb relented and put on a belt of her own. She handed one to Click. "Do you need me to cinch it on your thorax, sweetie?" she said.

"Aw, Morb, not in front of my friend," Click said, obviously embarrassed. "I'm not a larva anymore."

"You'll always be *my* larva," said Morb.

***

Per standard operating procedure I had avoided wearing my glasses as much as possible around people who were a) human, b) not related to me, and c) Leya. But I figured that seeing another alien planet was a big enough deal to bear the risk of looking like a dork. So I slipped my specs out of my pocket on approach to the planet.

I was glad I did. Bandia was even more beautiful up close. Surprisingly, the blue was vast fields of some kind of flora, and the orange was the color of the seas.

I turned to see what Chloe thought, and instead caught Leya looking at me. My desire to look less nerdy battled with my desire to clearly see the new planet. Social anxiety won.

I went for my glasses, but Leya's hand settled on mine. "Leave 'em on, rockstar," she said quietly. "Enjoy the sights."

She turned away and practiced what she preached while I tried to focus on the immensity of the new world we were about to land on and ignore the fact that my wrist and hand tingled where Leya had touched me.

"It's beautiful, isn't it?" she said, that same low whisper.

"Gorgeous," I said. Her eyes flicked toward me, and I looked away as fast as I could.

Not fast enough. "You talking about the planet?" she asked, her eyes half-closed, a subtle smile flickering at the corners of her mouth.

I looked at Noah. He still only had eyes for the control bank of the spaceship, watching everything Drxx did as we dropped to the planet.

I looked back at Leya. She was still staring. "Well?"

I gulped. "The planet is definitely beautiful."

I intentionally didn't answer her question directly, and leaving the ambiguity felt like about the bravest thing I'd ever done.

"Your glasses are smudged," she said. She carefully took them off me. Breathed on the lenses, then pinched them between her fingers and two layers of her t-shirt. Vision returned in full as she replaced the glasses.

There was a new planet in sight behind her. A new world, with experiences that no other human would ever have. And in that moment, the only thing I saw was her. Smiling.

"Smart is sexy, don't you know that?"

"I—" I looked at Noah, then swallowed, my mouth so dry it felt packed with sand. "Noah is…I mean—"

Leya shook her head and, seemingly to herself, added, "But not smart about everything, I guess."

"I don't understand."

She chuckled. "No, you don't. And I'm not sure how I feel about that. I guess we'll have to wait it out."

She turned away and looked at the planet and wouldn't answer any of my questions after that.

***

Once we'd gotten the mothership to about a hundred feet above Bandia's surface, we all split up into eggships. Feeling very much the veteran, I watched as Chloe and Click dropped to the surface in the first one. Noah and Leya followed. She stuck her tongue out at me while Noah wasn't watching, in case I wasn't already confused enough.

"What did that mean?" asked Drxx.

"If I figure that out I'll be the wisest man in the universe," I said, getting into another ship with Drxx and Morb.

We all landed at about the same time, but Leya was the first of the Earthlings to put her feet on the blue soil of Bandia. It bounced under her, like she was walking on a trampoline. "This place is *sick*," she said.

Click made a grunt—confusion—and Chloe put her hand on his head. "Sick means cool," she said.

Click did the confusion sound again, his parent-halves also joining in.

"It is sick to be cool? Does being cool make you sick? Is it too cool here? It's too hot for us, but—" Click's tentacles writhed, his concern for his friend touching.

"Our analyses of your system put Bandia well within your body's survival parameters," Morb said.

"The word she's saying means 'good,'" said Leya.

"Ahh," said Click.

Drxx's body bowed in half. "Your assessment is more correct than you may realize. Bandia is a welcome location for short excursions, but Celestians cannot breathe its atmosphere for more than a few days without getting sick. It is the warmth, but there are also trace elements that do not agree with us. Earth is far more compatible."

I noticed something: the brain-sponge had recalibrated, and I was actually hearing "Bandia" in my head, instead of "Band-Aid." It appeared I could influence the vocabulary it used to translate—like telling it I preferred Dictionary.com to the Unabridged Oxford Dictionary for communication purposes.

Cool.

Drxx pressed a button on one of the eggship discs. A hum sounded, then a metallic box about four feet to a side rose up from the disc. Drxx opened it and withdrew an enormous picnic basket.

"You really meant a *picnic*?" said Noah. Looking at me, he added, "They said we were going on a picnic while you were with Leya, but—"

"That's interesting I didn't know that a picnic do you say how interesting!" I shouted, the words exploding as a single, hurried breath, hoping to distract Noah from the fact that I'd had alone time with his girl.

Drxx provided a welcome distraction, throwing open the hasps of the huge basket with a flourish. "We have prepared this for today, based off our analysis of your Earthling customs, because we did not want you to feel bad about not going home."

"And you thought a picnic basket would fix that?" Noah sniped. "Full of Happy Meals, right? Well, it's gonna take more than that—*OH DEAR HEAVEN IS THAT A STEAK?"*

Drxx nodded. "We believe we have successfully recalibrated our ability to produce Earth food."

Inside the picnic basket, the now-loathed Happy Meals were nowhere in evidence. Instead, there were four plates. One held a thick ribeye steak and a baked potato with all the fixins. One held a salad that would have been at home at some five-star hotel. Another held an open-faced peanut-butter sandwich with bananas on it: one of Chloe's favorite "meals."

And the last plate had three slices of what looked so much like a Classic Pepperoni from Tony's Pizza back home that I had to focus to avoid drooling.

"We did an analysis of your biological waste deposits, plus chemicals we've found in your bodies while we measured your metabolisms during your sleep cycles, and cross-referenced them with popular alimentary establishments in your home areas to determine what we suspected would be—"

"Shut up, shut up!" shouted Noah. "Before I think about what this stuff probably is and don't want to eat it anymore." He inhaled over the steak. "That smells just like Mastro's."

"Yes, that was the location we used as a template for the secretions that—"

"Shhh!" Noah waved frantically. "Zip it!"

Leya was looking closer at the salad. "That looks like Garden Monsters. My parents—" She looked away and we all pretended not to notice her wiping her eyes. "I used to go there a lot."

Chloe was poking at the PB&B sandwich. "Can I have a Happy Meal?" she asked.

"If you would prefer," Morb said, "we can definitely secrete a—"

"Please!" shouted Noah, almost panicked. Then, in a whisper, "Please. Not another word until after I've eaten."

***

We bounced our way to a copse of lavendar trees, and Drxx and Morb pulled a legit gingham picnic blanket out of the basket and spread it on the ground for us. We all sat and ate. The Celestians as well.

I have not mentioned what their eating looked like. This is intentional, and you can thank me later.

Finished, pleasantly sated and the humans trying not to think of what we had *actually* been eating, we all lay back on the springy ground and stared at the sky. Well, the humans did. Morb and Drxx kinda just flattened out in place and grew new eyes at the top of their heads.

Chloe got bored the fastest (big surprise) and asked Click what there was to do. Click took her by the hand and led her back toward the ship. A few minutes later, two eggpods flew past. I'd taken off my glasses again, and the crafts were going so fast I only saw a fuzzy glimpse: Click, flying in the first one, bent double, then twisting to the side and the eggpod veering off, obviously steering the eggpod by weight shifts instead of the controls I'd seen used to this point. Seemed like that made the eggpod faster, but less precise in its movements.

I heard him scream, "Youuuuuu'rrrrre iiiiiiittttt!" as he disappeared. Then Chloe burst into sight as well, shifting her own weight to follow in the second eggpod, riding it like the coolest skateboard in the universe and laughing her brains out.

"I want one," whispered Noah.

"We only have two," said Morb.

"Then can I—"

"Wait your turn," she said. Moms are the same anywhere in the universe.

"Are they going to be safe in those?" I asked.

"The vehicles have safety measures sufficient to protect your soft-hard-soft bodies," said Drxx.

Morb reshuffled her eyes into forward position, then said, "Want to see something *cool*?"

Noah was on his feet in an instant. He offered Leya a hand and she took it, glancing pointedly at me as she stood. I got up too and followed everyone into the forest.

Drxx stayed behind; I think he was still more than a little mad at Morb, and trying to show it. Morb crossed her tentacles and made a rude sound to show she was still mad as well.

I was pretty mad myself. I understood what Drxx had done, and couldn't say I'd do differently. But recognizing yourself in a bad choice doesn't make it any better, or make it hurt any less.

28

Morb led me, Noah, and Leya through a "jungle" full of things that I'm calling trees even though they looked more like someone took crates of thirty-foot-long licorice whips, dyed them blue, and lashed them together at random intervals.

We huffed up a hill, then the forest ended abruptly and we were looking down on a small valley. It was a level plane, blindingly white, as though covered in salt or new-fallen snow.

"We're here," said Morb in a low voice. I slipped on my glasses, trying to step back a bit so I was behind Noah's and Leya's lines of sight.

Everything now in sharp relief, I saw that the white stuff was definitely granular—salt, sand, some mineral. In the center of the white was a small oasis of bright blue bushes, glinting in the rainbow light of Celestian suns. Walking around the periphery of the bushes: something that looked a bit like a saber-tooth tiger, if saber-tooth tigers were bright purple, twenty feet tall, and had six ears on each side of their head to match the six eyes on stalks sprouting from the snout. It skulked around the metallic oasis, sniffing and peering into the blue bushes.

"What's happening?" whispered Leya.

"A hunt," whispered Morb.

"Of what?"

The answer slid out of the bushes on the opposite side of the cat. An amorphous white blob rolled off the bushes and started oozing across the white field.

The cat instantly perked up. Sniffing the air, it dashed around the blue bushes. It turned too quickly at one point and I saw why it hadn't just crashed right through the oasis: it grazed one of the leaves that stretched over the white field. The leaf didn't bend at all, but the cat yowled and a line of blue blood welled from the cut the sharp "plant" left behind.

I squinted. "Are those metal?" Looking at Morb, I added, "Is this where you got the metal for the lase—"

"Quiet," she whispered. "Watch."

The little white oozeball was moving fast in our direction. It drew closer, and I could see it wasn't actually that little, probably taller than me. Still dwarfed by the cat though, and as it slid across the field it was plain to see the thing wasn't going to get to any kind of safety before the alien predator got to it.

Leya clapped her hands over her mouth, her eyes shimmering. "It's—"

"Amazing!" shouted Noah.

"Shhh!" hissed Morb.

"Amazing," Noah whispered.

"I was going to say, 'in danger,'" Leya said.

Noah shrugged. "Survival of the fittest."

The cat caught up with the blob monster and pounced. Leya gasped and I reacted like I would with Chloe, not thinking, just reaching out and putting my arm around her shoulders to give her a squeeze.

The cat hit the blob, which quivered and went still.

"Is it dead?" asked Leya.

I finally realized that I *had my arm around her*. I froze, just like the blob, only with more bones. And terror.

"It is not dead," said Morb.

We waited. I slowly moved my arm, not wanting to have Noah see me moving on his girl and maybe ending up as part of a hunt myself. Leya clapped her hand over mine, pinning it to her shoulder, making it impossible for me to remove the incriminating evidence of the social crime scene happening right next to my best and most aggressive pal.

No one moved, for various reasons. Not me. Not Leya. Not Noah or Morb.

The cat shifted. I could see now that its feet had sunk *into* its prey. It pulled, trying to escape, but the more it pulled, the deeper it sunk. It grew more and more desperate, jerking back and forth in terror and panic.

Noah wasn't impressed. "This is bori—"

The white field *erupted*. The sandy stuff flew into the air and we all had time to glimpse a blob the size of the mothership underneath. It split in half and the cat fell into its maw without a sound. Then it was over. All that remained was the blob, which moved back to the blue bushes.

"If *Blue Planet* ended like this, I'd actually watch it," Noah whispered, awed.

"We are on a blue planet," said Morb.

"No, it's a nature show. Like *Planet Earth* or—"

"We are not on planet Earth. We are on Bandia."

"Yeah, I know we're on Diarrhea," said Noah. (I *really* had to ask him about his brain-sponge's word choices; maybe he got a defective one.) "But I'm talking about a show that—ah, never mind." Nodding to the blob, which was now hanging from the tallest of the bushes, swaying in what I figured must be an inviting way to Bandia death-kitties. "Is that blob its baby?"

"It is more akin to your tongue. It removes itself from the body long enough to act as bait. Then, when the prey is stuck..." said Morb.

"Snack time," said Noah.

"Yes," said Morb.

"Coo—" he began, then stopped when the moment I'd been dreading finally happened.

***

Noah's eyes narrowed as he saw my arm around Leya. "What do you think you're—"

"Don't." Leya's tone was firm, cutting through whatever

Noah had been about to say.

I'd never heard someone talk to Noah like that before without getting their teeth rearranged, so I braced for the worst. Friend or not, there were things you didn't do to another guy, and putting your arm around his girl—or the girl he was interested in—ranked high on that list.

I felt my shoulders bunching, knowing that Noah wasn't going to hit Leya, but that I was the logical choice for dental remodeling.

Noah hit me. But it wasn't the fist to the face I'd expected. He just slugged me on the shoulder, then turned to Morb and said, "Are there any more hunting grounds?"

"Not many," said Morb. "But I think you might also like seeing the…"

Her voice trailed off as she disappeared into the woods. Celestians, I'd noticed, weren't big on human things like, "Follow me," or "It's over here." They just headed to the next thing, and anyone who was interested or supposed to be there followed along as a matter of course.

I figured Noah would prefer to remain with me, so as to begin the murder with as few witnesses as possible. But off he went after Morb, yelling, "Wait up! Is there more goo? Wait! I'm hungry. Do you have more steak?"

His voice was audible much longer than Morb's. I stared after them, happy about my stay of execution, but very confused. More so when Leya finally let go of my hand, then turned to me and said, "Well?"

"Sorry," I said. "I didn't mean to get between you and—"

"Gah!" she shouted. The blob on the blue bush twitched, and I wondered if this was a safe place for a conversation. Leya didn't seem to care. "You really are the dumbest smart person on Earth. Check that, we're not on Earth. You're the dumbest smart person in the *galaxy*. Is that the biggest thing there is?"

"Scientists actually think the cosmos is—"

"Why are you answering the question?" Leya shouted.

I almost answered, "Because you asked," but the second before I did, I realized: this was something my dad called a "Female Moment."

"It's not that it's illogical or irrational *per se*," he had told me once, right around the time he gave me the birds and bees talk (six years too late). "It's just a kind of logic and rationality that men as a rule are unlikely to understand. So if you ever find yourself in a Female Moment, you shut up, listen carefully, and confine your responses to either, 'That's rough,' 'You poor thing,' or—best of all—'I'm so sorry.'"

I almost said, "That's rough," decided to switch halfway, botched it, tried to switch to the third choice, and ended up with, "I'm so roughy."

Leya shouted wordlessly. "What does *that mean*?"

The shout did me in. Or maybe it was being called dumb, or just being close enough to her that all the blood had departed my brain. Either way, I deviated from Dad's Rules of Female Moment, instead shouting, "It means I have no idea what you're talking about! It means you make me nervous! It means you're smart and talented and when you write a poem it's like the entire world changes around it! It means you're the most beautiful girl I've ever seen and—"

Leya grabbed my face between her hands and interrupted me in the best way possible: with a kiss.

***

One time I bent over to grab an interesting-looking rock on the school playground. I was so focused on the rock I didn't notice other important details. As a result, I leaned forward right as a big kid tried to pump his legs hard enough to do a complete three-sixty around the swing set's support pole.

I don't remember it happening. I don't remember blacking

out, or being taken to the hospital. I do remember waking up, and feeling for the first few moments like I was in a glass bubble that distorted the sights and sounds of the world around me.

Being kissed was like *all* of that. Only nicer. The world vanished. No more Bandia, no more Celestia. Chloe and my parents evaporated from my mind. Even the threat of death-by-Noah disappeared.

There was just me. Just her. Just *us*. A perfect glass bubble separating us from the galaxy—or the cosmos—and everything that mattered was right here, right now, within my reach.

Sound came back first. Then sight. Smell and touch were already spoken for, bound up in the strawberry smell of Leya's hair, and the softness of her lips on mine, her hands on my face.

My arms rose to encircle her. I pulled her close. I felt a heartbeat, and the wonderful sensation of not knowing if it was hers or mine.

The kiss ended. All good things do, and the best we can hope for is that they find us again as we travel through the dark corridors of uncertain futures.

But dark as those corridors can be, they do allow glimpses into rooms of treasured memories, and I knew that no matter what happened, I'd look in on this room, this memory, this moment. Often, and for as long as I lived.

***

"What about Noah?"

It was the wrong thing to say from the point of view of wanting to keep this moment going. But it was the *right* thing to say from every other point. He was my best friend. I was his friend. I couldn't just—

"Wait, what was that?" I asked, blinking so hard I felt it in my toes.

Leya repeated the words that had only partially penetrated

my post-kiss stupor. "Why do you care what my cousin thinks?"

I felt like I'd been kicked in the head again.

"Wait, what? He's your boyfriend. Or wants to be. Right?"

She shook her head. "Where on Earth—or Celestia or even *Diarrhea*," she added with a chuckle, "did you ever get that idea?"

"You told me you were."

She cocked her head. "Pretty sure I would have remembered saying that. Which I don't."

"Then Noah did."

"Did he?"

I thought back. Recalling every conversation we'd had about her, and realizing that I'd barely mentioned her to him at all. She showed up at school with him, and I assumed she was his girlfriend. Then school rumor started telling its stories, and most of them centered around Noah being uber-lucky to have an in-home hottie, which always bugged me because I knew she was a lot more than that, but I never questioned it. I just assumed the truth of it. Because Noah was Noah.

And because you're you, I thought glumly.

I'd avoided asking Noah about her. Why ask, to hear about something forever beyond my reach? Why ask, to hear him talk about something I already knew was wonderful, and didn't want him to have.

But still…

"I think he did say he was interested in you. Something like that. Maybe."

Leya shrugged. "You'll have to ask him about it then. But *I* certainly never said I was with him."

I shook my head. "You never said you *weren't* his girlfriend though."

Leya rolled her eyes. "Guilty as charged. I'm also not an item with Adam Levine, Bruno Mars, or Harry Styles, or the evil clown from *It*. Would you like me to continue the list of people I'm not involved with?"

I looked into her eyes. I saw a bit of irritation. A lot of mirth. And something I'd never expected to see there: me.

I wondered if this was still a Female Moment. I wondered, oddly, what Dad would do. Even more oddly, I suddenly knew what he'd do, and that it was the best and *only* right thing in this moment.

I kissed Leya back. And this time I wasn't the kid getting kicked in the head. I was just me, now, with the girl of my dreams, on a blue and orange planet that would forever be my image of Heaven.

29

We walked back toward the picnic ground, but when we got close, both of us veered to the side. I think we both sensed the same thing: that to go back to where Drxx or any of the others might be waiting would be to end this pleasant dream, this perfect moment.

We held hands as we walked, fingers intertwined. Leya raised my hand toward her lips, and I wondered if she'd kiss it.

Not quite. She brushed it past her cheek, then she laughed.

"What?"

She looked at me through melodramatically half-lidded eyes. "I have to ask…"

"Yeah?"

She stopped. Turned toward me. Kissed me again—shorter than before, but still very nice—and then looked deep in my eyes and whispered throatily, "Do I really remind you of your mom?"

She cracked up as I gagged. "Ugh! Why would you say that?"

"I don't know. Just your mom's really sexy, you know?"

"Please, stop," I asked, waving my hands in front of my face.

She grabbed my hands again. "But, she's *hot*, Max. No shame—"

"Seriously, you have to stop or I'm going to tell Noah he can have you back as his girlfriend."

My turn to laugh at the look on her face. Because my smoothness and suave manners know no bounds, I swallowed spit halfway through the laugh and ended up coughing so hard my glasses fell off.

Laughing, Leya picked them up and went to put them back on me. "You do remind me of your dad a bit, when you wear these," she said.

"Leya—"

"What?" She shrugged. "You act like that's a terrible thing."

"Only because it is."

"He can't be that bad."

"You have no idea."

She was quiet a moment, and I felt the mood change. "I remember hating my mom, hating when my dad said I was turning out to be just like her. Then wanting to hear him say it again, just once. To say anything again."

I hesitated. "I've been watching you, you know."

She repeated her melodramatic sexy eyes. "Do tell?"

"Seriously. You know I've been totally into you since the first time I—"

"Saw me?" She laughed, a bit hollow, and I wondered how many times this beautiful woman had been fed that line.

I was glad not to give her what she expected. "No. I mean, I thought you were beautiful then, sure. But I kinda fell hard when I heard you read your poem. In English class."

She looked away. "Not that great of a poem."

I surprised her again: "No, it wasn't. Not as good as some of the stuff you wrote after that. But the way you read it was so full of feeling. Like every word you said was important, because you knew that all the words could end at any time. It was…beautiful. But sad."

Leya laughed, a bit bitterly. "I can't imagine why."

"Sure you can. But that's your problem." She swiveled to look at me, her expression veiled, and I heard Dad whisper, *"Careful, Max,"* in my mind. "I think part of the reason I thought you were with Noah is because he's the only person I ever see you with. Half the guys—heck, half the *girls*—in school would give their left arms for you to text them a smiley-face emoji, but you never hang out with them. You never look at them. Because you're still stuck in the accident."

Leya's expression darkened. She looked away.

"*Uh-oh*," Dad said in my head.

Shut up, Dad, I thought. I took Leya's chin in my hand. Gently, carefully turning her to look at me again. "They're gone. But you're not. You're alive. You should *live*."

She laughed, no humor. "What about you?"

I blinked. "My family—"

"Might as well be dead. Not Chloe, but you're always talking trash about your dad. Always complaining about your family ."

I didn't say anything. Neither did she. The day, so magical a moment ago, seemed suddenly overcast and gloomy.

"*Now, son, now!*" Dad practically shrieked in my head.

This time I took his advice. I took Leya's hands in both of mine. She didn't resist, but her fingers were limp, not returning the hold. I gave her hands a little shake, drawing her eyes to mine.

"I'm sorry," I said. "I know things have been rough." Then, ad libbing an extra line I thought my dad would approve of, I added, "I just want you to know you're not alone."

(*"Nice, kiddo."*)

Leya smiled at me. "Let's both just appreciate what we have."

I could have taken that any number of ways. All of them were good. And Leya made it perfect with another kiss.

Though I have to admit she harshed the mood by drawing back and saying, "So do you want to talk about Earth's impending doom now, or later?"

***

"You're right," Leya said. "I haven't been living. I've been getting by, and that sucks."

We'd resumed walking after Leya dropped her bombshell, again circling the picnic area. This time it felt different, like we were avoiding something dangerous at the heart of our existence.

"I can't imagine how that must make my aunt and uncle feel," Leya continued. I almost asked who her aunt and uncle were, then realized she was talking about Noah's parents.

Her cousin *Noah! Yippee!* I thought.

"They're my family now," said Leya. She bit her lip in an exceedingly cute fashion, then added, hesitantly, "And I'd really like to see them again."

"They told us we'd go home after the battle," I said, trying to sound more confident than I felt.

"Sure," she said. "But even assuming that's a possibility, did you notice what Drxx said? About this world?"

My brow furrowed. "That it's a vacation planet."

"'A welcome location for short excursions,'" she corrected.

"So?"

"So riddle me this, Abernathy: if Earth is their Plan B, what happens to everyone already living there?"

So much for magical days and perfect moments.

30

We finally ventured back into the picnic site, me wondering how the heck we were supposed to act after the day we'd had. Chloe came to our rescue though, showing up shortly after we did. And by "showed up" I mean Click *dragged* her into the picnic area, my sister covered in what looked like marshmallows the size of my head. Every square inch of her was covered, save only a small spot for her eyes, another for her nose and mouth.

Before I could start hollering questions, she said, "I crashed," in perfectly normal tones, like this was something I'd seen a thousand times before.

Turned out she'd gotten a bit overconfident in her eggpod, took a dive off the side of a rock, and the marshmallows exploded out of the base of her ride: the Celestian equivalent of airbags. They prevented her from being killed, even though according to Click she'd been going about forty miles per hour when she went flying off the mini-cliff. They also hit her with a mild narcotic effect, which was good because once we pulled the things off her, I saw that her leg was *very* broken.

Without the marshmallow buzz, she'd have been screaming. With it, *I* was the one screaming. "How could you let her do this?" I shouted, not even sure whom I was screaming at. "How could you let her—"

I stopped screaming when I realized that none of the Celestians were listening to me. And that they were glowing bright yellow.

"What are they—" Noah began.

"Shhh," Leya said.

A second later, Chloe jumped up, did a little jig, then started doing a move that honesty compels me to describe as a floss-dab-Fortnite dance.

"What—"

"Good," said Morb. "Our analysis was correct." Turning to me, she added a bunch of words my brain-sponge couldn't deal with in the least.

"Anyone else get that?" I asked.

None of the other humans had, but after a long Q&A session, I finally gathered that, as part of their studies of Earthlings, the Celestians had endeavored to discover why we were all so "crippled": stuck in a single form, without the ability to change it at our whim the way they could.

They hadn't figured out how to help us "evolve" to a better shape, but they had figured out how to use their own abilities on us—to a limited effect.

"Minor injuries are all we can assist with," Morb finally explained. "But we seem quite good at those."

"I'll say!" Chloe shouted. "Can I go riding again? I was about to perfect my kick-twist-flip-dab move and—"

"No!" I said. "One broken leg is enough."

"But I—"

"No!"

Chloe pouted for a bit, but scampered off with Click in search of more mischief, like nothing had happened and there was nothing to worry about. Ah, youth.

"Hey, I had a goose egg on my head when we got here," Noah said indignantly. "How come no one healed that, huh?"

"We thought your head was just shaped oddly," said Morb.

I thought about bringing up Leya's hypothesis, demanding answers, but figured that *she* hadn't brought it up to them, so I shouldn't either. For now.

***

The kiss, Chloe's accident, and the whole "we're getting kicked off Earth" thing made for a big day. The four Earthlings were exhausted when we got back to Celestia. Chloe was dead on her feet; I had to keep jostling her as we walked back to the lifepod. Click, Drxx, and Morb all said goodbye and walked into the other two lifepods, to do whatever it is they did while we slept.

As soon as they left, I pulled Chloe and Noah toward me. Whispering quickly, I brought them up to speed on humanity's impending eviction from Earth.

I wasn't sure who took it harder, Noah or Chloe. They both looked shockingly similar, both of them biting their upper lips. "But, Mom and Dad," whispered Chloe at the same moment Noah whispered, "All the football games," in the same stricken tones.

"Football games?" Leya was astonished.

"Yeah," Noah answered, angry. "We all have things that matter, right?"

"What are we going to do, Max?" asked Chloe.

The very question I'd been dreading. "I have no idea," I said. "I suggest we all sleep on it." I yawned, I couldn't help it. "I don't think the Celestians are likely to move on Earth without dealing with the Gro'nids first, so we've got some time. But—"

"Everyone put your thinking caps on," finished Leya. "We've got to figure out a way to stop them."

***

The dream I had that night was more vivid and real than any I'd yet experienced. I was Dad again, watching a news report that featured pictures of me and Chloe, the words "MISSING KIDS" in striking red letters at the bottom of the screen while a news reporter said, "The search continues for three teens and one eight-year-old who went missing over a week ago."

The TV cut to Graham the Granola Twin. His face was rough with several days' beard growth, his eyes wild and manic. "I already told you, news-dude!" he shouted into a microphone held by someone offscreen. "It was the aliens. Green men! Eyes in the forest!"

The TV cut off, and I (the me in the dream) turned to look at Marla Abernathy, wife to Sam, mother to Max and Chloe. "Maybe those crazies are right," she said. "Maybe our kids got taken away by—"

"Who?" I asked.

Marla looked past me, out the bedroom window and into the night sky. "I keep having these dreams," she said. "I feel like Chloe's inside my head. And I'm not talking regular dreams. I'm talking—" She put a hand to her forehead. "I don't know what I'm saying." She began sobbing. Her cheeks streaked with tears that kept coming, kept coming, wouldn't stop.

She slumped against me. Sobbed. "What if we…what if we never see them again?"

I pushed her back. "Don't say that. Marla, wherever they are, whoever they're with, we'll find them. I know we will."

Then Mom cried more, and I held her until she was asleep. I watched her for a moment, knowing somehow that I was watching a woman sleep from within the confines of my own faraway dream. Then I got up, whispering, "I will *never* stop looking."

I wrote a quick note to her so she wouldn't worry, and got in the car. It was only a short drive to Muir Forest. It was night, the public entrances were all closed. But I would find a way in. I'd look in the dark, as long as it took.

I'll find you, Max.

Something was tapping me. I was alone in the car, but I felt the tapping just the same. I ignored it. More tapping. Harder. Even harder. My whole body shook with it, and when I looked in the rearview mirror I saw Noah in the backseat, staring at me and saying, "I have a plan."

I sat up in bed, and found that whether I was bonkers or not, the shaking had been real. So was the Noah part. "Did you hear me?" he said as I blinked and sat up. "I have a *plan*, dude!"

***

"We have to warn our families that the Celestians are planning to take over Earth," Leya said. She squeezed Noah's arm as she said "families." I don't think it registered on him what she was doing, but it registered with me. I smiled at her.

"Yeah," Noah was agreeing. "We gotta get back there A-sap."

"I'm with you on the general outline," I said, "but the details of the plan are still a bit fuzzy."

"I've been watching how they fly those ships, right?" said Noah.

"You mean the mothership—"

Noah was shaking his head. "That was confirmation of a theory. I've been watching the smaller ships—the ones they used in the fight with the Gro'nids. I even got on a couple of them— what?" he asked, looking at me.

I pretended to wipe a tear from my eye. "You used the word theory correctly. I'm just so proud."

Leya laughed. "Har, har," said Noah. He tried to look mad, but then Chloe giggled and the effect was ruined. Noah cleared his throat. Started over. "Anyway, like I was saying, I've been watching how they fly the ships for days. The mothership thing was just the final check. I was pretty sure I understood the controls, but needed to double check with a live fire drill and— clutch, brake, accelerator, steering. It's not that different from a car."

"For the final approach, maybe," I said. "But I don't think an interstellar road trip is a great idea. Not like Google Maps gets out here much."

"I've got that covered," said Leya. "The nav-systems are pretty easy once you understand the basics."

"The basics? Of *stellar navigation*?" I said. "I think the world of you, Leya, I hope you know that. But figuring out interstellar navigational coordinates in the next few days is a pretty long shot, don't you think?"

"What do you think I've been doing with all my 'language lessons'?" she asked. "I've been spending most of my time with several nice young Celestians who just happen to be pilots."

My mouth swung wide open. "You devious—"

"Bet your booty, mister," she said with a wink. "Turns out piloting the ship is a lot like laser targeting a missile. They send out an unmanned—or unCelestianned—beacon probe to orbit the area they want to go, then the ship follows that trajectory in. And since there's already a beacon probe around Earth, we just program the ship to find it."

"And you have a lot of experience with laser targeting systems on an interstellar scale?" I asked.

Shaking her head, Leya said, "Not in the least. I'm not nearly smart enough to figure out intergalactic vectors based on totally alien technology."

"So—"

"But I *am* smart enough that my brain-sponge can read the labels on their systems, and to notice the button that says *Previous Destinations*, right by another one that says *Auto-Pilot*," she said, totally straight-faced.

"I stand corrected."

"Darn right."

"So you program the GPS and then Noah drives us the last little bit?" asked Chloe.

"Yeah," said Noah.

"But we need to use a ship with interstellar capabilities, and one that's been to Earth," I said.

"Right," said Noah. He looked over to where the Celestian buildings stood. The mothership hovered above the Temple of the Elders.

Leya pointed at it. "We steal it, I program it, Noah flies it. But there are a few other parts of the plan as well. We'll all have to help."

"What do you need me to do?" asked Chloe.

I expected Leya and/or Noah to explain that "all" meant "everyone who's already hit puberty," but Leya just nodded somberly and said, "You're the biggest part, actually. The mothership docks every morning on the top floor of the Temple building, and we need to get there, and get past everyone who might take issue with a crew of kids trying to steal a spaceship."

"We need someone on the inside," Noah said conspiratorially.

"Click," Chloe guessed.

Noah nodded. "But he can't know what we're doing. We can't risk him tipping the others off."

Chloe's eyes widened, and her lip quivered. "You want me to take advantage of my friend?"

Noah put a hand on her shoulder. "It may be the only way for us to get back home."

***

We ironed out a few last details, then got to it. Chloe asked Click if she could play tag again, and I was surprised to discover that during all the play on Bandia, Click hadn't managed to catch up to her once. "How is that possible?" I asked.

"I do a lot of skateboarding, duh," she said. Then, turning to Click, "So you wanna play tag?"

"And you will teach me some of your tricks?"

"Sure," she said.

Click's eyestalks quivered with excitement. "Thank you. Thank you so much. You are a good friend to teach me your Earth-board tricks."

If we'd been dealing with humans, Chloe would have blown it right there. Her distress at fooling a friend was so apparent that any human could have seen it from orbit. But Click wasn't human, so he just did a little hop and skip, then flitted into one of the lifepods and came out holding a pair of eggpod discs.

He and Chloe activated their pods, then ripped around the living pods, whooping with laughter. I saw I'd been right about my observations on Bandia: by using their weight to shift the pods' speed and direction, they got much faster results. And Chloe'd been telling the truth about Click not being able to catch her. Not because he was that bad with the eggpods, but because she was that *good*.

After a few minutes, Chloe leaned to the side, racing toward Noah, Leya, and I, and stopping expertly a few inches from us. She hovered in place until Click caught up.

"I think it's too open here, Click. We need somewhere with more stuff in the way. To help you learn how to steer better."

"Where can we go that would help me in this manner?" Click asked.

"What about the Temple?" asked Leya.

"Yes! That is an excellent idea! I approve!" Noah shouted, his voice so wooden and automatic I knew he had rehearsed his part in our little drama, word for word. "There are, after all, many spaceships parked in that area. They will allow you to practice. To zip right, and to zip left. To soar and...zip right again, and then—"

"What my big dumb ox of a cousin means," Leya interjected, glaring at Noah to shut up, "is that if you're really trying to learn how to play tag, the area around the Temple is good. It'll help you learn how to zig-zag around corners."

Click was bending back and forth. "I do not think that is a good idea. It is not allowed."

I read hesitation in Chloe's eyes, and gave a little nod: *Do it.*

She took a deep breath. "Look, Click, buddy. If it wasn't for you guys, we wouldn't be stuck here. And now I'm offering to show you how to play space-tag better than anyone and you're going to tell me it *isn't allowed*?" She shook her head sadly. "You've changed, man. You used to be cool."

Click held absolutely still. I could practically see him rolling options around in his head. "After this, we're even," he said.

"Even-Stephen," Chloe agreed.

"Who is Stephen?" Click asked.

"Doesn't matter. Let's go!"

And right on cue, Leya said, "Hey, can we come and watch?"

"Sure!" Chloe answered, not giving Click time to object. Perfect timing, just like Leya had suggested, but I could see in my little sister's eyes that this was killing her.

31

Click grabbed three more eggpods and we started for the Temple. A bad moment when we saw the mothership take off from the towers, but Click explained they were just doing flight checks.

"So it's coming back?" asked Noah. "'Cause we need it to—oof."

Leya had just elbowed him in the ribs. Click eyed them both. "What is going on? What do you need the ship for?"

Glaring at Noah, Leya said, "You have more suns than we do, so I'm sure Noah was just hoping it would be on the Temple so we'd have some extra shade."

My already-high estimation of Leya's intelligence kicked up another notch. I was in serious danger of falling in love. But my heart thumped into my stomach when I saw Chloe. She looked ill. All she'd wanted for years was to have friends. To belong. And right when she got her wish, events conspired to take it all away.

Okay, *we* conspired. What else could we do? The fate of the world was at stake.

The mothership returned to the Temple and everyone but Chloe relaxed. Once we arrived, Chloe tossed one of the eggpod discs on the ground. She stood on it, touched a button with her foot, and the eggpod lifted off. The transparent wall shield started to *snick* out, but Chloe tapped a spot on the disc and it withdrew again.

"Are you not going to fully engage the pod?" asked Click, stepping atop his own disc. He touched a button as well, and the shimmering "wall" of his eggpod enveloped him.

"Nope," said Chloe. She shifted, and her pod jumped toward Click. We all screamed, sure she'd crash, but with another minute shift the pod came to a halt only millimeters away from Click's pod. "The walls of the eggpod slow you down."

"They are part of the safety protocol," Click said.

Chloe shrugged. "The marshmallow things protect you if you crash."

"Those are a redundant backup system, not the primary defense," said Click.

"You can't be a hundred percent safe and still have fun. You can't be a hundred percent safe and do your best. You can't be a hundred percent safe and *live*."

Chloe smiled at me when she said it, and I felt a warmth that rivaled what I'd felt when Leya kissed me. Not the same, of course (again, we're not that kind of family), but Chloe had just said exactly what I told her the day I taught *her* to ride her skateboard. So scared, her little hands clamped to my arm as I walked beside her, then let go and gave her a push.

Click hesitated. Then he tapped a button with one of his toes and the eggpod's shields disappeared.

Chloe grinned. "You're looking faster already." She shifted her weight and her eggpod slipped to the side. "Do like I do."

Click did. The results were a lot sloppier than Chloe's smooth motion. "This is terrible," he said. "I am failing."

Chloe shrugged. "I ate pavement the first time I skated. Compared to me, you're doing awesome. Try again."

"I am better with the shield walls up," said Click. "I do not want to—"

"You can't get better if you hide behind walls," Chloe insisted. Then her voice softened. "And if you fall, I'll catch you. I promise."

Click nodded. He shifted, pushing his eggpod forward. Chloe went with him, zipping along at his side just like I'd done for her on the day she got her first board. It had been a present from me, and I never felt like I did anything so right as I did that day, handing over that gift. Watching her and Click brought it all back, to the point that I almost forgot what we were doing here.

"Nice!" Chloe shouted as Click turned a corner, then did a tight U-turn and headed back toward us. "You're rocking it!"

Click jabbed ten tentacles into the air in a Celestian fist-pump. "I am rocking it! I am—crashing! I am crashing!" He was careening right toward Noah.

I expected Noah to dodge out of the way, but instead he braced himself. "Grab my arm!"

Click did. As soon as his tentacle wrapped around Noah, *then* the football star juked and pivoted, using his body mass to redirect Click's momentum and turn what could have been a fall into a controlled spin that simultaneously steadied and slowed the eggpod.

Noah slapped Click on the shoulder. "Way to go, dude."

"I was crashing."

Chloe rode her eggpod to Click's side. "Nope. You were *learning.*"

Click looked deep in thought. "It is not our way to learn by failing."

Leya laughed. "It's pretty much the *only* way humans learn."

"That and your inability to," (clicks and whistles, the brain-sponge drew a blank), "is why you have been judged as a species of lesser—" Click stopped himself, a tentacle slapping over his mouth.

"Lesser what?" Noah said.

"Nothing. We are riding eggpods. I am rocking it!"

"Lesser *what?*" Noah demanded.

"Easy, man." I punched him on the shoulder. "Remember, we're here to give Chloe a chance to teach Click, right?"

"I want to know what he meant by—oof."

Leya's elbow again saved the day. "It's not important right now, right, *cuz?*" She smiled, but her eyes were deadly.

"Right," said Noah. "Yeah. Sorry, Click. Skate on."

I cocked an eyebrow at Chloe. She caught the cue. "Wanna play tag?" she asked Click. "Best way to improve on these things is chasing someone better than you."

Click's tentacles waved in excitement. "I would very much like to play the tag to improve my skills! See?" He flicked a tentacle in Chloe's direction.

She twisted and her eggpod slid her just out of reach. "Nice try, bud." Then she felt her chin with thumb and forefinger. "Say, you want to *really* get good?"

"I do," said Click.

"We should practice up there." Chloe pointed toward the top of the Temple. "The landing pad is perfect for tight turns."

"I do not think that is advisable," Click said. "I think my parent-halves would—"

"Click, what *did* you mean by 'lesser'?" Noah asked.

I saw Leya's elbow move into attack position. I grabbed her arm and held it tightly. "What are you doing?" she whispered.

"Wait," I whispered.

"So?" Noah pushed. "What was this 'lesser' thing you—"

"I think we should practice. On top of the Temple." Click was frantic to change the subject. He shifted, moving his eggpod close to Chloe. "We should go to the landing dock. There is plenty of room to practice there."

"Fine," Noah said. "But we're going to watch."

"All right," said Click. "But I am not good with Chloe's Earth-moves, so I will need absolute silence and no questions whatsoever about anything I did or did not say so that I may concentrate and not crash and can rock the free world like Chloe says."

Noah put on a show of thinking about it. "Fine," he finally said.

Click spun to look at me and Leya. "Agreed?"

"Well, I guess. If it's what you need," I said.

***

We rode a Celestian elevator to the top of the Temple. It was a lot like Earth elevators, but with a thick blanket of mucus on the floor: a byproduct of their secretion-based construction methods.

Once we'd exited the elevator and wiped the goo from our feet, Click and Chloe activated their pods again. I saw Chloe's expression change from guilty to mega-guilty, and suddenly knew that she was going to blow our cover.

"Boy," I said loudly, "I wish Mom and Dad could see this. It would be neat to show this to them someday, wouldn't it? *When we see them again?*"

Chloe stared at me, the conflict visible on her face. Then she turned to Click and said, "Just so you know, I've never had a friend like you. On *any* planet. I'm going to miss you when we go back."

Watery stuff started oozing from Click's eyestalks, dripping down and then snail-trailing over his ghost body. "I feel the same." Arm tentacles pointed at the streaks of silver on him. "I am leaking because I am sad. Earth-style!"

"Earth-style," Chloe said. She was fighting back tears.

"Chlo, better get going," I urged.

She wiped her eyes. "You're right about one thing."

"What is that one thing?" asked Click.

"You aren't quite fast enough. You know what I think you should do before we really get into this?"

"What is that, friend Chloe?"

Chloe blanched visibly, but kept going. "We have a game called hide and seek. One person counts to a hundred, while the other person hides. Then—" Her voice hitched, guilt stopping her prepared speech.

Leya stepped in without missing a beat. Did I mention how amazing she is?

"The other person hides, really well. When the first person finishes counting, like Chloe, for instance, then she goes to find the second person. Which is you, Click!"

Click glowed violet. "How does hiding help me better pilot my pod?"

"Because you have to move fast to find the hiding spot, then hold totally still while you wait," said Leya. "And everyone knows that holding still is the first step to moving fast."

"They do?"

"Totally," I said.

"And then," Leya said, warming to the story we'd prepared, "when you *are* found, the seeker—Chloe, just as a random example—is still 'it' until she tags the hider, which is you in the example."

"So I hide? And then play tag?" Click asked. The orange glow began to dim.

"Correct."

Click looked uncertain. "I'm just not—"

"Hey, that 'lesser' thing is still bothering—" Noah began.

"Start counting!" Click shouted, zipping away. Containers and machinery covered the docking platform of the Temple. Plenty of places to hide, and he disappeared quickly.

I jogged Chloe. "One...two...three..." she began in slow tones, allowing her voice to fade just like we'd planned. I knew it was hard for her, but she was acting like a trooper. I'd definitely get her a real, un-secreted Happy Meal when we got home. If we got home.

Noah eyed Chloe's eggpod. "That thing gonna get us to the ship?"

I looked up. We had decided earlier not to bring any extra

pods up here, so as not to draw attention or suspicion. But now, the mothership a good fifty feet above us, I was second-guessing that choice.

"It'll have to," Leya said.

Noah, Leya, and I all clambered aboard Chloe's eggpod, holding tight to each other, my little sister in the center. She shifted and the eggpod started to rise. None of us knew for sure this would work, but it seemed to bear our weight. So long as I kept from thinking about the fact that my heels were hanging into empty space fifty feet above a landing pad that was already at least two hundred feet above the planet's surface, everything was fine.

Another part of our plan we weren't sure of: if the mothership would open to us. It had every other time, but we'd always had a Celestian with us, and it wasn't like we knew the PIN code.

Again, fortune favored the brave, the bold, and the dumb Earthlings: an opening appeared when we were within five feet of the ship.

"This is going to work," said Noah.

***

Once inside, we hopped off and started running toward the command center. I was counting seconds in my head as we did all this, and figured Chloe would have gotten to sixty by now.

"We gotta hurry," I said, panting.

"Really? Are you sure?" Noah said. As always, he wasn't panting at all, but for some reason our physical disparities didn't bother me as much as they had before. Knowing you're cared for by someone amazing makes you suspect you might be a little amazing too.

We ran through the ship. Through the blue 'shroom room (say *that* ten times fast!), past the hummingbird-bat sanctuary, then a dozen more weird places, then the nav-room. Noah jumped into the pilot's seat.

"Here goes nothing," he said, and pushed a big button. Nothing happened.

"No biggie." Noah lost none of his confidence. "Just gotta pop the clutch." He pulled back on the control shaft, pumped the foot pedals, then hit the button again.

We all fell backward as g-forces slammed against us.

"Slow...down..." I managed. Noah shifted some things, and the g-forces diminished. I stood, helping Leya and Chloe to their feet.

"This is gonna make the best story ever at the next family reunion," Leya said. A mark of how happy she was, making a joke that involved the word *family*.

Noah caught it as well, and his grin almost stretched right off the sides of his face.

He flicked a few more levers, and a screen glowed. I saw the GPS controls that Leya had talked about, wondering how on Earth I'd missed them.

There were a lot of other things happening at the time, I thought. And I had to admit to myself that I was sorta glad, because I got to enjoy Leya doing her thing. She tapped a number of buttons, and a small dust-holo projection of Earth appeared.

"Got it!" she shouted.

"Nice!" Noah high-fived her. "You get us there, and I'll land us."

"She'll get us there," I said, which earned me a hug from Leya that made me feel like I could fly to Earth without a ship. "Next stop, home!"

"Hey, guys?" Chloe asked in a tiny voice. "Anyone know what the spaceship runs on?" When everyone turned questioning looks at her, she elaborated, "Like, do we have enough gas to get home?"

Noah shrugged. "Only one way to find out."

"Actually," said a voice from behind us, "there are several ways to find out. But none you should be using."

We all turned to see Drxx standing right behind us. He was holding a little blinking box and when he squeezed it, the ship lurched and the big viewscreen—which had been showing nothing but stars and space and, somewhere, an invisible dot where Earth was—spun to show Celestia.

"Guess we're not going home after all," muttered Noah.

Drxx looked at him and said, slowly and with more than a hint of threat, "You *are* home."

32

Drxx took us back down to the landing pad on one of the bigger eggpods, where a dismal welcoming party consisting of Morb, a dozen Elders, and Click waited for us.

The Elders' heads were glowing black, the green head-snake things writhing around so fast they were a blur. A dozen voices accosted us, all yelling, all angry. The brain-sponge tried to keep up but all I really got was the sense that everyone down there was angry, either at us or at Click.

"It wasn't his fault!" shouted Chloe. "I tricked him."

"Chloe, quiet!" I whispered.

Leya, eyes wide, agreed. "Yeah, these little guys look pretty ready to rage-murder us."

Everyone grew silent. The silence was worse than the yelling. One of the Elders slid forward. "Drxx, did you permit this?"

"No, Elder Thor," said Drxx. His head glowed black as well. "They will stay until we have defeated the Gro'nid."

"How did they get onto the ship?" demanded another Elder, the one that sounded like Darth Vader.

"I do not know," said Drxx. Then, turning his four eyes on the four of us, he said, "But it will not happen again. We will keep an eye on them." A dozen more eyes popped into existence on his face. "We will keep *many* eyes on them."

"So creepy," whispered Noah.

***

We were taken into the Temple, and escorted into a room in its center. Noah tried to resist, but had about as much luck as he'd had back on Earth. He didn't even have Hydro Flasks to wield as weapons.

Once we were shoved (or, in Noah's case, tossed) into the room, the hole in the wall-field closed behind us and wouldn't open no matter what we did or said. We were effectively sealed in a room with no doors, no windows, no openings of any kind. No table or beds, either.

The walls turned white. Circles started to appear all over them: what looked like Celestian eyeballs that stared, unblinking, at all of us.

"Man, they weren't kidding about the 'keeping an eye on us' thing," I said. It was a dumb joke, but I could tell Chloe was feeling about as low as a snake's belly, and dumb jokes were the only thing I could think of to cheer her up.

"Ever get the feeling you're being watched?" said Noah.

For some reason, the fact that Noah was joking too—and making a better joke than me, to boot—really irked me. I rounded on him, intending to chew him out. It wasn't his fault we were in here. But I was scared, and the only way my brain could cope with the fear was by lashing out at something.

Leya beat me to the punch. "That's not funny," she bellowed. "This is uber-creepy."

"Yeah," Chloe said. She put her fists on her hips. "What made you even think that you could fly that thing?"

Noah's eyes were perfect circles. "What? *I* was doing my part. If anything, we're in here because of Mr. Perfect." He jerked a thumb in my direction.

"How do you figure that?" I asked. The anger I'd been feeling doubled. Irrational, but that's humans for you. "How *exactly* do you think this is my fault, oh great Homecoming King?"

"*You* built the laser cannon, dumb-dumb." Noah jabbed a steel finger into my sternum. "If we weren't stuck waiting to see if it works or not, we'd be halfway home by now."

I gawked. "You *really* think that's what would be happening?" I could feel the moment reeling out of control, could feel myself losing any semblance of higher brain function. I didn't care. Anything was better than the yawning hopelessness that threatened to swallow my soul. "You didn't ask yourself why they were on Earth in the first place? Why they were scoping out our planet? Geez, Noah, I knew you were dumb, but—"

Whatever I'd planned to say after that evaporated into grunting as Noah tackled me. My glasses flew off. My arms flailed. I'd like to say I put up a good fight, but it only took about two seconds for Noah to pin me to the ground. His big fist drew back.

"Don't!" shouted Leya. She grabbed his arm.

Noah shook her off. "Why not?" His fist rose another inch. "Always perfect. Always knows the answers. Always the best at *everything* and you have to pick this moment? This moment to finally blow it?"

I stiffened. "What do you mean, *perfect*?" I whispered.

I realized, in that instant, something I should have seen long ago. I'd thought for years that I was a charity case. A pity project. But suddenly I saw everything through Noah's eyes.

He was strong, and handsome. He was popular. But whenever I spoke about anything but video games, he struggled to keep up. The only way to hang with me was to keep us doing things he was better at—sports, certain video games—because if he didn't do that he knew he'd fall behind.

Even in love, I thought. And the thought, though my own, took me by surprise. But it was true. I knew it was. I thought back to the first time I asked about Leya, and the expressions that had flitted across his face.

"You like her?" I'd said.

And he'd responded so carefully, first dodging the question, then giving me a non-answer that left me dangling in the wind. And I couldn't hate him for it, for the stress it had caused, because I saw it now for what it was: him struggling to compete on any level with me. Worried that I'd leave him in the dust. That I'd...

"I wouldn't," I said. "I would never laugh at you."

A single tear tracked down his cheek. "Bro, you *always* laugh at me."

It felt like whoever was in charge of the universe had pressed Pause so we could focus on the most surreal moment of my life: the moment I realized that Noah wished he was more like me. And then suddenly Noah was pulling me to my feet and we were hugging. Holding each other as we both realized that we had been best friends so completely and for so long that neither of us could even remember life before we were there for each other.

There was an instant where I almost shifted to a "bro hug." The kind where guys pound each other on the back a few times, like the only way we're allowed to express affection is tinged with violence. I felt Noah seize up a little too, and somehow knew he was feeling the same push to conform to that social norm.

I shoved it down deep, and just held my friend. Felt him hold me back just as hard, not letting anything get between what we felt for each other.

"Sorry," he muttered.

"Me too," I said. I hugged him harder than I'd ever hugged anyone before and whispered, "You're my best friend, man."

He went rigid. There it was, the truth, naked and unguarded, for him to allow or deny.

He nodded. "Same." And he hugged me his hardest—harder than I could. I groaned in very real pain. But it was a good thing. Perhaps the only way to *really* know someone was through a bit of shared pain. To hold one another through the fire and come out with the same burns, the same wounds, and know that you had done it together.

So nice, to know the truth. To feel that connection.

Something shifted, and I knew that, for all its good, the understanding Noah and I had come to had also highlighted the solitude of someone else, the way a single black ink spot on a page will highlight the white space all around it.

We both looked over at Leya, her face ashen, backing away from us like we were on fire. And that was true in a way, because there was this sudden warmth, and to someone frozen a fire is the most painful way possible to come back to life.

"What if I never see them again?" she whispered.

Noah shook his head. "You'll see the people you love," he said. He grinned. "And failing that, you've got us."

Leya didn't seem to hear. She kept backing away. Backing up to the walls, then pressing against the unyielding material as the eyes all around her shifted to watch.

"What if I never get the chance to tell them I love them? To thank them for what they're doing for me? To let them know they're my family?"

"You'll see them again. You'll get to do all that," I said.

"What makes you so sure?"

I had no answer.

"That's what I thought." She shook her head, back and forth so hard it was like she was trying to shake a thought right out of her brain. "You don't know. I'll never see them, I'll never tell them. I'll never feel like that, like I have a family, like—"

She stopped. Looked down. My hand was on her waist, and I didn't really remember how it got there. One moment, I was holding Noah. The next, my arm was around Leya, the other hand snaking around to pull her away from the wall, to pull her *toward* me.

"You have a family."

"But they're—"

"I'm not talking about the family you have on Earth. I'm not talking about your parents. Your father and mother are gone."

I saw her eyes fade, like her soul was leaving her body. I gave her a little shake. Hard enough that it couldn't be ignored. Sometimes we have to be shaken to see clearly. And I needed her to see clearly. For her, for me, for all of us.

"They're gone," I continued, "but you're not alone, Leya. You hear that? You're not alone."

"You have me," said Noah, his voice somehow both quieter and stronger than I'd ever heard.

"And..." I gulped. "And you have me. For however long we're trapped, and forever after that. I'm not going anywhere."

"Me either." Noah took Leya's hand in his own, a movement I'd have seen with jealousy only a few days ago. Now I saw it with gratitude. Noah was doing what he'd always done: protecting us. "We're family," he whispered.

The word was magic. I felt it, like cool water on a hot day. Life came into the room.

Holding Leya closer, I whispered, "You'll always have all of us, and together we'll get through anything."

The life and light I'd felt in the room flickered a bit. Leya pulled back. "How do you know?" she asked, tears in her eyes.

Sometimes we have to hold each other close. Sometimes all there is in the world is an embrace battling back the darkness of loneliness and fear.

But sometimes we have to let go. We have to step away from each other, not because each wants the other gone, but because stepping back is the only way we can see each other in our flawed, beautiful, ugly, amazing, miraculous entirety.

So I withdrew from Leya. I scooped up my glasses from where they'd fallen. Slowly, purposefully, with a care I hoped she understood, I put them on. I smiled, willing her to understand: that I wanted her to know that the way she saw *me* mattered. That her thinking I was better than I was had made that thought come true.

"I know because you've helped me see things more clearly." I grinned and winked. "And because I'm just smart like that."

Leya smiled. No confusion, no fear. Just the clarity that comes when we finally see all that we have, all that we are, and—if we're brave enough to dare—all that we may one day be.

In movies, this would be the moment where I swept the girl into my arms and we kissed. But I just held her hand. She held mine. Our fingers intertwined.

And in this moment—this real, true, unguarded moment— that touch of her hand was more than enough. I wasn't going anywhere, I told her with my touch. And hers said back, Neither am I.

***

"Who are you?"

Leya, Noah, and I turned to see Chloe standing beside the looming wall of eyes. They tracked her movement, unblinking. Mostly unblinking: one of them blinked quite a bit, and it was that one Chloe was talking to.

As though gearing up for a dreadful moment, she inhaled, held it, then said in a small voice, "Click?" The eye blinked. "Click, I'm so sorry."

The eye shimmered, like the light of the room had caught a tear. Then, slowly, it closed.

Chloe turned to me and the expression in her eyes, the sound of her words—they were hammer blows to my soul: "For once in my life, I had a friend. And I betrayed him."

It hurt. Not just the truth, but the quiet dignity of it. The way she held herself, like a queen at the moment of losing her crown. In pain, but controlled. Tortured, but refusing to bow.

Noah stepped forward. "You know what? It pains me to say it, but the betrayal thing? It's my bad." He took another step, then knelt before Chloe, like he wasn't kneeling down to bring her eye-to-eye with him, but because he needed to bow before her. "I'm sorry," Noah whispered, and then he *did* bow.

"What's happening?" Leya whispered. I glanced toward her.

She was looking at me, then Chloe, then me. She sensed it just as I did, this sudden feeling of awe in the air, of connection and understanding. She shook herself visibly, then knelt in front of Chloe as well. She put one hand on Noah's shoulder, one hand on Chloe's. "It wasn't just you," she said to Noah. And to Chloe: "It was all of us."

I felt myself drawn forward, pressed from inside by something I could almost—almost, but not quite—understand. I knelt beside Leya. One hand on her shoulder, the other on Chloe's back. All of us connected, by and through a little girl who in that moment felt like royalty.

"We pressured you to do it, Chloe," I said. I licked dry lips. "I'm sorry."

"*We're* sorry," said Noah.

I felt like she could fix it. Just say, "I forgive you," and everything would turn out all right.

I squeezed her shoulder, at the precise moment that I knew Leya and Noah were doing the same.

This can be all right, I thought. *Just forgive us, and we'll make it right. Together.*

And I believed it. We could fix this. If Chloe forgave.

She drew away. Our hands fell from her as she pulled back.

She went to the corner, and curled up into a ball under a wall of staring eyes. Everyone watching, none caring.

She cried, and in that moment I wanted to die.

Instead I spun, glaring at the wall of silent stares. "This was my fault," I said. "*Mine*. Not Chloe's, and not Click's."

I sensed Chloe's attention. I saw her out of the corner of my eye, shifting to watch as I spoke to what seemed like all of Celestia—

No. Not seems *like.*

Suddenly, I knew two things. The first was that this *was*

everyone. Every Celestian really *was* watching us in this moment. Joined to stare at an unknown.

Perhaps they are enemies, the Celestians were thinking. *They cannot be friends. Because…*

…because…

…BECAUSE…

And I knew. I knew the second thing: that the Celestians did not think humans were worthy of them. Because humanity did not understand the one thing that made *true* intelligent life.

Empathy.

I stared at Chloe, watching me from the corner, her eyes bright with new-shed tears. She nodded. I knelt beside her and held her hand, then, still holding it, I turned back to the wall, and made my case. Not aloud, but in my thoughts.

If you punish Click for what we did…well, then you're not as advanced as I thought.

As we *thought*.

I felt the second thought inside my head, but knew it came from somewhere else. A mind so much stronger, and brighter, and kinder than mine.

I looked at Chloe. She was smiling. Then she turned to gaze on the wall. I felt that strange, small, oh-so-*strong* voice. The voice of my sister.

The voice of a queen.

How do you call yourselves advanced, when your thought is to get rid of what you don't understand?

The eyes all blinked, like every Celestian had just flinched under the power of a little girl's clarity.

"Darn right," said Noah. I looked at him, and knew that he felt it like I did. So did Leya.

Chloe stood. She put her hand against one of the walls. The eyes there all shifted, leaving that part of the wall empty. Almost like they didn't want to let her touch them. Because they weren't worthy of her touch.

But you are *worthy, you dopes. Don't you see? That's the* **point.** *We're all worthy. We're all part of this universe, and the only way we figure things out is together.*

Everything came together in this moment. Somehow, I was holding Leya, my free hand slipping around her waist as I embraced her without letting go of Chloe. Big arms wrapped around us both: Noah, the big guy I'd thought was my superior, now acting as a kind of shield in what I suspected was the most important moment of any of our lives.

Leya touched Chloe's shoulder.

Not enough, I thought. *It's not enough. We're not...quite...*

Chloe didn't stop looking at the wall, or take her hand away from it. But her other hand reached for Leya. And when it touched her, it was like a circuit coming together. The energy flowed, and we were—perhaps for the first time in human experience—truly together. Truly one. Truly—

Joined, I thought.

Joined, Leya thought, her mind one of pain and loss, tempering her to kindness and understanding.

Joined, came Noah's thought, full of insecurity and concern, a longing to protect and to allow others to protect him in turn.

And then, finally, Chloe:

Joined.

The eyes flinched again, and all of them closed. They did not open. Just faded away.

Chloe didn't move her hand from its position against the wall and over Leya's hand on her shoulder. But she twisted to look back at us, and I saw confusion. "What's going—"

A thought intruded. Small.

No, not small, I thought.

Not small, came another thought. I knew it was Noah's, though he spoke not a word. *Weak. I know that weakness. It's fear, talking big.*

The thought came again, and this time I heard it more clearly, and heard with it the fear-smothering rage Noah had recognized.

This will be our

great moment of victory.

The thought fell away, a wisp of smoke in a windtunnel.

Then another came. A different voice, I was sure, though still possessed of that rage.

We will inhabit

their world.

And a third, more afraid than any of the other voices, and all the more terrible for wrath big enough to hide his terror:

And the vermin

will die,

or serve us

as our slaves.

"It's begun," said Noah.

So he knew too. As did Chloe and Leya.

And so did I, with such certainty that it was almost an afterthought when the shockwaves of the Gro'nid's attack rocked the room.

Then another, and a third. The world was shaking. Celestia was under attack.

Not under attack.

I looked at Chloe. The flat palm against the wall had shifted to a fist, and she was hunched over like a great weight had fallen on her.

It is the end.

"Of what?" Noah whispered.

Chloe's answer came with perfect clarity, perfect understanding, perfect conviction. The answer of someone who knew absolutely, without the impurities of hesitation or fear that overcome us as we age. The answer of a child, and the only answer that could be true:

It is the end of this world.

Of the Celestians.

Of everything.

PART THREE:

**Cry havoc, and
let loose the Petunia of War!**

33

A series of explosions rocked the room so hard that we tumbled in separate ways. Noah fell away first, his strength peeling away like armor torn in a joust. I tried to hold on, to Leya, to my sister. But the next explosion came so hard and fast that I felt like my knees had been driven into my spine. I fell to the side, and felt the separation like one more blow to my body.

I also felt a presence. The feeling of the Joining, but different. Something about what had happened between me and Noah, then Leya, and finally—most importantly—with Chloe, had changed us in some fundamental way. Always before, when we Joined it had felt like my mind was being batted around from place to place with no control of my own.

Now, I found myself...*dancing* is the best way I can describe it. My mind was skipping, hopping from place to place, mind to mind, person to person. I was everywhere and nowhere, but I was *always* in the place that I needed to be. I was Max Nathan Abernathy, in my deepest core, but I was also...also...

Drxx. I am walking down the street, my mind and heart aching for the loss of my brother-half. The pain will not go away, and I know I must do something or break.

A shadow passes over me, massive but fast. I look up and see the Gro'nid ship, its curve that should be graceful but is instead only terrifying for what it represents.

I stop walking. I concentrate and my head glows with the energy passing through my mind to send the message: We are under attack.

And the answer comes from the Elders, their minds speaking as one: WE KNOW.

The message received, I run, and—

I was back in the room. I reached out automatically. A hand took mine. Leya. I squeezed her hand, and—

I am Click. My head throbs, the black glow of terror stealing all light from the room to which I have been banished. I am alone. Forgotten.

I wish Chloe was here, *I think.*

A door appears in the wall-shield. I have been confined here, so I know even before Morb appears that my parent-half has come for me.

I am glad. I was so afraid. So alone.

"Come with me!" shouts Morb.

"Where?"

Morb does not answer. My parent-half's body explodes in appendages, all of them born for one reason: to hold me, the way I have not been held since I was younger than memory.

"I will protect you," Morb whispers, and I hear the words both with my aural receptors and within, in the parts of my heart where only truth can be heard.

I am still afraid. But I know I can bear the fear. For I am not alone. I will—

And back again. Another hand, reaching for me. The connection strengthened as I held Leya's hand in mine, and now Noah's arms surrounded us and gathered us close. We were three, together more powerful than Leya and I alone and now—

I move as fast as I can, dodging bits of things I cannot name as the city falls apart under the Gro'nid attack.

They are everywhere, *I think, leaping over a dead Celestian, one more of my people lost.* I must get to the weapon. Must save Morb. Save Click. I could not save my brother-half. But I can save my spouse and the child we created together.

I push myself, faster, faster.

And now I am at the cannon. I am Drxx. Brother-half to the dead, spouse and parent-half to the living.

And I will have the revenge I need.

I climb into the cannon. It is the only one we have that is fully functional, but it will serve. And I know that if I can strike the right target—

I will have my revenge.

The thought rings, echoes. Louder and louder until I have lost the faces of my family. I see only the dead, and wish only for more dead to join them.

I aim the cannon. The reticle appears in the air before me. Searching. Searching.

I find the ship. The one that belongs to the Gro'nid's leader.

I am aware that others are watching. Dozens have clustered around the cannon, waiting for the moment of salvation. And in my mind, Joined to me: so many more. All who are of our people, all the true intelligent lives in the universe. They are in me, and I in them. Together, we shall destroy—

Noah, Leya, and I all joined in a ring. I felt, in a way both distant and more present than anything I'd known, the presence of Chloe. She pushed into the center of our three-way embrace, like a baby climbing back into her mother, seeking an un-birth that will shelter her from the cruelty of life.

Then she was between us. We pulled closer, her at our center, and I realized I'd been wrong. Chloe wasn't trying to hide, to be unborn and so untouchable by life's trials. She was our center. The beating heart of what made us special: she was the child, and she was the humanity that made us fit to be called "intelligent."

Her arms went around my waist. She held me and I—

—press the trigger.

My people sigh, those nearby in audible whispers, the ones throughout Celestia gasping in my mind, ready for this moment of triumph.

The laser sighs too. Such a small hum for a blow to break the will of an entire race.

A red burst flows from the laser, the bright red eye of doom that will stare at the Gro'nid until they wither away and flee or die.

But it does not happen.

The glow dissipates. I am still staring at the reticle, looking at the space where the Gro'nid's lead fighter should have turned into vapor and smoke. But the fighter is still there. The winking Gro'nid on the body of the boomerang fighter seems to smile even wider as our doom comes for us.

I feel terror. Not just mine, but the terror of all our people as we realize, together, that the doom we thought to bring to our enemies has come for us instead.

My head glows black. The darkness of rage, of terror, the clouding that always tears us apart. I feel one last pang, the dark fear-glows of every Celestian coming into me like a laser scorching my center.

Then it is gone. The Gro'nid ship opens fire—

The world shook as explosions rocked the building we were in. I tried to hold onto Leya and Noah. Couldn't. They were flung away from me like paper dolls in a hurricane.

I managed to hold only to Chloe. Managed to whisper, "I've got you."

Another explosion, and I twisted as we flew through the air, shielding Chloe from the impact, using my own body to soften the blow to her as we hit one of the walls.

I fell, and whispered it again, willing the words to be real: "I've got you."

I felt her, arms around my waist, thoughts in my heart.

I know. The arms tightened around me. *And I've got* **you.** Then we—

Together. We are together. We are safe.

I try to send the thoughts into my child-meld, to Join so that Click may feel my presence, and know he is not alone. To tell him, "Morb is here with you, and your parent-half shall not abandon you, no matter what, you are not alone."

But it is hard to Join when fear is clouding your mind. And I am so afraid. For Click, yes. But also for Drxx.

"Drxx will protect us," Click whispers.

"I know," I say back. But it is a lie, as all spoken words must be.

Something hits the shelter, and I am thrown to the side, Click ripped away from me—

—and something was pulling me to my feet. Leya. Holding me as I moved through smoke and dust to find Chloe. I pulled her to her feet. Held her close. Noah pounded at the unyielding walls and screamed,

"Hey! Let us out! Let us—"

--out! Drxx, do you hear me? Get out of there! They will target the cannon!"

I do not know who cries out this way. One of the blasts hit near us and I feel like every part of me is on fire. So much pain. But I can move. I must move. Find my family. They were supposed to be in the shelter, and now?

An eye appears, my body knowing instinctively how to create the ocular nerves, the structures of the eye itself, and the supporting framework of the stalk that extends upward, allowing me as much vision as possible. Looking for the shelter where Morb and Click, my spouse and the child-meld we have created, were supposed to hide.

*It is a smoking wreck. Nothing there. Nothing. Nothing.
NOTHING.*

I am alone. Brother-half gone. Spouse and child-meld obliterated.

"Drxx!"

*I ignore the shouts of those around me, urging me to flee. So what if
I die? What do I have to live for?*

"Drxx, GET OUT OF THERE!"

*It finally penetrates: this is not the voice of some technician, some
random worker. It is—*

*"MORB!" I cry, even as my spouse reaches to hold me. Morb is
holding Click, and they are alive and I am alive and I have one bright
moment of joy before the darkness presses in and I see the Gro'nid ships
continue to pummel my home out of existence.*

*Morb holds me in its arms, but the bitterness and rage hold me even
tighter than my spouse. "The laser cannon has failed. The humans
betrayed us."*

*Morb looks at me. The eyes of my spouse blink slowly, the motion
fraught with sadness.*

"No," Morb says. "We betrayed them."

*I want to scream at Morb. To demand that my spouse take back those
words; demand that Morb understand my pain.*

Brother-half to a dead Celestian.

Child of a dead planet.

*Before I can say any of these things, Morb is running away, Click
still in the arms of my spouse.*

*They disappear into the smoke and destruction and I scream, and
that scream carries me back—*

"Come back, Max!" Noah was screaming. He was shaking me
too, but I couldn't feel him doing it. Impossible to feel someone
shaking you—even someone as strong as Noah—when the entire
world is bouncing like a cheap carnival ride.

Leya was pounding on the wall, screaming. "Let us out of here! Anyone hear me? Let us *go!*"

Noah screaming. Leya screaming.

I looked around, trying to find Chloe. She sat, still and calm, in the center of the room. She looked like she was waiting for something. What, I couldn't begin to guess.

Her calm faltered as another explosion hit somewhere nearby. Another, closer. A third that felt like a direct hit on the building we were in.

A tear appeared in the wall-field as the structure began to fail and—

No. Not a tear. A door. Someone was letting us out!

Morb appeared in the door, a battered-looking Click in her arms. "We need your help."

Chloe was already on her feet, standing right beside the spot where the door had opened, like she had known that help was coming and where it would arrive. "Is Click—"

"He's okay, he'll be okay!" Morb almost shouted. Then she swiveled and, visibly trying to calm herself, said, "The laser cannon is—"

"Misfiring," I said. Because I knew. I'd been there.

But it was a mistake to say. Morb didn't know. She hadn't felt us, watching it all. Her body pulsed black, blue, black, blue—mistrust, in the silent Celestian color-language.

"How did you know that?" she asked.

"We were there," said Noah.

If I'd said it, or Leya—maybe even Chloe—I don't think Morb would have believed us. She'd have left, certain we purposefully sabotaged the laser.

But Noah? For some reason—maybe his sincerity, maybe just that Morb kind of didn't feel like he was smart enough to lie—she bought it coming from him.

"Then how—"

"It's not important right now," I said. "What's important is that—" Another explosion sounded. Not right on top of us, thankfully, but close enough that we all took a step. "That," I finished.

Morb nodded. "The laser. Can you fix it?"

"Of course he can!" shouted Noah. And if I hadn't already known he respected me, I would've in that moment. There was no trace of hesitation or fear. He didn't believe I could do it, he *knew* I could.

And because he knew, so did I.

"Just let us out and he'll show you," Leya said. She looked at me. I didn't see the rock-solid certainty that Noah had. She didn't *know* I could do it.

But I did see this: she *believed* I could do it. And to act on that belief was more courageous than if she'd acted based on a bedrock of certain knowledge. She had faith in me, and that faith—that *hope*—buoyed me up beyond Noah's total conviction.

I dragged my eyes away from Leya's face—from her smile, from the newfound trust that infused her—and nodded to Morb.

"Take me to your laser."

34

We ran out of our prison room, and as always I could see farther than I expected as I looked through transparent walls to see...

Devastation.

Smoke curled up from dark craters where graceful buildings had once stood. Celestians, their bodies so gray and still there was no question they were dead, lay on the ground everywhere. I heard sounds I'd never heard, chittering noises the brain-sponge turned into screams that for a moment sounded so loud in my mind I thought I must go mad. I saw Chloe stumble, then Leya and Noah as well, all of them clutching their heads in a vain attempt to keep the noise out of our minds.

Just at the moment I thought I would die, the sound dampened. It was still there, the screaming a jagged undercurrent that felt like needles pricking the surface of my brain, but at a level that I could tolerate. Made sense: the brain-sponge was inside of us and I guessed that it didn't want to kill its current host.

Chloe, Noah, and Leya were already shaking off the effects of the painful mental burst. But they looked staggered. I knew *I* was. How could we not be? We were in a war zone.

And the closer we got to the outside wall, the clearer the destruction became. So many bodies, so many edifices torn to pieces.

Chloe stiffened suddenly and cried out. In the next moment I felt it as well: a familiar flutter against my mind. Fear channeled into rage, terror transformed to destruction. The Gro'Nid leader was out there somewhere, calling out—

"More firepower on that wretched structure! NOW!" I scream.

This is our last chance, our last gasp. I am the War Chief, and I must not fail! We must destroy the insects and take—

—then I was back to myself. Glancing at Chloe, I saw she'd felt it as well. This was the Gro'nid's final attack. Centered on the Temple of the Elders.

Which we were currently in.

"*RUN!*" Chloe shrieked.

We ran. All but Click and Morb, who stayed rooted to the spot for a moment, like they'd just been kicked in the Celestian version of a stomach.

"Come on!" Leya shouted. She grabbed one of Morb's tentacles and yanked it. Morb seemed to shake herself, then she grabbed Click and mimicked Leya's action. Click flinched, then looked around like he'd forgotten what was happening.

It only lasted a second. Which was five seconds too long. I felt the rage again—

"Targeting?"

"Yes sir!"

"Center the disintegration net upon it! I want NOTHING LEFT OF THAT VERMIN-FILLED STRUCTURE!"

—and then I realized I was flying.

Somehow, in that flash where I found myself in the Gro'nid's mind, someone had gotten me onto an eggpod. I was inside with Morb and Click, the three of us jammed so close it was hard to breathe. Through the transparent shell, I could see Noah in a second eggpod, standing beside an Elder—I think it was Elder Nicki Minaj. Noah looked terrified, but the Elder was stock still, obviously opting to forego piloting the eggpod like Chloe did, and using foot movements and psychic prompts to move the little craft through the Temple's halls.

I whipped my head to the side, praying I'd see—there! Leya and Chloe were in a third pod, flying with Elder Thor. Leya had her eyes clenched tightly shut, flinching with every swerve. Chloe had her hands pressed flat against the shield window, staring forward with determination, like she was racing not to escape destruction, but to bring it down on the—

—Gro'nid gunner has entered the coordinates and looks now at me. "War Chief?"

I clench my fist and shout the order: "Fire—"

—exploding all around. I thought I was dead. Nothing but smoke and flames all around for an eternal moment, what could only have been a nanosecond seeming to stretch to infinity.

Morb shouted, "GO!" and the eggpod surged out of the smoke, barely getting out before the Temple of the Elders crumbled to dust around us.

I whipped my head to the side, looking for Chloe's pod. Either I'd gotten shaken around by the explosion or they had, because instead of Chloe, Leya, and Elder Thor I saw the eggpod carrying Noah. He spotted me, gave me a shaky thumbs-up, then turned and barfed all over Elder Minaj.

I turned away, looking for Chloe. Not finding her. Panic like nothing I'd ever felt...

...and I saw her. Zipping away, the pod with Chloe and Leya and—

I squinted. Hard to make it out. But I thought I could see Elder Thor, covered in marshmallow goo. My heart skipped as I realized they must have been hit, whether by a piece of the Temple as it collapsed, or a direct attack from the Gro'nid fighters I didn't know, and the Elder who'd been driving the eggpod had been knocked out of action.

My heart skipped a second beat—or ten or twenty beats—as three boomerang fighters peeled out of formation and followed after Chloe and Leya's pod. The pod itself was spinning, out of control.

The fighters shot at them. Blinding light exploding from their bellies. The lights soaring toward Chloe's pod and then it was gone and I screamed because I'd lost my sister and there was no way I could ever live past that moment, but I was still alive and in the moment I ran out of breath and inhaled to scream again…

…I saw her! Chloe and Leya, their pod flinging itself right and left, but faster and more precisely than the now-comatose Elder had managed. Because now the pod was under the control of a master.

Chloe.

The boomerangs shot at her pod again, and again Chloe shifted, her pod eluding the attack by inches. But inches was all she needed.

I saw her face, lined with concentration, terrified, but alive. Doing what she'd been born to do.

Then I didn't see her anymore. She twisted, and her pod shot into the sky. The boomerang fighters tried to follow, but her turns were too fast, too precise. One of the fighters couldn't make the tight turn needed to avoid the falling towers of another Celestian building. The structure glanced off the boomerang fighter, spinning it out of control into the second fighter. The third managed to swerve out of the way, but the move took it right into the side of a different building, and it was gone too.

"She will be all right," Click whispered. I knew he wasn't talking to me—just saying it, in the hopes it would turn out to be true.

"Yeah," I said, for the same reason.

I craned my neck, looking for Chloe through the fire and

debris raining down all around. Couldn't see her. Again, panic pounded at me and I wondered what I was going to do next, how I was going to tell my parents.

A thought came into my mind. A gentle, quiet thought. One that was so familiar I knew it instantly, but so different there was no question about it being a thought of my own.

"There's a school with kids in it," came Chloe's thoughts.

"Chloe! Don't—" I shouted. She couldn't hear my scream, but she heard the thoughts behind them. And returned with her own:

"They're in danger. I can save them."

I shouted again. But no more thoughts came. One way or another, Chloe and Leya were now beyond my ability to help or protect.

35

We landed. No idea where, just that it wasn't the Temple (obviously), and the laser cannon was waiting for us.

We'd barely touched down when the shield disappeared and Morb was shoving me forward. "Go!" she screamed.

I ran toward the cannon. Trying hard not to notice all the boomerang fighters, the fact that they were drawing into that formation that I knew would drop a laser net over the city. Only this time it was much larger—obviously intending to skip over the "one building at a time" phase of the attack and simply disintegrate everything at once.

An explosion tore through the air, and fire belched up from somewhere deep in the city. I felt for Chloe, trying to reach her with whatever part of my mind had heard her before. Nothing.

Ahead of me, Drxx and several other Celestians were firing what looked like handheld—er, tentacle-held—versions of the laser I'd helped them design. A bit of a surprise, though it shouldn't have been, given how fast they absorbed information. But the small lasers didn't seem to do much. A few boomerangs had scorch marks and small cracks marring their hulls, but nothing more.

As I ran, several of the makeshift militia turned toward me. I blanched, thinking I was about to become a friendly fire casualty on a planet so far away from home I'd have thought "friendly fire" to be an impossibility.

"HOLD YOUR FIRE!" Drxx shouted. A half-dozen tentacles sprouted from his body, flaring to the guns that pointed at me and yanking them downward. One discharged, the laser hitting the ground only a few feet in front of me.

Drxx gestured for me to hurry. He didn't say anything. Didn't have to.

I ran to the gunner seat on the big cannon. Trying to ignore the flickering beam of the web weapon starting to trace rays across the sky.

I looked at the controls. Everything seemed fine. I flicked the fire button without thinking, and was rewarded by a flash and a familiar scream.

"You trying to kill me?" Noah shrieked.

I looked around the side of the targeting reticle and realized that the cannon wasn't pointed skyward, but had fallen roughly parallel to the ground. The laser had misfired, which was the only thing that saved Noah from being vaporized as he and Elder Nicki Minaj landed in their eggpod, directly in front of the cannon.

Just as with me, there was a scorched spot directly in front of Noah and Elder Minaj, only where the one that almost hit me had been about six inches in diameter, this one was the size of a house.

Noah ran over it, his feet barely seeming to touch the still-smoking ground as he rushed forward. Elder Minaj had to take a longer way around, terrified chitterings coming from her that my brain-sponge couldn't handle and so turned into a steady undercurrent of the song "Starship."

Great. Stuck light-years from home, trying to repel an alien invasion, and now I've got hip-hop pop music playing in my head.

"What do you need?" Noah huffed as he ran up. He looked at the reticle of the laser, which was flickering and flashing like there was a short circuit somewhere.

I didn't bother answering, just ran around to the back of the cannon and started tearing the housing apart, frantically looking for what was wrong.

A sound like a cross between paper tearing and sizzling bacon sheared through the sky. I looked up, and saw the boomerang fighters dropping slowly down. The sound had been the tallest remaining Celestian building being atomized one meter at a time.

"We better hurry, bro—"

"I know."

"I mean, like—"

"I *know*."

I looked through the machinery, trying to calm down, to focus. I'd tested the cannon. The Celestians had tested the cannon. It worked, we'd verified that. So what could possibly—

And just like that, I saw the problem.

And just like that, I knew we were dead.

***

It was a little thing, really. Just a connection that had fried. Things like that happened. Some dust got in, a spark flew. A power surge, and we had a fried fuse. A portion of the blue Bandian wire that had taken too much current and burnt to a crisp.

Back home, I could just go to my dad's tool cabinet, find a new one, and pop it back in. But here that wasn't possible. The Celestians had had to go harvest the materials I needed from Bandia.

Just a single wire. That was it.

The bacon/paper sound got noisier. The webs were consuming the lower towers of the buildings now.

"What is it?" Noah said.

"We're dead," I whispered.

Noah shook his head. "Naw, man. You'll fix it. You'll figure out whatever it is—" The screaming I'd been hearing this whole time amplified, and Noah must have heard it too because he winced and shivered before he said, "You can fix it, man."

"I can't."

"I believe in you, Max. Just—"

"I *CAN'T!*" Another building tumbled. The boomerang ships were within fifty feet of the ground. Celestians were abandoning the city, running to the outskirts, hoping to escape the extermination.

I looked at Morb and Drxx, holding Click tight to them. I wondered where Chloe was.

"Why can't you?" Noah's voice was so low I could barely hear it through the noise.

I pointed at the fried section of wire, careful not to touch it: whatever our problems were, I didn't feel like adding to them by grabbing the still-powered edges of a fried circuit. "We need a new fuse. A new conductor. The Celestians—what?"

Noah's face was undergoing a host of emotions that I couldn't pin down, before finally settling on a wide grin. In the next second, he was shoving me around the side of the cannon, back toward the gunner seat.

"What's going on, No—"

"Just get in there and get ready to go when the thing powers up or whatever!" he shouted. Then he was shoving me into the chair and running back toward the still-exposed guts of the laser.

"What are you—"

"I've got some conductor!" he shouted, then disappeared around the back of the laser.

I almost followed him. No way he was going to—

Zrrrp!

With a sudden hum, the laser powered up and the cannon shot into a near-vertical position. I had an instant to wonder where Noah had gotten the wire he would have needed, to wonder if he'd grabbed some of the wire-leaves from Bandia while we were there, to keep as a souvenir or something.

Then the targeting reticle flickered to bright life, and without thinking I centered it on the lead Gro'nid ship. The one I somehow knew was the command ship of the Gro'nid War Chief. I followed the rage that had touched me earlier, drawing a line in the sky from me to him, following that line with the muzzle of the huge laser cannon.

The reticle flickered. Something was wrong. The muzzle shuddered. Losing power?

The targeting image flared to life again. The muzzle lifted. Just one instant...

I thought of Chloe again, and thought as hard as I could, *I love you Chlo*, because I knew that I would probably be dead in the next second or two.

Incredibly, I felt like she heard. Like she was there with me for a second, whispering, "I love you too, silly!"

I smiled. And pulled the trigger.

The laser hummed, then bellowed, then went dead. The power shut off, and the cannon muzzle lowered to the ground.

I'd gotten off one shot. Had it been enough?

Yes.

I looked up, and saw the Gro'nid War Chief's ship explode. Twice, actually. First I saw a ball of flame shoot out of the top of the ship, then the whole thing exploded in a bright burst of orange.

The net that had been destroying the Celestian city flicked out of existence, and the remaining boomerang fighters spun and started fleeing as the Celestians who were left alive began cheering.

Check that. Most of the Gro'nid ships fled. A few wheeled in the air, then started firing again and I knew the fight wasn't over yet. Which meant Chloe and Leya—both of whom had to be alive, because I refused to accept the alternative—were still in danger.

I looked around. Spotted the small eggship that Morb had brought me here with. There was the other one too, beyond the smoking crater where I'd almost vaporized Noah. Me and him could grab the eggpods. Could find Chloe and Leya. Bring them to safety. We could—

And suddenly I thought, *Where is Noah?*

The big guy always cheered the loudest at sports events, always screamed and hollered with the glee of someone totally present for the victory. But he wasn't screaming with glee. He wasn't even in sight.

Sudden dread fell over me.

"Noah?" I shouted. Not waiting for an answer, I leaped out of the cannon and it was only then that I realized that Morb, Drxx, and Click were nowhere to be seen.

The dread increased. Celestians were cheering, the boomerangs were mostly running for the hills. But I was so afraid.

I ran around the back of the cannon, and saw Noah, and fear engulfed me as my subconscious put two and two together and came up shrieking as it remembered:

The flood of expressions that had passed over my friend's face. The sudden, forced grin as he pushed me around to the cannon. He had been terrified. Because he had known that we needed a conductor, and there was only one suitable one on hand.

I flashed to a conversation that seemed to have happened a million years ago:

"Blue Planet *is a snore. The last good show I ever saw in a science class was one about Albert Edison.*"

"*I think you mean Albert Einstein. Or Thomas Edison.*"

"*Whatever. Did you know the guy electrocuted an elephant to show off how dangerous electricity was? An elephant, man. They put him on a wire and zzzzap!*"

Noah was burned, terrible dark patches of his skin charred to the bone, and it was obvious that he'd found the simplest solution. Rather than worry about a wire, he'd just gripped the two loose connections and let the current run through *him.*

I knelt beside him. He had to be dead. But he wasn't. Noah was too strong to die that easily, that painlessly

He held out his arm, his burned, charred hand. I don't think he saw me—even his face was burnt to charcoal. But he knew I was there, and reached for me.

"Hey," he whispered.

"Hey," I said. I didn't want to take his hand; how much agony would my touch cause?

He didn't give me the choice. His hand quested for mine. Found it. Held it tight. Surprisingly strong for what he'd gone through, but far too weak for me to harbor hope.

"I make...a good...elephant...huh."

I was crying. "The best."

What was left of his face twisted, and I knew he was trying to smile.

Then his hand slackened.

Fell away.

And he was gone.

36

A curtain fell over my vision. I felt Morb, pulling me away from my friend's body. I heard Drxx, saying something about the heroism of Noah's decision. I heard Click asking for me to be calm, to wait and—

I pushed away from them all. I ran to the eggpod we'd come in. I wasn't Chloe; wasn't great at the controls, but I had seen and practiced enough that I got the thing airborne. Wobbled a bit.

As I rose into the air, I saw Click gesticulating down on the ground, calling out. Morb and Drxx flapping their tentacles over the still form of my best friend, glowing yellow. But this wasn't a broken leg—Noah was beyond anyone's power to help. Dead.

But Chloe isn't, I thought, praying it was true.

I leaned. Pressed the buttons on the floor. The eggpod lurched, then began moving.

Nowhere in particular. Just…away. Only two thoughts in my head: that I had to find Chloe and Leya if I could. And that I wanted, for the first time in my life, to kill something. Not to protect someone. Not for the Celestians we'd come to love in spite of the complicated relationship we had. Not for the chance of going home.

I just wanted someone—anyone—to hurt as bad as I did right then.

An explosion caught my eye, and I leaned my eggpod toward the boomerang ship hanging in the air, letting loose a barrage of bright, flaring lights that exploded as they impacted the remains of a building.

The school!

I rushed toward the fighter ship, thinking I'd ram it full speed. I'd probably die—I didn't think marshmallow goo would save me from a head-on collision with a warship—but I'd take someone with me. And the way I felt, that sounded pretty good.

Death in my mind, my friend's last touch in my head, I raced for the ship. Pushing my own little craft faster, faster. I just wanted to share my pain, to let it wash over someone else, and have us both burn up in the heat of that moment.

Like Noah, I thought.

And in that moment, it was like he was there with me. Right behind me in the eggpod, calling out, "Watch out!"

And imagined or not, he was right: two ships were behind me, tracking me. I leaned to the side, swerving the eggpod out of their path just as one of the ships loosed a barrage of plasma bursts that narrowly missed me.

"They're on our six, Max!"

"I know." I was talking to a ghost. But he seemed real. And the lie of that ghost was better than thinking of the loss I'd just suffered.

"On our six, man!"

"I know!"

"On our—"

"You say 'on our six' again and I'm going to stop dodging!"

"Why would you do that?"

"Because I'd rather be atomized by a Gro'nid plasma net than hear 'on my six' again!"

"But *you* just said 'on my six'! Does that count?" I didn't look at the imagination of him. If I looked behind me and saw him burned and blackened, that would have been horror. And if he'd been untouched, whole as I remembered him before his stupid, wonderful, heroic act?

Somehow, that would have been even worse. Even worse than seeing him burnt, even worse than the reality of this moment, where I was having a conversation with the imagined ghost of a friend.

I flinched as the fighter behind us fired again. I was lying: given the choice between hearing Noah say, "On our six" again and dying, I'd choose the first one.

But it was a close call.

"Max, he's still there. Still on—"

"Don't say it!"

"– our tail!"

"I know. I *know!* Couldn't you have just found a penny? A paper clip? A bobby pin?"

"Dudes don't carry bobby pins, dude."

"Well you should have done...have done...anything but what you did."

"But I *did* do it." I felt his hand on my shoulder, like it had been in the Temple, when we all were one mind. I felt him inside my head, and whether it was madness or memory didn't matter. It just mattered that I could feel Noah, and even though he was dead, I knew I'd carry him with me as long as I lived.

"So do that," he said. "Carry me with you, man. But *live,* okay? Live for both of us."

I didn't answer. The hand I'd felt on my shoulder fell away, and his voice was gone from my mind.

The ships behind me fired, another narrow miss. I was hurtling from death to destruction, with not the slightest clue what to do when I got to my destination.

I got there faster than I would have thought. Spinning through debris and flame, trying to ignore that continuing scream in my mind as the brain-sponge did its thing, shouting the agony that surrounded me directly into my mind. Juking and twisting like I was Noah, running for a touchdown during the Homecoming game.

Two more turns, and I found what I was looking for.

***

The school. Easy enough to spot, given that there were at least a hundred Click-sized Celestians huddled into a tight group. They stood in front of the glass-like shards that were all that remained of the building.

A single boomerang fighter had been hovering in front of them, drawing a bead, obviously ready to fire.

And who was there with them? Chloe and Leya, standing in front of the kids, arms spread wide, like that would do a darn thing if—when—the boomerang fighter turned its weapons on them. The single fighter held more than enough power to turn them to dust.

And what had I done? Brought several more with me.

Again, I heard Noah in my head: "It is what it is, right?"

"I guess so," I muttered, and did the only thing left to me to do: I pushed my eggpod downward, skidded to a halt, flipping the shields open and hitting the ground running.

"Get in!" I screamed to Leya and Chloe. Knowing that they wouldn't, even before both of them shook their heads and closed their eyes, either in terror of what came next or just so they wouldn't have to see me die too.

They weren't going to leave the Celestian kids behind. They'd been kidnapped, taken from their own homes, and now Chloe and Leya were laying down their lives in a useless gesture.

What could I do?

I stood there with them.

The boomerang ship that had totaled the school, now joined by the two I'd brought in tow, all shifted to point at the throng of Celestian kids—ready, willing, and able to destroy us all in a single plasma blast.

At least it would be quick.

"The force will be with you! Always," whispered Noah in my head. I almost started crying, surprised that the tears weren't for my own lost life, but because I'd never get to ask him about his nerdy obsession.

"For *Star Wars!*" I shouted, trying to sound brave, mostly succeeding (I thought), but the tears flowed for sure when Chloe and Leya both looked at each other and smiled. Leya's hands shot out, taking Chloe's hand, then mine. Two of the most important women in my life grinned and shouted it as well: "FOR *STAR WARS!*"

The boomerang ships hummed. Their weapons ports glowed.

And they fired, point-blank, right at us.

37

It was loud, I'll say that. So loud that I went down hard and for a few seconds all I could hear was a bell-tone ringing in my head at 150 decibels.

That was the first thing that clued me I might not be dead. A lot of theories out there about what happens after death, ranging from the whole Heaven/Hell thing to just plain oblivion. But they all had this in common: plasma-blast-based deafness figured in precisely zero of them.

I felt a hand, clutching mine. Looked up, expecting to see Chloe, or maybe Leya. Either one, I'd be glad of—I still suspected I was dead, and having some company for that particular adventure would be nice.

I did *not* expect something that looked like a fat, furry blue ogre. It reminded me a bit of one of the creatures in that Disney movie, *Monsters, Inc.*: obviously a monster, but kinda cuddly and cute, other than the bloody streaks across his fur and the necklace that looked an awful lot like it was made of spleens tied together.

The ogre helped me to my feet—then slapped me in the side of the head. I felt something wet there and felt it, expecting blood. Whatever it was was tacky, but my fingers came away clean.

The ogre started rapid-fire belching. Whiffs of something that smelled like lavender on burnt toast wafted over me. I would have thought I was having a stroke, but at the same time the smell hit, the wet feeling on the side of my head also intensified. I touched it again, and felt something pulsing. I started to freak out, but noticed the pulsing was happening in time with the ogre-thing's flower-toast burps.

I'd been attacked, chased, threatened, blown up—and that was just the last thirty seconds. So you'll excuse my brain for going bye-bye for a second, fleeing from pure panic and hiding behind scientific curiosity.

The ogre was burping. Roses now. Still on burnt toast, though, so mixed blessing there.

Burp-bur-bur-buuuurrr…

(And the thing on my head went *pulse-pul-pul-pulllllllssse…*)

Bur-burrrp-burrp—

(Puls-pulllse-pull—)

Then the thing gave one more twitch and suddenly, I didn't hear burps. Well, I did (and I still smelled the rotating bouquet of flowers on burnt toast), but I also heard:

"…General Petunia, War Chief of the Flower People, Slayer of the Wild Weeds, and Sower of Discontent among Those Who Would Prune Us."

The blue ogre bowed, so low his head almost touched the ground. He gave the longest, throatiest burp I'd ever heard, and the thing on my head pulsed, and with the pulse I heard General Petunia, War Chief of the Gro'nid, attacker of Celestia, and (apparently) guy who was way into flowers, say, "And I beg the apology of the one who has saved us from the great, grievous mistake we were about to make."

"Uh…I forgive y—"

The ogre gently but firmly pushed me to the side and, shaking his head, burp/pulsed, "Forgive me, but I am not speaking to you, though you are indeed a great warrior and no doubt many Thistles have fled the power of your Pruning Shears." Then he bowed even lower and said, "I speak to the Queen."

I frowned. Turned.

And there, of course, was Chloe.

Chloe, who barely managed to speak to Mean Girls Becca, Jessica, and Sierra.

Chloe, who wanted to belong but always felt apart.

Chloe, who had had to go to a different *universe* to find who she was.

Chloe, who bowed back and, in the most regal way possible, burped.

The ogre hitched a bit, like he wasn't really sure what to do with that. Then he bowed even lower. "You do me honor, my lady."

38

At this point, if you're thoroughly confused, you're not alone. It took a bit of shuffling and some *very* long burp-click-word conversations to hash everything out, but in the end here's what it all boiled down to:

The Gro'nid—the Flower People, in their parlance, as transmitted by their version of the brain-sponge (the tacky thing War Chief Petunia had slapped on my head)—had indeed come looking for a new place to live, and had found Celestia: a planet almost perfect for their species to continue and perhaps even thrive.

So far, so good.

But at this point, the Flower People's story diverged from the Celestians'.

The Celestians had seen an attacking, hostile force trying to exterminate them. The first attack had come with no warning, obviously designed to destroy them entirely.

But the Flower People? Basically, they had seen a very nice planet with "weeds" growing all over it—the Celestians' tower buildings, which were very similar to giant "ant-hills" (that's what the Gro'nid/Flower People's side-of-head-sponge translated the *very* stinky burp into). So they did the logical thing: destroy them.

When the Celestians resisted, they did so in a way similar to the Flower People's "ant enemies." And after doing everything possible to communicate—i.e., standing at the outskirts of the Celestian city several times and sending out their stinkiest belches—they determined that intelligent life did not exist on this planet.

Which made sense, to some extent. I mean, obviously the Celestians had technology, but it was all barf-based. So to creatures looking for two main things as signs of intelligence (machine-based technology, and prodigious burping), Celestians looked like—well, like ants would. *Just* like ants, in fact: very complicated society, big structures made of bodily fluids and natural components, and tossing stuff at attackers to frighten them off.

The Gro'nid (darn it, Flower People; still getting used to that one) sent their War Chief, Petunia, to clear things out. Which also fit, because to folks who called themselves "Flower People," an invasive insect species (ants, or Celestians) would be both terrifying and deadly.

Until the last fight, when everything changed.

At first, War Chief Petunia had thought he was dreaming as he felt the touch of something in his mind that he did not expect: intelligence. Someone speaking in his mind.

"There's a school with kids in it," followed by, *"They're in danger. I can save them."*

The War Chief hadn't believed it. Had thought he had taken one too many knocks to the fuzzy blue noggin. The "insect extermination" had continued, with the Flower People's laser net being the equivalent of an Earth kid shoving a firehose into an anthill. And it would have continued—and succeeded—were it not for what happened right before I blasted Petunia's ship out of the sky.

He felt that intelligence again. So strong this time that it could not be denied. He moved to the back of the ship, intending to call off the attack so they could regroup and see if they were making a huge mistake. So when the laser hit his ship, he had time to get into an escape pod and eject—the first explosion I'd seen, shooting out the back of the Winking Gro'nid—and then began looking for the source of the intelligence, the creature who had thought the words he felt so strongly they could not be denied:

"I love you too, silly!"

***

This didn't all come out at once, of course. There was a lot of hand-waving, clicking, and burping before one of the Flower People presented Morb with a side-of-head-sponge and convinced her to put it on, and even more before Chloe could convince Click to steal a brain-sponge and give it to War Chief Petunia.

But before any of that happened, I knew I'd have to deliver the terrible news to Leya. She'd just accepted that, though some of her family was gone, she had more family ready to keep and watch over her, to help her belong and give her a home where she could hang her heart.

That was in large measure thanks to Noah. And Noah was gone.

When I told her, I barely managed to choke out Noah's name before she knew.

"What...is he..." She couldn't finish the thought. It was just too terrible. She threw herself into my arms and I felt her body sag into mine as all the strength left her. Then we were both crying, weeping. Chloe joined us, as War Chief Petunia waited patiently and the Celestians all around us glared at the still-hovering boomerang ships, because we were still in the "no way I trust you" stage at that point.

We wept together, holding each other. So far from home, and somehow it had never once crossed my mind that we might have to go home without Noah. I'd worried about Chloe over and over, about Leya nearly as much. But Noah? He just felt invincible. He was a part of the landscape, as strong and steady as a mountain, and just as immovable.

But we'd lost him.

"He was the strongest..." It was all I could get out before weeping stole my voice.

"How...did...how did he..." Leya managed.

Between huge, wracking sobs, I managed, "A hero. He died

like a hero."

Then we were crying again, and kept crying until Noah said, "Wow, who died?"

***

Here's what I saw: Noah, burned to a crisp, beyond the ability of any possible medical aid. Holding my hand, dying, then me rushing off to find Chloe and Leya.

Here's what the Celestians—particularly Morb, Click, and Drxx—saw: Noah, heroically taking an electrical discharge for the sake of their people. His heart stopping, which they immediately knew because they'd been monitoring our bodies so closely they knew us down to our favorite foods, which entailed a *lot* of close watching.

Then they saw me running off, which struck them as inappropriate because they knew Noah needed help of some kind and thought I should give it to him rather than running away.

Back to what I saw: them glowing like suns over Noah. Bright yellow, the same as when Chloe had broken her leg on Bandia. They knew how to heal us, and though his heart had stopped, it had only *just* stopped, and he was still within the range of their aid.

So they fixed him. Broken leg, charred skin—it was all the same physiology to the Celestians, who were able to heal his "minor injury."

I resolved to have a talk with them about the difference between "minor injury" and "catastrophic death-burning." But later. Right now I was just glad to have my friend back.

***

The only downside was that they hadn't been able to heal his clothing (which they still didn't really understand as a concept). So when he asked "Who died?" we all turned and saw him, and our elation was tempered a bit by the fact that when I say "we saw him," I mean *we saw him. All* of him. And I'm not sure which of us was most embarrassed about that fact: me, Leya, or Chloe.

Noah didn't seem to much care. Which surprised me not at all.

Oh, there *was* a second downside:

Noah refused to tell us what the healing process actually *was*. He just went bright red and muttered, "No one should ever puke on that part of a guy's body," and then refused to say any more.

39

All right, back to Flower People/Celestian relations.

When I thought I heard Chloe say, "I love you too, silly," it wasn't my imagination. She'd heard me think the words, "I love you," and thought back her response.

And War Chief Petunia heard it. Recognized it as a) not his own thought ("I do not use terms like 'silly' when I profess affection!" he growl-burped), b) coming from someone who was not one of the Flower People (apparently they have a very distinct "smell" to their thoughts), and c) obviously intelligent.

So he was about to call off the attack when I hit their ship with the laser, he ejected, and landed in the middle of, obviously, a war zone.

All he could do was follow the "scent" of the thoughts he was hearing. He heard heroism, and love, and fear—all of which made sense given what Chloe was doing at the time: eluding boomerang fighters, getting to the school and barely convincing the kids to evacuate the shelter before it came down around them, and then taking up position with Leya in front of the doomed kids.

And the rest, as they say, is history.

***

Chloe was the key—not in that moment alone, but in everything that came before and after.

She was the one who had made contact with Click, sure, we knew that. But thinking back, we pieced together the fact that she was the one who had been touching me the first time I "Joined." Something in her had the power to pick up on the Celestians' wavelength, and she was able to somehow transfer that—albeit a less powerful version—to me, Leya, and Noah.

It was pretty cool all on its own, but the most important thing about her Joining was that both the Celestians and the Flower

People agreed that this was proof positive of intelligent life. Which made for a pretty big deal, because it also meant that the Flower People could not in good conscience exterminate the Celestians to take their planet. More important (at least from where I stood), it meant that the Celestians couldn't take *our* planet, either.

Surprisingly, Drxx was the one who convinced the Elders of this. I was there, and felt downright embarrassed as he recounted the help I'd given them with their tech development, as well as the bravery of Noah in offering up his body to what he had known would be a fatal shock to save the Celestians. And I got downright weepy when he called up the schoolchildren to talk about how Chloe and Leya had saved all of them, then stood between them and the firepower of the boomerang fighters. A few of them mentioned me as well—that I'd shown up and stood with my friends—but mostly they talked about what Leya and Chloe had done, sounding almost worshipful.

Which was just fine with me. They deserved it, and I felt a bit worshipful toward them myself (though for different reasons).

There was a lot of discussion and dispute, with Elder Nicki Minaj leading the argument to go ahead and "displace all the dumb Earthlings, yo!" and Elder Thor siding with those who agreed we humans were in fact intelligent life by all Celestian metrics.

It still might have ended in a tie, or with the Celestians viewing us as "less-than-intelligent"—particularly when Elder Nicki Minaj showed the other Elders a series of political attack ads from the last election, then translated the comments section of several YouTube videos as proof that no intelligent life could possibly exist on Earth. Heck, I was kind of leaning her way myself after watching the Democrats and Republicans go at each other, then reading a bunch of Internet trolls compare everyone who disagreed with them to Hitler.

It would have been a real problem, not least because if we

humans weren't "intelligent," that basically meant the Celestians could go to our planet and take whatever they wanted, feeling no worse about it than we did about destroying the rainforests (which was to say, not very bad at all).

The tie-breaker, when it came, was from an unlikely source. Elder Nicki Minaj had called for a vote after reading YouTube user UsernameUncertain74's comment about how the video of a box of kittens wasn't *really* just a cute video, but "jus 1 mor proof of the Illuminati conspirasee 2 put chips in our brains so they can control the masses!"

Yeah, things looked pretty bad.

But War Chief Petunia—who'd been granted diplomatic status and warned beforehand by Morb that he should show up to help out if he could, because Nicki Minaj was by far the most intelligent, refined, and convincing of all the Elders—stood up and said, "The humans have heard our thoughts. We have heard theirs, just as we have heard yours." He tapped his head, where a brain-sponge of his own nestled, translating the Celestian words to his burp-thoughts just as his burp-words were translated to Celestian clicks by the Elders' own new side-of-head-sponges. War Chief Petunia took a deep breath, then continued, "They are as intelligent as the Flower People, so if they are viewed as unintelligent life, then the Flower People will know the Celestians view them as enemies as well."

He let the implications hang in the air, along with the fading scent of daisies and toast.

The Elders began doing a glow-con. No sound, just brain-to-brain stuff that none of us—except Chloe—could understand. And even she, as special as she was, couldn't get everything they were saying. She was only eight, after all, and even an extraordinary eight-year-old isn't likely to understand intergalactic politics.

But she was smiling now, so I guessed that the vote was going our way.

"Way to *go*, Petunia," Noah whispered.

"Thank you, Space-Captain Noah," burped War Chief Petunia.

Yeah, when we'd introduced ourselves, Noah called himself "Space-Captain Noah" and it stuck.

"You're welcome, War Chief," Noah said. He burped. War Chief Petunia grimaced. "What'd I say?" asked Noah. "I was trying for 'thank you.'"

War Chief Petunia shook his head. "You insulted my radishes."

Noah frowned. "Okay, but—"

"Shhh." I hissed. I wasn't interested in burping, and Noah was sitting right next to me, still very naked.

The Celestians had offered to "make" him some clothes, but Noah went the same bright red as whenever he was asked about the healing process, said, "Never again," and that was that.

"Okay, I'll be quiet," Noah whispered back. "But Max?"

"Yeah?"

"Why don't you ever look at me anymore?" I sensed the wicked grin, even if I didn't see it.

"Noah—"

"Seriously. It's like you're *ashamed* or something." He crossed his legs.

"Noah, my sister is here. My *little* sister."

"Yeah. But it's nature, right? I'm like those nature people, like those Granola Goobers we met in the woods."

I grimaced. "Can't you just let the Celestians give you some clothes?"

Noah shook his head vehemently. "Never. Never again, no way, *never*."

War Chief Petunia was looking back and forth, from me to

Noah, then to Leya and Chloe, then back to Noah. "Ah," he burped. "Your people *do* typically wear clothing."

"Yeah," said Noah. "But *real* clothes. Like, pants and coats. Not something puked."

The War Chief looked a bit confused at the last, but then gave us the surprise of our lives as he shrugged, and suddenly there was a second, headless War Chief Petunia sitting beside us.

After the screaming (mostly mine) died down, we found out that the Flower People could shed their fur coats at will. It wasn't quite time for War Chief Petunia's "molting season," and he had planned to wear his full coat the whole time he was on Celestia, but now that he understood his "peer in the military, Space-Captain Noah" was in need, Petunia wanted Noah to take his old coat—a gift of some magnitude.

I thought Noah would balk at that, but evidently wearing someone's actual skin was cooler than a barf-sweater, so three seconds later he was wearing the War Chief's old coat like the biggest, hairiest, stinkiest onesie in the universe.

He looked pleased. I know *I* was, though for different reasons. Leya and Chloe were relieved as well—everyone had spent the last two days doing hard eye-contact with Noah, so it was nice to be able to look his way without danger.

The Elders stopped glowing, and when I glanced at Chloe, I saw confusion on her face.

War Chief Petunia somehow recognized it as well: "My lady?" he said. "Are you all right? If not, you have the power of" (a burp-series the side-of-head-sponge turned into "my hedge trimmer and my Garden Weasel") "at your command. But say the word and your enemies shall be mine!"

There'd been a lot of that over the past few days. War Chief Petunia had it in his head that Chloe was some kind of royalty, and his position as a leader of the Flower People demanded that he treat her with royal respect.

Now, Chloe waved him off. "I just don't know what they're going to do," she said.

Leya gave her a quick side-hug. "Don't worry, *my lady*," she said. "We'll just have a little faith."

"Indeed," burped the War Chief. "When hope is present, any fight can be won."

One by one, the Elders voted on the question of human intelligence, casting their lots by vomiting either blue (Yea!) or red (Nay!) in a pot in the center of the room.

One by one they voted, as the humans watched anxiously and War Chief Petunia shivered a bit without his coat.

When it was done, the vote was unanimous—all blue: humans were to be treated as intelligent.

Politics and social media notwithstanding.

40

The debate switched then from the question of Earth life to whether further discussions should take place in private. When War Chief Petunia asked why the Elders "wished to confer in secret, like weeds sprouting sullenly, without warning among the flower gardens of discourse," they answered frankly.

Sounding almost embarrassed, Elder Thor said, "Because your planet is still dying, is it not?"

"Yes," said War Chief Petunia. He was a military man, which meant he told it like it was, and he also understood what Elder Thor was implying. "You are worried we will take back our word and attack your planet again?"

"It is a concern," admitted Elder Thor, while Elder Nicki Minaj whispered, "Haters gotta hate, man."

So the vote for us had been unanimous. But there was still a lot of distrust.

Looking at what had happened, I realized how ridiculous it was: one species had almost wiped out another simply because they didn't understand how the other one thought, or the words they said.

Then I realized that, even more ridiculously, most human wars probably started for similar reasons.

Intelligent life?

Whatever the Elders' vote, I think all three of our species still had a way to go.

We have to start listening to each other, I thought. *Not just telling what we want, but trying to understand what the other people want...and what they truly need.*

"We'll get there," I said, talking to no one in particular. "We'll get there together. Some day."

I felt very proud of myself. But I'm a guy, and easily

impressed that way.

Leya was shaking her head. "You guys are so dumb," she said. But she squeezed my hand and smiled as she said it, so I couldn't help but smile back.

Noah, however, wasn't in love with his cousin—at least, not the way I was. Crossing his now-furry arms across his broad chest, he said, "Oh? Please, enlighten us, wise one."

"Gladly." Leya winked at me. Then, turning to the Elders, she said, "The answer is obvious." She pointed at War Chief Petunia. "The great warrior here is *shivering.*"

War Chief Petunia belched an upset, "I'm not shivering. I'm quickly clenching and unclenching all my muscles to make sure that I maintain a proper internal temperature."

Leya rolled her eyes. "Spoken like a true man," she said.

Again, she squeezed my hand.

Again, I realized how hard it was to understand people sometimes.

An onlooker might have heard Leya's words as mockery or derision. But the warmth of her hand, and the greater warmth of her smile told me clearly: she was just having a little fun. Just warming up for the reveal, whatever it was.

And it turned out my assessment of the moment was even more accurate than I could have guessed.

41

Leya asked two questions. Just two, and the unsolvable problems were resolved.

Question one, to War Chief Petunia, which he answered (a bit grudgingly) in the affirmative: "Are you cold?"

Question two, also to the War Chief, this time with a negative response: "Have your people surveyed the entire asteroid field just past Celestia?"

***

The reason War Chief Petunia had kept his coat from molting for so long was that Celestia was too cold for comfort. But people whose planet is dying can't be choosers, as the saying goes, so they had been ready to just survive in the (to them) frigid wasteland of Celestia as their best alternative...because they didn't know about Bandia.

Just as Click had explained to Chloe, the quantum asteroid fields beyond Celestia masked not only the asteroids' own locations, but the very *existence* of the planet in their center. It had taken the Celestians thousands of years to deduce its existence, and thousands more to figure out a way to travel into the field without having space rocks appear in the middle of their ships— or their bodies.

The Flower People had only been surveying for a decade, so no surprise that they'd missed it: a planet so close to perfect for them that, had they known it existed, they never would have bothered with Celestia at all.

It took a few days to repair the mothership after the attack, but once it was ready, Drxx flew the War Chief to Bandia. I would have expected him to be one of the ones who was still hostile toward the Flower People—Elder Nicki Minaj wasn't the only Celestian who still harbored mistrust for their once-invaders.

But Drxx seemed more embarrassed than anything. I think,

like me, he was shocked at how easy it had been for their people to war upon each other, over nothing but misunderstandings and a lack of communication. He and War Chief Petunia actually bonded quickly, and when I asked Click what that was all about, he Celestia-shrugged and said, "The War Chief is strong, and brave, and says what he feels without guile." He hesitated, then added, "And in all those things, he is much like Drxx's brother-half."

It hit me again, even harder: they were all people. The Celestians, the Flower People. They were so alike. All it took was time and listening, and friendships could begin.

Indeed, I realized, once you listened, and tried to understand, it wasn't hard for those friendships to happen—it was hard for them *not* to.

***

When War Chief Petunia returned, he was elated. Partly because he had just been shown a planet perfect for his people's relocation, but also because Drxx had shown him a fun game. He claimed to have invented it himself, but I recognized "Click-Boop-Beep" as a Celestian spin on the Rock, Scissors, Paper that Noah had played when we went to Bandia.

I think Noah knew it too. But instead of doing a Noah-esque thing like yell, "Hey, that's *my* game!" when he saw War Chief Petunia playing it with Drxx, he just called out, "Next game!"

They were laughing when I left them. Three of the warriors of their people, three species that had viewed each other with indifference at best, hostility at worst. Laughing like loons over a dumb game that just involved a willingness to sit close, play fair, and laugh when you lost—because you knew you wouldn't lose forever, and because you knew that even winning wasn't the point.

The point was being together.

42

There were so many things to iron out, and they hadn't even gotten to the question of how to deal with Earth. I got the feeling that the Celestians as a whole leaned toward letting humanity know they were not alone in the galaxy, but were sharply divided on whether to approach them with gifts of knowledge and barf-tech, or with the threat of extinction should Earthlings get too big for their britches.

Occasionally they asked for me or Leya to give our two cents, which was nice. Noah they asked once, but when he immediately started lecturing them about how the Evil Empire had started as a result of the Imperial Senate holding deliberations just like this—Noah was a closeted nerd of proportions I'd never guessed—and that even Yoda ended up having to hide in Dagobah, they thanked him and ushered him quickly out of the room.

Chloe? They wanted her there *all the time*. Both Celestians and Flower People seemed to view her as the hope of humanity.

And, as her big brother, I couldn't say they were wrong.

***

Like I said, there was a lot to do, and so many questions that still hadn't been answered.

"But we can't stay for all of it," said Chloe tearfully to Click after coming back to the life-pod the Celestians had bequeathed on us Earthlings as our own private residence.

"What do you mean, Chloe?"

"I mean, this is going to take forever. Like, *years*. But my dreams…they're so bad."

I was listening from my little bed, and sat up at that. Truth was, if Chloe hadn't brought it up that day, I would have. Because I knew. I'd been having the same dreams.

Mom and Dad. Drawn and tired after weeks of looking for their children. The hope in their eyes fading a bit more, day by day. It wasn't gone—I knew my parents, and there was no way they'd ever *completely* give up hope—but it was a shadow of itself. The shadow of two children they'd lost. Not to mention the visits from Noah's parents, the four of them getting together to compare notes, to check the social media feeds and the news and law enforcement websites.

They were dying. Hearts still pumping, lungs still pulling air in and pushing it out. But the sparks were gone. That was what I dreamed of, and what Chloe was feeling as well: the loss our parents endured.

What we were doing here had been—still was—important. We stood at the center of events that would shift the flow of human history, and our words and choices had affected the course of events forever.

But Chloe was right. The work we were doing would never end. But Mom and Dad—and Noah's parents, Leya's aunt and uncle—needed us to come back.

It was time to go home.

***

Like a lot of things, the lead-up was bigger than the moment of decision. Chloe said it was time to go, so it was time to go. The mothership was ready, the Elders had a nice new Temple being vomited up one invisible brick at a time by a team of dedicated Celestians, War Chief Petunia was busy surveying the best spots for the Flower People to relocate. Everyone had jobs that would continue on without us.

Part of me wanted to stay, to nudge that course of history a bit longer, see if I couldn't help our species get in on some of the best bits of Celestian and Flower People technology and culture.

But the rest of me knew, just as Chloe did, that any good we could accomplish here wouldn't matter if we had no home to go home to. Our parents were suffering, and an entire universe didn't weigh more than family for any of us.

So we went.

Click was hardest to convince. He wanted his friend to stay. And surprisingly, though it was mostly because Chloe *was* his friend, it was also because he had ascended to the Celestian status of "Cool Kid" by draping one of Chloe's socks over his head one day and parading it before the other Celestian schoolkids. Now it was a fad with all the youth, draping something over their heads and asking each other, "What is *your* clothings?" like they were comparing name brands at a Beverly Hills shop.

"How will I learn more clothings?" he wailed.

"Simple," Chloe answered. "You'll visit and I'll show you all the *other* clothings."

"Other clothings?"

"Sure! All we have is shirts and pants and socks and shoes and underwear—except Noah, because he just has the fur-baby suit so he—"

"Focus, Chloe!" Morb said from nearby, sounding just like my mom.

"Sorry." Chloe turned back to Click and shrugged. "I just have to go."

"But I'll miss you."

And Chloe, because she was still young enough to be wise, said, "I know. And you should. Because if you miss me you'll have to visit, and if you visit then you and me can help Earth people and Celestia people like each other." She cast a quick glance at me and whispered, "If we leave everything up to the grown-ups, they'll just mess it up."

Click thought for a while, then finally nodded. "That is true."

***

One more night, dreaming dreams of terror and sadness, the

emotions made all the greater by the knowledge Chloe and I had that they weren't really dreams at all. We were Joined to our parents, just like we were Joined to the Celestians and to the Flower People.

The dreams had actually helped us in the debates about how the Celestians (and by default, the Flower People as well) should treat the Earthlings. When we told the Elders about our dreams, it was just one more thing pointing to the fact that we could actually Join, and if we had minds powerful enough to connect at that level, the Celestians' culture demanded that the people of Earth be treated with kindness and respect.

And now it was time to return. To go back to the glorious, wonderful miracle of our everyday lives.

***

The trip back was like all trips back: it seemed to go much faster than the trip out had been. Noah, Chloe, Leya, and I got on the mothership, and a moment later Click was hollering that we were almost there, almost to Earth, almost "home!"

That was what he said: "home." Not *his* home, but the home of his friend. And the way he said it, the joy the brain-sponge translated, along with the way War Chief Petunia (who had insisted on coming along with "her majesty" Chloe) did a little happy-dance, was the best proof of all that we could have a future, the three species together.

Because for a Celestian and one of the Flower People to act like that, they had to feel our joy. They had to share our love of home—if only because they loved *us*, and we loved our little blue marble of a planet. Beings who share their hearts like that, who find things to love in common despite their many, many differences, well...

There would be problems, no doubt about that. Misunderstandings had happened before, and would inevitably happen again. Tragedy was never far when triumph was to be found.

But that shared love would be, I hoped, enough to see all our species through.

The four of us stood, as we had at the start, in the outer room of the mothership. We seemed to hang in the middle of space, supported by nothing but the need to move forward, and by the hope for what we now saw:

Just a speck.

Then a dot.

Then a circle.

And then we could see the features we knew. The curves of the continents, the white swirls of wind and storm above oceans so blue they seemed unreal.

We were home.

43

There it was. Earth, hurtling toward us after light-years of separation. So close.

Look, a lot had happened since we left. Lives had changed, the course of human, Celestian, and…uhh…Flower People-ian history had shifted. So I can't blame any of us for forgetting.

Okay, maybe a *little* blame.

Fine. I'm just going to say it:

What happened next was all Noah's fault.

***

We'd left Click and Chloe in the outer room, holding hands/tentacles, maybe crying a little in anticipation of separating, if only for a short time. "I'll come back," Click kept saying, to which Chloe repeated, every time, "You better."

The rest of us went to the nav-control room. Watching the big wall that was essentially a window to the universe's best view: Earth rising to meet us.

Morb and Drxx moved fluidly in their separate chairs, preparing for the delicate approach. The world spun in front of us, taking up the entire viewscreen, the greens and browns of North America dominating. I imagined I could almost see the Golden Gate Bridge, car lights winking their way across it as evening fell and commuters sped home. I could see the green patches that I thought might be Muir Forest, the place where everything had gone so terribly wrong, and so amazingly right.

Beside me, Leya gave my hand a squeeze. I looked at her and she winked. "Ready to go back, rockstar?"

I thought of it all. Of Mom, running in and out, smelling like fire. Of Dad, incapable of getting a single invention working without my help. Of the bills piling up and the stress of daily life trying to blend in to the mass of students at school.

I squeezed her hand back. "Absolutely."

Noah piped up. "Hey, could I drive?"

Drxx twisted back and forth: the Pac-Man ghost version of a head-shake. "I told you on Bandia, Noah. The approach is too dangerous. It calls for precision and an understanding of how to read the landing beacon and—"

"Aww, come on, man." Noah made as if to grab the controls.

War Chief Petunia stepped forward. Laying a giant blue paw on Noah's shoulder, he said, "My friend, your excitement is laudable, but perhaps we should retire. I have many an account of battles and glory, of gardens planted and weeds rent asunder—"

"Yeah, yeah." Noah leaned in front of Drxx, a move that would have obstructed the view for a human. Drxx just grew a few extra eyestalks and looked over the top of Noah. "Come on, Drxx. You owe us, right?"

A bright blast of light signaled we had just passed through the outer layers of Earth's atmosphere. I could almost smell the delicious, smog-filled air of home. So close, and I didn't want Noah messing anything up.

So, bright "me fix things good" kind of guy that I am, I gave Leya's hand a final squeeze, then let go and stepped toward Noah. I put my hand on his other shoulder as I said, "C'mon, Noah, let's let the drivers do the driving."

A lot had happened.

I keep telling myself that.

So it wasn't Noah's fault that he forgot. *I'd* forgotten. I think everyone kind of did. Even Morb and Drxx, right up to the moment where Noah tapped Drxx's shoulder, once…

"C'mon, big D…"

…twice…

"After all, if it wasn't for my heroic self-fricasee…"

...three times...

"...we'd have—"

Morb lunged at my friend. *"NOAH, DON'T—"*

And the rest of Morb's mind-scream was lost, because we had come home.

To Earth.

And were now inside its atmosphere.

Where Noah tapped Drxx's shoulder for the fourth time.

I heard it, the kind of snap you hear a thousand times a day if you live in a house with shag carpeting. No big deal: just a bit of static electricity.

While Noah was touching Drxx.

And Drxx happened to be touching Morb.

The Celestians had told us before that static discharges were "dangerous" and the results on Celestians were "unpredictable."

In this case, the dangerous, unpredictable effect was two Celestians exploding. Literally—there was a cross between a burp and a boom, and next thing I knew Noah had been thrown into the back wall at bone-crushing speed, covered in bits of goo that I quickly realized were Drxx and Morb, turned from their normal Pac-Man ghost forms to giant, sticky blobs by the "unpredictable" static discharge effect.

Oh, and guess who else got caught by the blast? Correct: War Chief Petunia and I, both of us touching Noah at "the big moment," had gotten hit as well. Like Noah, we were hurled into the back wall. Like Noah, we were more or less stuck to the wall by Celesti-goo.

The goo itself was highly unnerving. It had a consistency somewhere between peanut butter and Play-Doh. Angry violet, rippling like a snail. Morb's and Drxx's eyes appeared at random spots all over the goo, sometimes seeming to grow out of the same random eyestalk before the eyes (and stalks) pulled back into the

Morb-Drxx margarita.

The goo rippled, changed from violet to blue to yellow, then back to violet again as Morb and Drxx tried to get themselves under control. I thought I saw glimpses of both their heads, on opposite sides of the goo-ball that had engulfed us, like they were trying to separate from each other by force of will. But it only lasted an instant, and then they snapped back like a rubber band and the heads dissolved back into the sticky, eyeball-growing, sticky, color-changing, sticky, undulating, *sticky* mess.

The observant audience will notice I mentioned "sticky." Several times. This was intentional.

We—Noah, me, Petunia—were utterly stuck to the wall by Morb and Drxx. Which, again, the observant folks may notice meant that there was only one person in the room not caught in the goo-splosion.

Leya had missed the splash zone by centimeters, and now ran toward us. Reaching out to help, the movement cut short when I screamed, "Don't!"

Her hand stopped instantly, only inches away from us. "What?"

"It's super sticky, Leya. I don't want you to get stuck."

"I'll risk it," she said.

Noah'd been knocked cold for a second, but he came to right then and screamed, "Risk it! Risk it!"

"NO!"

I screamed, possibly louder than I'd ever screamed before. Again, she'd been reaching for us. Again, she stopped, this time millimeters from the rippling gootastrophe.

"What?" she demanded, seeming a bit put out.

"I just really need to make sure you don't get caught," I said, trying to maintain my calm.

"That's sweet," she said, in the tone of voice a girl uses when they want you to know you're definitely *not* being sweet, "but I think the circumstances merit the—"

"No, they don't!" I was shouting now, panic rising in my gut.

She put her hands on her hips. "And why the heck not?"

"Because we really need at least one person free, so that they can stop us from crashing into the mountain."

***

I have to admit, I was disappointed for a second. I figured that Leya would whip around, realize we were about to slam into a mountain that was growing *way* too large in the viewscreen, and grab the steering controls—girl power for the win!

Instead, she froze.

"Leya?" I said. "We're in a bit of a time crunch here."

Petunia had been totally knocked out. He woke up at that moment, saw himself covered in a slick of slime and eyeballs, and reacted in an appropriately alien way: he gave out the highest-pitched shriek-burp I've ever heard, then *grew a shell and curled up like the world's biggest pillbug.*

I guessed that meant we weren't getting any help from him.

Morb-Drxx shuddered, again tried to separate, then turned vomit green and somehow managed to get even stickier.

"Leya? Leya!" I was on full panic mode now, totally freaked. "Unless you do something we're going to—"

My mouth slapped shut, seemingly on its own, as I realized: of course Leya was petrified. This was how her parents had died.

Well, probably not *this* this, hurtling into the side of a mountain while coming home from an intergalactic adventure. But definitely an accident. A collision.

I didn't know what to say. What to do. Noah started howling, "Leya, please, Leya, please, Leya, please!" over and over, which didn't help.

Leya was still frozen. Her eyes were so wide I saw the whites

310

in a perfect circle all around those beautiful green eyes of hers.

It was just about the saddest thing I'd ever seen. Right up there with when I thought Noah died. I had no idea what to do, only that I couldn't help her.

At that low moment, the most surprising, strange, utterly perfect thought popped into my mind: *What would Chloe do?*

And again, my mouth moved without brain intervention. Opening, and the words coming out, soft and sincere: "Leya. You can do this. I believe in you."

Leya's eyes widened a bit more. A tear glimmered at the corner of one, but did not fall. She blinked it back, straightened, and ran for the controls. Stopped, and I worried that she had fear-frozen again.

"It's a stick!" she screamed, panic driving her own normally beautiful voice into glass-breaking registers. *"I don't know how to do stick!"*

I had just enough freedom from the Drxx-Morb-goo to turn my head. "Noah, help her!"

He was still chanting, "Leya, please, Leya, please, Leya, please," so lost in panic I don't think he heard me, or saw anything other than the mountain we were about ten seconds from hitting.

Morb and Drxx were still stuck together, but at least managed this: a hand-shaped appendage appeared in the goo right in front of Noah, and gave him a good hard smack upside the head.

The goo-slap knocked the panic out of him. He blinked twice, then in an utterly calm voice said, "Okay, just follow my instructions. Take a seat." She did, moving like a robot. "Good. Nice. Way to go. Now take the steering yoke—"

"The stick thingy?"

"Right, the stick thingy." Noah's voice was pure honey, sweet and rich. Even *I* felt calmer, and Petunia's shell started to turn back into hair.

Leya took the steering yoke/stick thingy. "Got it. Now?"

I successfully did not start screaming, even though I estimated we were about five seconds from having a bug-to-windshield moment.

"Now," Noah said, "just pull back. Not too much...nice...nice...Now grab that lever....not the blue one...yeah, that one. Give it a tug...good...now pull on the steering yoke—the stick—again...nice...and then...STEP ON BOTH THE FOOT PEDALS! NOW NOW NOW!"

To her credit, Leya did. She literally stood on them.

At this point, I was just screaming. And kept on doing it as the world rotated around us, and suddenly we were blasting back into space.

There was a funny little raspberry sound, and suddenly Noah and I were free. Petunia hit the floor, shelled up again, and rolled off into a corner. I envied him.

I turned and saw Morb and Drxx had finally bounced back from the static discharge. They rushed toward the nav-panel, yelling, "Move!" in a variety of interesting ways.

Leya did. Morb and Drxx settled back into their chairs, and I breathed a sigh of relief.

We're gonna be fine, I thought. Which is like challenging the entire *universe* to a dare.

"We are in trouble," Morb said calmly.

"Trouble?" I squeaked. "How? Why?"

"The system had been corrupted by our little 'accident,'" Drxx said, an eye appearing on the back of his head specifically to glare at Noah, who held up his hands and utterly failed to look innocent.

"What does that mean?" asked Leya.

Morb answered like moms everywhere, trying to soften the blow: "Well, that's complicated, really. There are lots of—"

Drxx answered like dads everywhere: "It means that we are doomed."

44

Lots of shouting ensued. I shouted some, Noah shouted some, Leya shouted some. Even Petunia finally un-bugged and hollered a demand for a quick summation (then turned into a pillbug again when the summation ended).

Basically, it boiled down to this: we were circling the planet at a ridiculous speed, our altitude dropping a bit with every second. The sensors that homed in on landing spots were fried, and the ship, lacking instruction on how or where to land, was trying to land us *everywhere*, all at once.

Chloe and Click showed up right in the middle of the conversation, of course. They were still holding "hands," and that didn't change as they listened.

I heard Chloe whisper to Click, "Isn't there something we can, I dunno, home in on?"

Click whispered back, "I do not think so. We would need a new beacon, something the ship would recognize as Celestian, and there is nothing like that here."

He was trying to sound brave, but I heard tears in his voice. If I hadn't already been panicking, I would have hugged them both.

But I *was* panicking, so I kept shouting questions at Morb and Drxx, all of which received the same answer: "No, that won't work," with the occasional addition of, "We are definitely going to die."

Click and Chloe put their heads together. They put their arms around each other. Well, Chloe put her arms around Click. He grew a bunch of tentacles that wrapped around her. Cute. Horrifying, but cute.

I thought they were commiserating. At peace with the idea of our imminent demise.

Then a thought came to me. Not mine, but Chloe's, and so loud it knocked me to my knees:

"DAD, WE NEED YOUR HELP!"

***

As I picked myself up, I got a bunch of weird images: things Chloe had been thinking "at" Dad, using her newfound psychic mojo to get him to help us.

It was enough for me to understand her idea. And it was pretty great—brilliant, actually. Because she realized there was one kind of Earth tech the mothership would definitely recognize, because we'd *made* it on Celestia, and the ship had been programed to understand it:

Lasers.

We'd made one on Celestia, the ship "knew" it, and, Chloe reasoned, if Dad could fire his StormLight laser into the sky, the ship could use it to home in on and land.

I also got an image of fire, which was unexpected, but not a high priority.

The high priority was Chloe's "Laser us home, Dad!" idea, which was fantastic—except for the one huge, gaping flaw.

I knelt next to Chloe. Hugged her. We were going to die, and there was nothing we could do about that. But we could die together, and we could die with her knowing how much her big brother loved her. It wasn't much, but it was all I had.

"We have one more revolution and we will likely crash," Drxx intoned hollowly. Tentacles shot out between him and Morb as they "embraced." Morb pulled Click to them, and a few even dragged the still-pillbugged Petunia over for a final, group hug.

Noah and Leya hugged too. I thought about going to them. Dying in Leya's arms wouldn't be a bad way to go.

But here was Chloe, crying. Here was where I had to be.

"Why is everyone sad?" she said. "Dad can shoot the

315

StormLight. He can—"

Her words trailed away. A tear tracked a lonely path down her cheek as I said, "Dad's never gotten that thing to work once, Chlo. Not without me, not even for a second. You know that."

"But...but he..."

I wiped the tear away, held her face between my hands. I kissed her forehead, and then gave her the biggest hug of my life. I crushed her tight, and tried to will her to hear—with her heart, with her mind, with every bit of her soul—how much I loved her, and how proud I was of her.

"Ten seconds," said Drxx quietly.

"Hey, guess what?" I whispered.

"What?" Chloe asked, her voice quivering.

"Petunia was right."

"About what?"

"Five seconds," said Drxx.

I pulled away. Just enough to look Chloe square in the eye as I said, "You are definitely a queen. And the best little sister any guy could ha—"

45

I'm just going to get this out of the way, to spare you the suspense: we didn't die.

I stopped talking, because the ship gave a gut-churning lurch, and I figured that this was the end. I hugged Chloe tight again, wishing I could shield her from what was coming, knowing I couldn't, but my body insisting on trying just the same.

The first lurch was followed by a another. Then nothing, until Morb let out a scream of pure joy and Drxx shouted, "We are saved!"

I forced my eyes open and looked out the viewscreen.

We were still flying. Straight and true, right toward the laser beam shooting into the air. No question it was the StormLight: what else could it be?

I looked at Chloe. She smiled. "I knew Dad would come through."

The ship gave a little shimmy. I looked at the nav-controls, my fear reigniting.

"It is all right," said Morb. "The ship's computer has reset. We have control again."

Everyone cheered. Hard.

When the cheering died down, Drxx said, "Now, we just need a good spot to land."

"Won't the laser get us there?" asked Noah.

"The laser reset the system," said Morb with a nod. "But we don't want to land there. We do not know if that is a populated area or—"

"It's populated," I said. "Very populated. It's our *house.*"

"Then we must find somewhere else." Morb looked at Drxx. "Are the sensors functioning enough for a scan?"

"Negative," Drxx said. "We must rely on our eyesight."

Which was going to be tough, because it was night. I could see the lights of San Francisco passing below us, but that was all populated, and I got the impression Morb and Drxx were a bit more worried about the all-manual landing than they were letting on. I didn't think vaporizing one of San Fran's beautiful neighborhoods would be a great end to our little story.

"What about the mountains? Muir?" asked Noah. "They're not populated, are they?"

"No, but in the dark we are likely to crash into the trees and perhaps fatally damage the ship or ourselves," Drxx answered. "We need a large area, with a lot of space. Empty but—"

"There!" I stabbed my finger out, pointing at a light that had appeared in a dark patch just outside the bright lights of San Francisco.

Drxx frowned. "How can you tell that is—"

"Just trust me!" I shouted. I looked at Chloe and winked. "Nice, kid."

She blushed, looking more pleased at the simple compliment than I'd ever seen her.

Which made me blush as well. Just seeing that effect on her made me realize how much this kid loved me. And that was good, because I loved her that much and more—all the way to Celestia and back.

***

We landed ten minutes later. There was a bit of turbulence right at the end, when Drxx banked to avoid a cloud of black smoke roiling upward, but at the end we touched down with (comparatively) little fuss. No hanging majestically above the planet's surface this time, to be ferried down via eggship. The mothership had been damaged, and we just set her down right beside the giant fire that had guided us through the last short leg of a long, long trip.

We left the ship. Noah, Leya, me, Chloe. The Celestians and

even Petunia, who had un-bugged and loudly claimed to have no idea what he was talking about when Noah asked why he freaked out so hard. All of us walked out of the all-but-invisible mothership, Chloe and I leading them straight toward the four old buildings that were burning merrily down.

Four humans, three Celestians, and a Flower Person. It was quite the menagerie.

And Mom took it pretty well, all things considered. She ran up and managed to hug me and Chloe both before fainting dead away.

***

She woke up a few seconds later, and hugged us both even tighter. Then she hugged Leya and Noah just as tight.

Then she fainted again.

***

The Celestians asked if they needed to heal-barf on her. Noah shouted, "NO!" his voice cracking hard in the middle. Then, getting himself under control, he said, "She'll be fine. She's just excited." Then, under his breath: "And the price is too high. Too high by far."

***

Mom finally came to, and stayed awake, though she did insist we move a bit farther from the still-burning buildings. "It was the strangest feeling," she said. "I was out putting up posters, and I just somehow *knew* I had to get out here and set this fire." She frowned. "Was that you, Chloe?"

Chloe started to answer, but Mom started kissing her and wouldn't stop, not even when she was calling Dad on her phone.

"Come [kiss kiss, hug hug] to the [kiss kiss kiss] controlled burn site [kiss kiss kiss-kiss-kiss], Sam."

I heard Dad shouting at Mom on the phone, asking what was going on, what was happening.

319

I took the phone from Mom's hand, and she flung herself onto Chloe and started a whole new round of kissing and hugging, before moving on to Noah and Leya, whom she treated with equal enthusiasm. Leya loved it. Noah did as well, even though he pretended not to.

And me? I raised the phone to my ear and said, "Dad? It's Max." Then, over the sudden, stunned silence, I added the words I'd been wanting to say for what seemed a lifetime:

"We're home."

EPILOGUE

Life changed.

Everything changed.

We got all swept up in it, the four of us. We were on a bunch of TV shows, and met with the leaders of just about every nation. Our return was cause for celebration. The fact that we'd returned with company was cause for a reexamination of the world we lived in, and the vaster universe beyond.

For a while, it seemed perfect. Things had changed so much, it was almost like humanity forgot how to act like the craziest life on Earth.

Wars stopped. Countries that had been openly hostile to each other for decades or longer opened embassies and began diplomatic conversations. Rancorous political parties, disagreeing theologies and ideologies—heck, even high school sports rivalries seemed less serious, less important.

We were all human. That's the way it had always been, but it took the arrival of a trio of Pac-Man ghosts and a blue furry ogre/pillbug to remind us that, even with all our differences, we were still more alike than we sometimes wanted to admit.

***

It wouldn't last forever, of course. People would start to grumble, there would be the usual crazies, the people who seemed to hold it as a sacred duty to be perpetually outraged, the folks who were more interested in looking for something to fight about than enjoying the many ways we got along.

But for now, the world was at peace.

Everyone except for me.

***

I was literally world famous. I had been appointed an official envoy between Earth and Celestia. I had beaten Noah on our last video game night. And, last but not least, I had the most amazing girlfriend in the universe.

Just the same, I'd taken shelter in the garage, hiding from the never-ending requests from government heads, world leaders, philosophers, and (weird but true) the Kardashians, whose agents called every five minutes to ask—again—about Celestian/Flower Peopleian/human branding opportunities.

Just sitting there, staring at the laser, the old question in my head.

"What's bugging you, kid?"

I looked up and saw Mom, leaning in the doorway between the garage and the house. I flinched instinctively; Mom had hugged us so much in the first few days after our return that the mere sight of her sometimes made my ribs ache.

But she wasn't in a hugging mood. Which was good, because I wasn't either.

"I don't get it," I said.

"What's to get?"

I tapped the StormLight. The laser that had guided us home had been inert since the night we returned. It had been a month, and every time I asked Dad about it, about how he finally got it to work—and just in the nick of time!—he shrugged and said, "I was wondering what you thought, actually—" and then asked me to come up with some idea about how to fix his newest non-working invention.

"Well?" Mom moved closer. She leaned on the laser, like it was nothing more than an armchair or a stair rail.

"Well? *Well?*" I snorted. "How did he do it, Mom? How did he start this thing up right at the perfect moment?"

Mom shrugged. "You know how. Chloe did her mind-beam thingy. Do you know where Chloe is, by the way?"

"She's over at Becca's with Click."

"Really? I thought she'd be back by now." Mom chuckled. "I never would have pegged Becca for the follower type."

"Hard not to be, when you're in the same elementary school class with a girl who saved the world."

"True," said Mom. "Still, it's—"

"Don't change the subject, Mom!"

Her eyes widened a bit. "Why is this bothering you so much? You know what happened. Chloe mind-beamed us, Dad shot the laser, I set fire to things. We did what parents do: we kept the lights on so you could come home."

"But *how*? How did he fix it, right at that moment, after all the years of failures, of needing my help, of—what?"

Mom was laughing. Hard, and loud, and long. And the harder and louder and longer she laughed, the more irritated I got.

"What's so funny?"

Mom visibly got herself under control. She tried to say something, lost it a bit, got it back together. Finally, she closed her eyes and took a deep breath. Then she opened them and said, "Max, your Dad never 'failed' once in his life." Her eyelids lowered and she got a bit of a dreamy look. "That was one of the things that attracted me to him. He was so brilliant. And he *listened* more than he talked. Smart, and a good listener? That's the brass ring for most women, kiddo."

I was shaking my head. "If he's so smart then why—"

"Why did he need you to finish all his work?"

I nodded. Mom pursed her lips. Then, more serious than I'd seen her in a long time, she said, "You're a smart guy too, Max. Just like him."

"Just like him? Smart? Brilliant? Mom, I don't get it. He never—"

I couldn't finish the statement. Impossible to talk when your jaw is scraping the floor.

Dad hadn't failed.

Ever.

He'd just wanted me to figure out the answers.

He set up the experiments. Silly things when I was a kid—"Max, can you help me set up this volcano mockup?"—then bigger and more complex tasks and inventions, each one flawed in some way that "only I" could fix—as soon as I digested all the lessons he was giving me.

We'd built so much of the StormLight together. That's what I thought. Just the two of us, working side by side, me guiding him to the right choices, trying to be subtle so he wouldn't feel bad…

…and him doing the same to me. Only far better, far more carefully. So subtle and crafty that his "brilliant" son was convinced that his father needed his help, and he had to study and learn to solve the problems only he could solve.

"He's been teaching me the whole time."

Mom nodded and kissed the top of my head. "Yep. To be brilliant, like him. To listen, like him. And, if you're very lucky…" She did a funny little two-step on the garage floor. "…to score a *chica caliente*, just like he did."

"Ewww."

She laughed.

"Am I interrupting anything?"

We both looked over. Leya was there in the doorway where Mom had been standing, smiling a confused smile, obviously wondering what was going on. My heart did a little flip when I saw her, same as always.

Mom shook her head. "Not interrupting anything at all, dear." Then waggled her eyebrows at me and said, "See? Your dad taught you *well*." She cast a quick look at Leya and whispered. "*Muy caliente, hombre.* Very hot indeed."

It was gross and embarrassing to have my mom discussing the girl I loved, even more so when she did that little dance, and everything got grosser and embarrassinger when Leya joined in, doing her own little two-step. And the universe put the cherry on the sundae by having Chloe arrive home right then. She squealed, "Dance party!" and started doing Fortnite dance moves while beatboxing.

It was dumb.

It was embarrassing.

It was silly.

It was everything that made me human. So what could I do?

I danced.

And we were still dancing when my dad got home, and started dancing with us. Noah came over, and we kept dancing. None of us needing explanation, because family didn't have to explain. None of us needing music, because the universe had a music we could hear perfectly in that moment.

None of us needing anything. Just what was there.

Just each other.

That's all any of us need: each other. Then, if we're very lucky, and we're willing to dance ridiculous dances to no music on a cold garage floor, we find each other, and reach out, and embrace. And, embracing, we accept who and what we are, the good and the bad, the dreary and the bright; in holding tight to what we love, we find what we love holding tight to us as well.

Which, as any person who's been to three different planets, fought in an interstellar war of extinction, and even realized his dad is a pretty cool guy will tell you...

...is enough for anyone.

GET A FREE BOOK!

Sign up for Michaelbrent's newsletter and you'll get a free book (or maybe a few!) with nothing ever to do or buy. Just go to bit.ly/mbcfree to sign up for your freebie, and you're good to go! You can also visit his website at WrittenInsomnia.com.

A REQUEST FROM THE AUTHOR:

If you loved this book, I would really appreciate a short review on Amazon (or anywhere else you'd like to post it).

Don't worry about anything fancy—just a single sentence is *beyond* wonderful. Even, "This book good. Me like this book. This book a booky book of bookness!" is fantastic.

And dropping a review really makes a difference, because the more reviews there are, the more likely retailers are to show this book to others, which enables me to take care of my family, and to keep sharing stories with the world.

Thanks again!

- MbC

Acknowledgments

About a year ago, I got a call from a woman named Kathy Muraviov. Kathy had worked as my manager for several years in the world of screenwriting, pounding the pavement on my behalf—much harder than I deserved!—for a long time before we amicably parted ways.

So when she let me know she wanted to talk "business," I was curious. Maybe a movie concept? Some bite on an old prospect that had never come to fruition?

Imagine my surprise when she told me that there was a gentleman in India who wanted to hire someone to write a book based on the screenplay for an as-yet-unmade movie...and that she'd immediately thought of me, as one of the folks she knows has one foot in the world of prose, another in Hollywood (okay, maybe not an entire foot, but at least a toe or two).

She set up an email introduction, and I got to know Gautham.

Gautham—the aforementioned gentleman in India—was a delight. Not only did he have a fun screenplay he wanted adapted into a book, but he was a bright and interesting fellow in his own right. When I asked him if he wanted me to simply call him "Gautham" or some other name, he responded...and then wrote me a full page on Indian naming practices. When I followed up with a question about his home, I got another wealth of information in an email I eagerly shared with my family.

As a writer—aka, someone whose job description could aptly be described as "professionally curious, perpetually ignorant"— I was thrilled. Not just because I had work, though the importance of that can't be overstated, but because I had met a new friend.

And, bonus: turns out having a pen pal in another country made me (at least momentarily) cool to my kids.

I began reading the script for *Light-Years From Home*, and had a blast with it. It was different from what I would have come up with—obviously, since someone else wrote it—but I saw a lot of things I liked, and even more I thought I could play off of, and add a bit of my own spin to while retaining the heart and spirit of the story: four kids who have to go all the way to an alien planet to find out who they really are as humans, as fellow-walkers in this strange thing called life. As well as being tickled that the planet they went to had the same name as a (pretty terrible) novel I'd written some years earlier: *Celestia*.

During the process of writing the book, our own world kept spinning: COVID continued laying waste to normal life. My kids continued growing, as kids so often manage to do. My wife got lovelier, as she so often manages to do.

And me?

I sat, and worked, and lived the lives of four kids who went light-years from home…only to discover that, no matter where they went, they took all their joys and sorrows, their talents and failings with them. To discover our lives are often so much more and less than the places we think of as home, and that love and kindness can carry the day wherever we find ourselves.

I'm sure there's a lesson in there somewhere. Perhaps, if I'm very lucky—and manage to slough off the "adult" parts of me that mistakenly think they know what's going on in life—I'll figure it out someday.

Until then, I'll be grateful. To Kathy Muraviov, who kept on watching out for me even after she stopped being my manager. To my new friend Gautham, who brought me so much fun and joy by providing a path I never would have thought to take.

Credit is due also to my Collings Cult, the folks who joke about flying off to a Utopia where chocolate is a health food and every book you read is a good one. Extra thanks to those who (as always) found errors and continuity issues and kept me from embarrassing myself *too* publicly—like Courtney Andrews, Tina Marie Baber, Mary Jo Bach, Julie Balla, Rita Bongiovi, Carol Brandon, Joan Combes, Bonnie Coponen, Mireva Coi, Judith Dickinson, Doreen Fernandes, Sean Flanagan, Carol Ford, Eddie "Awesome" Garcia, Julio Gilarranz, Anne Goehring, Audrey

Hammer, Debra Hartman, Emily Haynes, Christine Huff, Cindy Hulsopple, Steve Kane, Logan Kearsley, Jeff McMillan, Victoria Morton, John O'Regan, Tonia Schaef, Mary Jude Schmitz, Christina Smith, Dennis Smith (no relation), Cherie Spradlin, and Jayne Stenstrom, all of whom provided feedback and caught mistakes for their weird author friend.

And thank you, as always, to my family. Usually I read my books to my wife, because my books tend to be on the scary side and I don't want to scar my kids—at least, not more than all parents do. But because this was a fun space romp, I got to read the book to all of them...and will treasure the memory of a few days where I got to bring a few laughs and smiles to the people who have made my life a joy.

FOLLOW MbC

Twitter: twitter.com/mbcollings
Facebook: facebook.com/MichaelbrentCollings
YouTube: youtube.com/michaelbrentcollingsauthor
Patreon: patreon.com/michaelbrentcollings
Amazon: geni.us/MbCAmazon

*

SUPPORT MbC ON PATREON

Sign up for MbC's Patreon page and get EXCLUSIVE merchandise, free short stories, and chances at cool prizes like one-of-a-kind collectors editions and more! Just go to http://patreon.com/michaelbrentcollings and sign up!

*

GET MbC MERCH

Want to grab merch and swag? Check out MbC's merch page at http://teespring.com/stores/michaelbrent-collings, and grab tees, sweaters, mugs, and more fun than you can shake a stick at!

*

FOR WRITERS:

Michaelbrent has helped hundreds of people write, publish, and market their books through articles, audio, video, and online courses. For his online courses, check out http://michaelbrentcollings.thinkific.com

*

ABOUT THE AUTHOR

Michaelbrent is an internationally-bestselling author, produced screenwriter, and member of the Writers Guild of America, but his greatest jobs are being a husband and father. See a complete list of Michaelbrent's books at writteninsomnia.com.

NOVELS BY MICHAELBRENT COLLINGS

FUTURE TENSE: TALES OF APOCALYPTIC VISION
MALIGNANT
SYNCHRONICITY
STRANGER DANGER
TIRED: SO VERY TIRED
THE FOREST
STRANGER STILL
SCAVENGER HUNT
TERMINAL
DARKLING SMILES
PREDATORS
THE DARKLIGHTS
THE LONGEST CON
THE HOUSE THAT DEATH BUILT
THE DEEP
TWISTED
THIS DARKNESS LIGHT
CRIME SEEN
STRANGERS
DARKBOUND
BLOOD RELATIONS:
    A GOOD MORMON GIRL MYSTERY
THE HAUNTED
APPARITION
THE LOON
MR. GRAY (aka THE MERIDIANS)
RUN
RISING FEARS

THE COLONY SAGA:
THE COLONY: GENESIS (THE COLONY, Vol. 1)
THE COLONY: RENEGADES (THE COLONY, Vol. 2)
THE COLONY: DESCENT (THE COLONY, VOL. 3)

Made in United States
North Haven, CT
24 March 2023

34507023R00192